BBC

DOCTOR WHO

HARVEST OF TIME

DOCTOR WHO

HARVEST OF TIME

ALASTAIR REYNOLDS

BBC
BOOKS

1 3 5 7 9 10 8 6 4 2

Published in 2013 by BBC Books, an imprint of Ebury Publishing.
A Random House Group Company

This paperback edition published in 2014

Doctor Who is a BBC Wales production for BBC One.
Executive producers: Steven Moffat and Brian Minchin

The Random House Group Limited Reg. No. 954009

Addresses for companies within the Random House Group
can be found at www.randomhouse.co.uk

A CIP catalogue record for this book is available
from the British Library.

ISBN 978 1 849 90419 3

The Random House Group Limited supports the Forest Stewardship
Council® (FSC®), the leading international forest-certification organisation.
Our books carrying the FSC label are printed on
FSC®-certified paper. FSC is the only forest-certification scheme
supported by the leading environmental organisations, including
Greenpeace. Our paper procurement policy can be found
at www.randomhouse.co.uk/environment

Editorial director: Albert DePetrillo
Series consultant: Justin Richards
Project editor: Steve Tribe
Cover design: Two Associates © Woodlands Books Ltd 2014
Production: Alex Goddard

Printed and bound in Great Britain
by CPI Group (UK) Ltd, Croydon, CR0 4YY

To buy books by your favourite authors and register for offers,
visit www.randomhouse.co.uk

To all the Masters – past, present and future

PROLOGUE

The worst machine in the universe was a marble-grey box no larger than a coffin or shipping trunk. Its base was wider and longer than its lid, so that the sides had a slight cant to them. Three of the sides were blank, save for that marbling. The fourth, one of the two ends, had an angled console jutting out from it. The console's upper surface was set with a square matrix of white controls, each of which had been embossed with a precise black symbol in an alien alphabet. There were 169 controls, 169 different symbols, and the Red Queen's people understood about 75 of them. The rest had eluded their best scientists for centuries.

The Red Queen regarded the machine as possessing a quality of intrinsic malevolence. If anything could be said to be evil, it was this device. Yet she could not afford to ignore its transformative power. Of all the potent technologies recovered from the *Consolidator*, the ghost ship that had fallen into orbit around her adopted world, this was by far the most important and seductive.

The machine was called the Infinite Cocoon.

It was fitting.

'The volunteers are ready, ma'am.'

The Red Queen – her full title was Her Imperial Majesty Uxury Scuita – nodded at the aide who had scuttled up to her throne to deliver this information. Like all Praxilions – like all the native creatures of this world she ruled – the aide was a furry caterpillar, a pipe-cleaner bent into an upright 'L'. Its canine head reached the level of her knees when she was on the throne. The little Praxilions had many limbs, differentiated for function, and red and white longitudinally striped fur that made her think of toothpaste and seaside amusements. They smelled like sweet shops and perfume counters.

'Remind them again that they don't have to do this.'

'They know that, ma'am.'

'Nonetheless, tell them again. Let there be no doubt.' Without asking for assistance, the Red Queen pushed herself to her feet. She reached for the sceptre she kept clipped to the chair's side, using it as a walking stick as she made her hobbling way down the set of stone stairs at the throne's base. Praxilion aides skittered around her anxiously, ready to catch her should she fall. 'I'll be all right,' she muttered. 'Allow me a moment on my own, then bring the volunteers in.'

The evening air was cool on her private balcony. She waited until the door was shut behind her, then made her way to the ballustrade, sceptre clicking on the hard stone flooring. Her right hand gripped the gold-crusted sphere screwed into the top of the sceptre. She rested the other on the balcony's rail.

It was a long way down, but she had always had a head for heights. She thought of the sea, roiling far below, on a similar evening. But there was no sea visible from the imperial palace; they were too far inland for that.

Praxilion was a beautiful world, especially at twilight. Gently rolling hills, purple in the gathering gloom, ferried her eye to the pink-hazed horizon. Here and there, like clumps of pale frogspawn, were Praxilion villages and hamlets. She had grown accustomed to their alien architecture over the years, with its blobby preponderance of domes and small, igloo-like dwellings. It almost looked homely. They had been good to her, the Praxilions.

There. Her eye caught the rising spark of the *Consolidator*, climbing from the west. It was difficult to miss, being the only large thing in orbit. A ship as large as a small country, older than the very world it encircled – and one that her people had barely begun to explore, despite six thousand years of trying.

They had done well, given the difficulties. The technologies and materials they had already extracted from the *Consolidator*'s less impregnable vaults had accelerated Praxilion's industrial revolution to a tremendous degree. But there was so much more waiting to be brought down, if only they could get at it. And yet each new item seemed to cost them more than the last. The Axumillary Orb had taken a dozen lives to bring it into her grasp. Dozens more had been lost trying to understand the thing's safety mechanisms, which had been carefully locked when the fabled weapon was placed aboard the *Consolidator*. No wonder she kept it close at hand. Twice as many Praxilions had been lost bringing out the Infinite Cocoon – and many, many more had gone to their deaths by volunteering to test the machine itself.

It was late in the evening. The galaxy was old. Its stars had been through many generations of birth, exhaustion and rebirth. Praxilion astronomers had surveyed these ailing, metal-clotted suns and found scant signs of intelligence beyond their own world. But the records extracted from the *Consolidator* spoke of a different era. A bright, teeming period, when the galaxy held court to countless species, countless cultures. A period when even the ultimate barrier, time itself, had been shattered. The Epoch of Mass Time Travel, or the EMTT.

A time of wonder and miracles.

The Praxilions were haunted by a terrible sense that they had come too late to the party. But the *Consolidator* offered a glimmer of hope. Somewhere in the ship, so their intelligence led them to believe, was the secret of time travel – a fully functioning time-portal device. The Praxilions dreamed of forging a connection between their world and the distant past – a rejuvenating umbilical.

It was a good and noble ambition, the Red Queen thought. It would have been even better if it had not required the use of the Infinite Cocoon.

She returned inside. The volunteers were assembled next to the waiting machine, together with a small cadre of nervous technicians. The lid of the machine was open – it had slid off to the side, appearing to support itself along one edge. A greenish-yellow glow shone upwards from the open casket, illuminating the high-flung arches of the imperial palace.

The Red Queen walked to the machine's side. She leaned her weight onto the sceptre.

'I'm getting old,' she said. 'You all know this. I was younger when I came to your world, but that was thousands of years ago. Drugs and stasis have slowed the march of years, but they have not stopped it completely. The *Consolidator* would probably recognise me as a humanoid, were I to go aboard it. But there is just one of me, and I am far too frail to be much use up there. I am but a weak and feeble woman, as someone once said. That is why we have called for volunteers. That is why you are here, before the Infinite Cocoon. The people of Praxilion thank you for your courage. But you do not have to go through with this. There will always be others willing to take your place, and there will be no shame in turning away now.'

'I am ready,' said the first volunteer.

'Good,' the Red Queen said, studying the naked creature. They all looked the same to her, Praxilions, and divested of their belts and harnesses and armour were all but impossible to tell apart. Furry, friendly looking tubes of red and white, like draught excluders. 'And what is your name?'

The Praxilion said: 'We are Ver.'

They had three sexes, which even now the Red Queen had difficulty in distinguishing. Females, males, and a gender that translated, perhaps imperfectly, as 'sculptor'.

'Very well, Ver,' she said. 'Whatever happens from now on, you have the thanks of your people, your world, and me.

We take none of this lightly. Are you ready for the Infinite Cocoon?'

'I am ready,' the brave creature answered.

'Do you understand the risks? That, even if the transformation is successful, it cannot be guaranteed that the process is reversible? You may have to spend the rest of your existence shaped like me?'

'I understand.'

'We will of course do our best. You have that promise.'

'Thank you, your Imperial Majesty.'

'Then we shall begin.' The Red Queen nodded at the technicians. Four of them moved around Ver and lifted the Praxilion from the ground, then deposited their charge in the waiting interior of the Infinite Cocoon.

'Good luck, Ver,' she said.

The technicians shuffled back on their many legs. Two of them moved to the console at the end of the machine.

'We're ready,' one of them said.

'Proceed.'

The technicians did something. The Infinite Cocoon's lid began to slide shut, squeezing the greenish-yellow light down to a narrow bar, then eclipsing it completely. The box was sealed.

It began to hum and gurgle.

'Support medium entering the cavity,' said one of the technicians. 'All indications nominal.'

The white buttons were lighting up and going dim, in complicated fashion. The technicians responded to these changes calmly, but with great haste and seriousness. It took two of them, and they both needed to use three sets of upper-body manipulators. It was like a cross between brain surgery and speed chess.

'Commencing metabolic breakdown,' reported the other technician. 'Digestion proceeding along normal pathways.'

'Compensating for variance in absorption equilibrium,' stated the other. 'Stabilising... confirmed. Outer tissue and muscle mass now losing coherence.'

'Skeletal structure growing diffuse. Peripheral nervous system now fully attenuated. Tracking core neural functions.'

There was a question she had always meant to ask at this point. Was the subject conscious? Was the subject aware of what was happening to them, what might yet happen? The relatively few volunteers who had endured the Infinite Cocoon came through with puzzlingly different reports. Some were adamant that there had been a continuity of experience, an unbroken chain from the moment the lid closed to the moment it opened. That they had maintained a thread of narrowing awareness even as they were reduced to a kind of soup. Others spoke of no such continuity. It had been like falling asleep, or drowning, or being smothered in warm wet clay. Then there had been a nothingness, a kind of death, before the emergence, harrowing or otherwise. Sometimes they remembered their past lives. Not always.

Perhaps it was best not to know.

'Phase one metabolic breakdown complete. All indications normal. Beginning morphic patterning.'

The machine kept up its humming and gurgling. Beneath the lid was now nothing that resembled a Praxilion. A thing, in other words, not unlike the Red Queen herself.

'Growth symmetries established. Tissue differentiation proceeding normally. Ready to accelerate patterning.'

One of the technicians raised a two-fingered hand. 'Hold.'

The other technician glanced at the control matrix. 'Phenotype template's drifting. Try and lock it down.'

'What do you think I'm doing, for Praxil's sake?'

Haste now became panicked urgency. There had been a coordination to their efforts before; now their six pairs of hands threatened to become tangled up, like pianists fighting over a grand piano. The buttons were lighting and dimming at a quickening rate, almost too fast for the Red Queen to track. The Praxilions had speedy reflexes, but even they had their limits.

'Switch to procedure six!'

'I have! It didn't work! We're on seven now!'

'Not working either. Switch to eight.'

'Too risky!'

'You must! We're already past the point of no return!'

The Red Queen's grip on her stick tightened. The knot in her stomach had become a dark coiling horror. She had seen things go wrong before. It was very, very unusual for there to be a good outcome once this point was reached. The Infinite Cocoon was almost maliciously unforgiving.

'Stabilising,' one of the technicians reported. 'I think we can bring it back!'

'Perhaps.' The other sounded a cautious note. 'Re-imposing initial contours.'

The Red Queen whispered at an aide. 'What are they trying to do?'

'Trying to bring Ver back, I think. The morphic patterning failed, but if they can re-impose Praxilion anatomy...'

'I thought they were past the point of no return.'

'They were. A little. But if they can't go forward...'

'We have it!' called one of the technicians. 'Partial morphic lock reacquired. Lock firming up! Praxil be blessed! Ver, hold on in there! We've got you!'

'Hold on,' the Red Queen whispered. And in that moment her eyes met those of the other two volunteers, still waiting near the Infinite Cocoon. She nodded at them, sharing their concern. For an instant the barriers of species and rank were irrelevant. They were all thinking creatures and they wanted Ver to come through this. No matter if the attempt to impose human anatomy had failed; they just wanted brave little Ver to survive.

'Reconsolidating,' one of the technicians said, the dance of lights on the console beginning to ease.

'Biochemistry approaching Praxilion norms,' said the other. 'Ver is coming back!'

The Red Queen let out a sigh of thanks. So the Infinite

Cocoon had chosen to be merciful today. It was nothing that could ever be counted on, but she was grateful. Even if her hatred of the thing only deepened, that it could be so viciously unpredictable.

'Support medium draining away. Subject has regained full biological integrity.'

'Get the lid open,' she called. 'Now!'

Reluctantly, perhaps, the technicians hastened the process to completion. The machine stopped humming and gurgling. The lid began to slide aside. Yellow light flooded out of the widening gap. The Red Queen risked a step closer to the open machine. The technicians were peering in over the sides, straining their pipe-cleaner bodies to their maximum extension. She caught a flash of red and white within the box, a moving mass of bright coloured fur. A living, breathing form.

Ver was back.

Something sprang out of the box: It was a thin, tapering tentacle, striped like a barber's pole. It curled itself around one of the technicians and hauled them into the air, over the lip of the Infinite Cocoon, into the box. The technician screamed. The others, for a moment, were too shocked to move. Then another tentacle shot out, and a third, and the Red Queen halted, knowing that something had gone appallingly wrong, as it so often did.

Whatever had come back, it wasn't Ver.

A second technician was in the grip of the monster now, emitting a shrill note of pure terror, like a boiling kettle, even as its colleagues tried to grab onto it. And then a detachment of armed guards arrived, carrying gold stun rods that crackled with purple and lilac electrical discharges, and they looked to the Red Queen for her orders.

'Kill it,' she said.

And so they did, plunging their stun rods down into the machine, poking and prodding, the thing in the machine making its own terrible sounds, a kind of protracted slurping, and after a few seconds of that the technician that had been caught was hurled out, visibly dead, and the second was released, sprawling back, its body twitching like an accordion, legs and arms thrashing in the air.

It did not take long to kill the monster; it usually didn't. Confined within the machine, disorientated, they were seldom able to put up much of a fight. But even now, the Red Queen could not say for certain which were the worse sort: the monsters that wanted to break out and kill everyone, like this one, or the ones that wanted only to die.

'That was a bad one,' she said, when the technicians had finished recording the remains and cleaned what had once been Ver out of the machine. 'Almost the worst we've seen. I want a full report as to what went wrong, of course.' Then she added, though it hardly needed to be said: 'Poor Ver.'

'It will take some time to compile the report,' one of the technicians said. 'And even then, there probably won't be much we can say for certain.'

'Do what you can. In the meantime, all volunteers are to be released from their obligations. No one should have to go through that.'

'And the time machine project?' asked the other technician.

'Suspended, until we can be sure of not doing *that* to anyone again.'

'We'll never have that certainty,' the first technician said glumly.

'Your Majesty?'

It was one of the other volunteers speaking, one of the two that had been waiting.

'You are excused,' she said, with a generous sweep of her hand. 'You've proven your courage by coming this far. Go, return to your families. You owe Praxilion nothing.'

'We'd still like to go through with it,' said the other. 'We've been studying the statistics, and...'

'Technically, there's an improved chance of success after a major failure,' said the first volunteer.

'And by anyone's reckoning,' the second said, 'that has to count as a pretty major failure.'

'Did you know Ver?' the Red Queen asked.

'Ver was our friend. Ver would not have wanted Ver's death to dissuade us,' said the first. 'Ver understood what a difference the time machine could make to Praxilion. We must have that technology. No matter the costs.'

'Ver's bravery mustn't be wasted,' said the second forcefully. 'The technicians aren't to blame. We trust them. We are ready to take our chances with the Infinite Cocoon. We are ready to become like you.'

'And risk becoming something worse?' she asked.

'For Praxilion,' they said in unison.

The Red Queen looked down. Her instinct was to turn them away. They were courageous, it was true. But they also craved the glory that would come to anyone who managed to get far enough into the *Consolidator* to find the fabled time equipment. Fame, fortune, prestige beyond measure.

For now, she suspected glory had the upper hand.

The inescapable fact, though, was that sooner or later *someone* was going to have to get into the box again.

'Your names?' she asked.

'We are Hox and we are Loi,' they answered in unison.

'Very well then, Hox and Loi. I commend your dedication. Which one of you wants to go first?'

CHAPTER ONE

'Cromarty. Wind: variable three or four, becoming west or north west five or six. Sea state: smooth or slight, occasional moderate later. Weather: fair. Visibility: moderate or good, occasional poor. Fair Isle. Wind: variable five…'

The upper-class BBC-accented voice on the wireless was delivering the shipping news. It was an old battery-operated set, sheathed in imitation red leather with a circular plastic dial, perched between bottles and fishing weights on a makeshift plywood shelf.

Listening to the shipping news was one of the few pleasures Pat McGinty allowed himself. He imagined the man in a hut, much like his own – the shipping forecast passed to him under the door. Perhaps it was all this man did, delivering the forecasts. There was a practical component to McGinty's enjoyment, too. His livelihood depended on the weather, the storms and high tides.

Right now, though, what McGinty most needed was new batteries for the wireless. It was turned up to the maximum and still the voice was scratchy. He would turn if off in a little while, save the power a little longer. He looked at the toy crab he had found out on the beach after the last tide. The strange, nasty-looking thing was still skewered on the end of the harpoon McGinty took when he went out with his wheelbarrow. It was funny the way he'd found the crab, out on the beach, the seagulls picking at it.

He examined it again now, pulling it off the harpoon's spike, wondering what kind of toy it was meant to be, and if he could get at the batteries. Some kind of science fiction nonsense, probably. The main part of it, the crab body, its legs and feelers (or were they tentacles?) was made of a brittle silver. On its back, the size of a miniature whisky flask, was a glass cylinder. The body had broken easily under the harpoon, but the glass part had already been shattered when he found it.

McGinty turned the toy over and over, looking for screws, a hatch that he could open and get at the insides. There had to be batteries in it somewhere, didn't there? The thing still twitched every now and then.

'Forties. Wind: variable three, becoming east or north east four. Sea state: moderate. Weather: fair. Visibility: moderate or good. Forth. Wind: variable four...'

McGinty was just moving to turn off the wireless when there was a knock at the door.

Not exactly a knock, more a sharp but deliberate tapping, as if a seagull were pecking at the base of the door. McGinty frowned and rose from his chair. It might be one of the children from the village, come down to the beach to taunt him. Perhaps the same ones who'd sprayed 'nutter' on his hut.

The tapping came again.

McGinty fetched his harpoon. He crept to the door, unlatched and opened it in one easy movement. It was dark, but there was a moon out. A soft, salt-laden breeze drifted off the sea. The beach was colourless, receding to the water's margin where a phalanx of low waves broke into foam.

But on the ground was another metal crab. McGinty recognised it for what it was, and in that instant he recognised also that this crab was not broken; that the glass and metal canister on its back was as yet undamaged. Green light spilled from the container and the neat little joints in the crab's mechanical anatomy.

The crab looked as if it was squashed down, pressed into the sand by an invisible force. But the crab was only waiting.

McGinty raised an arm in a reflex defence, but it was too late. The crab sprang onto him, clutching its legs around his sleeve, and then – almost too quickly to believe – it was scuttling up the sleeve, up to his shoulder. The legs gripped hard enough to make him yelp. He dropped the hook and tried to paw the crab off him. Screaming now, he felt it scuttle around his neck. The crab's grip tightened. Those metal legs were tipped like talons… McGinty felt two stabs of pain and coldness. The crab had sunk its fangs into the back of his neck, beneath the base of his skull.

And then there was a pain beyond pain, a pain that smothered and consumed like the sea, rinsing away the last human trace of the man he had been. His body thrashed and whirled as if in the throes of some terrible electric shock.

And was then still. McGinty stood, his arms at his side. There was something not quite right about his stance, as if his entire body now hung from an invisible thread. A long line of drool spilled from his mouth.

'I am Sild,' McGinty said, his voice slurred and slow, as if talking to himself in his sleep. 'I am Sild and I must find the one. Find the one called the Master.'

CHAPTER TWO

An iron and concrete fist rammed its way out of grey waters, like the great gauntlet of some vast drowning knight. It was a production platform, an oil rig, located 200 kilometres from the Aberdeenshire coast.

A helicopter, much the same grey as the sea below, chugged its way toward the platform beneath an ominous cloud ceiling. The bulky craft had a military look to it: matte paint, various bulges and bumps suggesting weapons, sensors or countermeasures. But in the way of markings it was remarkably devoid of obvious affiliation to any of the regular branches of the British armed forces. Only a small circular logo betrayed the helicopter's current operational assignment. In truth, few people would have been any the wiser even if they had been close enough to read the letters and words on that logo.

UNIT: the United Nations Intelligence Taskforce.

Whatever *that* meant.

Certainly the young woman pressing her face to the helicopter's window had not had much of a clue about what she was getting into when she was first assigned to UNIT. Time travellers, ancient enemies from beneath the Earth, forces and factors beyond the planet – elements both benevolent and hostile and just as often imponderable in their

21

motives. Even now, years into her career as civilian scientific liaison, she was only just beginning to grasp the sheer scope of what her job with UNIT might yet entail. Literally, the fate of the Earth and human civilisation.

Dizzying, really.

Would she have accepted, had she known? It was a question Jo Grant came back to time and again. And always, upon due reflection, the answer was the same. Yes, and yes, and yes. Despite all the terrors, all the sleepless nights, it was better to know than not to know.

And sometimes, just occasionally, on the very good days, she had to admit that it could be quite good fun.

Today was not shaping up to be one of those days.

She wasn't overly fond of helicopters to start with, noisy, cramped things that they were. Helicopters and rough weather was a bad combination. Helicopters, rough weather, a long flight, an early start and a greasy canteen breakfast was about as bad as it could get. Jo doubted that she had seen anything less inviting than the production platform. But right now all she wanted to do was get down onto it, onto what passed as the nearest thing to dry land.

Above the four thick cylindrical concrete pillars that supported the platform from the waves – and vanished into the dark, roiling waters below – was a rectangular structure about the size of an office building or large multi-storey car park. Various extra rectangles had been stuck on the side of the main one, cantilevered out over the sea. The whole blocky mass was wrapped in a dense dark tracery of pipes and walkways and ladders, giving the unnerving impression that it was still some way from being finished, or indeed even safe. Rising above the main mass was a tapering skeletal tower, as tall again as the whole part of the rig below it, and off to another side, leaning at an angle, was a long crane-like boom with a dirty yellow flame burning at its tip. Near the base of the boom, Jo caught sight of a pair of tiny orange-suited oil workers. The scale of the platform kept tricking her: it was far too big a thing to be out here, surrounded by all this churning grey water. Even the fully enclosed lifeboats, perched far off the water on their drop platforms, looked tiny.

A big 'M' was painted on the side of the main rectangle, stylised to look like an oil rig itself.

'A dreadful waste, of course,' the Doctor observed, from the passenger seat next to hers. 'Burning fossil fuels – whatever will you think of next?'

'Don't approve, do you?' she asked, folding her arms.

'Hydrocarbons are no way to generate energy,' the Doctor said, in his best sanctimonious voice. 'Most mature civilisations realised that a very long time ago.'

'Petroleum's made up of hydrocarbons, isn't it?' Jo asked brightly.

The Doctor looked pleased. He had a dim opinion of Jo's grasp of scientific matters and was always glad when she displayed even the most rudimentary knowledge.

'Most certainly.'

Now it was Jo's turn to smile. 'Then I'll remind you of that the next time you take Bessie out for a spin!'

'That's different!'

'Oh, right. One rule for you, another for the rest of us.'

'It isn't like that at all!' the Doctor said. 'Anyway, when I've a spare afternoon, I fully intend to convert Bessie to run on pure hydrogen.'

'You had a spare afternoon yesterday – you spent it with your head stuck under the TARDIS console, driving everyone mad with your inane humming.'

'There was an excellent reason for that.' The Doctor left a weighty pause, which Jo resisted the temptation to fill. 'Time disturbances,' he went on. 'Someone seems to be opening up localised time ruptures. I thought I might see if I could pinpoint their origin.'

'And?'

'Didn't get very far. In hindsight I'd have been better off with my head stuck under Bessie's bonnet. Oh – and by the way – that inane humming happens to be a rendition of one of the greatest tragic operas in the history of the Venusian arts.'

'You're right about one thing,' Jo said. 'It was definitely tragic.'

They were coming in to land. On the top of the platform's main structure, cantilevered out over the sea, was the white square of a helicopter landing pad. The helicopter hovered over it and began to descend, pitching uncomfortably as it did so.

'You don't think those disturbances are anything to do with…?' Captain Mike Yates nodded out the window, at the nearing platform. 'This business? The thing that man said over the short wave?'

'I'm inclined to doubt it. It's well enough of Lethbridge-Stewart to send us out here, but I'm sure it'll turn out to be a fuss over nothing. Things do go missing at sea, after all.' The Doctor paused. 'Even quite big things.'

'Entire oil rigs?' Jo asked.

The Doctor offered one of his most infuriatingly inscrutable smiles. 'We'll just have to see, won't we?'

Jo felt the helicopter settle down onto the helipad. The rotors whirred down and at a signal from the crew Yates opened the passenger door. They stepped out into biting salty wind that pushed Jo's hair against her face. She wished she hadn't worn such a short skirt now. The Doctor tightened his cape, wrinkles cutting into his skin as he narrowed his eyes against the gale. Yates reached up and jammed his UNIT beret down firmly. 'Lovely day for it!' he muttered. 'Wish I'd brought my suntan lotion!'

A big man in an orange anorak was already on the pad. He walked over, raising his voice over the dying whine of the helicopter. 'Tom Irwin,' he said brusquely. 'Deputy operations, Mike Oscar Six.'

'This is Josephine Grant,' the Doctor said. 'This is Captain Mike Yates, and I'm the Doctor.'

Irwin nodded at the helicopter. 'You'll no be staying long, I take it?'

'I see Scottish hospitality's all it's cracked up to be,' Yates said.

'I was talking about the weather, Captain,' Irwin answered. He was a burly, bearded Scot, who looked strong enough to have swum his way out from Aberdeen. His anorak had a fur-lined hood and the same 'M' stitched onto the shoulder that Jo had already seen on the side of the rig. 'Nasty bit of work coming in from Norway,' he went on. 'You lot want to be back home in time for your Ovaltine, you'd best not dawdle.'

'We were asked out here, you know!' Jo said.

'That's between you and Eddie McCrimmon.'

'McCrimmon?' the Doctor said, raising his eyebrows. 'I used to know a McCrimmon once – awfully decent fellow.'

'Not Eddie's father, by any chance?'

'I doubt it – not unless Eddie's father was involved in the Jacobite rebellion.'

Irwin's eyes sharpened. 'I thought this was a military delegation, not a visit from the local nuthouse.'

Yates was making an obvious effort to sound civil. 'Actually, we are a military delegation.'

'You maybe, but your pals look like a pair of civvies.'

'We are,' Jo said. 'But we're on attachment to UNIT. And if that's a problem, you can take it up with Geneva.'

Irwin eyed her hand dubiously, but after a moment he offered his own gloved hand by way of reciprocation. Jo shook, but only maintained contact for an instant.

'I asked for that. First time on a rig, is it?'

'Last too, if I've got any say in it.'

This seemed to win her a flicker of grudging respect, judging by the twitch that creased the corner of Irwin's mouth.

'Aye, it's no picnic out here. You'd best come with me. Your boys on the helicopter need a brew?'

'They'll be fine,' Mike Yates said. He had told the pilot and co-pilot to remain aboard, so that they could make a quick getaway if the weather worsened. 'I suppose you know what this is all about?'

'Any reason I should?'

'Your boss was the one who called us in.'

'I can guess.' Irwin was leading them along a gridded metal catwalk, into a corrugated metal shed. 'That business two days ago?'

Yates continued: 'Your man sent a short-wave distress call which was picked up by every wireless station between here and Stavanger. Why was he so worked up?'

Irwin paused on a landing between two sections of staircase. 'He was on an oil rig that was collapsing into the sea. In his shoes, you'd be a bit "worked up".'

'This was another one of your rigs, was it?' Jo asked.

'Half the rigs out here belong to the company.'

'And was there anything special about this rig, the one that collapsed?' the Doctor asked, as they began to descend a clattering metal staircase.

'The boss'll tell you what we all know. Mike Oscar Four was ready to fall over. That's why it was being scrapped.'

'You don't sound as if anything unusual happened,' Jo said. They were on Mike Oscar Six now; Mike Oscar Four was the one that had had the accident. 'But rigs don't just collapse, do they? And there was that thing the man was supposed to have said, about the sea...'

'Pete Lomax was scared witless,' said Irwin. 'Not really cut out for this line of work. What he said he saw, and what he really saw, are two different things.'

At the bottom of the stairwell was a pair of double doors, with round windows in them, like the doors into an operating theatre. Beyond was a short corridor, metal doors on either side. The floor and walls were also metal, painted over in various uninspiring greys and greens. Other than the occasional equipment locker, fire extinguisher, first-aid box, safety notice or framed photograph of an oil rig or refinery, there was little in the way of comforting décor. No flowers or potted plants or delicate watercolours of trees and meadows. Compared to this place, UNIT headquarters was like the Ideal Home Show.

Irwin halted them at one of the metal doors. This one had a small white nameplate fixed above it, with stencilled black letters. He took off his glove, knocked twice on the door, then waited for an answer.

Jo heard an indistinct: 'Come in.'

Irwin opened the door, and beckoned the UNIT party to enter. The room was small, with a single large window overlooking part of the platform, and then out to the restless grey sea. A tough-looking grey-haired man in a chequered shirt was sitting at the desk, with a bulky computer positioned at an angle before him. He was tapping keys with blunt hairy fingers, while referring to a spiral-bound folder opened out next to the computer.

'Your guests,' Irwin said.

The computer the man was working on was a modern one, no larger than a television set, housed in a grey case with an integral keyboard built into it. Jo angled herself to get a better look at the data on the screen, the rows of flickering green characters. Computers were beginning to creep into UNIT operations but it was still fairly unusual to see one in an office.

'That's about all I can do for now,' the man said, with a defeated air.

'You did your best, Hopgood. Have them fly in a replacement circuit board as soon as possible. I can't manage without this thing now I've got used to it.'

The speaker was a woman. She had been standing at a row of filing cabinets off to the left of the door, so that Jo had barely noticed her presence when they entered. The woman slid a folder back into a gap in one of the cabinets, then closed the metal door.

27

'Computers,' she said, as the technician left the room. 'A year ago, I barely knew how to switch one on. Now I'm beginning to think they might actually make a difference. Maintenance schedules, parts procurement, shift management, real-time weather updates and sea conditions – it's all here. We even have a data link back to the mainland.'

She slid into the seat recently vacated by the computer man, then tapped away at the keys for a few moments. The rows of characters faded away, replaced by a diagram representing some kind of complicated flow system, rendered in wiggling green lines. Jo presumed it had something to do with the rig's functioning.

'Very sorry,' Yates said. 'But we were hoping to speak to Eddie McCrimmon?'

The woman slid a folder across the desk, studied the flow diagram, made a couple of felt-tip entries into the paperwork. 'You are.'

'Edwina McCrimmon?' Jo asked, glad that she had thought to do her research before arriving. 'I didn't know you were based out at sea.'

'Most of the time I'm not,' McCrimmon said. 'But I get out here as often as I can. It's the only way to get a real sense for what's going on. Feel the whirr of the drill under my feet, as my father says. And you'd be?'

'Jo Grant. This is the Doctor, and this is Captain Mike Yates.'

'I was about to introduce them,' Irwin said.

Edwina 'Eddie' McCrimmon was about twenty years older than Jo, although she still looked fit and able for her years. She was a tall woman, with ginger hair only just beginning to turn grey in places. She had tied the hair back with an elastic band, exposing a strong forehead. She wore work-stained trousers, a black knitted sweater. Over the sweater she wore a laboratory coat with the McCrimmon 'M' beginning to come unstitched from the fabric. She was missing a couple of fingers from her left hand, the one that she used to hold the felt-tip pen.

'Miss McCrimmon,' the Doctor said gently. 'Forgive my rudeness, but we do have rather a short weather window. Unless you'd rather have five additional guests for the next couple of days?'

'I'm afraid I've rather wasted your time,' McCrimmon said, continuing to tick things off. 'I had some concerns, I'll admit, after what happened with the decommissioned platform. Reason I got in touch with your Brigadier chappie.'

'Just like that?' Yates asked, unable to hide his scepticism. 'You just happened to have the Brig's phone number?'

'No,' McCrimmon said calmly. 'I have a friend I used to go to school with, who's now pretty high up in the Ministry. I mean, the MOD. I spoke to my friend, and my friend, who knows your Brigadier indirectly – they go shooting grouse together or something – thought it might not hurt to have a wee chat with him. But after I'd had time to think things over, and have a proper talk with Pete Lomax, I realised this wasn't a matter for UNIT.'

'Well, you could have called the Brigadier again!' Jo said.

'I did, actually. Twice. Told him not to bother sending anyone out. And despite that, here you are.' Like Irwin, McCrimmon spoke with a Scottish accent, but hers was softer and more mellifluous – Kirkcaldy rather than Glasgow. McCrimmon paused to look at Irwin. 'Tom, I want that blow-off valve replaced by the end of the second shift, if at all possible.'

'Already in hand.'

'The centrifugal separator?'

'Fixed and running.'

'And the thrust bearing on the number two drill?'

'It'll hold until spares arrive from shore. We'll get that draughty window of yours sorted, too.'

'Very good. I think that'll be all for the moment. You've got your pager on? I'll buzz when our guests decide they're not going to get much out of this visit.'

'Thank you,' Irwin said.

He closed the door behind him. McCrimmon continued writing in her file for a few seconds, then pushed it away, placing the felt-tip pen next to the file. The desk was very neat, with everything except the computer arranged at strict right angles. The computer had been given a dispensation to sit at forty five degrees, but even then Jo suspected that it was an exact forty five degrees, measured with one of those plastic protractors you got in geometry sets.

McCrimmon looked at her guests in turn.

'I don't want to be rude, but what I said to Tom Irwin was the truth: you really are wasting your time. What happened at Mike Oscar Four was deeply regrettable, I won't deny that. Lives were lost, as well as valuable equipment.'

'But you must have had some reason to contact the Brigadier,' Yates said.

McCrimmon tapped the tapped the index finger of her injured hand against the file: she'd lost the ring and little fingers at the knuckle. 'I was mistaken. I've got good men working for me, and I trust their judgement. When my extraction specialists say that the likely cause was a rupturing gas cell, why should I doubt them?'

'The Brigadier must have still thought there was something worth looking into,' Jo said.

'I'll answer your questions, let you speak to Pete Lomax – if that's what you insist on. But that still won't alter the fact that you've come out here for nothing. This was an industrial accident, nothing more.'

'A gas cell?' the Doctor enquired.

McCrimmon picked up her pen from either end and held it between her hands. 'I'll spare you the technical details. It's pretty complicated and unless you've a doctorate in geophysics I'm afraid it won't mean an awful lot to you.'

'Very considerate of you,' the Doctor said.

'An accumulation of gases has been known to build up under the seabed, especially in proximity to complex multi-

30

penetration drilling sites. When one of these cells ruptures – breaks through to the water – it acts like a huge bubble. If that bubble rises directly under an already compromised structure, like Mike Oscar Four... well, I'm sure you can imagine the consequences.'

'The rig collapses,' the Doctor said.

'Or suffers severe damage. Either way, it's not the kind of trouble we go looking for.'

'If there's a threat to British maritime operations,' Yates said, 'we need to know about it. Even if it *is* just gas cells. The sooner we have a word with this Lomax chappie, the better. Then we can all clear out and go back home to our Ovaltine.'

'Ovaltine, Captain?'

'Never mind,' Yates said. 'It's not really my tipple anyway.'

CHAPTER THREE

The wind stiffening, Inspector Archie Hawes breasted the highest point of the dunes and began his descent to the beach. The sand was getting into his shoes. He squinted, shielding his eyes from the sting of the wind. He could see the hut now, tucked against the fence line where the beach ended and the dunes began. He came here quite often, on his beat. Now and then he'd knock on the door and there'd be no answer. He'd peer through the window just in case, but if McGinty was out there with his wheelbarrow, off gathering scrap, it was just too bad. Hawes would retreat to his panda car safe in the knowledge that he'd made an effort, while not having to put up with any of that vile-tasting tea.

Not today, though. He could see a gentle glow coming from the hut's window. The gas lamp was on.

McGinty was home.

Hawes completed his descent of the footpath, onto the beach proper. The tide had already gone out and where it had reached its highest point was a sketchy margin of deposited items. Lengths of rope. Old bottles. Fishing net. Wood and plastic. Flotsam and jetsam, Hawes thought. He had the idea that there was some boring technical difference between the two, that the one was very specifically something and the other very specifically something else, not that it mattered.

33

The main thing was a nagging suspicion that McGinty would normally have cleared away this muck by now. He couldn't be *ill*, could he? That would be a turn-up for the books. District nurse, GP, even the giddy prospect of an ambulance... It would almost be more drama than Hawes could take.

He passed by the window on his way to the door, registering an impression of McGinty sitting at his table with a clean dinner plate before him. The yellow glow of the gas lamp almost made it look cosy in there, like a Dickensian Christmas card. Hawes wasn't fooled. He'd been in that hut often enough to know it was about as cosy as a public urinal.

Hawes stood at the door. He noticed that the word 'nutter' had been sprayed onto the wall to the right of it. Strange that McGinty hadn't painted over it, or at least tried to clean it off.

He knocked on the rough wooden door.

'Pat. It's me, Archie. Come for my brew.' No avoiding that particular obligation, Hawes thought.

There was no answer. He didn't think McGinty was deaf, but perhaps he'd nodded off at the table after consuming a lavish banquet of cold sardines.

He knocked again, spoke louder this time. 'Pat! It's Archie Hawes! Let me in.'

He heard the scrape of a chair, as of someone rising. There was a shuffling sound, the scuff of shoes on rough floorboards. The door was unlatched and opened.

McGinty stood in the doorway, still wearing his heavy oilskin coat. He was looking at Hawes, but also looking through him, out to the waves.

There was a long moment when Hawes expected the other man to say something.

'Pat?' he asked doubtfully.

'Hello, Archie.' McGinty extended a welcoming hand. 'Why don't you come in? I've got something to show you.'

'I see the kids have had a go at you again.'

McGinty closed the door behind them. It muffled the draught, rather than excluding it completely. 'Oh, don't worry about the children. They don't matter now.'

Something was off key, out of tune. Hawes would never have called the beachcomber a friend. But he knew McGinty well enough to sense that something was amiss. He thought of the way he'd been sitting at the table, bolt upright with the plate in front of him. Like a man with nothing to do but wait.

'Are you feeling all right, Pat?'

'I've never felt better, Archie. Please, have a seat.'

There were only two chairs in the hut. Hawes took the one opposite McGinty's seat. He studied the clean dinner plate as he lowered himself down onto the rickety platform. 'There's been a good tide,' he offered.

'And there'll be many more, while this planet still has oceans and a moon. But that's all behind us now.' McGinty had his back to Hawes now, as if he was preparing the tea. 'Here. I'd like to show you something.'

'What, Pat?'

McGinty reached up to relieve himself of his coat, freeing first the left sleeve and then the right. For a moment the coat hung on his frame like a cloak. Then he shrugged it the ground and remained standing with his back to the policeman.

Hawes stared, at first unable to process what he was seeing. Something was *stuck* to Pat McGinty. It was clamped onto him, fixed with prehensile metal legs to the lower part of his neck. It was a thing of silver metal and glass, sterile-looking, like some strange surgical attachment. Green light came from different parts of it. Fluid bubbled around in the glass part, and there was something *in* that fluid, a thumb-sized blob of indeterminate form.

'Pat…' he said falteringly. 'What's that thing?'

'Me, Archie.' McGinty turned around slowly and smiled. 'I am not Pat McGinty now. I am Sild.'

Hawes's mind flashed through the possibilities, but he could think of nothing that made sense of this. His only conviction was that it was wrong, dreadfully wrong, and that McGinty needed urgent help.

'We need to get you to hospital, Pat. Someone's done this to you.'

'Not someone, Archie. *Sild*. I am Sild; we are Sild. And now you will become Sild as well, and then we will find him. Find the man called the Master. And bring him to join the others on the *Consolidator*.'

'*Consolidator*? What are you talking about?'

'It's a spaceship, in the future. Orbiting a planet called Praxilion.'

'Pat, have you been on the funny tea again? I told —'

'Never mind, Archie. In a moment it will all be clear. Please stand by.'

'Stand by for what?'

That was when Hawes heard the scuttling behind him. He twitched around, just in time to see another of those things on the shelf behind him, crouched next to the red leather wireless set.

Chapter Four

Pete Lomax was sitting on the edge of a made bed, dressed in shirt and trousers. He was a slight man with tousled fair hair, spilling out over the bandages wrapped around his scalp. His room was just large enough for the bed, a bedside table, a desk and a steel-framed chair. He was putting aside a drawing pad when they arrived. Some sketches, mostly of scenes in and around the platform, were fixed to the walls with blobs of putty and drawing pins. These were the only concessions to homeliness in the room.

Eddie McCrimmon introduced them. 'This is the Doctor, Captain Yates, and Miss Jo Grant.'

Jo smiled. We're not here to make life difficult for you, Mr Lomax. It's just that something odd happened and you're our only witness.'

'I can't tell you much,' Lomax said, barely raising his head as he spoke.

'You managed to get to the wireless room,' Yates said.

At that moment a McCrimmon employee appeared at the door with a plastic tray laden with cups, jugs of tea, coffee and milk, and an assortment of stale biscuits. The drinks were distributed. Jo helped herself to one of the biscuits. Her appetite was coming back now that they were on firm ground.

'I had to call for the chopper,' Lomax said.

'There wasn't one on the rig?' Jo asked.

'It had come back here, to Mike Oscar Six. We worked shifts.' Lomax spoke in a quiet Northumbrian accent that reminded Jo of a driving instructor she'd once known. 'The chopper was due back that day anyway. When the thing happened...'

'You said something about the sea disappearing,' Jo said.

The Doctor gave her an admonitory look. Perhaps he'd been hoping to steer around to that topic gradually.

'What I meant was,' Lomax said, his coffee cup rattling on the saucer on he spoke, 'the sea conditions were rough. Seriously choppy. The waves were piling on top of each other. A trough opened up. It was like looking into a steep-sided valley, all black water and foam.' He gave a little shudder. 'I've seen some pretty bad seas, 50- or 60-foot swells, but that was the worst.'

'Just a trough?' Yates asked doubtfully.

'Aye.' Lomax looked annoyed. 'What else would it have been?'

'The transcript of your radio transmission,' the Doctor said, 'led us to think you'd seen something rather different. You said it looked as if the sea had been scooped out, as if there was a hole where the water should have been. A great, hemispherical hole, open for whole seconds, right under Mike Oscar Four, before the water crashed back in on itself.' Gently he added: 'That's what you *really* saw, isn't it, Pete? Not just a normal sea event, but something that didn't make sense at all?' The Doctor nodded at Lomax's drawings. 'You've got an eye for detail, we can all see that.'

They all caught it then: Lomax glancing at McCrimmon for an instant, as if seeking guidance or permission.

'Whatever I said on the wireless, I know what I saw.'

The Doctor nodded. 'Then in your experience, nothing that happened was in any way inexplicable? Just an unfortunate coincidence of bad weather and a rig that was already structurally unsound?'

Lomax frowned. 'What I said, isn't it?'

'Thank you, Pete,' McCrimmon said, her tone letting them all know that she considered that this interview had run its course. 'You've been more than helpful.' She paused and turned to the UNIT delegation. 'Pete was hurt, as you can see. Concussion, possibly a fracture; we'll know better when we get him back to the mainland. In the meantime, I won't have him put through any more distress. He lost friends in that accident. We all did.'

'Will you be returning to the rig?' the Doctor asked.

McCrimmon shook her head firmly. 'Pete has my personal assurance that he'll be re-employed on dry land, if that's what he wishes. He's been a good worker, an asset to McCrimmon Industries, and I wouldn't want to lose him.'

'I don't want to be able to see the sea,' Lomax said, in a half-mumble.

McCrimmon swallowed tightly. 'We'll... find you something.'

'It's just the sea,' Jo said. 'Isn't it?'

Lomax met her eyes. 'It's not just the sea.' He seemed on the point of adding something to this statement, some amplification or clarification on the tip of his tongue. But after a moment he went back to the business of staring into his cup. He was still frowning slightly, as if he'd seen something in the coffee's reflection, some brief swirling hint at an answer that might yet satisfy him.

Edwina McCrimmon watched the UNIT helicopter climb away from the rig and lose itself in the lowering clouds. Normally she did not welcome rough seas and heavy winds, but this time she was grateful for the adverse weather system. It had provided the perfect justification for the delegation to make their visit as brief as possible, and that meant slightly less of a headache for her.

The telephone on her desk rang. She sat looking at it for

a few seconds, willing the hateful thing into silence. But the phone would not stop ringing.

She lifted the sleek angled handset to her ear, certain she knew who was on the other end of it. 'Yes?'

'Don't "yes" me, young woman.' It was her father, calling from the mainland. 'They tell me the UNIT delegation's left. How much harm was done?'

'None at all.'

'I trust you didn't let them anywhere near that idiot Lomax.'

'I had no choice. But he didn't tell them anything.'

'For your sake, I hope you're right.' Calum McCrimmon – known to enemies and allies alike as Big Cal – broke off to bark something through to his secretary, the long-suffering Morag. 'You've made some serious errors of judgement in your time,' he resumed, 'but I've always believed you had what it takes in you to become an asset to this company. That's why I gave you the responsibilities I did. Now I'm starting to seriously question my faith in your abilities.'

'I told you, no harm was done.'

'You'd best hope so. In one rash action, by going behind my back, you've come very close to ruining everything. The men from the Ministry are furious and it's your neck they want on the chopping board – followed by mine for telling them you were a safe pair of hands.' Big Cal paused. She heard the sound of a cigar being snipped and lit, followed by a deep inhalation. 'I'll remind you that what we are involved with is vital to nothing less than the Scottish economy and the national security of the British Isles!'

McCrimmon remembered Mike Yates echoing a very similar sentiment. 'So what you're saying, Father, is that it's all right for one lot of government men to go snooping around our rigs, but not some others?'

'I'll thank you not to take that sarcastic tone, Edwina. You were told from the outset not to question things. You're enjoying your new computer, aren't you? I don't see you

40

complaining about that.'

'I'm not complaining... I just wanted to know *why* that rig collapsed. When your friends from the Ministry told me it was none of my business I decided to use my initiative to try to get answers from somewhere else. You can't blame me for that, Father.'

'The problem with you, Edwina, is that you've never known when to stop.'

'If I'd known when to stop,' she said, steeling herself to slam down the phone, 'I wouldn't be here now, would I?'

When she had terminated the call, she sat in silence for several minutes, shaking slightly and hoping no one would have the exquisite bad timing to disturb her. After a while she opened her desk drawer and took out a slim leather notebook about the size of a pocket diary. It was old and battered. There had been nine others once, all bought with pocket money from the local newsagents.

She opened the pages and leafed through. The paper was tissue thin. She had written on them in felt tip, the ink bleeding through from one side to the other. The pages were dense with a child's laboriously neat handwriting, the blocks of text squeezing around drawings of creatures and inventions and strange, alien landscapes. She had used lots of different colours, enough pens to fill an old tartan-printed shortbread biscuit tin.

Edwina's mother had died when she was 10, leaving her to be brought up by her father. Although she had not realised it at the time, writing in the books had been a form of escape for her, a way of managing her grief, channelling that emotional torment into creativity. By the time she was 12, she had filled the nine other books and half of the tenth, which was this one. She had kept this one under her pillow, working on it when she should have been asleep. Big Cal had found the others, but not this one.

The books were about an imaginary kingdom. Edwina had made it all up in her head. Actually, the kingdom was run by a queen, from a fine imperial palace floating in the clouds. The queen's subjects were talking animals, for the most part. It had started out quite simplistically, but over the course of the books Edwina had developed this world in increasingly lavish detail. She had thought up different countries, empires within empires. She had devised elaborate systems of magic and chivalry. She had made up adventures for the queen and her circle of courtiers. The imagined world had slowly become as real to her, and at least as complicated, as the actual one in which she lived.

This had become a problem. Edwina was not doing well at school. She didn't 'fit in', the teachers said. Always daydreaming, not knuckling down to work. Stern injunctions were issued. She had to apply herself, they said, if she was going to make something of her life. It was no good being 'off in her head' all the time. Her mother, who had always been practical, would not have approved.

When Big Cal had found the nine completed books, they had seemed to him ample evidence of a mind not being put to productive use. So he had taken the books from her bedroom, and thrown them and her big tin of coloured felt-tips into the bin.

'You're 12 now, Edwina,' he explained later, when the deed was done. And she was, too – it was her birthday. 'There's no time for that rubbish any more. You need to concentrate on your homework.'

The shock of it had been so great that she had not even cried. It was simply too far beyond any injustice that she had yet experienced. She had no words for the loss he had inflicted on her.

In that moment, she stopped being a child.

But in a way, Big Cal had done her an odd favour. She had started to knuckle down, if truth were told. She stopped being 'off in her head'. Almost as if to say: you want to see what I can do, do you? You want to see what you have awakened?

She became very scholarly, and very focused. Almost

frighteningly so. She had never been particularly interested in the more scientific areas of the curriculum, but she found herself taking to them with an intensity that left onlookers staggered and not a little perplexed. She turned out to be extremely good at mathematics and geology, and no slouch at physics, chemistry and biology either. She tore through secondary school, blazing a path onto a degree course in petrochemical engineering.

Big Cal, watching with a mixture of pride and vague apprehension, must have wondered what he had unleashed on the world, in that one afternoon of casual destruction. He had meant no great harm by it, of course. But the cruelty of that act never left his daughter.

By sheer force of talent and will, she had wormed her way into the family company, and then up through the hierarchy of power. Cal had resisted, to begin with, then reluctantly conceded that his daughter had real ability. Not everyone was cut out to work in oil. Edwina not only had all the right instincts, but she was fearless. Wanted to get out onto the rigs as soon as possible.

'I'm going to run this company one day,' she'd told him. 'And then we'll do things my way.'

He had laughed. But he wasn't laughing anywhere near as much now. Edwina had gradually gained control of a huge chunk of the business. One day, sooner than he or anyone else cared to think about, McCrimmon Industries would be hers. That was as unavoidable as night following day.

She dragged a finger along a line of precise text, inscribed in pink felt-tip. '… and the queen told her courtiers that they were not going to do things the same way any more. The courtiers were not very happy, but she told them she was the queen and they had better do what she said.'

She turned to the next page. It was blank, as she had known it would be. That was as far as the story went. The day her father destroyed the nine other books was the day she stopped dreaming.

'I'll forgive you,' she said quietly. 'One day.'

The Icelandic trawlerman was on deck, dealing with a recalcitrant winch, when he noticed the peculiar thing forming in the sky. Einar Sigurdsson was not, it had to be said, a man easily fazed by weather. In the forty years that he had been at sea, he had experienced just about every meteorological condition nature could throw at him, at least in this part of the world. The sea conditions today were not exactly pleasant, but this was hardly the worst he'd experienced in recent weeks. What was of more pressing concern to Einar was the dismal quality of fish his crew had been hauling in. He thought back to the stories his father had told him, and the stories his grandfather had told his father, their tales of plump nets and bulging holds, so much good silvery fish they couldn't bring it all home. Even allowing for a certain quality of exaggeration, things were obviously not as good now as they'd been in the old days. Einar would never have admitted as much to his crew, but in his darkest hours it began to occur to him that maybe, just maybe, there was something in what those busybody ecologists kept going on about, with their doom-mongering about overfishing.

Not that even the busiest busybody would have dared suggest that there was a connection between strange weather and depleted stocks. Einar took off his knitted cap and scratched at his thatch of wiry grey curls. What the hell was that thing anyway? Clouds blanketed the sky from horizon to horizon, but a little to the west was a darkening circle, turning from grey to mauve to purple even as Einar watched. It was as wide as a football field, easily.

Einar didn't like it. He had seen some weird things up there in his time, but nothing like this. The air felt tense, the way it did before a storm. It crackled with electrical foreboding. Einar muttered a dark Icelandic oath. The circle – foreshortened by the angle of view to an ellipse, like a human eye – was now as black as night. The clouds around the eye's edge were starting to curdle, pulled into feathery horsetails.

Einar was about to leave the winch and go indoors, get on the wireless and see what was happening, when the eye started crying.

A white cataract poured out of it, as if a waterfall had just switched on. It took a couple of seconds for the bottom of the water column to reach the sea. Where it hit, a great misty cloud of spray rose up like a veil. The roar hit Einar's ears. The cataract became broader, thickening to the width of the eye. It was a falling column of water, a white pillar bridging the sea to the sky. A seaspout in reverse, Einar thought. The sky giving water to the sea, rather than sucking it up.

He shuddered at the abject wrongness of it.

Einar stumbled his way to the cabin, glancing back over his shoulder at the impossible waterfall. The roar of it was now so loud as to smother all other sounds. The amount of water coming out of the sky – where could it all be coming from?

And then it stopped. The eye winked shut. The column of water, cut off sharply, descended like a white piston going into the ground. The roar faded away. The clouds knitted back together. Other than a threatening grey smudge where it had been, a smudge that was fading by the moment, there was nothing to suggest that the eye had been there at all.

Or that Einar Sigurdsson, trawlerman of forty years, was not going quietly mad.

The Ministry helicopter was smaller, sleeker and newer than the one from UNIT, painted glossy black rather than matte grey. It had waited for the other craft to clear the area before returning, holding station on one of the other McCrimmon rigs.

Now its shark-shaped body settled down on the helipad, and after the rotors had spun down three men got out.

Edwina watched them descend from the helipad and enter the rig. She was still trying to work out the relationship between the two Ministry men, Callow and Lovelace, and the third one. Sometimes they seemed like natural allies, at other times like enemies forced into grudging cooperation. She still didn't know the name of the third man.

'Go away,' she whispered. 'Finish whatever it is you want with us, then get the hell off my rig. And damn you, Father, for putting me through this.'

The terms of the arrangement, set out by Cal 'Big Man' McCrimmon, had seemed simple enough to begin with. Her father had made some arrangement with men from the Ministry of Defence. The less Edwina knew the better, it was made clear.

What it was, the MOD had some new equipment they needed to test. It was something to do with submarines. MERMAN, they called it – that was supposed to be a secret, but she'd overheard them once or twice when their guard was down. The gear was experimental and it needed to be deployed at sea from a number of fixed locations, for some reason. These fixed locations needed abundant power, and the ability to be visited by MOD scientists and technicians without attracting too much undesirable attention. Some existing Naval facilities were in the right place, but to test the equipment properly would have required developing completely new marine installations, far from land – not only expensive and time consuming, but difficult to hide from prying eyes. It was obviously better to make use of existing maritime infrastructure, and that was where McCrimmon Industries had come in.

The deal her father had set up permitted the MOD to use a number of the company's rigs and platforms as temporary sites for MERMAN equipment. The arrangement would last no more than a year. The impact on existing McCrimmon operations would be minimal: most of the oil workers wouldn't even be aware that anything was going on. Normal drilling operations would continue, but at the same time some of the rigs' power would be diverted to the MERMAN systems, located in sealed areas in the lowest levels of the rigs, safely distant from the normal work zones. The equipment was relatively compact and could be brought in and installed using normal helicopters and small teams. Once installed, it needed only the occasional adjustment or repair.

So far so good.

In return, McCrimmon Industries got a couple of sweeteners. The first was the off-the-record assurance that a number of legal barriers to further expansion would be expected to melt away – that, in other words, cooperation with the MOD would buy preferential treatment at government level, and in the procurement of overseas contracts.

All very shady, but this was the oil business after all.

The second was computers. In return for McCrimmon's assistance, the government men would install terminals and high-speed underwater data connections, linking the company's rigs and mainland operations into a super-efficient communications and control web, years ahead of the competition.

The Big Man barely knew a computer from a sack of tatties. But Edwina was well aware that this 'information technology' was the wave of the future. The company ignored it at its peril. When, in a few years, Edwina gained control of most of the firm – her father would have to retire eventually – she was determined not to be left behind. It would take imagination and boldness to stay ahead of the competition in the coming decades.

So, yes, she was willing to concede that there were upsides to the MOD arrangement. And it had seemed generous enough until it had occurred to her that they had probably needed to put in those underwater data connections anyway.

Not that she had ever been in a position to turn down the deal.

There was no knock at her door. The men just entered.

'Well?' queried Callow. 'Exactly how much harm did you do, McCrimmon?'

47

She disliked Callow. He had a thin, reedy voice and a habit of constantly patting his oily, slicked-down hair.

'I've already had the right royal ear-bashing from my father, thanks.'

'Your contacting UNIT was in express violation of the terms of our arrangement,' said Lovelace. She disliked Lovelace as well. He had a sharp, shrew-like face and a constant nervous twitch in one cheek. 'We've a good mind to pull out completely, and take our computer systems with us.'

'Aye, and be my guest while you're at it.' This was brinksmanship but she knew they wouldn't *threaten* her with pulling out, they'd just do it. 'I asked you whether there was a connection between the loss of my rig and the equipment you put inside it. You stonewalled me, so I looked elsewhere for answers. What did you expect?'

'They expected your absolute obedience,' said the third man. 'What they did not allow for was your natural intelligence and unwillingness to settle for anything less than the truth.'

The third man was always doing that: contradicting the other two, and often springing to her defence in matters where her judgement had been questioned. She ought to have liked him for that, felt that she had an ally, but he was the one she liked least of all. She felt she understood the other two: their easy assumption of power. She could imagine them lording it around Whitehall, going to the same clubs, trading stories of their time at Eton or Harrow. By contrast the third man was an unfathomable mystery. She had been alone with him once, while Callow and Lovelace were out of the room for a few minutes. It had been like being in the same room as a reptile.

The other men were clean shaven and usually dressed in suits. The third man was bearded, his hair combed directly back in a manner that made him both debonair and satanic. There were two notches of white in his beard but his age was otherwise hard to estimate. He moved like a younger man, with none of the occasional stiffness she saw in his companions. He looked foreign, but his accent was impeccably British. In his eyes was an amused youthfulness, when she permitted herself to look at them. Also something in those eyes that made her feel as if they were capable of sucking the living breath out of her.

He was always formally dressed, but it was never in a business suit. McCrimmon wasn't sure how she would have described the man's attire, put on the spot. He favoured the same type of outfit that she associated with political despots: a sort of buttonless black tunic with a high collar. He always wore gloves, and he had never once offered to shake her hand.

She was rather glad of that.

'She should not have called in UNIT!' said Callow. 'In doing so she has very nearly jeopardised the secrecy of this entire project.'

'She did her best to dissuade them from coming, once she had had time to reflect on the matter,' the third man said, tightening his gloves as he spoke. 'I have had experience with Brigadier Lethbridge-Stewart myself. Miss McCrimmon cannot be blamed for his tenacity.' He turned his gaze onto her. 'Doubtless they wished to speak to Lomax. You did of course limit the contact, in so far as it was possible?'

'I did my best.'

'Well?' Lovelace asked. 'What did the UNIT delegation go away with?'

'I told them that Lomax had had a fright. I was there when they spoke to him. He confirmed what he already told us. It was a freak event, a deep wave trough.'

'Just that?' the third man asked.

'That's what he said.'

'Then there was no more mention of...' Lovelace paused. 'Holes opening up. Ridiculous great gaps in the sea. No more nonsense of that kind?'

'No. But I can't stop them talking to Lomax again, when he returns to the mainland.'

'Let us hope,' the third man said, 'that they consider matters satisfactorily resolved.' He stroked his beard with one gloved hand. 'When is it intended to relocate Lomax, if I might be so bold as to enquire?'

'In a day or two,' McCrimmon said, 'depending on helicopter availability. There's no immediate grounds for concern, although he'll receive a thorough examination on the mainland.'

'Let us trust that he makes a speedy recovery.'

'He really couldn't have seen anything, could he?' McCrimmon asked, directing her query at all three of them. 'I mean, I know this is all top secret. But there's no way that he really *did* see the sea open up, is there? I mean, that can't have happened, can it?'

'Don't be ridiculous,' Callow said, smoothing down his hair where the wind had elevated a greasy flap.

'The people Lethbridge-Stewart sent,' said the third man. 'Was one of them an older man? White hair, about my height?'

'I'd say he was a bit taller than you, but yes, white hair, aristocratic looking – quite a peculiarly dressed man, too.' She resisted the urge to add: *like you*. 'Opera cape, one of those old-fashioned frilly shirts. He wasn't in a hurry to give his name.'

The third man chuckled quietly. 'No matter. We're adequately acquainted.'

'A friend of yours?' she asked.

'Of sorts. You might almost say we went to the same school.'

CHAPTER FIVE

The Brigadier was on the telephone. 'I see. Credible witness, and all that? Icelandic? What the devil was he doing fishing inside… Very well. Yes, I see. No, not at all. Thank you. And… anything similar… see that it's passed on directly.'

He placed the handset down. Halfway through his call, there had been a knock on the sturdy wooden door to his office.

'Come,' he bellowed.

Jo Grant and Mike Yates entered the room.

'We've just got back, sir,' Yates said, pausing to take a bite from a ham sandwich. 'Helicopter to Aberdeen, Hercules back to RAF Eastmere. Bit worn out, I'm afraid, and on top of that there's bally all to report.'

'I didn't send you halfway to Norway for "bally all", Yates.' The Brigadier, suddenly peckish, was irritated by the apparition of a ham sandwich. 'You met this McCrimmon woman? Did she cooperate?'

'More or less, sir.' Yates took another mouthful. 'She was a bit evasive, but then again I don't think she really appreciated a military presence on her rig.'

'She called us in, Yates – it's no concern of mine whether she appreciated the visit or not. And put that ruddy sandwich away, you're not on a picnic.' Set in front of the Brigadier was a dossier, containing a picture of Edwina McCrimmon, and a photocopy of a corporate report showing a cross-section of one of McCrimmon Industries' production platforms. 'What did you learn and... Good evening, Miss Grant. Where's the Doctor?'

'In his laboratory, sir.'

'I believe I requested a debriefing with the three of you.'

'I'm sure the Doctor will be along in a moment,' Jo said. 'He's going on about something or other – time disturbances, I think he said.'

'Related to this McCrimmon business?'

'Not sure, sir. We did speak to Pete Lomax – the survivor – but he wasn't very helpful.'

'In what way?'

'Bit shell-shocked, sir,' Yates said, stooping to dispose of the contraband sandwich in a nearby wastepaper bin. 'Poor bloke had obviously been in the wars.'

'The main thing,' Jo cut in, 'is that he doesn't back up his original transmission.'

'He denies that he made it? We have it on tape.'

'I mean, he's saying he was confused,' Jo said. 'What do you think happened, sir? Could he really have seen the sea disappear?'

'If you'd asked me that a couple of days ago I'd have been highly sceptical,' the Brigadier said. 'But since then, all hell's started breaking loose. Reports coming in from all over the place, all dashed peculiar, and more often than not there's a maritime connection, or at least proximity to the sea.' The Brigadier snapped the folder shut, pulled over a sheet of pink photocopied paper, and scanned a finger down a list of items. 'Loss of contact with a tanker off the coast of Sunderland. Visual report of a hemispherical area of sea disappearing, from a car ferry near Kirkwall in the Orkneys. Reports of an abandoned and empty police station near Arbroath – suspiciously close to the shore. And just now, the third consecutive report of columns of water falling from the sky.

Icelandic chappie, very het-up about the whole thing.'

'Is that why you were so determined we should speak to McCrimmon, sir?' Yates asked.

'The loss of the platform fits the same general pattern, yes. Someone's obviously got to her, and this Lomax fellow as well.' The Brigadier was on the point of saying something else when one of the several telephones on his desk started ringing. He picked it up, muttered his name and started listening.

When he placed the handset down, his expression was grave. 'That was Geneva. Apparently one of the Navy's Atlantic transmitters has just disappeared. They have the exact time it happened.' He looked up as the door opened again. 'Ah, Doctor. Good of you to grace us with your presence.'

Jo said, 'There's been another disappearance!'

The Doctor had arrived with a piece of the TARDIS in his hands. He cradled a lump of translucent machinery about the size and shape of an electric lemon squeezer. 'Did it by any chance happen about... oh, ten minutes ago?'

The Brigadier eyed the Doctor with familiar suspicion. 'How would you know that?'

'Because someone's interfering with time, Brigadier. Time anomalies, time ruptures – call them what you will. The TARDIS began detecting them several days ago.'

'And you didn't think to bring this to my attention?'

'Rather thought it might be an idea to have some idea of the strength and origin of these ruptures first,' the Doctor said. 'It's not unusual for time travellers to pass through the present moment, on their way from the past to the future, or vice versa. The TARDIS picks up these signatures in much the same way a boat bobs up and down when a larger vessel passes it in harbour.'

'Then that's all it is – other time traveller chappies, jaunting around?'

'Well actually, no.' The Doctor took the weight of the

object in one hand and stroked the side of his face with the other. 'That's what I wondered, but after the Mike Oscar Four business, I turned up the TARDIS's detectors to maximum sensitivity. If there was time-travel activity, I wanted to rule out it having anything to do with our friend at Durlston Heath.'

'You mean… him.' The Brigadier hesitated. Something was on the tip of his tongue, but he couldn't quite bring it to mind. 'The…'

'The Master!' Jo said.

'Yes. Him.'

'But you don't think he's involved, do you?' Jo asked.

'I would never rule anything out where the Master's concerned,' the Doctor said ruefully.

'But we've seen him in prison,' Jo said. 'About the only thing he's got is a television! You're not saying he could have made a time machine out of a *television*, are you?'

'Given enough time, the Master could make just about anything out of anything,' the Doctor answered gravely. 'Frankly, though, this doesn't look like his handiwork. If I'm right about these disruptions, they're originating from some *other* point in time and space, not on Earth – we're just on the receiving end. Nonetheless it wouldn't hurt to pay him a visit, all the same. We'll need the necessary paperwork, Brigadier. Can you sort it out with Childers? Say, for a visit first thing tomorrow morning?'

For a moment the Brigadier looked lost. 'With whom?'

The Doctor frowned. 'The Master, Brigadier. The chap you and I have spent a great deal of energy putting behind bars. The chap we were *just talking about*.'

The Brigadier pinched at the skin above his nose. 'Forgive me, Doctor: it's been rather a long day. I'll get onto Childers.'

'Very good, Brigadier.'

'And these time disruptions – if they're coming from somewhere else, any idea who or what might be behind them?'

'Only that whoever is involved, the energies and ranges involved are considerable.' The Doctor held up the piece of equipment he'd arrived with. 'This is part of the TARDIS's sensory apparatus – a chronometric stress analyser. I'm afraid the last pulse has damaged it entirely beyond repair.' The Doctor turned the piece of equipment over in his hands, eyeing it with all the sadness one might reserve for a broken Ming vase. 'My own silly fault. I had the sensitivity set too high. The temporal shear was a magnitude above the safe detection threshold.'

'In plain English, please, Doctor.'

'The force of that rupture, Brigadier, was beyond the capability of all but a handful of galactic species.' The Doctor raised a gently silencing hand. 'I've already run through a mental shortlist of candidates. Nothing that you or I have ever encountered fits the bill. And the fact the Daleks *aren't* involved may well be the last piece of good news I have for you.'

The Brigadier gestured at the damaged apparatus the Doctor was still holding. 'That... gadget. Can you get it working again, or patch in a spare?'

'This "gadget", Brigadier, was assembled by the Blind Watchmakers, the finest temporal artisans in history. Repairing it here would be like trying to mend a Swiss chronometer with a handful of crude Neolithic tools.'

'But you'll give it a go, won't you?' Jo asked. 'I mean, the Master could repair it, couldn't he?'

'I suppose.'

'And you're better than the Master, aren't you?'

The Doctor hefted the damaged equipment, giving it a shrewd second glance. 'I don't suppose it's completely beyond salvation. I'll see what I can do.'

Near midnight, just when he was beginning to think his head might have settled enough to begin to get some sleep, there came a soft knock on Pete Lomax's door. Who might it be at this late hour? Eddie McCrimmon had already come to speak to him after the earlier visit from the military people, and as far as he was concerned he was going to be left alone after that. McCrimmon had come to tell him that she had appreciated his cooperation, his wisdom in denying what he had said on the wireless transmission, as Mike Oscar Four was collapsing. 'No one thinks any less of you for it, Pete,' she'd said, sitting on the bedroom chair while Lomax rested, still fully dressed, on the side of his bed. 'Anyone who's worked in this business for more than a few years knows what it's like. This is a tough environment and it does things to us.'

He liked Eddie McCrimmon, it had to be said. She'd always struck him as a fair boss. A lot of the men – maybe most of them – had a simmering problem with the idea of a woman running a large chunk of the organisation. Even when they said otherwise. But Lomax had known Cal McCrimmon, and if the Big Man reckoned his daughter was up to the job, that was good enough for Lomax.

But when the door opened – Lomax hadn't even had time to say 'come in' – it wasn't Eddie McCrimmon.

'Good evening, Mr Lomax. I trust I haven't disturbed you?' The man sounded sincere enough, but no one who knocked on a door at midnight really cared whether or not they were disturbing someone. Of course they were.

The man closed the door behind him. Lomax had been sitting on the edge of the bed, wearing pyjama bottoms and a vest, looking through a week-old tabloid newspaper. The sheer mundanity of the news items – football results, an actor's drunken rampage at a nightclub – had been soothing his thought processes. It was good to be reminded that there was a real world out there, over the sea's horizon.

He'd had the main room light switched off, reading by the light of an angle-poise lamp on the bedside table. He'd been finishing off a cup of milky tea, with a shortbread finger perched on the saucer's edge.

He could barely see the man who'd just come into his

56

room. The man seemed to find the exact position to avoid being illuminated, as if the room's shadows were rearranging themselves to obscure this late visitor.

'Can I help you?'

'It's less of a question of you helping me, Mr Lomax, than of me helping you.'

The man was dressed in dark, formal clothes. He was bearded and gloved. Lomax had seen him already, skulking around. 'Are you... working for McCrimmon? I don't think I know your name.'

'I am known universally as the Master,' the man declared.

The state of relative calm that Lomax had begun to feel – the sense that the worst was behind him – evaporated in a stroke. The man seemed to have brought dread with him. It was in the room, hovering like an invisible gas.

'Away, man. I don't want to speak with you.'

'But we've hardly begun to get to know each other.' The Master, if that was his name, stepped closer. 'You've had quite a turn, Lomax. They say you'll soon be returning to a hospital on the mainland. I regret to say that we can't let that happen.'

Lomax had had enough of this. He made to move from the bed, judging that he was easily the stronger of the two men. But the Master was surprisingly quick. He placed a gloved hand on Lomax's shoulder, touching him gently. Although the contact barely registered as pressure – it was no stronger than the kind touch of a friend – something in the Master's hand compelled Lomax not to rise from the bed. He could only sit there, bewildered at his own paralysis. The Master maintained the contact. With no particular hurry, he leaned over to reach the angle-poise lamp, and directed the beam into Lomax's face.

'I am the Master and you will obey me.'

'Please,' Lomax said.

'The sea, the waves, Lomax. They're calling you, even now. You feel that call. You feel powerless to resist it. You know deep down that you will not be content until you answer that calling.'

'I don't want…'

The Master's control over Lomax was now as absolute and binding as if he was working a puppet. He removed the gloved hand on his shoulder, and touched his forefinger gently to Lomax's lips. 'Shush, now. There's a good fellow. We don't want you waking everyone, do we?'

Lomax whimpered another plea. But the Master only smiled. 'It's so close now, Lomax. The peace of mind you've been searching for. Those waves are waiting to welcome you. Hear them crashing against the platform, urging you to join them. Why resist a moment longer?'

'The sea. I have to go to the sea.'

'Yes,' the Master encouraged. 'You must. You know it is for the best. But take your time. Finish your cup of tea.'

The Master's vast experience told him that his hypnotic suggestion had taken sufficiently deep root. Seeing the almost willing ease with which Lomax had surrendered to his control, the Master could not help but feel a microscopic fondness.

He looked around, satisfying himself that there were no loose ends, content that Lomax could be left to follow his programming. He was about to leave the man when he spotted the shortbread finger, still uneaten He dunked the biscuit into the half-finished tea and popped it into his mouth, chuckling at his own excellent good fortune. He had been a prisoner for far too long.

Never mind. That was all about to change. 'Goodnight, Mr Lomax.'

CHAPTER SIX

The panda car attracted no particular attention as it beetled its way south along secondary roads, paralleling the bleak and windswept coast. Although it was still dark, the cloudless sky to the east carried the faintest hint that dawn was beginning to break, and with it a calming in the weather.

There were four people in the passenger compartment of the car: two up front, two in the rear. They were, respectively, PC Archie Hawes, the beachcomber Pat McGinty, and two occupants of the police station from which Hawes operated: DI Ian Staple and WPC Susan Cooper. All four sat bolt upright, staring straight ahead, as stiff as crash test dummies. All were now wearing police uniform, including the beachcomber. Occasionally one of the four would say something, but for long tens of minutes the vehicle's occupants sat in stony silence as they motored south. They did not really need to communicate verbally, not now, but it was good practice to use the speech mechanisms that came with their host bodies. They never knew when it might come in useful, if for example their primary communication channel was blocked.

'We should not have emerged so far north,' Hawes stated, after a long interval of wordlessness. 'We were meant to be much closer. It implies carelessness.'

'The technique is as yet imperfect,' said McGinty. His

voice was slow, deep and zombielike. 'We must use the signal as a homing aid. When the Assemblage is complete, Sild time control will become much more precise. Until then, be grateful that we are on the right world, in the right quadrant of the galaxy, in the right timeframe.'

'You are correct,' said Susan Cooper, speaking in the same slow, slurred tones. 'We should not complain about an error of a few hundred kilometres.' Slowly, she reached up to smear a strand of drool from her lips. All of them were having trouble with some aspects of motor control. 'All is in hand. The primary mission objective remains achievable.'

They continued south. There was not much traffic on the roads at this early hour but occasionally they passed another vehicle or lone pedestrian. The sky brightened by degrees. Now and then they slipped through a small hamlet or town.

'The unit McGinty found,' Hawes said, speaking of the beachcomber as if he were not present at all. 'The damaged ambulator. What became of its Sild?'

'McGinty's memories say it was consumed by indigenous fauna,' answered the body of the beachcomber. With a flicker of revulsion the Sild riding McGinty thought of the grey and white flying things, the raucous scavengers. So alien, so mindlessly carnal. *Seagulls*, that was what McGinty had thought of them as. The very word carried torrents of horror. To cross billions of years of time, to submit oneself to the glory of a one-way mission, only to end up being digested in the belly of one of those flapping, squawking, barely sentient nightmares...

'That could have been us,' Ian Staple intoned.

'Yes,' said Susan Cooper.

Pat McGinty chipped in with: 'I dislike this world.'

'Soon it will be different,' said Archie Hawes. 'The process of conversion has begun. The oceans and air of Praxilion will change it. Soon it will not be the same.'

'Take the next left.' A grubby road map was spread on Pat McGinty's lap. He had been tracking their progress since they had departed the police station. 'It will bring us to the sea. New arrivals should be coming in. We will meet them.'

Hawes shifted gears awkwardly as the car negotiated the sharp junction. It took them from a secondary road onto what was little more than a single-tracked country lane, bordered on either side by high dark hedgerows.

They met no other traffic. The hedgerows thinned away and the pothole-strewn road traversed a bare and windswept heath, before dipping gradually down to the sea. They passed a disused caravan site. At the end of the lane was a rubbish-littered dead end, a forlorn picnic area overlooking a short stretch of sand. The sea glittered in the morning light, low-breaking waves like lines of etched platinum. After a few moments the four occupants emerged from the panda car. They shuffled slowly to the top of the sand, their legs moving more than their arms. They walked like poorly animated figures in a cheaply produced cartoon.

Susan Cooper stretched a hand and arm before her like a rustic signpost. 'There. It forms.'

'Yes,' agreed Archie Hawes.

A lens-shaped hole appeared in the cloudless air. It darkened to purple, then black. A shaft of water emerged, ramming down. It hit the sea about a kilometre from the shore, drawing up a veil of mist. The inundation continued for several seconds, before ceasing abruptly.

'We must do better than this,' McGinty said. 'If we do not, it will take many centuries to drain Praxilion's oceans and atmosphere. There is always a risk that the native Praxilions will resist our efforts to bleed their world. Their Red Queen is clever.'

'We shall prevail,' Cooper said. 'When we have brought this facet into the Assemblage, our control will be limitless. We will hasten Praxilion's demise. This world will soon be fit for Sild occupation.'

'I see the newcomers,' Susan Cooper announced, lowering the angle of her arm like a railway signal.

From the froth and foam of the heavier waves stirred by the arrival of the water shaft, distinct bright things scuttled onto wet sand. Sild ambulators, in ones and twos, fours and fives and then tens and twenties, were coming ashore. The humans acting as Sild hosts had all seen similar sights on half-remembered wildlife documentaries, but this was no natural migration. The Sild pilots, drawing deep from the memories of their human vehicles, felt a prickle of awe. This was still no invasion force, not by the numbers that would come through in time. But at least there were enough to begin to get things done.

The steel crabs scuttled up the sand. They moved in straggly lines and columns. They were homing in on the four watchers.

'Ready the fifth host,' said McGinty.

Without a word, Archie Hawes and Susan Cooper went round to the back of the panda car. They opened the boot. They stared down at the policeman bound and gagged in the back of the car. This was their colleague, PC Nick Wheen. There had not been an ambulator available to control him when the police station was taken, so they had brought his body with them instead.

Wheen squirmed against his restraints. His eyes bulged in terror and incomprehension. He did not understand why his friends and colleagues had turned against him in this manner.

'We are Sild now,' Susan Cooper explained, with a blank lack of empathy. 'You are about to become Sild. The ambulator will attach itself to your nervous system and interface with your brain. You will retain some measure of consciousness, although there will not be free will. But you will begin to understand. Please stand by.'

Wheen tried to say or scream something. Susan Cooper and Archie Hawes reached in and extracted him from the car. They placed him down on the ground, still with his knees tucked under him the way he had been stuffed into the car.

They stood either side of him, their hands on his shoulders. Ambulators surrounded the kneeling form. Some began to scuttle nearer. Wheen's eyes widened more than seemed possible. He shook his head like a damp dog. He did some more muffled screaming.

Three of the ambulators were on him. Their pilots were keen to take first charge of a host. The crabs tussled and squabbled. Two dropped off, landing on their backs. The third made its nimble way up the top of Wheen's back. Wheen thrashed splendidly. The Sild tugged down the back of his collar, exposing a washing label. The Sild pulled aside the label, revealing an area of skin. It gripped tight with legs and tentacles. It pushed its neural probes into Wheen. The probes extended self-replicating structures deep into him, hunting for cortical matter.

Wheen jerked and spasmed.

Wheen became Sild.

He was still. The terror ebbed from his eyes.

Wheen stood. He brushed dirt from his knees. He was stiffer even than the others. It would take a little while for his pilot to learn how to use the host.

He looked down at his feet, at the many other scuttling crabs.

'There is room for me in the passenger compartment. The other ambulators can go in the back of the vehicle. There is room for them. We will find other hosts for them soon.'

The others agreed that this was a good plan.

'So you're off to see... so and so,' Yates said, shovelling a second helping of bacon onto his plate.

Jo looked amused. 'You mean the Master? Yes, Mike, that's why I'm having an early breakfast. The Doctor wanted to get going as soon as possible.' Jo used metal tongs to place two pieces of limp toast on her plate, then carried the tray back to one of the many vacant tables, Yates following close behind.

'You don't think he's mixed up in all of this, do you?'

'It's the Master, Mike. It'd be silly not to ask a few questions.' Jo settled into her plastic-backed chair.

'Have you met him?'

Jo looked up, thrown by this odd enquiry. 'Met who?'

'The chap we were just talking about! You know, old… what's his face.' Yates made a show of scratching his chin, signifying the Master's beard.

Jo was starting to wonder if this wasn't all some elaborate and not very tasteful prank. 'Mike, *of course* I've met the Master. Many times. So have you! What an odd thing to ask!'

Yates seemed unfazed. 'We deal with so many funny characters, it's hard not to lose track of them. If it's not the Yeti, it's the Cybermen; if it's not them, it's the Autons or the flipping Silurians. You can't blame us poor old military sorts if we get a bit muddled now and then.'

Jo spread some grout-like butter onto the toast. 'You remember all of them clearly enough.'

'It's not like they didn't give us a few headaches, is it? The Doctor and the Brig at loggerheads, the world in peril…'

Jo frowned, sensing that there was more to this than a bit of random mischief. 'So you remember the Autons and cave monsters, but you can't hold the Master's name in your head for more than a few seconds? And yet the Master and the Nestene Consciousness were working together to direct the Auton invasion – or that's what the Master thought, anyway.'

Yates jabbed a fork into his bacon.

'What who thought?'

'The Master, Mike! Are you really having that much difficulty remembering him?' Jo bit into her toast. 'But it's not just you, is it? There was that whole strange conversation with the Brig last night. He put it down to tiredness, but now I'm starting to wonder.'

'Wonder what?'

'Mike, something weird's happening. I need to talk to the Doctor.' Jo stood from the table with a feeling of profound foreboding, as if the ground under her might give way at any moment. It was not the first time she had felt this way during her time at UNIT, but that did not make the sensation any more pleasant.

'You've left some toast,' Mike Yates pointed out.

Jo pushed her tray over to Yates's side of the table. 'It's your lucky day…'

A sleek, shark-shaped black helicopter skulked low over the English countryside. The Master was enjoying the scenery, the deep-shadowed lanes, the frosted verges and neatly bordered fields still covered by a quilt of early morning mist. It was not that he took any great delight in these things in their own right, but they served as a pleasing reminder, reinforcing the fact that he would soon be leaving this planet and its deeply tedious pastoral vistas. He longed for space and the infinite, the playgrounds of chaos.

'You needn't look so pleased with yourself,' Callow said, from the passenger seat opposite the Master. 'One more slip-up, one more thing you can't explain, and we'll forget this arrangement ever existed.' He paused to pat down an aileron of stiff hair, lifting up from where it had been pasted onto his scalp. 'That business with Lomax was the last straw. You were supposed to intimidate the man, not drive the poor beggar to suicide!'

'Lomax was fragile,' the Master answered placidly. 'In his agitated mental state, his continued silence could not have been counted on. Or would you rather have run the risk of him speaking to UNIT again?'

Callow jabbed a finger at the Master. 'You overstepped your mark. Perhaps it *is* time to review our relationship. I should have listened to Lovelace… he never liked the idea of bringing you in on MERMAN.'

The Master shrugged. 'Without my technical assistance, you'd still be blundering around in the dark like the mental cavemen you are. But if you feel my usefulness has come to an end, so be it. I'm sure you can iron the remaining bugs out of your equipment, given about twenty years of trial and error.'

'You know we can't wait twenty years,' Callow said. 'We need it now. Before the Russians or Chinese get a march on us. Or, god forbid, the French. MERMAN must work!'

MERMAN: Marine Equipment for the Reception, Modulation and Amplification of Neutrinos. It was the Navy's latest piece of super-gadgetry, so secret that only a handful of top brass even knew that it existed.

For years, military men had struggled with a way of communicating with their submarine fleets while at sea. Radio could not penetrate to the necessary depths, and was susceptible to interception and eavesdropping. Ultra-low frequency sound waves had tremendous range, but could be easily jammed by enemy installations.

Neutrinos, on the other hand, were a gift from physics. These subatomic particles slipped through matter so effortlessly that it was possible to send a beam of them *right through* the Earth itself, from one side of the planet to the other. Of course, there were technical hurdles to be overcome before the idea could be made workable. The neutrinos had to be created, focused into some kind of beam that could be aimed in the right direction. The beam had to carry a signal. Harder still, the detection apparatus had to be compact enough to fit aboard a submarine.

None of that was insurmountable. But after years of trying to get it all to work reliably, the government had reluctantly decided that they needed outside assistance.

Who better than a resident alien, a humanoid genius with a grasp of science and technology far beyond anything known on Earth?

At the highest level of government, the Master's true nature was a matter of record. So Callow and Lovelace had come to him, even while he was still in prison. Their terms were simple. In return for offering technical assistance, the Master would be granted certain luxuries and relaxations in the terms of his confinement.

The Master, to begin with, had turned them down. Their concessions were insufficiently attractive. The problem of making the neutrino equipment function was as boring and trivial to him as a game of noughts and crosses. He could have done it in his sleep, if he had ever had need for sleep.

'Go and ask the Doctor,' he had said. 'He already works for the government.'

'The Doctor won't touch a military project,' Callow had pointed out. 'You, on the other hand, should have no such qualms. You love weapons and warfare. You've maimed and murdered thousands. You kill without the slightest hesitation.'

'You're too kind.'

But when the Master had had time to reflect on their offer, he had begun to see a possibility quite beyond anything Callow and Lovelace might have had in mind.

Their neutrino generating and receiving equipment was exceedingly primitive. They barely understood how it worked. With a tweak here, a tweak there, the Master could easily make it do all that Callow and Lovelace wished. Instantaneous, unbreakable communication with submarines, no matter where they were in the world.

But more than that? Why not?

Could MERMAN also offer a way to achieve his complete freedom?

It had seemed almost too good to be true. And yet the evidence was already mounting that he had been right to take the initiative. He had sent out a plea for action. The plea had been answered – or was at least in the course of *being* answered. In a very little while, he felt certain, help would arrive. No mere terrestrial prison could hold him – not even the elaborate measures of Durlston Heath. The Master would be free again. And he would have no one to thank but himself.

He liked it that way.

'We're nearly there,' Callow said. He dug into his pocket

and came out with a stubby grey box, the size of a match case. 'You know what I have to do now. Are you ready?'

There had never been a moment when the Master had not been aware of the bite of the metal collar fixed around his neck, just under the fabric of his tunic. 'Is it really necessary?'

'You know it is. Childers must keep believing you're being taken away for interrogation.'

'The man is a fool.' The Master settled back into his seat. 'Do what you must, Callow. It must be some compensation for the torments you endured in boarding school.'

There were three buttons on the grey box, each of which was protected by a flip-up cover. The first one armed the unit. The second delivered an incapacitating electrical pulse, enough to kill most men and easily stun a Time Lord. The third, if depressed, would trigger a small but lethal explosive charge. The Master was in no doubt that Callow or Lovelace would use that button, if they thought he was trying to make a run for it. They had used the stun option many times.

'Steel yourself,' Callow said, flipping up the protective cover and hovering his thumb over the second button.

'I am.'

Callow delivered the stun. The electrical shock hit the Master. He grimaced, barely able to move, even as the pain consumed every conscious thought. And then there was dreamless oblivion. Of course it was dreamless. The Master had never dreamed in his life.

CHAPTER SEVEN

Jo found the Doctor bent over a cluttered brown desk in the UNIT laboratory. A jeweller's lens was jammed into one eye. Clamped before him on the desk was the TARDIS chronometric stress analyser, into which the Doctor was poking and prodding a pair of tweezers. The Doctor broke off from a piece of particularly unmelodious humming.

'Just a moment, Susan...'

'It's not Susan! It's me, Jo! Remember?' She plonked a mug of coffee down on the bench next to the apparatus. 'I thought you wanted to make an early start! Don't tell me you've been up all night fiddling with that thing?'

The Doctor sighed, withdrawing the tweezers and popping the lens from his eye. 'And I was getting somewhere, until you created a small seismic shockwave with that mug.' But the Doctor's irritated mood was temporary. He glanced at the wall clock. 'Goodness – it really is time to leave, isn't it? I'm afraid I got carried away.'

'Have you nearly repaired it?'

'That's the thing. I *think* I have, but it's giving very strange readings. Either the thing's broken beyond repair, or the time disruptions are about ten times stronger and more frequent than they were yesterday!' The Doctor took a cautious sip from the coffee. 'I suppose we ought to have a word with

Lethbridge-Stewart, see if there haven't been more reports...'

'Doctor, I'm a bit worried about something.'

Give the Doctor credit: he could be dismissive and absent, but when Jo really had something on her mind, he took her perfectly seriously. 'What is it, Jo?'

'Who's the man we're going to visit today?'

'That's rather a peculiar question, if you don't mind my saying so.'

'All the same, would you mind answering it?'

'The Master, of course. He may or may not be mixed up in all this, but we'd be remiss if we didn't have a word.'

'The Master, yes. Oh, that's a relief.'

The Doctor put down the coffee cup and folded his arms. 'What's up?'

'Do you remember that thing that happened last night with the Brig, when he seemed to lose track of who the Master was? Well, the same thing's happened to Mike. It's like they keep forgetting! I was starting to think it was me going potty, but at least *you* remember him. Don't you?'

'Quite frankly, Jo, I'd give anything to forget the Master.' The Doctor rubbed at the back of his neck. 'Something's obviously happening, if you say it's spread to Mike Yates. Have you spoken to any other UNIT people about this?'

'Not yet. I wanted to see you first, and then...' Jo hesitated. 'How could it spread, Doctor? How could amnesia work like that?'

'It may well not be amnesia, Jo. That's what worries me. I'm afraid what you've described sounds very like the early onset of PTF, or progressive time-fade.'

Jo frowned. She'd spent long enough around the Doctor to pick up a lot of Time Lord lore, but this was a new one on her. 'Time-fade?'

'I may be jumping the gun.'

'And if you're not?'

'We're dealing with something very worrying indeed. Time-fade is an extremely rare phenomenon – so rare that there have only been a handful of documented cases. Or rather *undocumented*… because even the memory of time-fade itself eventually fades away.' The Doctor looked aggrieved, as if this was the sort of thing it was very bad form to talk about. 'Well, it settles one thing. We really do need to have a word with the Master. And the sooner the better. If this is time-fade, it will eventually spread to everyone and everything who has ever had contact with the Master. Every memory, every record.'

'But we're immune, aren't we? Whatever it is, it's not affecting us?'

'For now, Jo. It doesn't mean that the fade won't reach us in the end.'

'But what does it *mean*, Doctor?'

'It means, Jo, that the Master is ceasing to exist. Ceasing to *have* existed. If this time-fade is real, the Master is being unstitched from time.'

Director Childers, chief of security at the Durlston Heath facility, was there to meet the prisoner when the black helicopter settled onto its rooftop landing pad. Two of his uniformed staff flanked him, carrying light machine guns. Another two stood behind him, either side of the prisoner's wheelchair. They had become well used to the prisoner being taken away, sometimes for days on end, and then brought back, usually the worse for wear. The routine had become… well, almost routine.

It was windy on the roof and Childers was more than usually glad of the heavy lambs-wool coat he had thought to bring with him from his office downstairs. He disliked the British winter, with its long weeks of cold, damp weather, calculated to sap anyone's morale. To think he'd once used to *look forward* to winter, because that was the main rugby season. To think that he'd once imagined having a professional career with Hull Kingston Rovers. The closest he came to a Hull KR game now was the final scores in the newspaper.

The helicopter's rotors whirred to a halt. The door opened and Callow got out. The prisoner was still in his seat, head lolling to one side. He looked like he was asleep, or drugged.

Childers nodded at the guards behind him. 'Bring the chair.'

The chair was driven by a remote-control unit, being operated by one of the guards. It sped forward, its electric motors emitting a high-pitched whine. Callow urged the guards to come closer.

Childers walked up to the government man. He'd long ago made up his mind about Callow. Thought that the world owed him a living. The problem was that the world seemed to agree, most of the time. Doors opened for men like Callow, into the right clubs, the right professional circles. Childers couldn't imagine him ever drinking Double Diamond over a packet of pork scratchings.

'I don't know what you've done to him, don't want to know either.'

'That's good, Childers.'

'But it makes me sick. He's a prisoner of Her Majesty's Government, not some animal. Might be how they treat people in other countries, but we're better than that.'

'Yes. Very good.' They were both keeping their voices low, allowing the wind to muffle the conversation. 'Got that off your chest, have you, Childers? I'll remind you that if it wasn't for Her Majesty's Government, you wouldn't have a job. And part of that job entails doing what you're told – especially when national security is at stake.'

'Security – that's the answer for everything, isn't it?'

'Mind yourself, Childers. You've been made more than aware of your responsibilities here. Now help me get him into the wheelchair.'

Childers did as he was told. That was what it always came down to, in the end: doing what he was told. Accepting his place in the scheme of things, just another willing cog. 'I thought this was the right thing to do, once upon a time,' he muttered, as they manhandled the unconscious prisoner from the helicopter to the wheelchair. 'I was ready to go along with whatever it took. But now I'm wondering whether I shouldn't start asking around. I had that Lethbridge-Stewart on the telephone this morning, you know. Bit of a toff, of course. But there are toffs and there are toffs. I've always liked Lethbridge-Stewart.'

Callow's response was icy. 'Lethbridge-Stewart?'

'He's sending some people out.'

'You should have refused them.'

'He's allowed to let his people have visiting rights, you know.'

'I'm well aware of the Brigadier's rights, Childers. He means well and his heart's in the right place. A bit like you, really – dim but loyal. But if a word of this gets out to him – or to anyone else in UNIT, or Geneva, or C19 – I'll need look no further than *you* for the source of the leak.' Callow stepped back from the wheelchair, while the guard with the remote control activated the automatic restraining mechanisms. Metal hoops closed around the prisoner's ankles and wrists, locking him to the wheelchair. The prisoner was still out cold. 'Looking forward to your retirement, Childers? Looking forward to spending a bit more time with the wife?' Callow touched a finger to his lips. 'Oh, wait, you can't. She's jetted off to the Costa Brava. But never mind. I'm sure you'll still find something to keep you occupied. It'd be a shame to jeopardise all that. Wouldn't it?'

Childers looked at the edge of the building, with its low metal fence. 'Take a running jump, Callow.'

'I don't need to,' Callow said, standing with his hands linked, watching as the guards steered the wheelchair toward the entrance to the rooftop lift, the prisoner's head bobbing up and down as the chair bounced along. 'I brought my own helicopter, you see.'

Tom Irwin was the first to break the bad news to Edwina

McCrimmon. She was in her office, fielding one worried enquiry after the next from her oil workers. Word was getting around that the loss of Mike Oscar Four had not been what they liked to call an 'isolated incident'. All sorts of strange and worrying things were happening, and a lot of them seemed to be concentrated on the North Sea. In times of unsettled weather one could expect the odd boat or ship to be lost, but there had been a puzzling cluster of such events in the last couple of days. The worrying thing was that the losses were continuing, even though the weather had become calmer. Not just losses, either. Eyewitness reports of all sorts of madness. Holes in the sea, columns of water dropping from clear skies. Even mention – as yet unsubstantiated – of belligerent metal crabs. Clearly the last was nonsense, but it was a sign of how agitated people were getting. Edwina was largely immune to the usual nautical superstitions, but it was hard not to shake a feeling of impending dread. And we haven't even shot dead an albatross, she thought.

Her first priority, when she could find a clear five minutes, was to have another word with Pete Lomax. She had been all too willing to go along with the idea that Lomax's story had been the product of an overheated imagination. Now she was starting to have doubts. The reports of holes in the sea chimed with Lomax's claim that a great void had opened under the decommissioned rig. Not just the trough of a big wave, fearful as that could be, or an area of water affected by rising gases, but an actual void, like the hole scooped out of a bowl of ice cream.

Callow, Lovelace and the other man had been all too keen to nudge her into the idea that Lomax had been confused. Lomax, too, had seemed willing to accept as much.

Now she wondered if she had done him a grave injustice, by not taking his word at face value.

'Ah, Tom,' she said, as Irwin pushed his head into her office. 'Can you hold the fort for a few…'

'It's Pete Lomax.'

'I know. I want to have another chat.'

'He's gone.'

She blinked. 'Gone?'

'I just went to check up on him. There's no one in his room. The bed's made. And there's no sign of him anywhere else on the platform.'

'It's a big platform, Tom.'

'I've already got a couple of guys on search duty. But I'm worried, Eddie. It's not like Pete to just up and vanish.'

'No,' she said, on a falling note. 'It's not.'

'Did you speak to him last night?'

'Yes, around teatime. Not long after the UNIT people left.'

Irwin nodded. 'I saw him a bit after that – maybe eight o' clock. After that, I don't know. Those government men were still hanging around, weren't they?'

'Like a bad smell. You don't think they…'

'What?'

She was about to say 'got to Pete', but that was ridiculous and melodramatic. 'I saw the helicopter leave in the middle of the night. Callow and the other man, the scientist, were aboard. Lovelace is still on the platform. There's no way they smuggled Pete out without our knowing.'

Irwin planted his hands on either side of his hips, like a gunslinger ready for a shoot-out. 'Eddie, don't take this the wrong way. But I think it's time you were straight with me about what's going on.'

'I've been as straight as I can, Tom.'

'We've lost a platform, there's all sorts of weird stuff going on, and now Pete's missing. All of this is connected and it's starting to worry me. I can only do my job if I'm kept in the picture.'

'I made a mistake,' she said. 'I should never have given the UNIT people the brush-off. Maybe it's time to get back in touch with them again.'

'And hope they've never heard the story of the boy who cried wolf?'

It was a point, but not one she wanted to hear. 'We need to find Pete, if he's still aboard. Two men isn't enough. Put another four on search duty – and I don't care what it costs us.'

'Putting employees before profit? Make sure Big Cal doesn't hear you, he'll have a fit.'

'I'm not Big Cal,' McCrimmon said. 'I'm Eddie.'

Bessie, the Doctor's bright yellow Edwardian-style roadster, made an incongruous sight as it pulled up at the heavily defended checkpoint. Other than the red and white striping on the lowered security barrier, the open-topped car was the only colourful thing to be seen for miles around. The flat-topped buildings of the Durlston Heath complex, beyond the high, razor-wired perimeter fence, were blocky studies in various dispiriting hues of grey and off-white.

'Bit on the early side, mate.'

A guard had come out of the armoured kiosk, toting a sub-machine gun. He wore a black uniform and a jaunty black beret.

The Doctor offered an accommodating smile. 'Didn't hit any traffic, old chap. If Director Childers isn't in yet, we'll be more than willing to wait in the canteen.'

'That sounds like a good idea,' Jo said. After the long, cold drive from UNIT headquarters, it sounded idyllic. 'A nice cuppa, maybe a slice of hot buttered toast?'

'Haven't you already had your breakfast?' the Doctor asked.

'That was hours ago! And before you had me shivering in this contraption!'

'Bessie's a perfectly serviceable form of transport.'

'Provided you're an Eskimo!'

The guard coughed. 'When you two are done arguing, do you think I could see your passes?'

Jo showed the guard the accreditation for the two of them. The guard took their passes, muttered something unenthusiastic, and disappeared back into his kiosk for a couple of minutes. They could see his silhouette through the glass, on the telephone. Eventually the call was concluded, the guard came out again with their passes, and the barrier was raised. 'Mind how you go.'

'We will,' the Doctor said.

He thanked the guard with a wave, slipped Bessie back into gear and drove under the barrier.

'What exactly are you hoping to get out of the Master anyway?' Jo asked, as they trundled down the main service road, threading its way through the complex of buildings.

'That'll depend on him. But I can't say I'm not looking forward to seeing the old fellow.'

'I don't know how you can say that.'

The Doctor looked amused. 'Why ever not?'

'Well, for a start, he's tried to kill you on several occasions! In really horrible ways!'

'We've had our differences, it's true. But he's still one of my kind. I'm afraid we have rather more in common than I'd care to admit.'

'More in common than with someone like me?'

'I didn't say that, Jo.'

'But you meant it, deep down. Didn't you?'

The Doctor could not bring himself to answer. And she would never have expected him to offer her a consoling lie, anyway. The Doctor had too much respect for Jo for that. She knew how he saw her. With affection, certainly. A companion he valued, whose opinions and instincts he had come to prize. A necessary foil for his own vanity. Someone he enjoyed showing off to. Beyond that, though, she was under no particular illusions. The Doctor was fond of her.

But only the Doctor and the Master knew what it felt like to be the Doctor and the Master. No human being in history had ever come close to an understanding of how they experienced time and eternity. Not even Einstein on the best day of his life.

Oh well, Jo thought. At least the Doctor didn't actively disdain her. That was something. And of all the people now alive, only she got to spend a significant part of her existence in his company. Only she got to see some of the things he spoke of. That also was something.

But being around the Doctor could burn as well.

Durlston Heath sprawled across hundreds of acres of flattened land near the sea, resembling in its blocks and cubes a kind of neurotic toy town. Jo was certain she would not have felt quite so negatively about it had the Master not been here, but it was hard to imagine anyone *liking* this place. She supposed it provided employment and security for many workers and their families. The facility had been here since the dawn of the nuclear age, constructed in that false dawn of post-war optimism, when it had genuinely seemed as if it might be possible to generate power on a scale and efficiency that made it too cheap to meter.

There had obviously been a misprint on Jo's last electricity bill, in that case.

At length they came to one of the oldest parts of the complex. Jo's apprehension rose: it was as if she could sense the Master's presence, leaking through barriers of concrete and lead. Durlston A had been the original reactor, a prototype which was later souped up to provide power to the National Grid. After decades of service it had now reached the end of its operational lifetime. As far as the public were concerned, the reactor was in the costly process of being readied for the long and difficult business of decommissioning.

Jo knew better. The reactor would be decommissioned, eventually, but only when it was no longer needed to contain the Master. Given the fact that Time Lords were extremely long-lived, it was anyone's guess as to how long that might take.

In truth, it wasn't much to look at. A being of the Master's stature demanded a prison on an unprecedented scale: a citadel of eternal incarceration, an impregnable monument to his cosmic crimes. Something black and spired and soaring, Jo reckoned. Durlston A, by contrast, was a dingy white cube, like a scaled-up washing machine, gristled in pipes and scaffolding. Connected to it was a dreary blue-grey office and control complex, a few floors lower than the cube. The entire structure looked about as impressive and threatening as a municipal ice-rink.

The Doctor eased Bessie to a halt by the main entrance of the control building. He switched off the engine, engaged the external handbrake, turned to Jo and said softly: 'You don't have to come inside, you know.'

'Come all this way, may as well go the last mile.'

'He can't hurt us, Jo. Not now. But I still want to know if there's something going on.' The Doctor touched a finger to his nose. 'Watch him, and keep watching him. Two pairs of eyes are always better than one. He may give something away.'

'I'll do my best.'

The entrance was up a short flight of steps. Jo and the Doctor went through a revolving door into a brightly lit lobby. Beneath a low ceiling set with strip lights was a horseshoe-shaped console, arrayed with television screens and dials, and equipped with banks of push-buttons and colour-coded telephones. Two uniformed operatives, a man and a women, were sitting on swivel-chairs within the console. They were constantly switching television views, punching controls, picking up and putting down telephone handsets. It was as efficient and technical as a space mission. Jo was able to see several of the television screens, and via them glimpses of the Master, caught from different angles as he moved within the confines of his interconnected room.

She felt a tightening in her belly. Bad enough knowing the Master was still on the Earth, let alone that she was about to be in the same room as him.

'Well, let's get this over with. Some of us have work to be getting on with.'

'Ah, Director Childers,' the Doctor said, greeting the man who had just come into the lobby from another door. 'It's very good of you to accommodate us, at such short notice.'

'You're supposed to give at least a day's warning, you know. The only reason I've conceded is that Brigadier of yours, raising merry hell in Whitehall.'

Childers was a tall, solidly proportioned Yorkshireman. He had a lantern jaw and bullet-shaped head; his remaining hair shaved close to the scalp. His frame looked too big for the suit into which he'd been stuffed. He reminded Jo of a bouncer. She had done her homework on the man before a previous visit. Working class, risen up through the ranks by sheer force of will and ability. Not a man to be underestimated.

'I see he's up and about,' the Doctor said.

'Beggar hardly seems to sleep.' Something in Childers' gruff manner had eased. 'Must be due to that thyroid condition of his.'

'Thyroid condition?' Jo asked mildly.

'You remember,' the Doctor said. 'Prisoner M... has a rare medical condition, Jo. It's the reason he needs to be kept immersed in a constant low-level radiation field. What would be harmful to us, over an extended period, is beneficial to him. Sort of like radiotherapy, only the dose is constant.'

Jo did her part and nodded. She had forgotten about this nonsense cover story. The truth was that the Master's physiology ensured that he was unaffected by the radiation field. But it was a very effective way of keeping others away from his influence.

'You'll be needing your dosimeters, before you go in there,' Childers said, as if they might have forgotten that detail.

'In recent days... have you noticed anything unusual?' The Doctor asked. 'Not so much about Prisoner M – although I'd be interested to hear if you had – but in your memories, your recollections of him?'

'My *recollections* of him?' Childers creased his meaty features into a frown. 'Is this some daft idea of a joke?'

'I realise it's an odd question.' But the Doctor forged on. 'When you woke up this morning, or yesterday, how long was it before you remembered the prisoner?'

The odd thrust of this conversation had drawn the interest of the two console operators, who risked glancing up from their screens and telephones for an instant. Childers glared at them. They returned to their surveillance.

'I don't have to remember him. He's on my mind all ruddy day. He's never ruddy *off* my mind. Does that answer your question?'

'Excellently. Now do you think we could see him?'

They went into a second room, a windowless office adjacent to the lobby. There was a door in the opposite wall, a cabinet to the left of it, a smaller console and chair to the door's right. Childers beckoned to the cabinet. 'It's open. Take your dosimeters.'

Jo went to the cabinet and took out two of the radiation detection badges. She passed one to the Doctor and clipped the other to her coat. The badges were white rectangles, with strips of black film fixed across them. While she did this, Childers moved a newspaper off the swivel chair and eased his frame down onto it. He put the newspaper on the right of the console: it was yesterday's edition, turned to the sports section, with a black and white picture of a rugby match above the final scores.

Childers touched a series of switches. Screens lit up, echoing the views they had seen in the lobby.

There was the Master, pacing around with his hands clasped behind his back, as if in deep and restless concentration.

Childers tugged a flexible microphone to his lips. 'Prisoner M. Can you hear me?'

The Master halted in his peregrinations and turned to face a hidden speaker. His urbane, pleasant voice came out of a grille. 'Go ahead, Director Childers.'

'You have a pair of visitors. The Doctor and Miss Grant.'

The Master had his back to the camera, so Jo could not see his expression. 'What an unexpected treat.'

'Go to your chair.'

'At once.'

The screens flicked from one camera to another as the Master moved through his rooms, before finally coming to rest next to what appeared to be a wheelchair. The Master lowered himself into the chair, resting his feet on the metal supports at the front. His arms rested on the padded supports either side, black-gloved hands dangling over the edge.

'Your glasses.'

'Of course.'

The Master reached into the waist pocket of his black tunic and came out with a pair of black sunglasses. He snapped them open, fitted them to his face double-handed, obscuring his eyes, then allowed his hands to return to the wheelchair's supports.

'Be still.'

Childers touched another control. Via the camera, Jo saw a pair of heavy clamps whirr into place around the Master's wrists, binding him to the chair. Another pair fixed his legs into place. A single clamp curled around from behind the chair to secure the Master's neck. The Master squirmed against the hard metal restraints.

Childers looked down, studying a set of lights as they flicked from green to red. 'He's secure now. I'm opening the main door. It's on a timed entry code: you've two minutes to get to it, then it will lock automatically.' His hands moved to a small keyboard, covered by a black plastic cowl. The Doctor heard four digits being entered, then another row of lights flicked to green.

'You've tightened arrangements since my last visit,' the Doctor said.

'Can't be too careful. You know what he tried to do to that psychiatric team from Geneva, when they turned their back on him. They're the poor fools that need psychiatric help now!'

The Master's voice crackled through again. 'Is there some difficulty?'

'No,' Childers said. 'Your guests are on their way through right now.'

'I await them with great interest.'

Childers touched another couple of controls. 'I'll be watching on these cameras the whole time you're in there. So will my team in the lobby.'

'And listening in?' the Doctor asked.

'Would that be a problem?'

The Doctor put on his best apologetic face, one he reserved for all manner of officials and bureaucrats. 'I'm afraid so. Matters of national security and all that.'

'I hear that a lot these days,' Childers said, reaching over to flick off a microphone.

The Doctor smiled. 'Sometimes it's the truth.'

CHAPTER EIGHT

They walked into the main reactor building. It was a huge enclosed volume, a large armoured cube, boxing a space large enough to swallow a good-sized cathedral. There were galleries and walkways everywhere, spidering up and down the interior walls. The floor was a grid of walkways running between the bulging forms of turbines and associated equipment, hulking snail-like forms mostly painted a uniform mid green. In the middle, occupying at least half of the building's internal volume, but sunk down into a pit in the floor to at least half its height, was another cube. It was also wrapped in ladders and catwalks. A small number of guards, wearing radiation-proof clothing, patrolled the chamber with machine guns and walkie-talkies. Jo glanced down at her badge, bending it to get a better look at the strip. It was already speckled with little white stars, like bird droppings.

'This way,' the Doctor said.

They ascended a spiral staircase up the side of the inner cube. At the top was a door, which in turn led to a short passageway through to the cube's interior. Bathed in yellow light, it made for an impressively complicated scene. Occupying most of the floor was a water-filled trench, sheerwalled and deep. Above this pit was a heavy-duty crane, running on a gantry. The crane was presently lifting a blocky object out of the water, a thing about the size of two luxury caravans stuck together side by side. It was made of metal, and it had no windows.

The crane stopped when the object was out of the water. A swing bridge moved automatically into place. Jo and the Doctor descended a short flight of stairs down to the level of the swing bridge, then walked across it. Warm water bubbled beneath. The flooded pit was deep and lit by submerged lights. At the end of the swing bridge, where it met the side of the accommodation unit, an armoured, watertight door had swung open. The Doctor knocked politely

Jo checked her dosimeter again. More white speckles. Twenty minutes, Childers had said. She had a feeling it was going to be the longest twenty minutes of her life.

'Doctor, Miss Grant – please make yourselves at home.'

The Master, confined to his wheelchair, could not rise to greet the Doctor and Jo. But the chair swivelled on their approach. The Master's gloved hand rested on a small battery of controls set into the right armrest. The chair whirred forward to a table, facing two seats that had been welded in place. 'I am afraid you may find my hospitality leaves a little to be desired.'

The combination of beard and heavy sunglasses masked much of the Master's face. Jo was glad of that: she didn't have to look into his eyes. But she was more than aware that those eyes would be looking back at her, boring through the plastic.

'We won't be staying long,' the Doctor said, tapping a finger to his dosimeter.

'Nonetheless, do sit down.'

The Doctor and Jo sat in the welded metal seats. 'Caught you at a busy time?' the Doctor asked.

'As a matter of fact, I was indulging in some light reading.' The Master's fingers jerked in the direction of a heavy leather-bound textbook spread out on the table. 'A history of early surgery. Quite remarkably barbaric, Doctor: scarcely distinguishable from a torture manual.'

'I'm sure you found it thoroughly entertaining.'

It was a lie, Jo thought. He had not been reading at all, certainly not when they arrived. They had seen the Master pacing around his cell like a caged animal.

'We've been concerned about you,' she said, reciprocating with her own lie. What she meant was: *we've been concerned about what you might be up to.*

'My dear Miss Grant: such a touching concern for my welfare. But I assure you, there is no need to worry yourself on my account.' His fingertips curled to gesture at his surroundings. 'Look around you. My every desire is catered for. What more could I wish for, beyond these walls?'

'The chair seems a bit of an indignity,' the Doctor said.

'The small price I must pay for the pleasure of guests,' the Master said. 'Think nothing of it, Doctor. I am allowed a degree of mobility, the inconvenience is small, and I shall not have to put up with it for very much longer.'

'Director Childers is going to relax the rules again?' Jo asked.

'The man is an irrelevance. I merely state that my present conditions will prove temporary.'

The Doctor smiled. 'You're not telling us you've hatched a scheme to break out of here, are you?'

'And if I had, Doctor, would I be so foolish as to reveal that scheme to my greatest adversary, the architect of my incarceration?'

'If it allowed you a chance to boast, you might.'

The Master chuckled. 'We know each other too well, Doctor. But the truth is, I have no plans to escape. "Plans" would imply a state of affairs that has yet to come to pass, something that might yet be derailed by circumstance. That I *shall* escape, Doctor, is as cold and irrevocable a certainty as the ultimate heat death of the universe. I could not prevent it coming to be even if that were my desire. Wheels are in motion. I am quite powerless to stop them.'

Jo looked at the Doctor. 'Why would he tell us that?'

'Because he never learns, that's why.' The Doctor reached over and turned around the anatomical textbook. It was open at a series of grossly unpleasant line drawings, annotated in Latin. He turned over a couple of pages, hesitated, then turned back to the place where he had started. The Doctor touched a smudge and lifted his finger to his nose, sniffing the bouquet. 'He's arrogant, Jo: that's always been his downfall. Never misses a chance to brag. And no matter how many times he fails, he never accepts that the fault might lie in the over-estimation of his own competence.'

'One of us failed basic chronic navigation, Doctor. One of us passed with the highest commendations in temporal engineering the academy has ever granted. Need I labour the point?'

'It's never stopped you before.'

'Will you please stop bickering?' Jo asked exasperatedly. 'We've been here five minutes already and all you've done is snipe at each other like a pair of old washerwomen!'

'Five minutes, five million years: it makes little difference to Time Lords,' the Master said. But he sealed the remark with a smile. 'You are quite right, Miss Grant: it is entirely unbecoming of us. In fact I am *delighted* that you have chosen to drop by – both of you. I know we have had our differences, but I cannot say that my time on Earth has been without its compensations. You have both added a certain *spice* to my stay. But all good things, as they say, must come to an end. Perhaps now would be the ideal time to bid *adieu*, while maintaining the fond hope that our paths may yet cross again, in some other time and space?'

'So you can have another go at murdering us?' Jo asked.

The black mirrors of the sunglasses reflected her own face back at her. 'Leave me to my affairs, Miss Grant, and I shall leave you to yours.'

'That's reassuring.'

'So you really think you're getting out of here, do you?' the Doctor asked.

'Without a shadow of a doubt.'

'Childers' men would pick you off in seconds. You may be a Time Lord, but you're not immune to bullets. Even if you managed to regenerate, you'd be incapacitated long enough to be recaptured.'

'You are labouring under an unfortunate misapprehension, Doctor. You presume that my escaping would depend solely on my own actions. Needless to say, I would never be so foolish as to attempt such a thing. Fortunately, I have no need to. My departure from this state of confinement will be facilitated by external factors.'

'Help – from outside?' Jo said. 'But apart from a handful of people, no one knows you're here.'

'I do,' the Master said.

'What on Earth do you mean by that?' the Doctor asked.

'Use your imagination, my dear fellow – what little of it you possess. I am a *Time Lord*. I travel through *time*. There are iterations of me spread across all eras of history. Past versions, future versions. I am legion. This version of me, trapped here, is but one facet of my multi-temporal existence.'

The Doctor directed a concerned glance at Jo. 'You think you can call on some other incarnation of yourself?'

'Not "think", Doctor. Know. And the deed is done. My call has gone out, and I am pleased to inform you that it has been answered.'

The Doctor's tone was grave. 'If you cross your own time stream, you risk catastrophe. The Blinovitch Limitation Effect…'

'Is nothing but a story told to children, designed to keep the real power in the hands of the High Council.'

'Wait,' Jo said, raising a hand. 'Let's get this straight. He can't have sent a message to himself, can he?'

The Master chuckled quietly.

'Tell us,' the Doctor urged. 'If you've already put something in motion, what harm can it serve? Have you sent a message into time? How do you know it's been answered?'

'I do, Doctor. An event… has occurred. The nature of this event speaks of temporal manipulation on an impressive scale.'

The Doctor leaned forward. 'The disappearance of that oil platform? How would you know about that?'

Jo tried to read the response in the Master's expression, but the supercilious smile conveyed nothing useful.

'If such a thing were to happen, it could only be me, or iterations of me, launching a massive temporal assault on this time.'

'But you're still here,' Jo said.

'Patience, please, Miss Grant. Skaro was not destroyed in a day.' The Master gestured to his little television set, on which the test card was currently showing. 'I see from the news that there have been reports of unusual weather phenomena. Water falling from the sky. Ships vanishing. Clearly my time interventions are gathering strength, their energies being calibrated and focused.'

The Doctor folded his arms. 'And you're certain it's you, are you?'

'Who else, my dear fellow?'

'Well, you've sent a message, somehow, and *something* is responding. But isn't it a bit of a leap to assume that the time intervention is down to you?'

'I encoded my psychic patterns on the time signal. No one but me could have decoded it.'

The Doctor picked absently at a piece of fluff on his sleeve. 'Well, I hope for your sake that you're right about this. And I suppose the time-fade is all part of your grand plan as well, is it?'

The Master budged his seat forward. He seemed to strain against the metal hoops binding him place. 'Time-fade? What are you talking about?'

'Oh, come on – it's obviously your doing. First the Brigadier, then Mike Yates – for all we know, it could have spread to the whole of UNIT by now. Very clever, I grant you.'

'I confess I don't know what you're talking about.'

'Nice try, old chap.' The Doctor winked at Jo with theatrical over-emphasis. 'Thing is, we've seen the evidence for ourselves. Classic PTF. It's as if their specific memories of you are being progressively scrambled and erased. But of course you know this. The amnesia will create a level of confusion and disruption that will help you to make your escape, when the moment comes. It's all part of whatever dastardly scheme you've been hatching.'

The Master's voice was level but threatening. 'I assure you it's nothing of the kind.'

The Doctor looked at Jo. 'I think it's high time we were on our way, don't you? The tone's turned a bit frosty all of a sudden.'

'I warn you,' the Master said, squirming in his seat. 'Do not trifle with me. Time is on my side! Time has always been on my side!'

'It may well be,' the Doctor said, pausing. 'But... who are you, again?'

'No!' the Master called. 'I will know of this! I demand it! Tell me about the time-fade!'

The Doctor made a show of sniffing his fingers again. 'That smell... I could barely place it, to begin with. But I think I recognise it now. It's *oil*.'

'Oil, Doctor?' Jo asked innocently.

'Very definitely. Crude oil, the kind that comes straight out of the sea. The only question is, how did it ever get in here?'

Dave Giles, luxury coach driver, flicked a cigarette butt through the open sidelight of his rakish red and white vehicle. He performed the action with a certain studied nonchalance, fancying himself as the sort of laconic character who featured in Spaghetti Westerns, the kind of man who seldom shaved, kept his hat drawn down low and never uttered a word of more than one syllable. That was the kind of bus driver Dave

Giles was. A High Plains Drifter of the commercial vehicle world. A Pale Rider of day trips to Minehead and school outings to the West Midlands Safari Park. This illusion, fragile as it was, lasted exactly as long as it took Dave Giles to catch his reflection in the rear-view mirror. Not exactly Clint Eastwood. More Cliff Michelmore, if he was going to be honest.

But even this crushing realisation could not take the sparkle out of Dave Giles. He was having a good day. The bus was going well, they were making good time, and even the frequent interjections from Mrs Gambrel, stern organiser of the Women's Institute daytrip to Scarborough, could not dampen his mood. She had stationed herself in the passenger seat immediately behind the driver's position, the better to tilt forward at regular intervals, like one of those bobbing glass birds.

'Are you sure this is the right way, Mr Giles?' she asked for the nineteenth or twentieth time. 'These roads do seem *very* narrow. If we'd stayed on the A road...'

'Trust me, Mrs Gambrel. I know these roads inside out. We'll be at *le Chef Petit* in two shakes of a donkey's tail.' And then I can buy another pack, a have a crafty fag or two, and your ladies can relieve their bulging bladders, Giles thought.

And he did know the way – sort of. He was fairly sure he'd taken these back roads on a school trip, a couple of years ago, and just as confident that he knew roughly where they'd come out. The key thing was that cement works in the distance. He recognised it from last time, a huddle of square grey and white buildings looming over the low countryside, like a collection of giant shoe boxes. It was the cement works, wasn't it?

Not a power station, by any chance?

Actually, the more he looked at it, the more it began to look like a power station and less like a cement works. Dave Giles grimaced. Perhaps they should have stayed on the A roads after all.

92

'Mr Giles, you've been promising us the fabled services for nearly an hour now. We are not trying to find Shangri-La, the lost kingdom of the Incas or the final resting place of King Arthur. We are merely searching for a roadside refreshment area with adequately hygienic toilet facilities. Some of my ladies are beginning to find it *very* difficult...'

But it was turning into his lucky day, obviously. Blocking the road ahead was a police panda car, turned side-on to obstruct both lanes of this narrow highway. Standing next to the car were five – *five* – police officers.

'Oh dear,' Dave Giles said, slowing the bus to a halt.

In fact, he couldn't have been happier. He didn't care why the police had closed the road, only that it saved him the bother of driving further and further into the unknown. A tree down, an accident, a crazed axe murderer around the next bend, it didn't matter so long as it got Mrs Gambrel off his back. Better still, he'd be able to have a sly word with the police, find out where he'd taken a wrong turn. And then turn the bus around and get back on the right road with no one thinking it was his mistake.

'Just a second, ladies,' Giles said, putting the bus in neutral, engaging the brake and opening the power-operated door. 'I'll just have a word with the boys in blue, see what's up.' If he'd had a cowboy hat, that would have been the moment to jam it down and step out of the saloon, an Ennio Morricone tune playing in the background. He imagined wearing boots with those big cog-wheel spurs, rather than his current polished black slip-ons with ornamental gold buckles.

Leaving the bus chugging away, Giles walked over to the five policeman. It was strange the way they stood like that, all in a row in front of the car, like footballers awaiting a penalty shootout. One of them didn't even look like a policeman. He looked more like a tramp, dressed in a policeman's clothes which didn't fit very well. Greasy grey hair came all the way down to his collar. Must be special branch.

'Road's blocked, is it, officers?' Giles asked cheerily.

'Where are you going?' asked the only female policewoman in the line-up.

'Scarborough, love.'

'Your passengers?' queried the oldest of the male policemen. 'Have they reached maturity?'

Giles looked back at the bus. He could see the paisley-bloused Mrs Gambrel leaning over her seat to look through the front windscreen. 'And then some.'

'They are of able body and mind?' asked the tramp. 'They have no cognitive or motor impairments?'

'Well, other than the odd dicky hip...'

'They will suffice,' said the woman. 'They will all suffice. He will suffice.'

'Open the boot,' instructed the youngest of the male policemen. 'Release our fellows.'

'The thing is,' Giles said, 'I think I took a wrong turning anyway. I'm trying to get back onto the A road, the one with the services on...?'

'We know of no services,' said the tramp.

The woman and the oldest male policeman had the back of the panda car up now. They were looking into the boot. 'Emerge,' the woman said. 'Emerge and take your hosts. The time has come!'

Giles felt himself drawn to the open boot of the panda car. Part of him wanted to run away, sensing the basic wrongness of this situation. Another part had to know.

The back of the car was full of silver crabs. Giles watched, rooted with shock and fear, as they began to spill out. They had too many legs and too many fine, whipping tentacles. There were glass things on their backs, and things inside the glass things. The crabs were pulling themselves over the lip of the boot, dropping down onto the ground. Ones and twos and threes and fours, fives and tens... dozens of them, an impossible silver tide brimming from the back of the car. They must have been packed as tight as sardines.

'There are still too many of us,' the woman said. Her voice

was as flat and emotionless as a sleepwalker's.

The first crab was on Giles. It was whisking up his leg. He screamed and tried to bat it off.

'No!'

'We are Sild,' the woman said. 'You will become Sild. Please stand by.'

'This is a good start,' said the tramp. 'We will dispose of the police car here. We will take the bus. We will find more hosts soon.'

Giles screamed.

Giles stopped screaming.

And then Giles was Sild.

He turned around stiffly. Mrs Gambrel was still looking through the front window. She had seen something of what had happened, although it was doubtful that she understood. But that she had seen enough to be frightened, that was not in doubt. Giles – what had been Giles – watched as Mrs Gambrel frantically tried to find the control that closed the automatic door. How many times had she seen him work the door, without paying attention, Giles wondered?

Silly woman.

The tide of crabs surged toward the bus. Giles and his five new friends followed in their wake.

CHAPTER NINE

The Doctor watched the Master's accommodation block sinking slowly back into the flooded pit, trailing the dark umbilicals of electrical, air and water-supply cables as it descended beneath the glowing waterline. Jo, anxious to be out of the enhanced radiation environment, had gone ahead of the Doctor. He did not much blame her for that, feeling no great inclination to linger himself.

But he needed time to marshal his thoughts, to think through the implications of their conversation with the Master. Absently, he lifted his fingers to his nose again, as if doubting that initial impression. But no, there it was again. The subtlest of chemical messages, but one that led to an unavoidable conclusion. The Master, normally meticulous, had brought contamination back with him into the cell. Such an error could only have been made in haste, as if the Master had not had time to rid himself of all traces of the oil platform. The Doctor was certain now that this was where he had been, perhaps within the last twenty-four hours.

The Doctor's mind spun through the possibilities. Why would the Master allow himself to be taken outside, and then brought back again? Many times the Master had proven himself ruthlessly adept at escape – even if the act of escaping necessitated the deaths of innocent bystanders.

To the Master, such deaths were regrettable only in the sense that they marred the elegance of his plans.

He wouldn't allow it, the Doctor thought. Not unless he had no choice. Not unless he was being coerced into something, and then brought back to the prison.

But again his experience of the Master gave him profound misgivings. It was true that the Master had, on occasion, imagined himself in control of forces that would eventually turn against him. But by the same token many other intelligent beings had deluded themselves into thinking they had some control or influence over the Master. Without exception, these unfortunates had learned that the Master was only going along with the pretence of coercion while it suited him. Usually that was the *last* thing they learned.

So who was stupid or arrogant enough to think they had a rein on the Master now?

Not UNIT, the Doctor was sure: the Brigadier had his failings, but underestimating the Master was not one of them. Someone else. Someone who knew about the Master, knew something of his capabilities, and might not be able to resist the temptation of using him...

But who knew about the Master, beyond the highest levels of government?

'It's time to go now,' said one of the masked guards. 'Your badge is at maximum dosage.'

For a moment the Doctor was on the verge of boasting that he had survived prolonged exposure to radiation levels ten times as high as this. But the guard meant well, and the encounter with the Master had put the Doctor in a troubled state of mind. He allowed himself to be escorted back out of the high-security area, to the small office where Childers was still waiting, studying camera views on his console.

'Miss Grant is outside, Doctor. Had a nice little chinwag with the prisoner, did you?'

The Doctor waited until the guard had left them alone. 'What have you allowed to happen?'

The insolence of this statement caused the other man to look up properly for the first time. 'Begging your pardon?'

'The Master... your prisoner... has been allowed in and out of Durlston Heath. That could only have happened with you turning a blind eye.'

Childers elevated his bulky frame from the chair. 'Not sure what daft ideas the prisoner has been putting in your head, Doctor, but I'd thank you not to take that tone. Rest assured that I'll be speaking to Lethbridge-Stewart about this.'

'Speak to him all you want. I'm sure the Brigadier will be very interested to hear that the most dangerous man in the world is being allowed to come and go at his leisure. Are you *quite* out of your mind, Childers?'

'Enough.' Childers leaned over to a flexible microphone stalk on his console. 'Security, please. Observation Room One.'

It took only a few seconds for the door to open, and for a guard to present himself.

'The Doctor's forgotten his way out,' Childers said, his meat-coloured face turning a rosier shade than normal. 'See that he reaches his companion, and that the two of them find their way to the exit checkpoint.'

'I'll do that, sir.'

Childers seemed about to leave it at that. But as the Doctor was ushered gently to the door, he added: 'I don't need any reminders about the prisoner, Doctor. I know full well what a threat he poses to national security.'

The Doctor nodded, making a mental leap. 'Which is why you'd be willing to sanction some off-the-record interrogation? It's useless, you know. Torture never works. There isn't a mature civilisation in the galaxy which hasn't learned that lesson.'

Childers' complexion deepened beyond rose. The blood seemed on the point of bursting out of him.

'See the Doctor out.'

When they emerged from the perimeter a UNIT Land

Rover was parked by the side of the road a little way from the checkpoint. Sergeant Benton was waiting by the side of the vehicle. He gave a cheery wave to Jo and the Doctor.

The Doctor pulled Bessie up alongside the Land Rover.

'What's up?'

'Escort back to headquarters, sir. Brig said he didn't want you dilly-dallying on the way. It's getting worse.'

'The amnesia about the Master?' the Doctor asked.

'Him, yes. Now we know that we have to keep remembering… him… we're making an extra effort. Talking about him all the time, putting notes everywhere, getting these posters printed…' Jo noticed that Benton had donned a white armband. He caught her looking at it. 'These as well. They help a bit. But we only have to stop concentrating for a second or two…' Benton looked momentarily foggy. 'What were we…'

'The Master,' the Doctor said gently.

'I'm sorry, sir. I'm trying really hard. But it's like trying to do long division while tying my shoelaces on backwards.'

'Not your fault, old chap. Something is happening to your knowledge of the Master, something very fundamental, and you can only resist it so far. Whatever you do will only slow the fade, not stop it. Unfortunately, the rate of progression is very steep. I'm not sure how much time we have.'

'Before what?'

'Before none of us remember the Master.'

'What would that actually mean?' Benton asked. 'I mean, if we don't remember… him… would that really be so bad?'

'I don't know,' the Doctor said, and Jo knew he was speaking the truth, and that worried her more than anything. She could deal with almost anything when the Doctor seemed on top of events. 'The Master has done something, that's clear. If he's not lying, then he's managed to squeeze a signal into time, a kind of mayday code, broadcasting his temporal whereabouts. And he thinks that that signal has been intercepted and decoded by another version of himself, in some other timeframe.'

'Is that possible?' Jo asked.

'I rather fear it is. But the time-fade... if my instincts are right, that's not something he anticipated. He seemed frightened. I've almost never seen the Master frightened. I'm not sure I like it.'

'Because if something's got him frightened... what does it mean for the rest of us?'

'Exactly,' the Doctor said.

Benton opened the door and made to get back into the Land Rover. There was a piece of paper sellotaped to the windshield. Presumably it was there to remind him why he was on this errand in the first place.

'I think you need to see this,' Tom Irwin said.

Edwina McCrimmon was on the outside walkway of Mike Oscar Six, trying to clear her thoughts. It was her usual remedy, a dose of bracing fresh air, the sea below, the smell of oil and the hum of heavy industrial machinery. Getting closer to what the business was all about, Big Cal had always said. Drilling into rock. Being at war with the weather and the waves, always and for ever.

It usually did the trick. Today it wasn't working.

One of the company's other platforms, Mike Oscar Three – a little over fifty miles closer to Norway – had dropped off radio and subsea data-link communications. Mike Oscar Seven was reporting some kind of 'disturbance', the messages presently too garbled to make much sense. Had an intruder got aboard? Had one or more of the regular oil workers had some kind of psychotic episode?

McCrimmon had called back to headquarters. It turned out they were monitoring on-going 'incidents' across a number of platforms and support vessels, not all of them belonging to McCrimmon Industries. In view of the uncertainties, head office had instigated the standard emergency evacuation procedure. High-capacity helicopters were already starting to shuttle back and forth from the mainland, extracting non-essential personnel. McCrimmon had been told to curtail normal drilling operations until the extent of the difficulties could be assessed.

It might be nothing. McCrimmon had seen her share of storms in a teacup. Oil workers were a twitchy bunch at the best of times. But with the disappearance of Mike Oscar Four, and now Pete Lomax, she could not help but jump to the obvious conclusion. It was all connected, somehow, with the MERMAN experiment. She had a good mind to confront Lovelace, finally give him a piece of her mind. All she could do with was one piece of good news.

At Tom Irwin's arrival she dared to allow her hopes to rise. 'Please tell me you've found Pete?'

'Not exactly,' the big bearded man said. 'Searched every square inch of this place – the bits we're allowed to get into, anyway. There's no trace of him.'

She looked down over the railing, watching the gulls orbit the legs of the rig, dashing in and out of view under her. She envied them their absolute indifference to gravity. To the gulls this metal imposter was just another landmass. It churned up the water around it, it offered sanctuary, warmth and scraps of kitchen swill. They had come to depend on it. In their tiny minds it was geologically old.

'You'll just have to keep looking.'

Irwin had made his way along the catwalk to stand next to her. Not too close – there was a good couple of metres between them – but near enough that neither had to raise their voice unduly.

'Let's be honest, Eddie. We know where Pete is.'

'I don't want to think about that.'

'None of us do. But out here, it's the easiest and quickest way out.'

McCrimmon had always had a fear of heights and drowning. 'No matter how fed up I got, that's not the way I'd choose.'

'Something happened after we left him alone. Something that – I hate to say – pushed him over the edge.'

One of the helicopters was coming in, big as a bus with its rows of passenger windows. She wouldn't have minded being on that when it took off back for the mainland. But even if the evacuation went all the way, she would be among the last to leave the platform.

'How can you know he was pushed?'

'Because there's this.' Irwin had produced something from his pocket. It was a small drawing book, a tablet with ring-bound pages. 'I found this in Pete's room. It had slipped down between his bed and the bedside table. You know how he used to like sketching.'

'What made you look there?'

'I wondered if Pete was under the bed. Sorry, but I wasn't going to leave any stone unturned.'

'You were right.'

Irwin approached close enough to hand McCrimmon the book. She took it carefully, thinking how easy it would be to let go, to watch it flapping its way down to the waves like a square-winged bird. If there was something in this book, something that complicated things, something that made her job even harder than it had already become, she wouldn't be at all sorry to see the book plummet gannet-like into the sea.

But she had to know what was in it.

She opened the book and flicked through the pages. McCrimmon was no art critic – she would never have claimed to be – but she could see a certain undisciplined vigour in Lomax's sketches, an energetic roughness that made the drawings look more alive, more artistic, than if they'd been more finished and refined. Lomax had used a black felt-tip pen for all his drawings, and he had worked with evident speed, his strokes contrasting between light sketch work – barely there at all – and thick black lines where he had almost dug the pen into the paper. The sketches had all been done on the missing rig, perhaps in his last tour of duty. Some of the

DOCTOR WHO

drawings were of scenes on the rig itself – items of equipment, vistas of the accommodation block, the helipad, and so on. The sketches never extended to the limits of the page, but merely faded out into barely hinted at details. Lomax had also drawn people: quick snapshots of workers, usually anonymous, going about their daily business. McCrimmon could imagine him snatching out the sketchbook in odd moments, perhaps when he was technically on duty. The sketches had an impromptu, unforced look – it was as if his subjects had not been aware they were being sketched. He must have completed the individual drawings in a rush of pen strokes, before the view altered.

She turned the pages. More sketches, not all of them completed. Abandoned efforts. As she progressed through the book, it became obvious that the latter half was still blank.

Eventually she reached the final image.

It was another figure, but not one of the rig workers. It was also someone that McCrimmon recognised immediately, even though the sketch was exceedingly rough and unfinished, little more than a scribble forced into the shape of a man.

'The third man,' she said.

Irwin gave a slow nod. 'Hard to miss.'

The man had been drawn facing out of the page, as if Pete Lomax had been standing in front of him while sketching. The form of the drawing was of a tapering wedge, with the man's head swollen to almost comical proportions, like a balloon bobbing toward the viewer. The rest of him was suggested, rather than drawn in any detail: a converging inverted triangle of furious black strokes. McCrimmon couldn't help but think of a malevolent jack-in-the-box. She still didn't know the name of the man.

But there was no doubt that this was him. The fastidious beard, bracketed with two symmetrical strokes of white. The prominent brow, beneath a receding fringe of greying combed-back hair. The eyes, boring out of the paper like twin drill-holes. There was a terrible commanding force in his stare. Lomax had made the eyes into vortices: circles of blank paper, surrounded by tight constricting spirals. It was almost as if they had been paper-punched right through to the next blank sheet.

Beneath the sketch, one word, scrawled in jagged strokes, as if gashed with a dagger:

MASTER

That was all.

'I don't like this,' she said.

'Didn't think you'd be over the moon,' Irwin said.

CHAPTER TEN

Men and women had been busy at UNIT headquarters, and the activity was still on-going. Posters, economically printed in black and white, were being pasted or pinned onto every available surface. They were all identical. Each poster showed a grainy full-face photograph of the Master, his head tilted slightly down, his eyes staring out of the image. Above the picture, printed in bold capitals, were the words THE MASTER! Beneath the image, in slightly smaller type, was a more detailed explanation:

THE MASTER IS OUR GREATEST
ADVERSARY.
HIS CRIMES HAVE ALREADY ENDANGERED
THE EARTH AND COST MANY LIVES.
ALTHOUGH HE REMAINS IN CAPTIVITY,
THE MASTER IS USING HIS POWERS TO
AFFECT OUR MEMORIES OF HIM.
WE MUST RESIST THIS INFLUENCE!
STUDY THIS POSTER.
COMMIT IT TO MEMORY.
TRY AND BRING THE MASTER TO MIND
FREQUENTLY.
MENTION HIM TO YOUR COLLEAGUES.

CARRY REMINDERS ABOUT YOU!
COLLECT A WHITE ARMBAND FROM THE
QUARTERMASTER'S OFFICE AND WEAR IT
AT ALL TIMES.
RECITE THE WORDS
'I MUST REMEMBER THE MASTER'.
TOGETHER WE CAN RESIST THIS
INFLUENCE!
REMEMBER THE MASTER!

Periodically, a recorded announcement would come over the general address Tannoy, as a woman with a cut-glass accent recited the same words: 'Remember the Master!'

As impressed as he was by this industriousness, the constant interruptions were making it very hard for the Doctor to concentrate on the task in hand. Perhaps that difficulty (he was normally very good at blocking distraction) was the first faint sign that he, too, was being affected by the time-fade. If so, he just hoped he could keep the worst of it at bay, until he had an idea what they were up against.

He was still struggling with the damaged chronometric stress analyser. Such a shame that he had been careless with it! It had been hard enough dealing with the Blind Watchmakers in the first place. Large mole or bat-like creatures (opinions varied), with a highly developed sense of acoustic perception, and whiskers so acutely attuned that they could literally see by touch, right down to the discrimination of colour, they lived in tunnels, under the ash-black, airless crust of their battle-sterilised husk of a planet, and they had been living in these tunnels for numberless aeons. Despite their highly refined non-visual senses, Blind Watchmakers were famed for their almost comical clumsiness, their inability to squeeze past each other without a collision, and the many accidental indignities, injuries and deaths they inflicted on their hapless guests. No one ever paid them a second visit unless there was very good reason.

But they were worth the trouble. Despite this clumsiness they were instrument-makers of unparalleled ability. Their clocks made pulsars look slipshod. A Watchmaker compass was sensitive enough to detect the nervous system of a gnat, half a continent away. Their chronometric recording devices were without equal.

The Doctor's was fixed in place in a makeshift cradle on the laboratory bench, wrapped in a nest of coloured electrical cables and Christmas tree lights, the substitute parts rigged in with crocodile clips, electrical tape and dollops of plasticine. From this uninspiring chaos extended several dozen peripheral tangles, connecting the instrument to the grey metal boxes of a number of hefty government-issue oscilloscopes. As primitive as these analysis devices were, the Doctor had long ago learned to make the best of what was available to him.

Adapt and survive. Make do and mend. These were good mottos for a time traveller.

By careful manipulation of the dials and switches on the oscilloscopes, and by painstaking observation of the flickering green sinusoid traces on their little gridded screens, the Doctor had made considerable headway. The time ruptures, if he could believe the readings, were increasing in frequency, magnitude and longevity. Whoever was doing this – whoever was opening ruptures to the present – was definitely getting better at it. That water falling from the sky was coming from *somewhere*, the Doctor felt certain. He just wished he knew where that place was, and when.

Another world, perhaps – elsewhere in space and time. And the logical conclusion was that the occupants of that world, or at least someone, was intent on transferring their oceans across time to here, Earth. It was small beer right now – mere billions of litres of water. But it was continuing, and the amount coming through in each event was increasing. It might take years or decades, but the effects would eventually be hard to ignore. Earth's seas would swell. The oceans would swallow the land. The good people of this planet, who the Doctor had come to like, would drown under the impossible, endless deluge.

Who – what – would do such a thing? And to what purpose?

The Doctor had the vaguest inkling that he already knew the answer to that question. Somewhere in the deep past. A vanquished foe, a singular alien menace. Tiny creatures, deceptively beautiful in their unarmoured form. Little gemmed things, like ornaments.

Stealing oceans, draining worlds and flooding others, was the way *they* had always done things.

But that had been so long ago. They had been locked away. Put aboard that terrible ship. And that terrible ship had been fired into the black hole, and destroyed. It could not possibly be them.

Could it?

That was when the telephone rang. The Doctor picked it up grumpily, knowing exactly who was on the other end.

'You know, Brigadier, a chap can't be expected to do any useful work if—'

'Never mind, Doctor.' Lethbridge-Stewart had that certain manner about him, the one that betokened a particular kind of military seriousness. It usually meant the balloon had gone up, metaphorically speaking. 'We've found something. I'd rather like you on site before we bring in the big guns.'

'The big guns, Brigadier? I bet you can barely contain yourself.'

'There's a helicopter on standby. I'd like you aboard it, with me, in five minutes.'

'For pity's sake, man. Aren't you going to give me at least some explanation?'

'Crabs,' the Brigadier said succinctly.

'Crabs? What do you mean "crabs"?'

'Metal crabs, Doctor. Coming ashore. In rather large numbers.'

*

110

The serenity of a lightly travelled secondary road was shattered by the approach of a red and white luxury coach, tilting on its suspension as it took a bend at reckless speed. A roadside observer, of which there were thankfully none, might have found the excessive velocity troubling. The coach appeared to be in the hands of a maniac – a thief, perhaps, who had stolen the vehicle and was now determined to get as far away from the scene of the crime as possible. But the driver of the coach appeared in no way perturbed or out of the ordinary. He was a respectable-seeming middle aged man in a crisply ironed shirt, tie and blazer. He sat bolt upright, both hands on the wide horizontal steering wheel. His face was a mask of utter composure. Behind him, compounding the sense of ordinariness, were rows of patiently seated passengers, most of them women of at least middle age. They seemed surreally unfazed by the coach's careering progress, its cavalier tilting, the way it bounced and swayed from one pothole to the next, the manner in which the back end swung out on the more slippery parts of the highway. The women leaned to the left and right in their seats, but in curious metronome-like unison, as if they had been practising for weeks. The same was true of the five police officers who had taken seats on the same coach.

The woman behind the driver leaned forward. She wore a paisley-patterned blouse. She tapped him lightly on the shoulder. 'Slow down. We are not yet ready to breach the facility.'

The driver rotated his head to the extent of its travel, taking his eyes off the road for an alarming interval. 'We have sufficient force of numbers. Now is the time to strike.'

'We must have more hosts. Not all ambulators were provided for. Those without hosts must gain hosts.'

This was correct. All of the passengers were under Sild control now. But they also carried ambulators in their laps and handbags, waiting for more hosts. And more Sild were coming ashore with each successful time rupture.

111

'What do you propose?' the driver asked, swivelling his eyes back onto the road. The bus, which had veered to one side of the highway, clipped a farm gate with its rear end.

'If we strike before success is guaranteed, the authorities may organise a counteroffensive.'

'They will not win. Sild forces will eventually overwhelm this world. The process has commenced.'

'That is true.' The woman – the former Mrs Gambrel – spoke in the same uninflected tones as the driver. 'But occupation and control of this world is only our secondary objective. Our primary objective is the Master. We know from our other encounters that the Master is resourceful. If we do not achieve success on our first strike, the Master may elude us.'

'He cannot escape. We will find him, wherever he goes.'

'That is true,' the woman said again. 'But needless delay and confusion must be avoided. We will not strike until all local ambulators have hosts.'

'That could take hours. Days.'

'It need not. Remember, our hosts need not be human.' The woman was looking over the speeding hedgerows, into the fields beyond. Huge and docile creatures grazed there, supremely oblivious to the coming end of their world. 'They need only be useful,' the woman added.

The Doctor stooped against the blast from the helicopter's rotors. It was a smaller machine than the one that had taken them out to the rig, a waspish craft with a bubble canopy, skeletal tail, exposed engine parts, and room for no more than four occupants.

'Are you quite sure this is necessary?' he asked.

'I can't wait until we can capture one and bring it back to headquarters,' the Brigadier said. 'Whatever these things are, they're coming ashore in waves. Hundreds of them, all up and down the coast. I need to know what they are, and ideally how to blow them up.'

'I wondered when we'd get to blowing things up.' But the Doctor was willing to accept that Lethbridge-Stewart had a point. Not that he really needed the evidence of his eyes to know what they were dealing with. That earlier suspicion, of an ancient foe returned from time, was now looking all the more plausible. But it would be good to know for sure.

He planted a foot on the helicopter's landing skid.

'Doctor!'

It was Jo Grant, running to catch up.

'I'm afraid the Brigadier's got me on an errand,' the Doctor said, offering an apologetic shrug. 'But we shan't be too long.'

'It's Eddie McCrimmon,' Jo said. 'She's on the telephone! Called the Brigadier's office, because that's the number she had. But she really wants to speak to you, Doctor.'

'The perishing woman was no use to us at all when we flew out to meet her,' the Brigadier said, employing 'we' in the loosest possible sense, since he had not actually met McCrimmon. 'I fail to see why we should jump at her beck and call now.'

The Doctor had to fight to be heard above the roar of the engine. He was half on, half off. The helicopter was almost ready to lift off. 'What does she want, Jo?'

'I don't know, Doctor – she says there's some kind of evacuation going on – but she really wanted to speak to you.'

'You can deal with her on the Doctor's behalf,' the Brigadier said, snapping shut the Perspex door on his side and leaning over to speak to the pilot.

'Perhaps I ought to have a word after all,' the Doctor said, as Jo backed away from the whirling rotors. 'If the Master really has been allowed to come and go from Durlston Heath, and if he *was* on that platform…'

'Whatever it is, Doctor, I doubt very much that it is quite so urgent as an advancing army of metal crabs. Miss Grant can deal with the woman. Now please get into the helicopter.'

'It's all right,' Jo called. 'I'll talk to her! We ought to at least hear what she has to say.'

The Doctor nodded, easing into his seat and closing the door.

And then they were airborne, rising above UNIT headquarters. The helicopter put its nose down and surged for the coast.

CHAPTER ELEVEN

'Hello? Yes, it's me, Josephine Grant. We met on the platform. I'm afraid the Doctor's had to be called away on urgent business. No, nothing medical – he's not *that* kind of doctor. Well, actually he's all kinds of doctor at the same time, I suppose.' Jo halted – she could sense Eddie McCrimmon doing her level best to get a word in. 'What I mean is, you're going to have to talk to me for the time being. Is it about Pete Lomax, the man we spoke to?'

'In a manner of speaking. Are you certain I can't talk to someone in authority?'

This needled Jo, the presumption that she was no more than a glorified tea-maker, but she was used to it. 'I am in authority, Miss McCrimmon – I wouldn't have come out to your rig if that wasn't the case. I've exactly the same UNIT security clearance as the Doctor.' Jo felt like adding that Eddie McCrimmon was the last person she should have had to lecture about the presumption of authority in a female professional. But she decided to let it go for now. 'So what is it about Mr Lomax?'

'Mr Lomax is dead, I'm afraid. At least, it's looking increasingly that way. After you visited him, he seems to have decided to jump off the platform. We've searched top to bottom. There's nowhere else he could have gone.'

115

Jo was momentarily stunned. She had barely known Pete Lomax, but in the brief meeting they'd had, she had formed the opinion that he was a decent enough sort. The thought of him jumping into the cold North Sea, falling through the open air, knowing he was going to drown, was awful. What could drive someone to such a thing? If she had learned only one human truth in her time with the Doctor, it was that she would choose life over death, over and over again. Where there was life there was hope, always and for ever.

She wanted to believe that.

'That's terrible. He seemed like a really nice man.'

'He was. I liked him a lot.'

After a moment Jo said: 'You don't think we had anything to do with it, do you?'

'No, you only asked him fair questions. It's the other lot I've concerns about. Especially one of them.'

'The other lot, Miss McCrimmon?'

'Look, call me Eddie – it's easier. And I'm sorry for what I said to you just now. I shouldn't have doubted your credentials. I'm guessing you've worked hard enough to get where you are in UNIT.'

'And I'm guessing it hasn't been quite as tough as getting where you are in the oil industry.'

'A few ups and downs on the way – although there are some who'll always refuse to believe I could have got anywhere without Big Cal's influence.'

Jo nodded to herself at this remark – she couldn't help but think of her own uncle, how he had pulled strings to get her into UNIT, and how that meant she had to work even harder to prove herself.

'The fact is,' McCrimmon went on, 'my father never wanted me in this line of work. It scared the living daylights out of him.'

'Maybe he had a point, if people are starting to jump off oil rigs,' said Jo.

'That's the thing, though. Pete Lomax wasn't the type to

do that. That's why I think someone got to him. Look, I'm going out on a limb here. But I have to talk to someone I can trust outside of McCrimmon Industries. Do you know of something called MERMAN?'

'No,' Jo answered truthfully. 'I'll need a bit more to go on.'

'It's a project – a government project, something to do with submarines... They needed our help to test it.'

Jo sensed tremendous hesitation in the other woman, as if she knew that every word might end her career. 'Go on.'

'I don't know much more than that. But men have been coming out here, putting MERMAN equipment on our platforms. Including the one that sank... or vanished. And now we've got this problem with two other rigs, and a full-scale evacuation in progress...'

Jo could barely contain her exasperation, remembering how unhelpful McCrimmon had been during their visit to the platform. 'Why didn't you say something at the time?'

'They put me in an impossible bind, I'm afraid. Even now, I'm taking a big risk by talking to you. There were lots of them to begin with, technicians, scientists. Now there are just three. One of them – Lovelace – is still on the rig. But it's not him I'm calling about. There's another man... I don't even know his name, but he's usually with them. I think he's another scientist, a technical consultant or something. To be honest I don't much care for him.'

Jo had a nasty suspicion she knew where this was leading. 'What about this other man?'

'I think he might be the one who got to Pete. There's more to it than that, though. After you'd gone... this man asked about your friend, the Doctor. As if they knew each other.'

'Can you tell me what this man looked like?'

'Beard, slicked back hair – something of the Devil about him. Always wearing the same black clothes.'

'That sounds like the Master,' Jo said. She thought back to the oil that the Doctor had found on the Master's book, presumably carried back from the rig by accident. There

117

could be no doubt now.

'That's the word on Pete's drawing,' McCrimmon said after an uncomfortable silence. '*Master*. It's the same man, has to be. Do you know his name?'

'That is his name.'

'Just that? *The* Master? Like *the* Doctor?'

'Yes. And they do know each other. In a manner of speaking.'

'I can't trust him, can I?'

'No, you can't. But the Master's in prison. We saw him. He might have been able to come and go before now, but it's not going to happen again, not with the Doctor and UNIT keeping an eye on him.'

'I hope you're right about that, Jo. That only leaves Lovelace to worry about, and the equipment.'

'What about the equipment?'

'I don't know. But somehow this is all connected, isn't it? The MERMAN experiments, the Master, and all these strange things happening. The sea opening up, the weird weather... the problems with the other rigs... all those odd things I keep hearing on the radio.'

'I wish they weren't,' Jo said. 'But I think you're right. It *is* all connected. But UNIT are involved now. If you'd only...' She halted, all of a sudden becoming aware of a kind of absence on the other end of the line. 'Eddie? Are you still there?'

But of Edwina McCrimmon, there was no answer.

'Put the handset down,' Lovelace said. 'I won't ask twice.' He had a gun in his hand, a slim black automatic. That was as much as McCrimmon knew about weapons. Real or fake, she was not about to take the chance.

'You brought a gun onto my rig? You've got a cheek, pallie.'

'Our rig, Miss McCrimmon. Or were you somehow under the impression that you retained control out here? Your father understood perfectly well that it was never a question of *choosing* to cooperate with us. We needed the use of your facilities. We would have taken them one way or the other. Now.' Lovelace twitched the gun. 'Away from your desk, please. You've done enough harm for one day.'

'What are you going to do – throw me overboard, the way you did Pete Lomax?'

'A regrettable complication. Neither Callow nor I wanted things to end that way. But our colleague is a man of great persuasion. I'm afraid we should never have let him speak to Lomax.'

'The Master, you mean?'

There was no surprise in Lovelace's face. 'Yes. I overheard your conversation with the UNIT woman.' He nodded at the telephone. 'Doubtless you neglected to remember that all communications between Mike Oscar Six and the mainland are now routed through our seabed data link. We have been monitoring your calls since we initiated the MERMAN experiments. My only regret is that I did not terminate that data connection before you had a chance to speak to UNIT. An oversight on my part. There will not be another.' The barrel of the automatic twitched again. 'Move.'

'You can't take control of an entire rig, Lovelace. There's just one of you.'

'Beyond the continued functioning of the MERMAN equipment, what happens on this platform is of no concern to me. I merely wish to ensure that matters do not deteriorate any further.'

'By killing me?'

'If you insist. But I'm perfectly satisfied with locking you away, until you pose no threat to our operations. Move away from the desk, McCrimmon.'

She did as she was told, confident that Lovelace would make good on his threats if she pushed him. He was already implicated in one death, after all.

'Just tell me,' she said. 'Did Pete really die?'

119

'I'm afraid so.'

'That friend of yours is a snake.'

'He's no friend. In fact his usefulness to us is almost complete.'

'Good, because if I never see him again…'

Lovelace opened the door to her office. He glanced out into the corridor, making sure it was clear. 'Quickly, please.'

'Where are you taking me?'

'The one place where I can be absolutely sure no one else is going to stumble upon you.'

'We're in the middle of an evacuation, Lovelace – in a little while they're going to notice me missing!'

'You overestimate your importance, McCrimmon. I doubt very much that you will be missed.'

The corridor was still clear when they emerged. McCrimmon was half hoping that Tom Irwin or someone else was going to come along. But at the same time she did not want anyone else dragged into this trouble. 'You really think you're doing the right thing here, Lovelace? National security and all that?'

'I would hardly be pointing a gun at you if I did not believe in the rightness of my cause.' They were in the corridor. He closed the door behind them. 'Walk ahead of me, a few paces. I'll have the gun on you the whole time. If we meet anyone, you act normally.'

'You're not going to get away with this.'

'There is nothing to "get away with", McCrimmon. I am acting in the national interest. This is a time of heightened international tensions. Britain's independent nuclear deterrent must remain competitive. MERMAN is a vital element in the continued effectiveness of our submarine fleet.'

'It doesn't even work! If it does work, it's not in the way you think it does! Haven't you been paying attention? Everything's going to pot! We've lost one rig, lost contact with another and there's all hell breaking loose on Mike Oscar Seven! Don't tell me that's none of your doing!'

Lovelace pushed open the door to a stairwell, descending into the rig's lower levels. 'All tests have proceeded satisfactorily.'

'And who told you that – your creepy pal with the goatee?'

Seeing that the coast was clear, he closed the gap between them and gave her an encouraging prod from the automatic. 'Down the stairs. Quickly.'

'Don't you get it, Lovelace? Something weird's happening. The loss of Mike Oscar Four, all these reports of strange phenomena… it's all happened since you switched on your stupid equipment.'

'Nonsense.' He was on the stairwell above her, keeping the automatic aimed at her shoulders. 'You're a resourceful woman, McCrimmon. Doubtless you already know something of our experiment. Our equipment generates neutrinos – the most harmless particles in the universe. There are countless billions of them sleeting through you all the time, whether or not our equipment is switched on!'

'Then there's obviously something about your equipment you don't understand. Or did that not occur to you? You've started something, Lovelace.'

'Keep descending. And remember you're on an oil rig in the middle of the sea, so forget about making a run for it. If you do, I'll kill you.'

CHAPTER TWELVE

The helicopter swooped low as they neared the coastline. The Doctor, despite his growing misgivings, could not quite suppress his natural curiosity. He hoped it would not prove to be *them*, but if it did, there was a genuine mystery waiting to be unravelled. 'You know, Brigadier,' he said into his radio mouthpiece. 'I almost wish the Master were with us. He and I might have a lot to talk about.'

'The who… Oh, I see. Him.'

'Do try and concentrate, old man.'

'I'm doing my best. We're all doing our best. But have you ever tried to remember something that wants to keep slipping out of your head? It's like trying to hold onto a bar of soap in the bath! Of course you wouldn't have that problem, being an alien.'

'I assure you I am not immune to the effects of the time-fade… merely better equipped to resist them. Now, concerning these crabs…'

'If you've met them before, I need to know everything you have. Their defences, weapons… tactical weaknesses… everything we can use against them.'

'If I'm right, Brigadier, the enemy we're dealing with are lightly armoured, minimally weapon, and susceptible to just about everything above small arms fire. Get in close

123

enough, and you can kill them with a well-aimed pebble.'

'That's very good news, Doctor – and it chimes with what I'm already hearing from my men on the beach. They're taking these blighters apart as if there's no tomorrow!' But the Brigadier's tone wavered. 'You don't sound as if any of that was *meant* to be good news.'

'It's not. These creatures – if I'm right about them – are also responsible for billions of deaths, for the wholesale slaughter and oppression of entire planetary civilisations. They are as ultimately ruthless and unstoppable as any adversary we've yet encountered.'

The UNIT forces had the enemy pinned down on a stretch of sand, still wet where the sea had retreated. The helicopter touched down on a patch of hard ground near an assortment of military vehicles perched just above the start of the beach. Sandbags and barricades had been hastily installed around the vehicles and landing area. Further down the slope of the beach, UNIT forces were dug into small sand holes, with rifles and bazookas resting on sandbags. The Doctor heard the crackle of automatic weapons fire, punctuated by the occasional grenade or bazooka blast. Overhead, helicopters loitered. Further away, lost behind cloud cover, a jet or two circled, making an endless scraping sound like fingers down a blackboard. The stench of war filled the air.

The Brigadier and the Doctor jumped out of their helicopter, stooping against the down-blast. Benton was already on site, handing the Brigadier a pair of sturdy military-issue binoculars.

'Situation report, Sergeant,' Lethbridge-Stewart said, as he raised the binocs to his eyes and fiddled with the focus wheel.

'Almost too easy, sir. We're picking them off like sitting ducks. Their armour can't stop even light rounds. We've called in air support, but it's almost not worth the bother.'

'Are they still coming out of the sea?'

'In waves, sir. I mean, in *military* waves. Not sea waves.'

'At least make an effort to get to the point, Benton.'

'We're holding them, sir. Isolated reports of more coming ashore up and down the coast, but it's nothing we can't contain with a few mobile units and close air cover.'

The Doctor's keen eyes made out the remains of the aliens, where they had been butchered in their dozens. Pieces of shiny silver crab, dismembered and smoking, littered the shoreline. The UNIT soldiers had already killed hundreds of them.

'This is how it always begins,' he said grimly, when Benton had wandered off to talk to another group of soldiers.

'I'm sorry, Doctor?'

'You are dealing with Sild, Brigadier. This is how their planetary offensives always begin. With relatively small numbers of lightly armoured invaders. You'll think you have the upper hand, and indeed for a little while you will. But these Sild are coming ashore in hundreds. Will you be so confident of taking them all out when they arrive in thousands? Tens of thousands? That's their *modus operandi*, you see. Force of numbers.'

'We'll just keep shooting them.'

'Eventually some will get through.'

'But they have no weapons, no obvious armour.'

'You don't understand, Brigadier. They have no need of weapons or armour because they are ready – eager, even – to accept tremendous losses. But all it takes is one Sild to reach one of your men. Then that Sild has control of that soldier, with *his* gun and armour. And then everything changes.'

'Preposterous. My men would sooner die than turn against their fellows.'

'Your man would already be dead, to all intents and purposes. The Sild establish direct neural control of their hosts. They gain access to memories and tactical knowledge, as well as the ability to move around undetected. It happens in ones and twos to begin with. Then tens and twenties, then hundreds, then thousands.' The Doctor paused for effect.

'Then millions. That's how they take over a world. They've done it countless times.'

Something of this grim diagnosis seemed to reach the Brigadier. 'What can we do?'

'Very little. The more you throw at them, the more likelihood there'll be of the Sild eventually co-opting one of your soldiers.'

'And the alternative is…? Just let them take over?'

'The net result will be the same.'

Benton came running back. 'We're ready for an extraction, sir – robot's in position, and we've identified a candidate.'

The Brigadier looked at the Doctor. 'We have a chance to bring one of them back in more or less one piece.'

'It's a dreadful risk.' But the Doctor added: 'If you let me examine it, the risk would be reduced. And then at least I'd be confident it's the Sild we're up against.'

The robot was the kind they used for bomb-disposal operations. The Brigadier had gone to considerable trouble and called in several favours to borrow this latest technology. About the size of a large toy tank, it had tracks, a camera and an extensible remote manipulator arm. It was guided by an operator using a hand-held control unit, squatting behind the cover of the sandbags.

'Send it in,' the Brigadier said.

The robot trundled down the beach, electric motors making a high whine. The bursts of automatic fire continued, but for now the UNIT forces were concentrating their efforts away from the area of beach where the robot was moving. Most of the Sild, as far as the Doctor could see, were either dead or incapacitated. He could not see any new units emerging from the waves.

But it would not stop here, he knew. It never did.

The robot reached the damaged unit, which was upside down and with two of its main limbs blown off. The arm lowered, extended, and then clamped its claw around the body of the alien.

'Gently,' the Doctor urged.

'My chap knows what he's doing.'

The robot had the Sild. The creature's remaining legs and tentacles were thrashing now that it had been lifted from the sand. It looked rather helpless and pathetic, although the Doctor knew it would be a very grave error to think that. While they could still move, Sild remained lethal.

'Reverse,' the Brigadier instructed. Then, to his other men: 'Resume fire!'

The robot backed its way up the sloping beach, until it was back on level ground. A detachment of soldiers surrounded it, aiming the muzzles of their guns at the thing in the robot's grip. The Doctor jumped over the barricade and made his way down to the scene. 'Be careful!' he shouted. 'Keep well away from the legs and tentacles. One touch, and they'll reach your nervous system.'

The ambulator was damaged, but the travelling compartment – the glass cylinder on the crab's back – remained intact. The claw had closed around the body without crushing or trapping the cylinder. The Doctor approached warily. The thumb-sized thing inside the cylinder was twitching nervously, like a maggot on a hook.

'Well?' Lethbridge-Stewart called.

'Definitely Sild, Brigadier. I'm afraid the Earth is in very great peril.'

The Doctor eased between the soldiers. The ambulator's remaining limbs were still thrashing, trying to loosen the robot's grip. But now the Sild became aware of the Doctor's approach. The Doctor halted and rolled up his sleeve, not wishing to be encumbered by folds of loose fabric.

'What are you doing?' the Brigadier demanded.

'Something I may well have cause to regret.' The Doctor positioned himself before the Sild. He moved his hand slowly in, aiming for the cylinder on the crab's back. The legs and tentacles jabbed for his flesh, but failed to make contact. The Doctor pulled back his arm.

'Good grief, man. Are you quite mad?'

'Far from it,' the Doctor called back. 'I was taught the rudiments of snake charming by the finest swami in old Calcutta. Just before the siege of Khartoum! If I can just time my strike...'

He darted in again, but lost his nerve at the last moment. The Sild was quick – very quick. He would have to bluff it. He made another approach, a feint this time, and withdrew the instant the legs and tentacles began to whip in his direction. But then he struck again, and this time continued the movement, allowing the tentacles to strike his bunched-up sleeve, and his fingers closed around the cylinder. He only had one chance, and it had to be fast. He snapped the cylinder free, and fell sprawling back onto the sand. The glass was still intact. He held the little canister in his hand.

The ambulator, denied its pilot, had become still. The Sild – the true Sild – was in the container. And now it really was harmless.

The Doctor scrambled to his feet, dusted sand from his knees and elbows, and made his way back to the Brigadier.

'There's your enemy.'

The Brigadier took the glass cylinder between his fingers. He held it up to the sky, squinting dubiously. 'That?'

'That,' the Doctor affirmed.

'But it's just...'

'A tiny little thing, yes. Barely larger than your little finger. And rather beautiful, wouldn't you agree?'

'It looks like a seahorse. And those colours – blues and greens. It's almost like it's lit up. Like little illuminated gems.'

'What you are looking at, Brigadier, is one of the most vicious and belligerent life forms the universe has ever thrown up.'

'What did you say these little blighters are called?'

'Sild. A small name, for a small terror. One I'd rather hoped we wouldn't hear from.'

'You've never mentioned them before.' The Brigadier was

still fascinated by the thing in the glass container.

'For a very good reason. They shouldn't exist. The last Sild were rounded up and locked away a billion or so years ago, under the authority of the Time Lords. They were locked aboard a ship, along with a thousand other horrors. And then the ship was destroyed.'

'Evidently not. Well, what of this one? Can we extract any information from it?'

'Not unless you've experience in the interrogation of tiny alien sea creatures.'

'I thought as much. You say these things are ruthless?'

'As ruthless as anything we've ever encountered.'

The Brigadier nodded. 'You know, I've a good mind to drop this thing on the ground and step on it. But I don't suppose you'd approve of that, would you?'

'Categorically not.'

'Benton!'

'Yes sir!'

'Coordinate the delivery of this specimen to the boffins at Porton Down. We may be able to take these things out with bullets, but if they start arriving in droves we'll need some biological or chemical agent we can disperse over a large area. We'll secure as many live Sild as we're able.'

The Doctor shook his head slowly. 'You're wasting your time. There's nothing that will work on them in that fashion. There's only one way you'll stop more Sild arriving.'

'Which is?'

'We must find a way to block their time ruptures.'

'That sounds more your area than mine.'

The Doctor smiled wryly. 'Yes, it rather does, doesn't it?'

Atkins, the guard at the Durlston Heath checkpoint, had been keeping half an eye on the bus for some minutes. It had been parked some way up the approach road, just sitting there with its engine ticking over, no one coming or going from the thing. It was a privately operated touring coach, red and white, the kind that took people on daytrips. A bit old-fashioned looking, but otherwise in fair nick. What on earth it was doing loitering near the power station, miles from anywhere, was anyone's guess. The driver was sitting behind his wheel, literally just *sitting there* – he wasn't reading the paper, or drinking a cup of coffee, or blowing his nose. Just sitting upright, with both hands on the wheel, like a plastic figure in a die-cast toy. The guard had made out the forms of other passengers. They might just as well have been moulded as well, for all the moving about they were doing. What an odd bunch! Perhaps they were all listening to *The Archers*. That would send anyone to sleep.

Atkins returned to his reading material. He was flicking through the densely illustrated pages of the latest number of the War Picture Library series. It was a wartime story, goodies versus baddies, lots of explosions and shooting. The Germans always shouted 'Aiiieeee!' as they died. Atkins wondered what he would choose, confronted with similar circumstances. 'Aiiieeee!' seemed to him to lack the necessary gravitas and originality, as well as sounding a bit, well, German. But then who knew what might come to mind, in those final moments?

He looked up again. Finally, the coach was on the move again. That was good. He'd been on the point of putting a call through to central security, alerting them that something a bit odd was going on. But he didn't need to do that now, and anyway he would have felt like a right charlie getting everyone all hot and bothered over a coach. It was probably full of old ladies!

But the bus was picking up speed now. Rather than turning around, it was still coming down the approach road. Actually, it was going at a hell of a clip.

Atkins put down his edition of the War Picture Library. He was on the point of reaching for the telephone when he realised that the coach would be at the checkpoint long before he managed to get through to anyone.

Atkins reached for his sub-machine gun. He ran out of the kiosk, the barrier still lowered. The coach was only getting faster now – he could hear the crunch of its gears being selected, the scream of its transmission as the driver floored it. What was up with that maniac? He was still sitting there, bolt upright.

Atkins moved in front of the barrier. He raised his sub-machine gun, aiming not at the coach but at an angle over its roof. He released the safety catch and let off a short burst, gratified by the show of muzzle flash. If that didn't let the coach driver know he meant business, nothing was going to.

But the coach wasn't slowing. In fact, at the speed it was now going, slowing was scarcely an option. It was going to hit the barrier whatever happened.

'Hey!' Atkins shouted. Nothing for it now – he aimed the sub-machine gun at the coach's front, spraying a burst across the radiator grill and the leading wheels. The driver didn't even flinch! It was as if he was made of wood.

Atkins kept firing. But he had to think about himself now. He dived aside just as the coach hit the lowered barrier, the vehicle missing him by inches. Sprawled on his side, he retained sufficient presence of mind to keep firing. The coach had sailed right through the barrier, shattering it to matchwood. It had even demolished the kiosk, clipping it as it passed. And still the coach was continuing, rocking and rolling on its suspension as it powered further into Durlston Heath. From somewhere, tripped by the damage to the checkpoint, a siren began to wail.

Atkins pushed himself to his feet. He didn't know if he'd managed to hit anyone or anything on the coach. Dazed, he stumbled over to the remains of the kiosk. The telephone handset dangled from its receiver. Atkins picked it up, hoping that there might still be a connection. But the line was silent.

Stumbling – he had twisted a knee in his dive – Atkins limped after the coach. Someone was going to get a right ear-bashing for this.

CHAPTER THIRTEEN

The Doctor took the walkie-talkie and pressed the bulky object against the side of his face. 'Jo? Yes, it's me. We're at the coast. I'm afraid my worst fears have been confirmed. We're dealing with—'

He fell silent, because Jo seemed to have equally urgent news of her own. He listened intently, nodding at intervals, asking questions of his own. He disliked walkie-talkies, the awkward business of remembering to press the 'talk' button, remembering to say 'over' when he was done, but he and Jo had had their share of practice with the two-way radios and were at least as fluent in their use as the UNIT regulars.

'I see,' he said finally. 'Well, stay put – I've a feeling merry hell is about to break loose here. What? No, it's much too risky. No, I don't want you going back out there!'

When he had finished with the call, Lethbridge-Stewart said: 'News, Doctor?'

'Yes, and not at all good.' They were standing next to one of the UNIT operational control vehicles, a thing the size of a horse transporter. From the beach, out of sight, came the intermittent crackle of gunfire.

'I thought we'd had our share of bad news for one day.'

'Jo spoke to Edwina McCrimmon. It seems the Master was definitely on the platform.'

133

'Then why in heaven's name didn't she tell us?'

'She was frightened – caught between two powerful branches of government. Brigadier – does the name MERMAN mean anything to you?'

'Should it?'

'It's some kind of covert military experiment, something to do with submarines. From what Jo got out of McCrimmon, some men from the government persuaded McCrimmon Industries to let them use their rigs as part of their test set-up. It also seems that they brought the Master in as technical consultant.'

'The… We've come across him before, haven't we?'

'The Master, Brigadier? Yes. As a matter of fact you and I were discussing him only a short while ago.'

The Brigadier contorted his face with extreme mental effort. 'I remember. But it can't be him. We've got him in… some kind of prison, I think. I know the chap in charge. Childers, that's the fellow.'

'Well, it would seem our friend the Master's been granted day-release status.'

'You think he summoned the… what are the blighters called?'

'Sild, Brigadier. No, I think it rather unlikely. I think the Master put out a call for help *from himself*, but someone else answered. The question is, is it a coincidence that the Sild have emerged here, and are seemingly intent on advancing into dry land? Or are they actively looking for the Master?'

'The…'

'Brigadier, listen to me carefully. You remember Childers and Durlston Heath. We have to secure that facility.'

'It's a prison, Doctor – how much *more* secure could it be?'

'Prisons are generally built to stop people from escaping. The danger now is of hostile forces breaking in.'

'I see.'

'Whatever resources you can spare, you need to start placing them in a position to defend Durlston Heath. Soldiers, tanks, air support – whatever you can muster. We need to protect the Master. Shield him, and if necessary break him *out* of that prison ahead of the Sild.'

The Brigadier nodded, then seemed stuck on something. 'Run that last bit by me again, Doctor.'

Lovelace had taken Edwina McCrimmon deep into the lowest levels of the platform. There had never been any part of the rig that felt completely unfamiliar to her – she had made a point of that not being the case – but it was true that her day-to-day business seldom brought her down into these uninviting levels. The lowest accommodation and recreation floors were two flights of stairs above her head, the canteen, medical and administrative areas even higher. They were still high off the waves, but down here – where for some inscrutable reason the rig's designers had felt no need to specify the installation of windows – it felt oppressively dank and claustrophobic, like being in the lowest parts of a ship. She had no cause to come here very often and the constant on-off rattle of generators and air circulators made it no place to stay unless you had good reason. Beneath her feet were a few layers of rusting bolted metal and then an awfully long drop to the sea below.

But it was here that Lovelace, Callow and the third man – the one she now thought of as the Master – had set up their operations, and that had meant even less incentive to spend time down here. Part of the deal her father had set up with the men from the Ministry was that they would be allowed to operate in conditions of secrecy, free from distractions and prying eyes. Access to their whole operational area, which took in two whole corridors of stores, generators and switching rooms, was controlled by a set of newly installed security doors. McCrimmon had accepted these terms grudgingly, but she had known that there would be little impact on the rig's routine operations.

Lovelace stopped at the security door, the automatic still clenched in his fist. Although put in recently, it was the usual sort of door found throughout the rig, with a metal body and a circular porthole in the upper half. The only difference was the heavy-duty lock and the keyed-entry pad next to it. Lovelace flipped up a plastic lid and tapped his code into the pad. The door made a loud clunk and unlocked.

'Walk on,' he said.

'You can't hold me prisoner, Lovelace. This is a civilian facility.'

'Write to your MP.' He prodded her with the automatic, bidding her to go through the open door.

He walked her along a short stretch of corridor, past several closed doors, until they reached what McCrimmon knew to be a small stores room. It was windowless, little more than a large walk-in cupboard set with shelves and a couple of grey filing cabinets. No telephone, no handy ventilation grille to crawl out through, like they always did in television series.

'UNIT are on their way, Lovelace. What do you hope to gain by locking me in here?'

'What I hope to gain, McCrimmon, is you not meddling in matters of national importance. Sit down.' He jabbed the gun at the only seat in the room, positioned next to a very narrow desk. Then something caught his eye. 'Wait a moment.'

She had seen it too: several bulky ring-bound documents sitting on the desk. They were too new and dust-free to have been here before, which could only mean they were connected to MERMAN. Lovelace moved to scoop up the documents and tuck them under his arm, evidently not wanting to leave McCrimmon with some choice reading material.

This was her one chance and she took it. She had dismissed the idea of simply running away – she wouldn't be able to easily close any of the doors behind her – but the room had given her a weapon. While Lovelace was momentarily distracted, she sprang for the wall and snatched the fire extinguisher from its mounting. Lovelace dropped the files and began to turn, bringing the automatic to bear. Would he?

She wasn't sure. He had a snivelling sort of look to him, the kind that made her doubt that he was capable of following up on his threats. But maybe he also had the necessary meanness to shoot a woman at point-blank range, merely to protect some stupid national secret. Either way she wasn't going to take the chance. In the half-second in which she had formulated her plan, she had meant to spray him with the fire extinguisher, smother him in foam. She could even visualise him, stumbling around like a crazed snowman, while she sped off. But there wasn't time for that. The fire extinguisher felt nice and heavy in her hands, like a solid iron bar. She raised it and whacked it against Lovelace, hard, catching him high in the shoulder. Lovelace yelped and dropped the automatic – she heard it clatter to the metal floor. She came in again with the extinguisher: not trying to kill him, or even do him a serious injury, but put him out of action long enough for her to scoop up the gun and get out of that room.

But Lovelace was quicker than she had been expecting. The second blow caught him at an angle, not hard enough to do any real damage. Lovelace gave a grunt of pain and rage, and then he grabbed the chair by its back, swinging it at McCrimmon as if he were a lion tamer and she the lion. One of the chair's metal legs caught McCrimmon's wrist. She let go of the extinguisher – it hit the floor with a resounding, bell-like clang, narrowly missing her feet. Lovelace tossed the chair aside and grabbed a heavy black document file from the shelves, bearing down on McCrimmon and swinging the file as if it were a rectangular boulder. McCrimmon raised her right arm defensively. She kicked out and caught Lovelace in the crotch. Lovelace groaned but maintained his attack. McCrimmon ducked as the third blow came down, sinking to her knees and reaching for the automatic. She had no idea what she was going to do with it but she felt certain she did not want Lovelace anywhere near that weapon, now that he had demonstrated his keen willingness to use violence.

Lovelace, though, was just a fraction too quick for her.

Her hand was almost on the automatic when he jammed his heel down onto her wrist.

'Now, now. Let's not get carried away with ourselves, shall we?'

'Let go of me,' she said, the pain excruciating.

'You lost two fingers, I see. Did it hurt?'

'Aye, it hurt – what do you think?' She was looking up at him, standing over her. With the other shoe he kicked the automatic out of reach. He was bleeding from his nose, great scarlet rivulets of it. He smeared his other hand under the nose.

'Look what you did to me, McCrimmon.'

'Nothing compared to what I'll do to you later, sunshine.' She paused. She wanted to cry from the pain but there was no way she was giving him that satisfaction. 'You want to know how I lost those fingers, Lovelace?'

'Not particularly.'

'I got my hand caught in a power-operated winch. On the deck of an oil rig. Took them off at the knuckle. I heard them go *pop, pop* as they came off. I was lucky I only lost the two, you know? Watched them go into the winch, too. That's not something you want to see every day.'

'Your point being, McCrimmon?' Still with his shoe on her hand, Lovelace knelt down and picked up the automatic. His nose was still bleeding, red dots spattering the floor.

'I got careless. I was messing around with something I didn't understand properly. And it came back and bit me.'

'I see. And you think this little parable has some relevance to…'

'You're in over your head, Lovelace. Whatever you think that box of tricks of yours was meant to do, it's not doing it. Or it's doing something else, as well.' She studied him carefully, still refusing to show the pain he was inflicting. 'That friend of yours… the Master. How well do you really know him?'

Lovelace relinquished the pressure on her hand. He pulled away quickly, closing the door before she had a chance to do anything. McCrimmon heard the sound of a metal latch being slid into place.

There was no lock on the inside. Not that she had expected one.

'Why does he want this thing moved around anyway?' The UNIT lorry driver looked suspiciously at the battered blue police box he had been asked to relocate. It was sitting on a wooden pallet, the pallet and its load currently straining the lifting capabilities of a green-painted forklift lorry, which was in turn under the temporary control of the UNIT driver himself. 'Come to think of it, what's it doing here in the first place? Why do *we* need a police public call box – haven't we enough blinking telephones as it is?'

'Orders from the Brig, mate. That's all I know.' The UNIT soldier in charge of operations handed the lorry driver a slip of paper with directions on it. 'That's your rendezvous – about five miles from Durlston Heath power station.'

The lorry driver turned the piece of paper the right way up. 'Miles away – who do they think I am, Fangio?'

'Roads shouldn't be too bad.' The soldier paused, allowing a military jet to pass overhead, the sound of its engine like fingernails scratching the sky. 'Bit of a flap on, so the Brig wants it there fast. You'll get a couple of cars as escorts, and the fuzz have been told to make sure you get through in one piece. Once you've delivered the box, you can get back here sharpish.'

'Delivered the box,' the driver repeated. 'So there'll be a crane or forklift at the other end, will there? This thing weighs a ton!'

'Not sure. But the Brig said not to worry about that bit. Apparently it's all taken care of.'

'What does he expect it to do? Sprout wings and flap its way off?'

But this was a rhetorical question, not one that the driver really expected answering. Still muttering under his breath, shaking his head at the utter stupidity of his superiors, he loaded the telephone box onto the back of the lorry. After that it was a simple matter of tying it down, then screening the load with the tarpaulin cover. He set off cautiously, taking bends carefully. It was just a blue telephone box but it felt like the thing was stuffed full of lead ingots. He had considered opening the door to have a shufti inside, but the box was locked.

Never mind. If the driver had learned one thing in his military career, it was that there were some things you just weren't meant to ask too many questions about.

CHAPTER FOURTEEN

The Brigadier's helicopter scudded rapidly over the flat fields and marshes of the coastal home counties, on its way back to UNIT headquarters. In this winter light it was a landscape of browns and greys, variations on a theme of drab. Even the trees stood skeletal and forbidding, as if they aspired to grow into electricity pylons when they were taller. The Brigadier was not one for the countryside, it was true. Its chief function, as far as he was concerned, was to contain things that could be hunted and shot during the appropriate seasons. It was also quite good for military exercises, provided you could find enough of it to blow up or strafe.

But, as always, a new and looming threat to the Earth sharpened his appreciation of things. It wasn't much to look at, this colourless tapestry, but damn it all if some aliens were going to try to take it off him. That wasn't on at all. That was anything but cricket.

The Brigadier had already used the helicopter's radio to call ahead to headquarters and coordinate transportation of the Doctor's TARDIS. The convoy would be at the rendezvous point within half an hour, if all went according to plan. Ideally, they would just drive in and extract the… chap, the man they were after, without incident. If difficulties did arise, then Yates had an armed detachment under his command.

And if force proved insufficient to get the job done, the Doctor ought to be able to get inside via the TARDIS. Doors and walls were no obstruction to a machine that could slip in and out of time. That was what the blasted thing was designed to do.

But the Brigadier would not have reached his very considerable rank without having learned the value of foresight. There was a truism that no military plan survived first contact with the enemy. In his many encounters with terrestrial and extraterrestrial foes, Lethbridge-Stewart had learned the grim wisdom of that aphorism. A good soldier learned not just to think one step ahead, but to think three or four in advance. Assume not only that Plan A will fail, but that so will Plans B and C. It always paid to have a Plan D in hand, no matter how desperate it might be. In his long career, the Brigadier had fallen back on Plan D more times than he cared to admit. Sometimes the necessary action was obvious. Sometimes it was anything but.

Today, as the helicopter headed home, the Brigadier had no difficulty grasping the shape of Plan D. It was awful in its clarity. The objective, as far as the Doctor was concerned, was to get *the chap* out of that prison, before the Sild got to him. But in truth that was only the most desirable outcome. If all else failed, then it would merely be necessary to prevent the chap falling into Sild control. That was what you did.

But the fellow... the chap... The Brigadier concentrated hard, yes, him, the Master, him, that one... the one they were supposed to not keep forgetting... he was inside multiple layers of reinforced concrete, specifically designed to guard against any conceivable accident or terrorist attack.

If no conventional forces could reach him, then something decidedly *unconventional* would need to be considered. The kind of weapon that every commanding officer hoped they would never have cause to deploy.

The Brigadier tapped the pilot, requesting use of the radio. 'Get me Geneva.'

He was going to have to go to the very top for this one.

'Local yokels!' Yates said, braking the Land Rover so abruptly that the Doctor had to brace himself against the dashboard. 'Can't they take more care of their gates?'

They had come across the obstruction as they approached the agreed rendezvous point five miles from Durlston Heath. Their convoy consisted of three vehicles: two Land Rovers, the Doctor and Yates in the first, and a truck bringing up the rear, with Benton behind the wheel. At first glance, the thing before them appeared to be a kind of abstract roadblock: a misshapen mass of black and white barriers, like large painted sandbags on white stilts, squashed into a haphazard barricade. But the sandbags were *moving*, jostling each other and shifting position, and they had heads and eyes and mouths, and udders.

'I don't think,' the Doctor said, 'that the "local yokels", as you so colourfully put it, are entirely to blame.'

'Someone let those cows loose,' Yates said. 'If it wasn't the country bumpkins, then...'

'They're under Sild control,' the Doctor said sharply.

'What?'

'Look closely.' The Doctor pointed at one of the nearest cows – it was looking right at them, its pink-lined mouth hanging open in extreme bovine stupefaction, as if it had never seen anything quite so strange as a Land Rover. 'On its neck.'

A Sild ambulator was clamped onto the back of the Friesian, at the base of the neck. The tiny silver crab was almost lost against the massive animal, submerged in hair and folds of fat.

'Three... four...' Yates counted, with mounting horror.

'Enough for their purposes. They only need to control a few cows; the herding instinct will do the rest.'

'They can't do this,' Yates said. 'It's just... *wrong*.'

The Doctor looked at him tolerantly. 'Worse than

controlling human hosts, Mike? To the Sild it makes absolutely no difference.'

Yates unclipped a radio handset from the dashboard and spoke to headquarters, shaking his head as he clipped the radio back into place. 'Our rendezvous point is on the other side of these cows, and there's no way for us to get there without a long detour.'

'What about the other lorry, the one carrying the TARDIS?' asked the Doctor.

'Coming in on the coast road. Hasn't reported any difficulties yet, so this may be the only obstruction they've managed to organise. But I'm afraid we'll have to get through it if you're to get to your TARDIS.' Yates took the radio, selected a different channel and said: 'Benton – we're going to attempt to push through. We'll try our Land Rover first. Advance slowly behind us, but be ready to reverse.'

He slipped the Land Rover back into gear, and began to approach the animal roadblock at a little above walking pace.

The Doctor, sensing what was to come, braced a hand against the dash. 'Here they come,' he said.

The road remained obstructed, but the cows were now moving to meet the convoy. Only a few of them were under direct Sild influence, but the herd instinct was so strong that the others may as well have been. The Sild cows broke into a heavy, shambling trot, and then the trot became a stampede. The ground was wet and muddy, so some of the cows slipped and fell under the hooves of those following. But still the mass advanced: less a group of animals, more a single shifting wall of concentrated meat and muscle, an organism as wide as a road. The mass of cows bellowed and snorted, their heads lowered like battering rams.

Yates's hands were tight on the steering wheel, his jaw set as he leaned forward, the Land Rover whining as he held it in first gear. The Doctor willed him to keep accelerating, but at the last moment Yates's resolve seemed to fail him.

It was a mistake to steer. The Land Rover had begun to

turn to the right when the first wave of cows collided with it, and the off-centre impact was enough to tilt the vehicle onto two wheels. The Doctor redoubled his brace and waited for the worst. The vehicle crunched onto its side, the engine racing and then cutting out, and then all the Doctor could see through the windshield was a press of cows, like black and white dough expanding to squeeze against the glass. The Land Rover jerked sideways, the road crunching past through the broken side window.

Yates had the driver's side door open. He heaved himself out, straddled the open doorway and reached down to help the Doctor. 'Quickly!' he called.

The Doctor extracted himself, judging that now was perhaps not the ideal time to point out that they would have been far better meeting the cows head-on. Precariously, the two of them stood on the side of the tipped-over car. The Land Rover was fast becoming an island in a sea of cows. Seeing his moment, the Doctor jerked down in time to rip a Sild ambulator from the neck of one of the animals. It came free with a slurp of embedded tendrils, their silver metal now pinkened with blood. The spider legs thrashed the air, the tentacles trying to whip around the Doctor's wrist. The cow the Sild had been operating dropped as if it had been shot with a captive bolt.

'We're surrounded!' Yates called.

The other Land Rover, still upright, was powering back in reverse. But the sea of cows reached almost to its bonnet. 'Now, Mike!' the Doctor shouted, and sprang off the toppled Land Rover onto the spine of the nearest cow, hopscotching his way from animal to animal until, in a few deft bounds, he had reached the sanctuary of the other vehicle. Still clutching the ambulator by its glassy cylinder, the tentacles constricting the circulation into his hand, trying to force him to relinquish his grip, he looked back and beckoned Yates to follow him. Yates, surveying the prospect confronting him, looked about as enthusiastic as a man instructed to swim a shark-infested lagoon. 'Hurry!' the Doctor shouted, as the Land Rover he was standing on backed slowly away and the sea of cows increased in number and width. 'It's now or never, Mike!'

Grasping the truth in this, Yates followed the Doctor across the shifting landscape of ridged backs. Months of training on assault courses could not possibly have prepared him for this scenario, but to his credit Yates managed to keep his balance until the last moment, then he slipped and seemed on the point of falling into the yawning crevasse between two cows. But the Doctor leaned over and grabbed Yates's sleeve with his free hand, and then the two men were safe, for the moment.

The Land Rover backed away at higher speed, until it had cleared enough space to execute a turn. Yates and the Doctor hopped off and jogged to the lorry. The cows were still advancing, and the Sild ambulator was doing its best to disengage itself from the Doctor's grip, constricting and probing at the same time. It was like an iron tourniquet.

'That thing!' Yates said.

'I'd rather hoped… this…' The Doctor paused to smash the ambulator against the side of the lorry, 'wouldn't be necessary.'

The transparent container shattered, exposing the Sild occupant, and for an instant the Doctor hesitated, his deepest convictions tested. But the tendrils were cutting his skin now, seeking a path into his peripheral nervous system, and if he did not do something the Sild would either kill him or have him under its agonising control. Again he smashed his hand against the side of the lorry, sickened by his own actions but knowing he had no choice. Only then did the ambulator fall limp, tendrils loosening. The Doctor dropped it to the floor. The blood rushed back into his hand.

Yates was staring at the mess left by the Sild. 'That… was one of them?'

'Nastiness comes in all sizes,' the Doctor said. 'The mile-long city slugs of Esquenal are among the gentlest, kindliest

146

of souls in the galaxy. Their slime-trail poetry...'

'Point made, Doctor.'

The Doctor signalled to the lorry driver to back up over the smashed ambulator, just to be sure that it couldn't be used by another Sild. The lorry reversed, crunched over the empty machine, halted, and then UNIT soldiers began to spill out of the covered rear compartment. Benton emerged from the front and then joined Yates, the two of them directing the UNIT forces to coordinate small arms, semi-automatic, machine gun and anti-tank fire on the cows.

'Is this really necessary?' the Doctor wondered out loud. But deep inside, he knew the answer.

It was a terrible thing to witness. The UNIT forces did their best to target the Sild-controlled cows to begin with, but in the chaos of moving animals, and with the Sild able to move from host to host, it was all but impossible. The Doctor, already appalled by his own actions, could barely watch.

But there came a point where the guns fell silent. There were no cows left by then, and the Sild ambulators – those that had survived the slaughter – had by then scuttled for cover.

'I'll tell you one thing,' said Benton, surveying the resultant carnage. 'That's put me right off my dinner.'

'There won't be dinner for any of us unless we get through,' Yates replied.

Having lost his Land Rover, Yates assumed control of the lorry, the Doctor and Benton taking up the passenger seats to his left. In low gear, the lorry navigated a slick red passage over the barricade of carcasses, wheel-slipping its way up and over the vile, squelching mass. The remaining Land Rover could not get through at all, and so was abandoned.

After that, although the road was strewn with abandoned vehicles, they encountered no significant resistance before they reached the rendezvous, the other lorry waiting about a mile further down the road by a T-junction with its lights on and engine still running. The driver gave them a funny look as they pulled past, doubtless taking in the quantities of blood and gore still adhering to the other vehicle. The two lorries continued in close formation, until at last the blocky structures of the power station began to jut above the treeline.

'Smoke,' the Doctor said. 'And it looks to be coming from within the perimeter.'

CHAPTER FIFTEEN

Edwina McCrimmon did not give up knocking and shouting until her knuckles were bruised and her throat raw. It had been a valiant try, but it was obvious from the lack of response that she was on her own. She was not simply locked in the storeroom, as objectionable as that would have been. The storeroom itself was screened off from the normal comings and goings of the rig, with access to this whole area controlled by the automatic security door. The door was airtight and soundproofed. She had heard Lovelace walking away, but once he was on the other side of the door she had not even been able to hear him tapping the code back into the keyed-entry device. Not that she had any doubts that he had done so.

So no one was going to hear her, and no one was going to just stumble on her by accident. There would have to be an organised search of the platform, and that would not happen until she was established as definitely missing. Hours, maybe.

You want something done, Big Cal had drilled into her often enough, do it yourself.

McCrimmon scooped up the fire extinguisher. It felt as solid and heavy in her hands as when she'd used it against Lovelace. Pity she hadn't put a bit more swing into it, with hindsight. But at least she'd left Lovelace with something to remember her by.

She grasped the extinguisher double-handed and used it as a battering ram against the door, targeting the area corresponding to the padlocked latch on the other side. The first blow did nothing except jar her painfully. But on the second she felt something crunch in the door's frame, a giving of its integrity. It was wood and metal, after all. Callow and Lovelace had not installed any additional security measures since they had expected their main door would be sufficient.

She drove the extinguisher home again. It was hard work, sapping strength with every swing, but on every second or third impact she felt that same splintering crunch. This was probably not the way fire extinguishers were meant to be handled, it was true. She just hoped the door would give in first.

'And then you and me, Lovelace, we're going to have words,' McCrimmon said.

At that same moment, oblivious to the escape attempt going on below, Lovelace was making his furtive way through the rig. He had the automatic in his hand, but concealed behind his back, just in case he had the misfortune to bump into anyone along the way. He knew his way around the place by now, but it was never an environment in which he was going to feel at home. Corridors of metal and plumbing, with tiny windows or no windows at all, made him nervous, as if he was a rat in a laboratory maze. Nice whitewashed corridors of power were more his thing. The sooner this mess was sorted out and he could go back to the calm hierarchies of the Ministry, the better.

He didn't like what he'd had to do to the McCrimmon woman, but it wasn't as if she hadn't been asking for it, poking her nose into government business she'd been told to keep well out of. Trouble had been brewing from the moment the other platform vanished into the sea. It would have been a lot easier for all involved if the Lomax man hadn't had the bad form to actually *survive*, and start blabbing about the sea opening up. Of course they would have had to shut him up one way or the other. But it had been a mistake to let the other one anywhere near him.

Lovelace froze, momentarily troubled. The other one, the man they arranged to extract from the prison when he was needed, and return when he was not... *him*. But the man's name felt elusive, like one of those puzzle pictures where you had to squint to see something in the picture, something that kept flickering in and out of focus. The Bast... the Master. That was it, the Master.

The alien. The Time Lord.

Him.

Concussion, Lovelace thought. The woman had delivered a good whack with that fire extinguisher. Deserved all she got in return, too. The upstart Scot was lucky he hadn't shot her and dumped her body overboard. With everything at stake, he'd have been within his rights. Did she honestly think her life counted for more than national security?

Lovelace smeared a hand under his nose – the blood was beginning to dry up, though his nose made an ominous and painful click when he touched it.

He opened a metal door, climbed the staircase back up to the administrative level, still keeping the pistol tucked into the small of his back. Quickly he reached the corridor where McCrimmon kept her office. He thought of her down below, kicking and screaming against the electronically locked door. With all the noise that came with a working oil rig, even one in the middle of a phased shutdown of normal operations, there wasn't a chance of anyone hearing her.

He touched his nose again. Felt like there was something hard and bony moving around in there, some cartilaginous thing that was no longer connected to the surrounding tissue.

'Where's Eddie?'

Lovelace stopped. It was Irwin, McCrimmon's burly deputy – he had just come around the corner at the other end of the corridor. Another Scot with a chip on both shoulders –

it was like they had a production line running. Lovelace had taken an instinctive dislike to the bearded Glaswegian from their first meeting.

'Miss McCrimmon?' Lovelace hammed. 'I was wondering the same thing! She seems to have abandoned her duties.'

'Not too likely, if I know Eddie.' The Scot's eyes were naturally squinty and suspicious. Now he made them ever squintier. 'What's up with your face? Why are you keeping your hand behind your back?'

Nothing for it. Lovelace brought the automatic into plain view. 'Shut up.'

'What have you done? Where's Eddie?'

'Safe. More than you'll be, if you don't shut up.'

'You've locked her somewhere, haven't you?'

Lovelace jabbed the pistol threateningly. 'I said shut up.'

'Listen to me carefully, Callow. I don't know what you or your pal are up to, and frankly I don't care.'

'I'm Lovelace,' he said.

'Callow, Lovelace, you're both interchangeable, like Tweedle-dee and Tweedle-dum. And you know what? It disnae matter. I've got more important matters on my mind than some bampots from the government. We're in the middle of an evacuation! We've lost one rig, lost contact with another, and there's something not right on a third! I'd very much like to have a wee chat with my boss. And you've got the cheek to think you can point that thing at me?'

Lovelace opened the door. 'Get inside.'

Irwin looked at the automatic, seemed to weigh his chances, before thinking better of offering resistance. 'You're mad, Lovelace. Totally doolally flip.'

'I said get inside.'

He stood away from the opening door, waggling the automatic to encourage Irwin to enter the office. 'Stand over there, by the filing cabinet.' Lovelace followed Irwin inside and closed the door behind them.

'What are you hoping to get away with?'

'Stand still. One move, and I'll shoot you. And don't give me any nonsense about critical systems. We're a long way from the drilling gear here.'

Lovelace pulled the office chair out on its castors and settled into the desk, his back to the window. Good, the computer was still switched on. He placed the automatic within easy reach and hammered at the keys, until the lines of flickering green text on the screen began to update. Irwin twitched and Lovelace proved how quickly he could pick up the automatic again. 'I'm quite serious, Mr Irwin. I shall not hesitate.'

With the secure connection to the Ministry established, Lovelace picked up the telephone handset. 'Yes. Yes, it's Lovelace. Get me Callow, immediately. No, I can't wait.'

'Having a chinwag with your pal, are you?' Irwin asked.

Lovelace ignored him, waiting for Callow to come on the line. He heard the rattle of typewriters, the hum of traffic through poorly insulated windows, the distant chime of Big Ben. He had definitely drawn the short straw, having to nurse the equipment back here while Callow returned to the familiar comforts of town.

'Yes?' Callow sounded irritated.

'It's Lovelace. What the blue blazes is happening? Who authorised this evacuation?'

'I tried to reach you,' Callow said suavely. 'There's some disturbance on the coast – army and air force mobilised, UNIT involvement. Cover story is it's an exercise, but I think we can draw…'

'Never mind that. What about the platforms?' He glanced at Irwin again. 'Is it true? Has another platform vanished?'

'Communications are a bit muddled at the moment – lot of misinformation flying around. I'd sit tight if I were you. Probably all have blown over by morning.'

'I'm not an *idiot*, Callow. It can't be a coincidence that all this has happened since we initiated the experiment…' He directed another look at Irwin, debating with himself how much he dared reveal. If he was going to have to end up shooting or silencing Irwin, it really didn't matter. 'The man. The chap.'

'The chap, old boy?'

'The one in the prison. Him. What's his... status?'

'Status?'

'For pity's sake, it's a simple question!' Lovelace used his free hand to knead his temples. 'Perishing woman hit me with a fire extinguisher. I think I've suffered local amnesia. Can't seem to hold the chap's name in my head...'

'No,' Callow said, a wondering tone in his voice. 'It's not just you. I've been having... difficulty. Ever since we returned him to the prison. Him... his name.'

'I almost had it just now. The M... The M...' But that was as far as Lovelace could go.

'Something's wrong,' Callow said.

'I know.'

'It's tied in. The platforms... the military activity. The amnesia. We've opened a can of worms, Lovelace.'

'I want to get off the platform,' he said decisively, all of his options suddenly crystallising. 'There's a queue to get aboard the helicopters. But I can use government privilege to secure a seat.'

Irwin shook his head, disgusted.

'What about the equipment?' Callow's voice was a buzzing little irritant on the other end of the telephone. 'You can't just leave it unattended! If the platform isn't lost, and the Russians...'

'I'll destroy it. That was always the plan, wasn't it? Scuttle the equipment, if there's any chance of it falling into enemy hands?'

'Is it still operating?'

'As we left it. But I can power it down, and initiate the self-destruct.'

'After all we invested...'

'It has to be done, Callow. There's no other choice.'

154

'Behind you,' Irwin said.

'Shut up.'

'I'd look behind you, if I were you.' The Scotsman's voice was icily calm. 'There's something crawling up the outside of the window.'

Yates swerved hard as a middle-aged man, wearing wellingtons and a brown overcoat, ventured into the path of the lorry. The lorry clipped the man and sent him flying into bushes along the road. Yates made to brake, but the Doctor touched a hand to the steering wheel.

'Carry on, Mike. That man's long past any help we can give him. He was dead from the moment the Sild took control of his body.'

Yates breathed out heavily. He had seen some dreadful things in his time with UNIT, but little to compare with what the day had already brought. But he nodded and continued, trusting the Doctor's word.

After that, it only got worse. The vehicles, skewed across the road, presented no hindrance to the heavy UNIT lorries. Even a double-decker bus, parked diagonally, was not too large to be shoved aside. But the Doctor eyed the empty bus with extreme trepidation. The Sild took their hosts in ones and twos to begin with, but always their operational objective would be to claim larger groupings. No sooner had this fear crystallised than a trio of elderly women emerged from behind the cover of a white Transit van, tipped over on its side. The women shuffled out into the middle of the road, arms hanging stiffly at their sides, heads lolling as if they had nodded off halfway through a game of bingo. Again Yates's reaction was to swerve, though there was barely room for the lorry.

Yates's hands had a death grip on the steering wheel. His eyes were nearly closed.

'I can't do this.'

'Mike, listen to me carefully. These people are already

dead. What you are driving towards are alien creatures, no different from the Axons or Autons – you understand? They're not people, not any more. Now, in all likelihood there are dozens of Sild waiting in hiding, waiting for us to slow or hesitate. If one of those things gets aboard this vehicle, we've had it.'

'It still seems like you're asking me to drive through innocent people.'

'They're not people any more. They're Sild weapons.'

They drove on. Yates kept his nerve, even when three police officers stepped out into the road and raised their hands, in stiff unison, as if all three were being worked by the same puppeteer. The lorry hit the police and bounced over them, exactly as if they were speed bumps.

The horror of it, the unspeakable horror, the thing the Doctor dared not communicate to his friends, was that Sild control was nowhere near as simple as instantaneous death for the host. True, death was guaranteed from the moment of Sild attachment. True also that the host had lost all volition, all conscious control of their own body and to a degree their own higher mental processes. But something remained – enough residual awareness to know that they were being ridden and controlled.

'Director Childers on the radio for you, sir,' said Benton, passing the Doctor one of the handsets.

'We see smoke,' the Doctor said. 'It looks to be coming from inside the perimeter. Have you managed to keep them out?'

Childers sounded faint but otherwise his normal self. 'For now. The smoke's coming from outside – they've crashed some cars against the fence and set fire to them, trying to break through. Where are you?'

The Doctor glanced at Yates. 'About a mile from the gatehouse. It's getting pretty thick out here, but we should be able to make it through. Is the Master... the prisoner... still under observation?'

'The… man? Yes.' Childers seemed to lose himself. 'What were we talking about?'

'Director Childers, listen to me carefully. For reasons that I won't go into, you may be finding it very hard to keep the idea of the prisoner in mind.'

'Yes…' Childers said, with a peculiar mixture of relief and suspicion. 'I thought it was me. It's only started happening in the last hour or so.'

'It's not just you, but it is very, very important that you cling on to the idea that there's a man in your care. Nothing matters more than this, Childers. You've got to keep that man safe. Don't let him out of your sight, and don't let anyone near him.'

So it had reached Childers. That was a measure of how far the fade was progressing. Childers, who knew nothing of the Master's true identity, who knew him only as Prisoner M, was beginning to lose grip on his memories as well.

'Checkpoint ahead, sir,' Benton said. 'Looks like they're still holding the fort.'

'Slow down,' the Doctor said.

The approach to the checkpoint was a chaos of cars, smashed, toppled and burned. Scarves of smoke and mist obscured the view. People were moving between the vehicles, and some of them had weapons. Rifles, shotguns – enough to trouble even a fully armed UNIT detachment. As one of the figures, a milkman, turned his back to the lorry, the Doctor made out the glass-and-silver ambulator clamped to his neck. Some of the other hosts bore evidence of recent gunshot injuries, gruesome enough in one or two cases that it seemed impossible that the human could be still breathing. Indeed, they didn't have to be. Sild could make corpses move, for a while.

Once again, revulsion touched the Doctor to the absolute core of his being. This could not continue.

'Shouldn't there be a barrier here?' Benton asked.

The Doctor nodded. The kiosk and barrier were gone,

but the entrance was still under guard. Four uniformed men waited at the entrance. Every now and then one of them would aim their sub-machine gun over the heads of the gathering hosts, warning them to move back.

The Doctor nodded. 'Benton's right. It's too easy. Those guards are under Sild control.'

'Are you sure?' Yates asked. 'I know one of those chaps – Atkins. He was in my old regiment.'

'Look at the bulges at the backs of their necks,' the Doctor answered. 'They've been clamped. Including, I'm afraid, your friend Atkins.'

'But Childers said…' Benton began.

'Childers was mistaken.' The Doctor settled his hand on the lorry's steering wheel. 'Something's broken through the perimeter. Durlston Heath has already been compromised!'

CHAPTER SIXTEEN

Picking up the automatic, Lovelace swivelled the chair just enough to bring the window into view, while still being able to keep half an eye on Irwin.

The Glaswegian had not been lying. Something *was* on the other side of the window. Lovelace's first impression was that it was a very strange kind of crab. They were hundreds of feet above the waves and somehow this crab had managed to climb out of the water, all the way up the outside of the platform, clinging on against the wind and the spray, or had perhaps been scooped out of the water by a bird, then somehow dropped here, on the high levels, and not been broken or killed in the process. But, as his second glance confirmed, it was not really a crab at all.

'That thing...' he said slowly. 'Is it... something to do with the rig?'

'Are you out your mind, Lovelace? Does it *look* like it's anything to do with the rig?'

The crab was mechanical, Lovelace now saw. It had a fist-sized central body, made of some silvery metal or plastic, and long spindly legs radiating out from the middle. It was spread across the window, from one part of the frame to the next. In addition to the legs, it also had whip-thin tentacles or feelers. They were tapping the glass, moving up and down the edge where the glass slotted into the frame. Tap, tap, tap, gentle enough that he had not been aware of it during the telephone conversation. But now it was quite clear that the crab-machine was trying to find a way into the room from the outside.

'It's a robot... or something.'

'There's something on its back,' Irwin said. 'I can see it from this angle. A sort of glass pod or bottle. Has this got anything to do with your experiment, Lovelace?'

The crab's tapping had intensified. Lovelace remembered the telephone. 'Callow... listen to me. There's something trying to get into the rig.'

The glass made a scraping noise, jarring in the frame.

'It's going to have that window loose any moment now,' Irwin said. 'Eddie was always saying it was draughty in here!'

Callow said: 'You're imagining things, Lovelace. That concussion of yours is obviously—'

'Shoot it!'

For once, it seemed to Lovelace that Irwin offered excellent advice. He did not like that crab at all. It seemed profoundly wrong on any number of levels. He aimed the automatic at the window, put down the telephone handset to screen his eyes against splintering glass, and fired.

The gun made a surprisingly loud crack. The window shattered. The crab was still there, still spread across the frame, even though jagged pieces of glass were stuck into it. A snap of cold, salty air came through the broken window. The bullet had gone right through the body of the crab. He could see sky through it: a perfect circle of cloudy grey.

Lovelace left the chair and walked slowly to the window, the gun in his hand, ready to turn it on Irwin if needed. At least now he had proven that he was willing to fire the weapon.

He tapped the body of the crab with the nozzle of the automatic. The crab dropped away, falling back towards the sea.

160

'Do you think there was just the one?' he asked.

'Aye,' Irwin said. 'And the Clangers, they're real as well.'

Yates scanned the sky with watchful eyes. Aircraft had been coming and going since they had arrived at Durlston Heath, but far overhead, on their own urgent errands. 'Then where are they?' he barked into his walkie-talkie. 'We were promised helicopter cover by now! What do you mean, twenty minutes? We haven't *got* twenty minutes.' He signed off, gritting his teeth in frustration as he telescoped down the aerial. 'I'm sorry, Doctor. I'm afraid we're not going to get much help here, at least not for a while.'

'We can't delay,' the Doctor said. 'The Sild may already have reached the Master.'

'The *who*, sir?'

'Try and keep a grip on it, Mike. The man we're here to rescue. As bitter a taste as that leaves in my mouth.'

'Right, sir. Chap in the posters, right?'

'Chap in the posters, Mike, yes.'

They were standing next to the lead lorry, parked askew so that it served as cover between the UNIT officers and the entrance to Durlston Heath. The guards had not so far opened fire, but the Doctor was under no illusions that the lorry would simply be allowed to drive on through. The Sild-controlled guards were hoping that they would make exactly that assumption, whereupon they would attack when the UNIT personnel had nowhere to hide.

'We have no choice,' he said, with bitter resignation. 'Those men will never let us pass, and if we try to force our way through it will become a bloodbath.'

'But those men aren't really men any more, are they? Any more than those people we hit on the road?'

'Those people on the road threw themselves at us, Mike. But are you really ready to open fire on those guards without provocation?'

'Well, not without provocation, but...'

'Get the cover off the TARDIS! I can't attempt precision dematerialisation with a *tarpaulin* draped over the old girl!'

'Are you sure, sir? You said you'd need to be inside the perimeter, to be absolutely certain.'

'I was rather hoping,' the Doctor said, 'that if we managed to get inside the perimeter I wouldn't need the TARDIS at all. As you are all so fond of reminding me, she's hardly the most reliable transport just at present.'

Benton came over with a walkie-talkie. 'Brig for you, sir.'

The Doctor took the handset. 'I was just about to take the TARDIS for a little spin, Brigadier.'

'Sorry to spoil your fun, Doctor. How long do you think you'll need?'

'How long have I got?'

'Reports show Sild elements closing in from different directions. If there's the slightest chance of them reaching the... um...'

'The chap,' the Doctor said.

'Him – yes.' The Brigadier made a harrumphing sound. 'Well, it can't happen. I can give you twenty minutes, but if you're not out by then, I'll have no choice but to pull out my men and resort to an airstrike.'

'And what type of airstrike did you have in mind?'

'The kind that requires Geneva authorisation, Doctor – which I've just been given.'

'I see. Twenty minutes?'

'It should be sufficient. If you haven't reached... the objective... get back in the TARDIS and leave. Is that understood? No heroics, Doctor. I don't have time for them.'

'I shall do my utmost to ensure there are no heroics, Brigadier. Might I speak to Jo?'

'She's on her way to Scotland, as you well know. We can get through to the Hercules if necessary, but it ties up communications...'

'Why on earth did you allow her to head to Scotland?'

'Because you wanted her up there! Against my wishes,

but she was very persuasive.'

'Yes, I imagine she was.' The Doctor's tone softened. 'I don't suppose we should be too surprised. We can't very well hire people on the basis of their independence and initiative and then complain when they demonstrate exactly those qualities.' He paused. 'She'll find her way to that platform one way or another, even if she has to hire a rowing boat. Can you make sure she has as much assistance as you can spare?'

'I'll do what I can. Twenty minutes, Doctor. From the end of this sentence.'

'Thank you, Brigadier.'

The Doctor handed the handset back to Benton.

They went back to the second lorry. Its tarpaulin covers had been pulled back in readiness. The TARDIS rested upright on a wooden forklift pallet, the time-space machine's pseudo-mass straining down on the lorry's already weary suspension.

The Doctor climbed onto the rear platform as the UNIT men removed the temporary rigging which had kept the TARDIS from shifting around. 'Well, old thing,' he said, rubbing a hand against the battered blue exterior. 'Think we've got it in us?'

He fished out his keys, opened the TARDIS, prepared to disappear inside. But he hesitated before closing the door. 'If all goes well, I'll return directly to UNIT headquarters. Tell the Brigadier to prepare a cell for the Master – and make it a strong one.'

The Doctor shrugged off his cape, moved to the central console, hands trembling with the magnitude of what he was about to attempt.

Working quickly, but still with great care, the Doctor adjusted all the navigational presets he had carefully locked down while still at UNIT headquarters. If he had his calculations right, he should be able to use the residual energy from the time distortions to override the Time Lords' control of the TARDIS. *If* he had it right.

'Just this once,' he muttered, as if he was talking to Bessie. 'Just this *one time*. Work.'

The Doctor pushed down the dematerialisation control.

The central part of the console began to rise and fall as the TARDIS initiated reluctant entry into the Time Vortex. More warnings lit up. The Doctor danced around the console, cancelling indications, making small adjustments. The wheezing, groaning sound of dematerialisation intensified, and then died away to a gentle rhythmic hum. Time flight had been achieved. The subjective interval, inside the TARDIS, bore no linear relationship to the objective interval. But it would still take only seconds. The Doctor busied himself adjusting temporal trim controls.

Abruptly, the TARDIS lurched. The wheezing and groaning returned. The console slowed, and then ceased its rise and fall. Time egress had been achieved. The TARDIS had emerged from the Vortex.

The Doctor made a quick appraisal of the console readouts, satisfying himself that the numbers were not too far from where he had hoped they might fall. He turned on the external viewer. He was hoping to see the interior of the Durlston A reactor, but perhaps that had always been an unrealistic expectation. He was not so far off after all. The TARDIS had come to rest on a stretch of sand, drab and windswept, hemmed by dunes on one side. The Doctor made the view track around through 360 degrees. The sky was a cloudy grey, squatting low above a band of grey water that could only be the North Sea. He had obviously not come very far from his point of departure. The Doctor watched as the scene tracked around, expecting the blocky outline of the power station to hove into view at any moment. Once he knew exactly how far off course he had come, he could refine the parameters for the next attempt.

The Doctor stopped the viewer's tracking. It had locked on to some figures, dragging something out of the water.

Curious, the Doctor touched the zoom controls. The figures resolved into bearded, wild-haired men clad in bedraggled costumes of leather, fur and simple metal armour. They had horns on their helmets, and the thing they were dragging out of the sea was some kind of wooden-hulled boat, with a crude dragon carved into its prow.

'Ah,' the Doctor said to himself. 'Close in space, but a little *off* in time.' With a twinge of self-directed irritation, he realised that he had failed to engage one of the temporal lock overrides. Now one of the helmeted men had broken away from the boat-hauling party and was running toward the TARDIS in a state of some excitement, waving an axe and screaming. 'Terribly sorry for the intrusion,' the Doctor said, entirely for his own benefit.

He threw the dematerialisation control again, and the TARDIS lurched back into the Vortex.

The time flight lasted a little longer this time, but the re-entry was smoother, and when the Doctor reactivated the viewer he was gratified to see that he was very definitely indoors, in what was clearly a modern industrial structure. He checked the readouts, encouraged to see that the spatial and temporal indices all appeared correct, within an allowable margin of error. He had travelled less than a second from his original moment of departure on the UNIT lorry, and much less than a mile in space.

He was in the reactor building.

But the Doctor had learned his lesson and before leaving the TARDIS he was careful to complete a 360-degree sweep of the building's interior. He was inside the main hall, but not yet within the cube which contained the Master's accommodation unit. The lights were still on, and there was as yet no sign that the Sild had reached this far. Perhaps there was still time.

The Doctor opened the door, ignoring the TARDIS's warnings that the air outside was moderately radioactive. He slipped on his cape and stepped out into the reactor hall.

The TARDIS had come to rest on a section of elevated metal flooring between two huge turbines. Alarms were sounding, orange lights flashing all around the echoing space. There were no guards around: the Doctor presumed that they had been called away to defend the perimeter. He locked the TARDIS, then made his way quickly to the steps which led up the side of the central cube. But at the top he found his way blocked by a heavy metal gate, barring entrance into the cube. The Doctor struggled with it for a few moments, then dug out his sonic screwdriver. Glancing around nervously, doing his best to shut out the distraction of the alarms and the lights, the Doctor struggled to bypass the heavy electromechanical lock. But it was to no avail. The sonic screwdriver could get through most things, given time, but time was exactly the thing in short supply. Muttering to himself, the Doctor returned the screwdriver to his pocket.

There was nothing for it.

He descended the stairs and found his way out of the main hall, along the connecting office that led to Childers' observation room. An automated voice was blaring from speaker grilles in the wall: 'Security Warning. Perimeter has been breached. Level one lockdown is now in effect.'

The Doctor found the observation room. The door was ajar. He pushed it open, flicking on the room light as he entered.

Childers was sitting at his console.

The Doctor looked at him, expecting a response. Childers was awake, but his mind seemed to be elsewhere. His hands sat limply in his lap. His eyes were fixed on the screens and controls of the console, but there was no focus in them.

The Doctor spun Childers around in his swivel chair, snapped his fingers to bring the man out of whatever trance he was in. 'For pity's sake, man – snap out of it!'

Childers blinked and frowned. He seemed not to have noticed the Doctor until that moment.

'I've failed, haven't I?' Childers asked distantly, as if not really expecting an answer. 'Let everyone down.'

'Now's not the time for that,' the Doctor said. 'Whatever you did, or allowed to happen, you thought it was for the best. But now we need to think about the Master.'

'The Master?'

'Prisoner M. *Think*, Director. Concentrate. Prisoner M. You remember him, don't you?'

'There was a Prisoner M once...' Childers said. 'That was a long time ago, though.' A childlike questioning tone entered his voice. 'Why are you asking about him now?'

'Childers, listen very, very carefully. That man is still in your care – just. He's in the main reactor core. But the people... the things... breaking into Durlston Heath want to get to him very badly. We have to get to him first!'

Childers squinted like a man looking into the sun. 'Get to who?'

'Never mind.' The Doctor could see that this was hopeless: Childers' amnesia was too far gone.

The Doctor leaned over and threw a sequence of switches on the console, watching until lights turned from green to red and red to green.

'What are you doing?'

'Paying a visit to an old acquaintance, before someone else does. I've opened the gate to the main cube.' The Doctor flicked another bank of switches. 'This initiates the elevation of his accommodation unit. Now all I need is to enter the override code to open the main door into the unit.' The Doctor tapped the sequence he'd seen Childers use on his last visit, then turned to regard the row of status lights under the keypad. They flashed red three times, emitting a shrill buzz at the same time. 'What day is it today?' the Doctor asked, before his gaze chanced upon a tear-off calendar sitting next to one of the telephones. 'Monday, of course. And you've changed the code, as you were meant to do.'

'Is there a problem?' Childers asked.

'I'm rather afraid there is. I need to know the new code,

167

Director. Four numbers. Do you remember them?'

'Be a daft wazzock if I didn't, wouldn't I?'

'Then tell me the numbers.'

But the Doctor drew breath, freezing on the last syllable. He was no longer looking at Childers, but at the thing creeping up the back of Childers' chair. With Childers facing him, all that the Doctor could see was the extremities of its legs, the tips of its probing cilia. 'Director,' he said softly. 'Would you... slowly....' He beckoned gently, hoping to coax Childers out of the chair, before the Sild had a chance to clamp on.

It was, however, a vain hope. The Sild clasped itself around Childers' neck, and in an instant Childers seemed to break out of his shell-shocked state, reaching up frantically, trying to claw the alien thing away from him. He shrieked. The Doctor, no less horrified, sprang forward, spun the chair and tried to rip the Sild away from the rear. Childers thrashed and gurgled as the Sild's tentacles locked tighter around his throat. It was not trying to strangle him, but to incapacitate him sufficiently to enable full integration.

The Doctor stumbled back. Childers was turning a liverish purple, the Sild adjusting itself as it prepared to sink its nerve taps. Only seconds remained. Even as this urgency gripped him, the Doctor's eyes scanned the room in fear, wondering if another Sild was close at hand.

He remembered the sonic screwdriver. He pulled it out, adjusted its settings, and turned it to maximum sonic disrupt. The screwdriver made a rising whine, a note that rose in frequency and intensity until it was at first audibly painful, then beyond pain. He steered the beam in the rough direction of the Sild and hoped that this might work. Childers was slumping in the chair, losing whatever fight he had possessed. On the console, one by one, the glass-fronted dials and readouts began to shatter. The Doctor hoped that the glass in the Sild's container might also succumb, but it was proving far more resilient to sonic disruption. The screwdriver was turning hot in the Doctor's hands, approaching power overload.

Suddenly the Sild released. Its legs had turned momentarily ineffective, allowing the Sild to dangle away from Childers. The Doctor pocketed the still-hot screwdriver and ripped the Sild from its host. Inches of blood-smeared cilia slid out of the man, and then as the tips popped free, they emerged with little specks of grey-pink matter. Brain tissue, the Doctor realised. The Sild had already touched Childers' mind. Ordinarily, the severance of contact would be fatal for the host organism. But if it had only been seconds…

The Doctor kicked the Sild away. It was spasming, unable to right itself. The Doctor grabbed at a metal waste basket. He upended it, tipping out its paper contents, and dropped the empty receptacle over the struggling Sild.

'Director! Can you hear me?'

Childers coughed. He coughed again, drew breath and let out an appalled shriek. He tried to pull himself out of the chair, but the Doctor held him gently down.

'Easy, old fellow.'

The shriek turned to a moan. The moan abated long enough for Childers to say, quite clearly: 'Sild.'

'I know,' the Doctor said, feeling a combination of terrible pity and empathy. 'It's all over now. The Sild has gone.'

But the damage it had done, that was very much not gone. This was what happened to the Sild's victims. They either died straight away or not long after.

'Hurts.'

'Director, you've been a very brave man. But now I need you to be a little braver. In a few seconds, you're going to start feeling very drowsy. Before that happens, I'd like you to tell me the numbers.' The Doctor was cupping Childers' head now, supporting him gently, not wishing to cause this poor man any more pain. 'The numbers, Director. It's very important.'

'It's all over now,' Childers said.

The Sild was rattling around inside the waste bin.

'There's still time. Give me the numbers.'

'No, there isn't. It's over. Relegation time.' Childers voice was slurred. He sounded like a man on the edge of consciousness, about to drift into sleep. 'They'd have needed to score against Blackpool to stay in the division...'

'Childers!' The Doctor was about to slap the man. 'This isn't about rugby!'

'Relegation time. Down the flipping table.'

Childers slumped. The Doctor allowed the man's head to loll, knowing it was over; that sleep had taken him and that death would follow quickly. The Sild had done too much damage to his mind, in the moments it was coupled. The Doctor's revulsion sharpened to a keen hatred. It was an abomination that a living creature could to this to another.

Then his eyes chanced upon the newspaper again. Now that he looked closer he saw that the paper was folded to the sports pages. The Doctor snatched it up and glanced down the long columns of rugby results. Hull Kingston Rovers versus Blackpool Borough. Hull: 3, Blackpool: 5. The score had been ringed in faint red biro.

Was it possible?

The Doctor moved back to the keypad. He tapped digits: a zero, a three, a zero and a five.

The lights flashed once, then went out. A set of green lights had come on.

The Sild was beginning to find its way out of the bin, poking thin legs and tentacles under the rim. The Doctor's rage boiled over. He stomped on the bin, crushing the Sild's limbs. The Sild's glass container shattered and the creature was still.

'Thank you, Director,' the Doctor said, addressing the now dead Childers. 'You didn't let the team down, in the end.'

CHAPTER SEVENTEEN

Lovelace's hand was trembling on the automatic. The thing on the window had unsettled him. Were it not for the fact that Irwin had been present as a witness, he would have gladly accepted Callow's theory that his concussion was getting to him.

He had returned to the telephone after shooting the crab, but when he picked up the handset there was nobody on the other end of the line. He tried reconnecting to the Ministry, but something was wrong with the sub-sea link.

'If I were you,' Irwin said, 'I'd be thinking about a change of career.'

'We're all in this together,' Lovelace said.

Irwin had his arms folded. He looked perfectly relaxed and affable, not at all like a man being held at gunpoint. It was an act, Lovelace was certain, but a thoroughly convincing one all the same. 'Aye, but what is it we're "in", Lovelace? That's the question. What mess have you brought down on all of us?'

'The less you ask, Irwin, the less need I'll have to shoot you.'

'That's mightily reassuring.'

At that moment the general alarm began to sound. It was a fierce electronic tone, signalling one of several calamitous things that could happen on an oil platform. It was coming out of a grille in McCrimmon's office, but the same sound would be transmitted throughout the rig.

'What is it?'

Irwin shrugged. 'Could be a fire, could be a blow-out, or a structural problem. Or could be more of those crab beasties scuttling around. So are you still going to do what you told Callow over the phone? Blow up your equipment or whatever it is you said? Wouldn't want the nasty old Russians getting hold of it, would we?'

'Never you mind.' Lovelace's intentions had been thrown into disarray. Ideally, he had been planning to scuttle the MERMAN equipment before abandoning the platform. But the coming of the crab, and now this alarm, made him anxious not to spend a minute longer on the rig than necessary.

'Take me to the helicopter deck. We're leaving.'

'Not until you tell me what you've done to Eddie McCrimmon.'

'I said we're leaving. You know I'll use this weapon if I must. So take me to the helicopter deck!'

'Find it yourself. You've come and gone from the rig often enough.'

'You misunderstand me. You're my hostage now, Irwin. You're the man who's going to get me on that helicopter ahead of the others.' And he waggled the automatic for emphasis, just in case he had not made his point with sufficient authority.

By the time the Doctor reached the immersion tank, the Master's accommodation unit was halfway out of the water, being hoisted by the overhead gantry. The connecting drawbridge was in the process of folding out, ready to provide access to the module.

But the Master was already standing at the open doorway, braced against the frame, looking down into the flooded pit, as if he half fancied his chances of jumping and swimming.

'Doctor,' he called, raising his voice over the alarms, Tannoy announcements, and the labouring whine of the overhead gantry. 'You do me a great honour, by arriving to witness the moment of my escape. But I advise you not to interfere.'

'I haven't come to interfere, I've come to rescue you,' the Doctor shouted back.

'Rescue me? My dear fellow, all is in hand, as should be evident even to you. I have sent a message into time; this is the response.'

The accommodation block came to a halt, swaying slightly. The Master kept his balance, waiting for the connection walkway to lock into place.

'You're wrong,' the Doctor called, the two of them now facing each other from either end of the walkway. 'You're wrong, and what's worse, you know it!'

'Step aside, please Doctor. I have work to be getting on with.'

'The amnesia – aren't you curious about it? Doesn't it worry you?'

'A mere side effect of my temporal intervention, Doctor.'

'It's a lot more than a side effect. Even the UNIT records of you are starting to degrade. It's progressive time-fade! You are being unstitched from time.'

The Master had begun to advance across the connecting drawbridge. 'Then it can only be part of my plan.'

'It's the Sild.'

'Do not mock me, Doctor. We both know that the Sild are long gone. I transmitted my message into the future, not the remote past.'

'I don't understand it either. But I've seen Sild units coming ashore. Somehow or other, the Sild are responding to your transmission.' The Doctor paused for effect. 'But not in the way you were hoping.' He looked over his shoulder. 'They're here – individually, and in control of many hosts. They've reached Childers, and you'd have been next.'

173

'And is that why you're here? To turn me over to them?'

'My TARDIS is nearby – at the very least it'll get you away from the Sild.'

'And then what? Further incarceration? Forgive me, Doctor, but I may just take my chances with the Sild, assuming they are not a figment of your overheated imagination.'

'They're stronger than you.'

'But I am quicker, and vastly more intelligent. Stand aside, please.' The Master advanced another couple of strides: he and the Doctor were now close enough to touch.

'You'll never make it out of this building.'

'You underestimate me, as always.'

'You can't do your usual bargaining with the enemy, Master. It may have worked with the Axons and the Nestene Consciousness, but they *needed* your cooperation. The Sild don't need cooperation at all. Whatever they want from you, they can get it by sheer force.'

'They are very welcome to try.'

The Master pushed forward, trying to barge his way past the Doctor.

'No!' The Doctor cried, grappling with his old adversary, hoping to pin the Master in one place long enough to reason with him. 'I won't let the Sild have you! They want you very badly and that's reason enough to stop them!'

'I warn you, Doctor!' The Master gave the Doctor a violent shove, enough to topple him over the side of the low-railinged walkway. The Doctor grabbed for something, anything, to stop his fall. His feet flailed over open air. His fingers grabbed onto the lower lip of the walkway, and he hung there.

The Master tugged his sleeves down and adjusted his collar, regaining what little composure he had lost during the struggle. His hair, oiled back, remained immaculately undisturbed.

'Farewell, Doctor.' The Master planted the toe of his boot on the Doctor's fingertips. He pressed down, like a man stubbing out a cigarette. The Doctor let out a yelp of pain.

'You fool! I only wanted to help you!'

'Is that true, Doctor? Or are you really only concerned about what the Sild want of me?' The Master worked his boot to one side and the other, until the Doctor could no longer maintain his grip. He let go, the bones in his fingers feeling as if they been turned to shards, and hung by the other hand, over the immersion tank. The Master set his foot down on the Doctor's other hand. He did not have to press very hard this time. The Master chuckled.

And then the Doctor was falling, and the Master was free.

Jo had just passed through the checkpoint at RAF Eastmere airfield, flashing her UNIT accreditation, when the orderly passed her the radio.

She took it with trepidation, fully expecting to be reprimanded, perhaps even given notice of her dismissal. She had exceeded her authority in arranging this last-minute dash to Scotland; still worse, she had pulled the wool over the Brigadier's eyes by letting him think the Doctor fully approved of her plans.

'Lethbridge-Stewart here,' said the voice on the other end of the connection. 'I've told them to stop you getting on that Hercules…'

'I see, sir.' Jo had to speak up over the four-engined drone of the military transport, squatting on the ground while it was being readied for departure. 'Look, I realise I overstepped—'

'… until help arrives,' the Brigadier continued, speaking over her. 'In a very short while, my ground forces at Durlston Heath are going to be surplus to requirements. As soon as I can free those men, I'll helicopter them to Eastmere.'

Jo gulped. This was the last thing she had expected. 'And… um… the Doctor, sir?'

'I'm afraid the news is mixed.'

'Has he managed to get to…'

'The Doctor's gone into the power station on his own, in an attempt to reach the… objective… ahead of the Sild. He had to take the TARDIS – there was no other way through the perimeter. At least, that's what we think. We've had no contact with him since he dematerialised, and that was...' There was a pause as the Brigadier consulted his watch. 'Twenty-eight minutes ago, precisely.'

'I'm sure he'll be out sooner or later.'

'I wish I shared your optimism, Miss Grant. I gave him twenty minutes to get in and out. I have now exceeded that time by a considerable margin.'

'What are you saying, Brigadier?'

'I'm saying I have no choice but to authorise an airstrike.'

'But you don't know if the Doctor's still in there!'

'Believe me, I would far rather wait until I have concrete news of the Doctor's whereabouts. But I simply don't have that luxury.'

Jo nodded to herself. She had crossed swords with Lethbridge-Stewart on many occasions but she had never had cause to doubt his integrity or his indebtedness to the Doctor. This must be one of the hardest decisions he had ever taken in his military career.

'How long, Brigadier?'

'The Phantoms will be in position in... just over two minutes.'

CHAPTER EIGHTEEN

During the short trip to the helicopter deck, Lovelace made no attempt to hide the fact that he had a pistol aimed squarely at Tom Irwin. The more obvious the situation the better, in fact. As they passed other oil workers, waiting their turns to board one of the helicopters, Lovelace barked: 'Let us through! Any of you tries anything, I won't hesitate to shoot him and you.'

'I'd take him at his word,' Irwin said through his beard. 'Man's got a serious case of the heebie-jeebies.'

'Where's Eddie?' someone shouted.

'He's got her locked away below, in the secret area,' Irwin called back, before earning a hard jab in the kidneys from the automatic. 'Assuming he isn't lying, and he killed her the same way him and his pals bumped off Pete Lomax!'

'What the…' another worker shouted, as Irwin's words hit home. The man had a hefty spanner in his hand, and seemed to debate swinging it at Lovelace.

'Get down there,' Irwin said back. 'See if you can find Eddie. Tell her this nutcase has slipped a gear!'

The alarm was still sounding, louder now since it was coming from one of the deck-mounted speakers, its shrill blare echoing off the high steelwork of the crane, blow-off tower and drill derrick. Lovelace prodded Irwin up the final flight of stairs, onto the flat grey apron of the vacant helipad.

One of the transports was coming back in from the mainland, the steady thump-thump of its rotors already cutting through the sound of the alarm.

'What do you think this is going to achieve, Lovelace?' Irwin asked, crouching down against the wind and the anticipated arrival of the helicopter.

'You worry about yourself, Irwin; I'll worry about me.'

'Oh, I get it. Pals in high places. You lot can worm your way out of any old bother, can't you? Is it something they teach you in public school?'

'Tom!'

The two men paused. The speaker was another oil worker, but Lovelace had never bothered to keep tabs on more than a handful of them. It was a young man with long hair, like a layabout or footballer, running out onto the operations deck with his arms flapping.

Irwin said, 'What's up, Bill?'

'It's Gerry Evans, Tom – I don't know what's got into him!' Then the young man appeared to notice the unusual situation before him: the man with the gun, aiming it at Tom Irwin. 'Tom?'

'Never mind us, Bill. What's the matter with Gerry?'

'There's something stuck to him, like a metal crab! He's walking around like a sleepwalker, tried to grab hold of me before I cottoned on! I closed the fire door, sealed him into D section! Is that what the alarm's about?'

Irwin looked at Lovelace and nodded slowly. 'There are more of the sods. Someone must've seen enough to raise the alarm.'

The helicopter was completing its final approach, settling slowly down onto the platform.

'The nick, as they say, of time,' Lovelace said.

'If you still have contact with your pals in the Ministry,' Irwin said, 'you'd better get word to them that we could use a bit of help out here.'

'No need. As Eddie McCrimmon was so good to point

out, UNIT are on their way.' Then Lovelace smiled. 'Unless she was bluffing.'

Lovelace walked to the door of the helicopter, still training his automatic on Irwin. He rapped on the pilot's door. 'Open up! If you delay, I will shoot this man!'

The pilot had flipped up his visor. He looked perplexed, then shocked.

Irwin nodded at him. 'Better do as the idiot says. He can have a seat at the back, and talk to the police when he lands. I can still get twenty men off the rig if they budge up.'

Lovelace shook his head. 'No. I'm not waiting.' He worked the side door, which was now unlocked, and hopped up into the cabin, crouching down to keep the automatic trained. The pilot and co-pilot were talking furiously.

'At least take some of my men!' Irwin called. 'It's no skin off your nose – you're on the helicopter already, and I won't stop you! My day starts getting better the moment you leave!'

'No,' Lovelace said. 'We're going now. Take off, pilot – unless you'd like a bullet as well!'

Irwin shook his head resignedly. 'You'd better do what he says – he's already well off the deep end.'

'Very sensible of you, Irwin.' Lovelace dragged shut the door, and began to scuttle back to one of the passenger seats. 'Take off!' he snapped again.

The helicopter began to rev up – the rotors had hardly slowed after touchdown – and with a moment of dreamy disconnection from the rig and its manifold difficulties, they were aloft. Lovelace allowed himself to sink back into the padding of the seat. It was not exactly the case that his troubles were over. There would, as Irwin had correctly predicted, be some questions to answer when he reached the mainland. Equally, it was true that he did have connections where he needed them. His actions, though committed with a certain haste, were eminently defensible. He had worked to protect vital national interests. He had not actually *killed* anyone. And if it looked as if he was running away from trouble now, in flagrant dereliction of duty, then it was only because he had an obligation, a pressing moral responsibility, to protect the sensitive information in his head. He was Lovelace! He couldn't risk himself, not to shut down equipment which probably wasn't going to last long anyway.

Something moved under the seat, across the aisle and a couple of rows back. He heard it quite distinctly, even above the throb and thump of the climbing helicopter. A kind of scratchy metallic whisking and tapping. A dread beyond dread seized Lovelace. It couldn't be, could it? One of those things couldn't have found its way aboard the helicopter while it was on the pad?

But there it was, emerging from under the seats – the same as the one he had shot through the window. Not the same one, though. There was no bullet hole in this one. The fist-sized body was intact. Now that he was seeing the crab the right way up, he had no difficulty making out the glass pod Irwin had seen on the other one. A squishy little thing was moving around in that bottle, twitching like a worm on a hook.

'Land!' Lovelace shrieked. 'Put us back down!'

The pilots twisted round in their seats, but they couldn't see what Lovelace could see.

'Land!' he screamed. 'Go back!'

The crab was on his side of the aisle now, climbing up the back of the seat behind him. The silver tentacles were groping ahead of it. His thoughts flashed back to what the young man had said, about a crab stuck to another oil worker. Lovelace had eased from his seat and was now moving forward, back toward the cockpit. The pilots were still trying to work out what he wanted. Take off, go back – no wonder they were confused.

He aimed the automatic at the crab, fired once. The crab dropped off the seat. He'd killed it, hadn't he? One clean shot, the way he'd dispensed with the one in McCrimmon's office.

No. The crab was damaged – he'd blown off one or two

of its limbs, but it was still capable of movement. He aimed again, panicked, and missed completely, blowing a hole in the hull. It wouldn't matter; the helicopter wasn't pressurised.

Now the crab was scuttling onto the ceiling. It was just as nimble upside down as the right way up. The thing was coming down the centre of the aisle, straddling it like a nasty modern light fitting. Lovelace aimed again and fired. This time he bit off a good chunk of it. The crab hung lopsidedly. He wasn't going to take any chances. There had to be only one of the things on the helicopter, didn't there? If there was another one he was stuffed anyway.

Empty the whole automatic into it, that was the only solution. Clutching the pistol double-handed, he fired and kept on firing, shot after shot through the crab, through the insulation of the ceiling, into the whirling iron guts of the helicopter's motor.

And all of a sudden the helicopter started making a very sick sound indeed.

The Doctor paused on the ladder, halfway out of the immersion tank. For a moment, exhausted and bedraggled, it was all he could do. Nothing had prepared him for the sheer visceral shock when he hit the water. He had gone under, the shock of the impact jolting the air from his lungs, and he had gulped down a throatful of water before he was able to regain some measure of self-control. Even with the benefits of a respiratory bypass system, drowning was a very real possibility.

But he forced himself to the surface, gasping and coughing, and even as the cold began to sap his muscles of their strength and coordination, he paddled his way around the perimeter of the tank to the white metal service ladder which rose from its depths. He heaved himself out of the water, shivering and coughing, and only managed to ascend a couple of rungs before he had to stop.

What a fool he had been, to think that the Master would

simply accept his word without question. In his shoes, would he have placed any more faith in his adversary?

Probably not.

The Doctor delved into his deepest resources and resumed his ascent of the ladder. With a final grunt of exhaustion he reached the same level where the connecting bridge had swung into place, and was at last able to stand on his feet. At least two minutes had passed since the Master had forced him from the platform.

His shoes squelching, his muscles still in shock, the Doctor nonetheless forced himself to run out of the central chamber, into the connecting corridor where his progress had originally been obstructed by the security gate. It was open now, of course – no one had been at the console to close it after the Doctor's passage. Beyond the gate, he found himself back in the main reactor hall, with its high walkways and ranks of snail-like turbines. He was looking down on it, from the top of the spiral staircase. There, on a stretch of flooring between two turbines, was the waiting TARDIS.

And the Master trying to get inside – stooped by the door, attempting to force it open.

The Doctor was grateful that old habits had made him lock the TARDIS upon leaving. 'Stop!' he called, trying to make himself heard above the din of sirens and warning announcements. His voice echoed and re-echoed. Something must have reached the Master, for he turned around and acknowledged the Doctor with a nod, before returning to his work.

'You can't open it!' The Doctor shouted. 'You're wasting your time!'

The Master did not deign to turn round this time. But something flashed in his hand, brought to his side for a moment as if he wished the Doctor to know what it was he held, the way a stage magician might flash a card for the audience's benefit. The Doctor stared. He had recognised the silver device in an instant – the handle and angled head, like a clever little dental drill. It was a sonic screwdriver.

There was nothing for it. The range was extreme, but the Doctor would have to try jamming the Master's sonic screwdriver with his own. He reached into his sodden pocket, his hand expecting to close around the handle of his own sonic screwdriver.

It wasn't there.

The Doctor had begun to search his other pockets when he realised what should have been obvious all along. In the struggle on the platform, the Master had pickpocketed him. From time-meddling, to the genocides of entire species, from strangling to petty pilfering: the scope of the Master's criminality was absolute.

The Doctor couldn't just watch, doing nothing. He started down the spiral staircase, skipping treads two and three at a time, his cold-numbed hands riding the bannister. The Doctor had come close to losing the TARDIS before but that was something he could almost accept. Having it *taken* from him was an affront beyond imagining.

Yet when he reached the bottom of the spiral staircase, the TARDIS was still there. It emitted no sound and its blue light remained unlit. The Master was still near the door, but no longer attending to the lock. He was on his knees, his hands now reaching behind his neck.

The Doctor quickened his pace, even as every instinct compelled him to move in the opposite direction. A Sild had clamped on to the Master. He was fighting it, as best he could, but the Sild was resisting, its legs and tentacles redoubling their hold. An ordinary person, the Doctor knew, would surely have succumbed by now. But the Master had a Time Lord's nervous system and extreme mental fortitude. The Sild, in turn, was touching a mind quite unlike any other it was likely to have encountered.

And yet the Sild would triumph. The Doctor was sure of that. It was simply a question of how long it took to overcome the Master's defences. Minutes, perhaps, rather than the usual seconds. But of the outcome there could be no doubt. The Master, after all, was why the Sild were here.

The Doctor reached the other Time Lord. By now the Master was on his side, legs drawn to his chest in agony. His face was a mask carved of equal parts pain and concentration.

'Doctor,' he managed to say, the word half-choked. But if the Master was on the verge of begging for help, he could not yet bring himself to that humiliating state.

The Doctor stooped down, collecting the sonic screwdriver which the Master must have dropped when the Sild reached him. A scuttling sound came from further down the walkway. Two more Sild were advancing along the elevated walkway, while a third was working its way over the back of one of the turbines. If they were here in ones and twos, then they would soon be here in dozens, then hundreds. The Doctor fished out his key and opened the TARDIS, stepping neatly around the writhing Master. He paused on the threshold, part of him ready to close the door, engage the dematerialisation circuit, prepared to abandon the Master and this planet to their mutual fates. There was a whole universe out there, with miracles and wonders enough to fill a thousand lifetimes. Nothing bound to him to this miserable corner of space and time except a handful of friendships.

But there was no force in creation stronger than those friendships. Jo, the Brigadier, the rest of his colleagues in UNIT… and by extension every human being alive on this planet. He couldn't abandon them to the Sild.

Even the Master deserved better than that.

The Doctor directed the sonic screwdriver at the Sild. It jerked in his hand, as if it had been left in an odd setting. Whatever it was, the Sild did not care for it. The alien creature sprang off the Master, twitching on its back in a kind of electrocuted palsy. The Doctor glanced at the sonic screwdriver, as impressed and disturbed as if it had changed into a snake.

The Doctor dragged the now slumped Master by the

shoulders. He pulled him over the threshold, into the TARDIS. The other Sild were very close now. The Doctor squirted the sonic screwdriver at them. At close range, the effect was one of instant debilitation. At longer range, it only slowed or deflected the advance. The Doctor ducked back inside and started closing the doors. A Sild crawled around the top of the doorway, tentacles whipping. The Doctor slammed the door, but not quickly enough. The Sild was inside, dropping to the floor, righting itself. He aimed the sonic screwdriver at it, delivering a close-range energy pulse even as the Sild seemed about to pounce for his own neck.

The Sild twitched like a nerve-gassed spider.

The Doctor propped the Master against the control room's wall, then tried to straighten his head so that it didn't loll onto his chest. There was something hard under the Master's collar, like a second collar of metal. For an instant the Doctor was inclined to investigate, but for once his sense of urgency prevailed over natural curiosity. Leaving the Master alone, he strode to the console and initiated dematerialisation. He danced around the instruments, flicking switches and turning knobs, until he had locked the TARDIS on to UNIT headquarters. The console's central element began its reassuring rise and fall. The Doctor allowed himself a moment's relief – there had been no real danger of the Sild penetrating the TARDIS, but it was still good to be out of there.

Something slammed the TARDIS. It was less a lurch, more a hard jarring collision: the temporal equivalent of ramming a multidimensional iceberg. The Doctor slid from one side of the control room to the other, cartwheeling his arms – it was as if the level floor had become the deck of a capsizing ship. Then he was sliding back the other way, almost falling this time, until he was able to find an anchor in the central console. The Master, too, was being thrown around like a rag doll. The controls had gone haywire, the central element jerking up, down, up, up, down, up, down,

down. The Doctor made frantic adjustments to the controls. The TARDIS's environmental readings were either scrambled or nonsensical. Sifting through centuries of experience, the Doctor could only conclude that the TARDIS had been exposed to some violent energy field in the instants after dematerialisation had commenced. Had the Sild, against all his judgement, managed to bring a powerful weapon to bear? Something with the energy density of a stellar envelope?

No. There was, now that the Doctor put his mind to it, a vastly simpler explanation.

'Lethbridge-Stewart,' he said, for nobody's benefit but his own. 'You actually went and did it...'

CHAPTER NINETEEN

There was, of course, no sense in which the events of the Doctor and those of Captain Mike Yates could be said to be cotemporaneous, not now that the Doctor was hurtling through the Vortex, neither part of time nor entirely detached from it.

But in the moments before the TARDIS vanished from the reactor hall, Yates, from a distance of two miles, trained his glare-proof binoculars on a single red-finned and shark-grey Phantom. He watched the jet curl away to the north east, twin afterburners bright as miniature suns, its bunker buster package having been deployed successfully. Invisibly to Yates, for it was far too small to be seen at that distance, the jet was already in the process of being guided home via a laser-designator, shone onto the reactor building from a second Phantom loitering far beyond the Durlston Heath perimeter.

Yates lowered his binoculars. He reached for a pair of flash goggles and slipped them on. It was almost unnecessary. The bunker buster did not detonate until it had already penetrated both the outer and inner layers of Durlston A, so there were already two layers of well-protected building interposed between him and the initial flash. Through the goggles it registered as an instant of muted brightness, as if the reactor building were a giant opaque cube in the heart of which some illuminating light source had just been switched on and off. Yates felt the kiss of the heat pulse. And then an eruption of billowing bright light punched apart the hall in a kind of cone formation, dragging fire and gas and dirt in its wake, and an instant later there it was, the incipient mushroom cloud, hauling itself into the sky like a vast swollen cerebellum, propelled upwards on the piston of its own monstrous knotted spinal column. The brain seemed to churn and writhe, like a thing in transports of mental anguish. Under Yates's boots, the road quivered.

Yates was not impressed. He had seen bigger bangs.

Then it came: the sound and the fury. A hot wind, a muffled but still appallingly loud thunder crack, echoing and echoing, until a second sound, a crunching endless roar, swallowed it. It sounded like the world being torn in two, over and over again.

Yates extracted the earplugs from his ears and lowered the flash goggles.

There was a squawk from his radio. He lifted it to his ears. 'Greyhound Two.'

'Status?' the Brigadier queried.

'Bang on target, sir. Couldn't have asked for a cleaner strike.'

'No,' the Brigadier said, with a distinct absence of enthusiasm. 'I don't suppose we could have.'

'And the Doctor, sir? Do you suppose...?'

'We gave him as long as we could,' the Brigadier said.

Tom Irwin had watched the helicopter go down with a sick feeling in his stomach. It had been bad enough observing Lovelace's departure, knowing that the helicopter was almost empty, but at least it had taken the man out of his hair. Yet the helicopter had barely been two minutes away from the rig when something had begun to go badly wrong. The normal sound of the rotors had gained an ominous grinding undertone, like a Glasgow Corporation bus crunching its gears on its way up Sauciehall Street. Smoke had begun to billow out of the rotor assembly in unfeasible black quantities, like ink from an octopus.

It had gone down fast. Irwin had been trained in helicopter crash scenarios, how to survive a ditching in water, how to escape from a capsized helicopter – but at the back of those simulations – cold, wet and terrifying as they were – was the unstated and frankly optimistic assumption that the initial descent was inherently survivable. That had not been the case here. The phrase 'dropped like a stone' had never been more appropriate. Shorn of lift, some mechanical fault preventing the normal auto-rotation of its blades, the helicopter had fallen out of the sky like the cumbersome metal thing it had always been. It had tipped over and aimed itself nose down, arrowing into the water like a gannet. Irwin couldn't have given a stuff about Lovelace, but there was no way those pilots were surviving an impact like that. After only a few seconds bits of the helicopter were seen floating on the surface.

Under other circumstances a helicopter crash would been the most significant development in weeks. Right now it was just another troubling incident on a day that was going from bad to worse. With the crew left on the platform, Irwin did not even have enough spare manpower to organise a rescue attempt. Not that there would have been much point.

Fortunately that was not the only helicopter shuttling between shore and sea. Brushing aside questions – dismissing the fact that he had just been held at gunpoint – Irwin returned to Eddie's office and tried to get a line to mainland operations. But the telephone was still dead, the way Lovelace had left it.

He went down the corridor, to the wireless room. The door was shut but unlocked. The wireless room had hardly been used since the sub-sea cables went in, but it was still kept in operating order. Irwin knew his way around the equipment well enough. He pulled a seat up to the desk, settled on the headphones and called up mainland operations. The signal was poor – whatever was going on was causing radio interference – but he was able to communicate news of the helicopter crash and request continued assistance in the evacuation. Another helicopter was already on its way.

'Eddie's somewhere in the rig,' he told the wireless operator on the other end. 'I'm going to see if I can find her – she might be in the secure area. Any word on that UNIT party, let me know.'

Irwin delegated one of his men to keep watch on the wireless equipment, while he gathered two more workers and told them to follow him down into the platform's lower levels, hoping and trusting that this hunt was going to come to a happier conclusion than the one for Pete Lomax. It was no time to mount a search, with the alarm still blaring, the men spooked by what they had seen out on the deck and reports beginning to filter in of more crab sightings. Irwin pushed all that from his mind, for the moment. Find Eddie, establish some order. That was priority number one.

But finding Eddie turned out to be the easy part. Irwin heard the banging long before he reached the security door at the start of the restricted area. Through the little window in the upper half of the door he could see Eddie herself, swinging a fire extinguisher against the door from the other side. What should have been a clang came through as a muffled thud.

Irwin tapped the glass and held up his hand. 'Easy! We're here!' he called, as if raising his voice was going to make much difference.

Eddie came to her senses. She looked flustered but otherwise in one piece. She dropped the extinguisher and ran off down the corridor. He waited until she returned, perhaps thirty seconds later, with a notepad and pen. She scrawled something on the pad, then jammed the pad against the window.

LOVELACE

Irwin looked around to his men. 'Get me a pen and paper, someone.' Then he turned back to the window and dragged a finger across his own throat, tapping the other hand against the name Eddie had written. 'Dead,' he mouthed.

Eddie mouthed back: 'Dead?'

Irwin nodded. She would just have to accept that; there was no way he was going to be able to mime a helicopter accident.

Eddie wrote something else in the book.

LOCKED IN STORES. SMASHED WAY OUT. CANT GET THRU THIS DOOR. CODE ON OTHER SIDE?

Irwin nodded. There was a keyed-entry device, but he had tried the obvious combinations – all zeroes, all ones, one, two, three, four, with no success. He gave a hopeless shrug.

Eddie wrote again.

IF U CANT FIND OUT CODE, CUT THRU DOOR.

'Cut through?' Irwin asked.

OXY-ACET, DRILL, WHATEVER. ON A BLOODY OIL RIG. USE YR IMAGINATION.

He grinned. The day was not shaping up to be the best of his life, but there was still life in his boss, and that was enough to lift his spirits.

Someone slipped Irwin a notebook and chunky black felt tip. He bit the cap off and jotted down his own note.

BIG PROBS. ATTACK OF THE KILLER CRABS. LOVELACE HELI CRASH. EVAC IN PROG – HELIS AND LIFEBOATS. GOT TO GET YOU OUT FAST. THEN WORK OUT HOW SMASH GEAR.

She nodded, composed her own reply. CRABS?

Irwin said: ROBOT CRABS. INFESTING RIG. NASTY.

She asked: CONNECTED MERMAN, LOMAX ETC?

Irwin replied: THINK SO.

Eddie wrote: UNIT ARRIVED?

Irwin replied: NOT YET. BUT LOVELACE PLANNED SMASH GEAR. CHICKENED OUT. NOW WE HAVE TO DO IT.

Eddie wrote: IN ROOM HERE. BUT BEHIND ANOTHER DOOR. CANT GET IN. NEED TOOLS.

'We're on it,' he said, trusting she'd get the message.

She wrote: WATCH OUT FOR CRABS.

Irwin nodded. Watching out for crabs was very near the top of his agenda.

CHAPTER TWENTY

The TARDIS tumbled through the Vortex like a house brick tossed down a well, glancing from one pseudo-dimensional wall to the other. The Doctor had managed to regain some measure of stabilisation, but that was not remotely the same as saying that he had managed to bring the TARDIS back under true control.

As he moved around the console, trimming this, adjusting that, it began to dawn on him that there was more to this current lack of control than the jolt the TARDIS had received from the nuclear blast. Something about the Vortex itself was not right. There were currents and eddies where things should normally have been placid. A flow was pulling the TARDIS along.

The Doctor strove to apply more power. The TARDIS protested. The stresses on it were mounting.

'It won't work, you know.'

The Doctor had been so absorbed in his struggles that he had almost forgotten that he did not have the TARDIS to himself. But even then, it was a surprise to see that the Master was conscious, let alone capable of speech.

'And you're in a fit state to have an opinion on the matter, are you?'

The Master was still slumped against the wall where he

had last come to rest. But his eyes were open and his head no longer lolling against his chest. 'Even a simpleton, based on the evidence of his senses, could deduce that we are caught in some kind of temporal slipstream.' His voice was thick, slurred, like a man waking up with a terrible hangover.

'Well, obviously.'

'Continue with unbiased field retardation and you'll rip your precious TARDIS to shreds.' The Master, with great effort, forced himself to his feet. He rubbed the back of his neck and stumbled toward the console, almost tripping before the Doctor caught him.

'Steady on, old chap.'

The Master braced himself next to the console. 'Field retardation will get you nowhere. Have you tried flux injection?'

'Of course.'

'Tachyon dampening?'

'Naturally.'

'And counter-gravitic torque equalisation?'

'An *Ogron* would have tried counter-gravitic torque equalisation.'

'And where did it get you?'

'Insufficient quasi-mass. I tried to compensate, but all pseudo-time buffers were on overload.'

'With a magnitude three disturbance, that scarcely surprises me.' Without asking, the Master tapped some controls. He squinted at a set of dialled instruments. 'How do I adjust your charged vacuum resonator to the next harmonic?'

'You don't.' The Doctor coughed. 'Because I haven't got one. They didn't start fitting them until the Type Forty-Fours.'

'I see. And if I were to suggest cross-linking the output from your metric coupling module with the input from your neutron exchange?'

'You'd be making a preposterous suggestion. You know, you *really* should sit down. A few minutes ago you had a Sild clamped to you. Just because you're a Time Lord…'

'A temporary inconvenience, no more than that.' But the Master had no sooner completed this statement than he collapsed to the floor, lying half under the console's overhang. The Doctor stepped over him gingerly, as one might a sleeping dog.

'Cross-link metric coupling to neutron exchange – what a ridiculous idea,' he muttered. 'But if the flow is orthogonal to the Vortex, I suppose it *might* just work.' Hurriedly, he made the necessary alterations. The change was not instantaneous, but gradually the flight of the TARDIS became smoother, more like her usual self.

The Doctor consulted the temporal indicators. They were still being pulled into the future at high velocity. This was still not independent time travel of the kind the TARDIS used to be capable of, before the Time Lords banished the Doctor to Earth – but either that injunction had been lifted remotely, to allow him to follow the Sild signal, or the temporal flow was simply too strong to be resisted.

But the Master's suggestion had decoupled the TARDIS from the worst effects of that suction. With the right application of power, at the right time, it might even be possible to snap free and resume normal Vortex flight.

He studied the instruments again, and hovered his hand over the fat red mushroom of the emergency power boost.

'Well. What are you waiting for?'

'I don't know.'

The Master hauled himself up from the floor and leaned against the console. 'The Vortex flow is evidently the result of Sild interference.'

'Then you believe me, finally?'

'I can hardly doubt the evidence of my senses. The flow will eventually pull us forward to their time, like water running out of a sink. If you do not break us loose, we will be carried far beyond the Epoch of Mass Time Travel, to whenever and wherever the Sild have their primary concentration. Very few individuals have ever travelled as far beyond the EMTT as we are about to!'

'I'm well aware of that.'

'Then why don't you snap us out of the flow?'

'It won't end, even if we break free. The Sild want you very badly, and they'll find you again. No matter where you go, they'll track you down.'

'But for you, Doctor? You have no business with the Sild. They have no business with *you*, either. This petty little world we have just departed… why let it concern you?'

'Because that petty little world is the nearest thing I have to a home. Something you wouldn't understand. And even if I turn back now, the Sild won't stop attacking the Earth. They have a taste for blood.'

'Then you leave me no choice. I must fight you for control of the TARDIS.'

'In your present state? You couldn't fight your way out of a paper bag.'

The Master chuckled quietly. 'I confess, Doctor, that for once you have the better of me. I am… weakened.'

'You're lucky to be alive.'

'I had the benefit of a little extra protection.' The Master tugged down the edge of his collar, exposing a gleam of silver. 'Callow and Lovelace fitted me with this device months ago. A simple mechanism, designed to ensure my compliance.'

'Callow and Lovelace?'

'The government men, Doctor. From the Ministry of Defence. When they had me away from my prison, they didn't want me escaping. This collar ensured that. A primitive radio circuit, wired to a small explosive charge. Crude, but I won't deny its effectiveness. Thankfully for me, it also served to obstruct the Sild, when it attempted to achieve nerve-linkage.'

'If you hadn't pushed me into the water, we'd both have been away from there before the Sild arrived!'

'Hindsight, Doctor. A foolish distraction, even for time travellers.' The Master nodded at the Doctor's hand, still poised over the power boost. 'Well?'

To the Master's visible surprise and suspicion, the Doctor stepped back and offered his upturned palm to the control. 'It's all yours. If you feel so strongly about this, use the boost.'

The Master's eyes were narrowed. 'I presume there's some subterfuge involved?'

'Nothing of the sort. But since this involves you, the decision should be yours. Hit the boost, and the TARDIS will return on its homing setting to UNIT headquarters. Given the chaos back home, it shouldn't be too difficult for you to contrive an escape.' The Doctor shrugged. 'I won't even stop you, old chap. But I'll tell you this. It won't end. The time-fade will progress so far that even *you* don't remember who you are. And whatever it is the Sild want of you, they'll keep looking. They've reached back into the EMTT from the extreme end of history. That means their range is effectively infinite. That means there's nowhere at all for you to hide.'

'You paint such an attractive scenario, Doctor. And the alternative?'

'We ride this stream, all the way to the Sild. And then we find what it is they want of you. And then – if there's a chance – we try and stop whatever it is they're doing. If we can reverse their time interference, begin to undo the time-fade... so much the better.'

'I always knew you had an optimistic streak, Doctor. I never realised it shaded into the basest idiocy.'

'The Sild are undermining time,' the Doctor stated, ignoring the Master's insult. 'If we wait too long, time travel itself, as we understand it, may become impossible. And then the Sild will truly have won.'

'That would be... unfortunate.'

'As I said, the choice is yours. You can accept this fate, or we can try and do something about it.'

The Master touched one of the white flashes in his beard. 'I admit I have some curiosity. Coupled with a natural instinct for vengeance.'

'For what they have done to Earth?' the Doctor asked, surprised and encouraged.

'For what they have done to me. The Earth can rot, for all I care.'

Though it stuck in the Brigadier's craw, there was nothing for it but to extract his men from the vicinity of what remained of Durlston Heath. With Sild-controlled elements advancing from all directions – you could tell as much from the reports coming in from frightened and confused civilians – the small detachment of UNIT soldiers would have been easy prey. Air support was coming in now, helicopter and fast jet, and for the time being this was the only effective countermeasure – strafing and bombing anything that even looked suspicious, even a herd of animals moving in peculiar formation. A curfew had been established, people told to stay indoors – by now it was clear that the cover story of a military exercise could not be maintained.

But the Brigadier knew that the Sild advance could only be slowed, not stopped, and it would not just be the British Isles in peril. The time ruptures were continuing, reports coming in from other UNIT bases and personnel. More Sild were coming out of the sea, stretching the coastal defences to the limit. Despite UNIT's best efforts, the aliens were managing to find hosts.

The Brigadier could only hope that he had done the right thing in attacking the power station. It was up to the Doctor now… if the Doctor was still alive.

Lethbridge-Stewart snatched up one of his many desk telephones. 'Any news on those over-flights? I want photographic coverage the instant the dust settles. If you find the TARDIS in the ruins, I want to know the instant it happens. If you don't find the TARDIS I want to know that as well.'

It was Yates on the other end, raising his voice above the thud of rotor blades. 'Where do you want to deploy us, sir? If we're being pulled out of the Durlston Heath area…'

'I want you to rendezvous with Miss Grant at Eastmere – I've told them to hold that Hercules on the ground until you arrive.'

'I see, sir. And Miss Grant – what do you want us to do with her – escort her back to headquarters for a dressing down?'

'Don't be an imbecile, Yates. I want you to go with her to Scotland. I have three helicopters on standby. If we can't stop the Sild here, then our next best chance is where this mess all started, with the MERMAN project.'

'MERMAN, sir?'

'I'll have briefing notes ready for you in Scotland.'

Lethbridge-Stewart placed the telephone back down, his mind in turmoil. He had given the Doctor more time than he had promised. It had been the right action, hadn't it?

Not for the first time that day, the Brigadier thought back to those happy, innocent days of his early military career, when the only enemies you had to be concerned about were foreign powers, and where 'time' was something you only worried about at the end of a long evening in the officers' bar. Back before he had to bother himself with Yetis or Cybermen or strange men in blue boxes.

'Come back to us, Doctor,' he whispered. 'Much as I may rue the day we ever met, things do seem to make fractionally more sense with you around.'

Chapter Twenty-One

The Master was the first to sense the transition. 'The flow's grip on us is weakening. We must be getting very near the origin.' With the Doctor's tacit consent, he threw switches and tapped keys on the console. 'Turbulence setting in. Multiple time streams bunching, cross-threading. It may start getting rough again.'

'Perhaps we should try and break free before it does,' the Doctor said. 'We'll still arrive somewhere near the origin, but under our own control.'

'And possibly undershoot by centuries, even thousands of years. No, Doctor! You have persuaded me that I must confront my adversary head on.'

'In which case, remind me to be somewhat *less* persuasive in future.'

'The future,' the Master declared sternly, 'is a luxury we may both soon find in short supply.' He had braced himself against the console, facing the Doctor across the central pillar.

Neither the Doctor, nor the Master, or even the TARDIS itself had any real notion of how far they had come, except that the temporal distance was at least billions of years. They were adrift in deep time, without maps or compass. All they could be sure of was that neither of them had ever travelled this far into the extreme future of the galaxy.

Or was ever likely to again.

When the Vortex did at last release the TARDIS, it was with another series of lurching jolts and bumps. The Doctor and the Master fought to maintain stability as the TARDIS barrelled down these temporal rapids. The Doctor dared not think how much power it would take to return home again, fighting against this vicious current.

But at length all was quiet. The central column had ceased its rise and fall. The external environment sensors registered conditions that were almost unsettlingly normal. A little on the cold side, but there was air and gravity out there.

'Let's take a look, shall we?' the Doctor said, activating the external viewer.

He swept through 360 degrees. It was a panorama of gloom and darkness. The sensors registered an enclosed volume, but it was a huge one. They could have been in a collapsed building or an underground cave. The only thing that was clear was they had arrived *somewhere*, rather than just floating in empty space.

'There's a cyclic oscillation to the gravity,' the Master observed. 'At the microsecond level.'

The Doctor cursed himself for not noticing that. 'Yes, I noticed. Implying…'

'That the field is artificially generated, not produced by the mere concentration of bulk matter. That, in other words, we may have arrived in a station or ship of some kind, with a functioning gravity generator.' The Master tugged down the hem of his tunic. 'I propose an investigation. I take it there are torches somewhere aboard, or would that be a presumption too far?'

'Before we step outside,' the Doctor said, 'I think you and I need to have a little discussion.'

'You have some doubts about my trustworthiness?'

'Well, now that you mention it.' The Doctor rubbed his chin. 'There is the small matter that you've tried to kill me on a number of occasions.' The Doctor's hand wandered down to caress his neck. He was remembering how it felt to have an animate telephone cord strangling the life out of him.

'We were at odds then, Doctor. Our goals were opposed, and you placed me in an insupportable position. Things are very different now.'

'Are they really?'

'If it's concrete reassurance you want, this collar of mine is still activated. The triggering circuit is coupled to a bi-state antenna with a resonant frequency of...'

'Never mind,' the Doctor said.

But when the Master was not looking, he slipped his hand into his pocket and found solace in the sonic screwdriver.

Better safe than sorry.

'Brig on the line for you, Miss Grant.'

Jo took the handset with trepidation. They were halfway to Scotland, Jo and Mike Yates, Benton and the rest of the UNIT detachment in the noisy, draughty whale-ribbed hold of the Hercules. It had been bumpy all the way out from Eastmere. The Sild time ruptures were beginning to cause local weather anomalies, presaging the world-changing storms and havoc that would follow.

'Jo here, sir,' she said, taking the handset from Benton. 'Any... news?' She had to gulp down hard before finishing her sentence. 'I know you had to go ahead with the strike.'

'If there had been any other way, Miss Grant.'

'And the Doctor?'

'We don't know. All we *do* know is that the TARDIS has not returned to headquarters, and there's been no sighting of it anywhere near the power station.'

Jo could hardly believe that the Brigadier was delivering this devastating news in such an offhand fashion. Didn't he also count the Doctor as a friend, even if that relationship was sometimes a bit strained? How could he sound so detached?

'Then what you're saying... the Doctor's dead.' A sudden coldness entered Jo's tone now. It was infectious. 'Is that it?'

'That's a possibility,' the Brigadier answered. 'The Doctor knew that there was a great risk in going into the power station ahead of the Sild. He knew that we'd have no choice but to use this weapon of last resort. But there's a glimmer of hope, Miss Grant!'

'Is there?'

'The blast cloud has cleared. Radiation levels are low enough that I've authorised helicopter over-flights, with spotters and photographic equipment. The strike was a precision attack, and it succeeded in destroying exactly the area where the… chap, him, the objective, was incarcerated. But there's no sign of the TARDIS.'

'Maybe the TARDIS got blown up.'

'The Doctor always insisted that it was indestructible, Miss Grant. I think on this occasion I may be inclined to take him at his word. Of course, there's rather a lot of rubble to sift through, and we can't begin to do that until… well, you take my point. But until I have evidence to the contrary, firm evidence, I will continue to base my judgements on the assumption that the Doctor is alive and well.'

'But where is he, in that case?'

'An excellent question, Miss Grant. To which the only possible answer is: anywhere, and anywhen.'

Two torch beams scissored the air like searchlights, barely able to penetrate the depths of the chamber in which the TARDIS had come to rest. It had emerged from the Vortex at a slight angle, on what appeared to be a rubble pile or garbage heap. The Doctor placed his footsteps carefully, the loose ground shifting under him with treacherous intent. It was hard to see his hand in front of his face, let alone cracks and crevasses in the ground.

'There is a glow in that direction,' the Master said. 'Faint, but quite unmistakeable. It appears to be another chamber, connected to this one by a throat.'

'If the Sild are present, they're keeping rather a low

204

profile,' the Doctor said, pausing to tighten the coat he had slipped on over his cape.

The Master, who had spurned the offer of extra clothing beyond his usual minimalist black outfit, said: 'And I will avoid drawing hasty conclusions, until we have some measure of this place. I advise you to do likewise.'

They crept slowly down the rubble pile, sweeping torches this way and that, alert to the presence of any other parties. Once in a while, the Doctor risked a backward glance at the TARDIS, all but invisible save for the lit-up letters of the words POLICE PUBLIC CALL BOX and the fretted yellow rectangles of its windows.

'So you think this is a ship of some kind?' the Doctor asked.

'Or a station, as I allowed. But clearly artificial. Not of Sild manufacture, either.'

The Doctor agreed. The Sild built their ships to suit their own modest dimensions: riddled with a plumber's nightmare of finger-thick fluid pipes. They had no use for huge, air-filled chambers, even less for terrestrial gravity.

'Then what it is doing here, and why have we been brought here?'

'In time, Doctor, we may yet have some answers.'

The Master had been right about the glow from the adjoining chamber, though even when the Doctor's eyes had achieved full dark adaptation, it was no more than a ghostly suggestion; the promise of light rather than the thing itself. They had reached a relatively level floor – hard and metallic – although even then their progress was occasionally hampered by some rubble pile or dark obstruction of indistinct shape. If they were on a ship, the Doctor decided, it was obviously long past its prime.

He gave the TARDIS one final glance and then their torches picked up the fact that the ceiling was lowering, as they traversed the connecting throat between the chambers. He was beginning to make a little more of the chamber ahead.

It was lit, but only dimly, and there was an impression of galleried levels, row upon row of alcoves or nooks climbing to a dizzying height. There were things in those alcoves, like carved stone figures, but that was much as the Doctor's straining eyes could perceive.

'Quickly,' the Master called.

He had wandered to one side of the throat, where the floor curved around to form a wall. The Doctor stabbed his torch in the Master's general direction. The beam caught an impression of a deeper darkness against the wall, an oval of absolute black against which the Master stood, with his face to the blackness and his hands clasped against the small of his back.

'What have you found?'

'Unless I am very much mistaken, the outside.'

The Doctor walked over to the window. It was as wide and long as a banqueting table, set at a convenient height for humanoids. A fine spray of micrometeorite impacts peppered the glass. The Doctor guessed that it had been in place for centuries, perhaps much longer than that. It was conceivable that until recently a force field had protected the glass.

Beyond the glass, nothing but swallowing blackness.

'It's lovely,' the Doctor commented. 'I wish I'd brought my Box Brownie.'

The Master raised gloved hand. 'Your impatience does you no credit, Doctor.'

He waited, and was soon rewarded. A planet hove into view, then tracked slowly from the top to the bottom of the window. Clearly the Master had witnessed the planet's previous passage.

'Do you recognise it?' the Doctor asked. There were a hundred billion habitable worlds, far too many for any one mind to retain, but it had often been said that Time Lords had an uncanny memory for such things.

'I don't,' the Master said. 'Although it's clearly a world near the end of its lifetime. If it once had oceans, landmasses, it might ring a bell. Reminds me a little of Skaro…'

'It's definitely not Skaro.'

'I said *reminds*,' the Master corrected testily. 'I merely note the extreme desolation, the sense of a world exhausted beyond its limits. A place of stagnation and decay, of entropy made manifest.'

'Your idea of holiday heaven.'

He waited for the planet to appear again. It took ninety seconds to return to the top of the window. It was, the Master's opinion of the place notwithstanding, a dismal-looking place. The planet was a dim red, like a hot coal that had nearly cooled down to being black again. It had no visible atmosphere, no seas or icecaps or indications of surface vegetation.

But it was not lifeless, or at least had not always been lifeless. 'Cities,' the Master commented. 'Or if not cities then some kind of technological installation.' He clenched his first. 'I curse our unpreparedness. We should have long-range sensors, communications devices…'

The Doctor waited for the planet to come around again. 'There must be a sun,' he said. 'How else would we be able to see it?'

But the Master had become bored by the view already. He was on his way to the next chamber, with its milky luminescence and layers of rising galleries. The Doctor followed, his mood unsettled by the view of the time-ravaged world. He wondered what relationship this ship or station bore to the inhabitants of that planet, if any of them yet lived.

'We can't have just landed in this place by accident,' the Doctor said, calling ahead to the Master. 'It must have some connection to the Sild. Something drew us here!'

'This place speaks to me,' the Master said, pausing to face the Doctor. 'I know of it, on some level – almost as if I was here once before. Its scale and size… It's a ship, of that I'm certain. A vessel of immense age, older than some solar systems. But how can I *know* that?'

'We've both got around a bit,' the Doctor said, indulging

in cosmic understatement. 'Maybe you popped in here once, during a previous incarnation.'

'I cannot deny it may have happened,' the Master allowed. 'But it almost feels as if I've been here a thousand times. How is *that* possible?'

'Some side-effect of the time-fade, perhaps. If this is the epicentre, the origin of the fade...'

'Quickly please, Doctor. Tell me I am not deluded. Tell me I am not seeing what I *think* I am seeing.'

The Master had reached the entrance to the next chamber. The level of the flooring dropped shallowly away from him, so that he surveyed proceedings from a slight rise. The Doctor caught up with him, standing to the right of the other man. He could not tell whether the thing he had heard in the Master's voice was horror or awe or some chimerical combination of the two.

The chamber was hemispherical, with a gently dished floor. They had come in through a gap in the wall at the chamber's base; there was a similar gap in the opposite wall. Circles of pale blue light, like lines of latitude, ringed the chamber from floor to pole. These circles were the source of the milky radiance. Between each ring of light was a gap tall enough for an entire circle of alcoves, each of which was easily high and broad enough to contain a man. As the rising chamber curved over to form its own ceiling, so the alcoves tipped gradually toward the horizontal. There were hundreds in the low rings, but far fewer in the high levels.

'How many?' the Master asked. 'I have an idea, but I'd like to hear yours.'

The Doctor had already performed the same rough calculation. 'More than seven hundred alcoves. Of which perhaps two-thirds are presently occupied.'

'Four hundred and seventy occupied spaces, by my reckoning. Give or take a few.'

'Give or take,' the Doctor agreed.

'Do you recognise any of the occupants?'

The Doctor hesitated over his answer. 'One or two.'

'Let's take a closer look, shall we? It would be foolish to jump to conclusions, however utterly inescapable they may appear.'

They walked to the right. The lowest three levels of alcoves formed two incomplete half-circles, broken by the two entrances. The Doctor studied his companion, hardly daring to wonder what was now going through his mind. The Master was unpredictable at the best of times, but even the sanest of beings would be tested by the knowledge of what lay in this chamber. The Doctor's hand slipped into his pocket, touching the sonic screwdriver for reassurance.

A third of the alcoves were empty, but the rest held bodies. Each lay behind a frontage of curving glass. The bodies were all humanoid figures, although that was as much as some of them had in common. Here were men and even a few women, representing a spectrum of ages and builds and ethnic types. Some were very old, while others were still children. A fraction were alien or ghoulish in appearance.

'Notice the confining devices,' the Master said, as if he was conducting a guided tour. 'Shackled and restrained. Escape would have been quite beyond them. They would have been barely able to move. Note also the life-support mechanisms, the nutrient lines and direct nerve taps.'

They were playing a kind of game. The Master knew that the Doctor knew. The Doctor knew that the Master knew. But he wasn't sure if he was expected to state what was by now blindingly clear.

These bodies all belonged to the Master.

Chapter Twenty-Two

'Tom!' McCrimmon said, when at last Irwin and the other oil workers returned, coming back down the corridor to the door behind which she was sealed. 'I was starting to wonder where you'd got to.'

The statement was largely for her own benefit, since the door's soundproofing made it impossible to communicate verbally. But her relief was sincere and palpable. The security door had proven resistant to various improvised battering rams, delivered from both sides – even a fire axe hadn't done more than dent it – but somewhere in the platform there surely had to be something that could cut through metal, even metal of the two-inch-thick armoured kind. And these were McCrimmon workers, after all: supposedly the best in the business, and she had no reason to doubt it. Someone was always drilling or cutting something when McCrimmon needed to sleep, so the least they could do was drag out the necessary equipment now. It would be embarrassing in the extreme if her own people hadn't managed to extricate her by the time the UNIT forces arrived, as she was confident they would.

Irwin had reached the door now. McCrimmon took her pad and wrote: WHAT'S UP? HOW IS EVAC GOING? MORE CRABS? She held the note up to the window in the air.

Irwin looked through the glass at her message. His expression seemed strangely nonplussed, almost disinterested. Instead of writing out his own reply, he looked to one side. His hand had moved up as if entering a sequence into the keyed entry code.

She smiled, understanding – although still a little troubled by Irwin's blank lack of acknowledgement. Lovelace might be dead, but somehow or other Irwin had managed to uncover the numbers for the door, sparing them the bother of cutting through. 'OK, good,' she said, again for her own benefit.

But the door had not opened yet. Irwin was still standing on the other side, arm stretched out as if tapping numbers into the pad. Now that she paid due attention, there was a certain rhythm to his movements. He would enter a code, then glance down at the lock as if looking to see if it had opened or not. Tap, tap, tap, tap, glance. Tap, tap, tap, tap, glance.

'Oh, no.'

Understanding was coming upon her and it was not a good sort of understanding. Something was wrong with Tom Irwin. Wrong with the lot of them, in fact. Other than Irwin, the others were standing around like zombies. Waiting for something to happen, with nothing to say or do until it did. Not one of them had moved, or appeared to speak to another, since the party had arrived.

'Oh God.'

Tap, tap, tap, tap, glance. She knew what was happening now. Irwin had not managed to uncover Lovelace's code. But he was working through the permutations regardless. Zero, zero, zero, one. Zero, zero, zero, two. Zero, zero, zero, three. That was how it was going to be. All the way through the possibilities until he hit the jackpot. Her mind reeled. Nearly ten thousand possibilities – but odds were he wouldn't need to go through all of them before finding the right one. Say, five thousand, give or take. How long was he going to need to do that? Hours, definitely. But not tens of hours.

Not tens of hours at all.

The system had been set up so that an alarm sounded on the other side, but that was hardly an issue now.

She wrote another note. Her hand was shaking so hard she dropped the pen twice. TOM. WHATEVER'S GOT INTO YOU, THIS IS ME. YOUR FRIEND EDDIE.

He looked at the message. For a moment, something interrupted his machine-like rhythm. He dug into a pocket and came out with the pad and thick felt-tip he had used earlier. He wrote a message onto the pad, then turned it around for McCrimmon's benefit.

It was not Tom Irwin's handwriting at all. It looked as if it had been done with a ruler, all angles and parallels.

WE ARE SILD NOW. YOU WILL SOON BE SILD. PLEASE STAND BY.

Irwin chose that moment to present his back to her, allowing her to see the silver thing clamped to the base of his skull, a kind of mechanical crab. She did not need to see the others to know that they were similarly afflicted.

Under the circumstances, McCrimmon did the only reasonable thing to do.

She screamed.

'This way, Miss Grant!'

Three military helicopters, fuelled, weaponed and with their engines running, sat in an arrowhead formation only a short stroll from the loading ramp of the Hercules.

'Any more news?' Jo asked Mike Yates, glad to be out of the Hercules, if only for a few minutes.

'About the Doctor? Nothing that I've heard. The Brig says the Sild have given up their assault on the power station – it's as if they sense that the objective has been lost. But that's the only bit of good news! They're continuing to gain hosts and move inland. They've got to be stopped!'

'They came here for the Master,' Jo said. 'But now they've had a taste of Earth, they'll take it anyway.'

'Do you think the Doc'll be able to do anything? I mean, assuming he…'

'It's all right,' Jo said. 'It's all I've been thinking about. But you know what? If the Doctor *did* get to him, to the Master… and if they did manage to get out of there in the TARDIS before the airstrike… that would explain why the Sild have given up on the station, wouldn't it? They can *tell* the Master isn't there.'

'Or dead.'

'No, they'd still want to get to his remains, I think. They must know he's not there. And that can only mean the Doctor made it out, can't it?'

'I suppose so.'

'I'm trying to look on the bright side, Mike. You could help me along a bit.'

While the Lynxes were being crewed, they kitted Jo out with UNIT camouflage gear, helmet, goggles and headphones. There was time to grab a coffee and a bacon sandwich, and then it was out to the apron and into the helicopters. Waiting on their seats were hastily photocopied dossiers covering the essential elements of the MERMAN project – what the Brigadier had been able to weasel out of Whitehall, and piece together from his own discussions with the Doctor – as well as technical blueprints for Mike Oscar Six, the rig where Jo had first met Eddie McCrimmon.

'Any word from Edwina herself?' Jo asked, wondering if there had been an update since she had left UNIT headquarters.

'Not a sausage,' Yates said. 'And I've just checked back with the Brig in case something came in while we were en route. It's worse than that, in fact. After declaring a state of emergency, the rig's gone radio silent. The last thing anyone heard was something about a helicopter going down… Apparently one of these Whitehall bigwigs was on it.' He was

214

tapping the first page of the dossier. 'Erm... so basically we haven't got a clue what we'll find when we get out there. It's not just Mike Oscar Six, either. Rigs and ships are dropping like flies. Still sure you want to be on this expedition?'

'Do you think the Doctor was really keen to go into the power station, Mike?'

'Not really.'

'There's your answer, then. I don't want to do this either but that's no excuse, not when the Doctor put his neck on the line for us.'

When they were aloft, chugging in formation for the coast, Jo scanned the dossier. There wasn't much to it, to be frank. MERMAN: marine equipment for the reception, modulation and amplification of neutrinos. A project to develop the means to communicate with submarines, while they were still at sea, using streams of sub-atomic particles.

Jo could just imagine what the Doctor would have thought of that. If only you'd put a little of that ingenuity to something peaceful, instead of working out increasingly clever ways to blow yourselves up... or something along those lines. That was the Doctor, all right. A basic fondness for humanity tempered by great disapproval, or great disapproval moderated by an undeniable fondness... She had never worked out which was the case, and perhaps now it did not matter. They were on their own.

He's still alive, Jo thought. She had to cling to that. She had to believe that, deep down, she would feel differently if he were truly dead, truly extinguished.

But what if she were wrong about that? What if this was how it felt to live in a universe without the Doctor in it?

'So let me get this straight,' Yates said, riffling through the notes. 'They couldn't get this stuff to work properly, so they had the bright idea of bringing in...' He stumbled, squinted. 'Look, it's gone all smudgy! Why didn't they give us decent copies?'

'They did,' Jo said. 'But the bits that are to do with... him, the Master... they're being affected by the time-fade. That's why we have to work quickly – not just because of the Sild, but because if we leave it too long we'll forget why all this ever started!'

'Boffins. Why can't they leave well alone?'

'The point, Mike, is that the Master must've pulled a fast one. That's what the Doctor reckoned. Used this signalling equipment to send a message into time. And that's what brought the Sild!'

Even Jo was now finding it difficult to keep the facts about the Master straight in her head. It was like trying to remember a long telephone number while searching for a biro and a scrap of paper. The details kept slipping around, blurring, interchanging. The Doctor had been right; they weren't immune to the time-fade just because they'd travelled in the TARDIS, just a bit better equipped to resist it.

'But the Master couldn't have wanted the Sild to come,' she went on. 'That can't have been in his plans at all. And now the Sild are coming through in stronger and stronger numbers, and it's got something to do with homing in on the MERMAN signal. So we've got two chances: deal with the Sild at their origin, somewhere else in space and time, or try and stop them coming through at this end. Maybe one won't be enough without the other.'

'We're stuffed then, unless the Doctor can deal with the other bit.'

'Well, yes,' Jo said. 'But the TARDIS wasn't in the wreckage of the power station, was it?'

'They couldn't *see* it,' Yates pointed out, not needing to elaborate that this was not quite the same as it not being there.

'Even if the TARDIS got buried under all that rubble,' Jo said, 'it wouldn't have been damaged. Provided the Doctor was able to get back to it in time... Look, I'd rather believe he did, all right? And I'd rather believe he's out there now, somewhere or somewhen, doing whatever he can to stop the Sild coming through. And counting on us to do our bit here!'

As Jo spoke, the helicopters sped out into open water. Nothing now stood between them and Mike Oscar Six except miles and miles of cold North Sea.

CHAPTER TWENTY-THREE

'You cannot have lived this many lives,' the Doctor said.

'Why ever not?'

'Please tell me it isn't so. Please tell me you don't recognise all these incarnations.'

'Of course I don't *recognise* them all, Doctor.' The Master's answer was scornful. 'But enough of them to be sure. That's what happens when you see yourself in the mirror.'

The Master's many faces, for the most part, were partly concealed by some sort of breathing apparatus, a mask with a long flexible trunk curling away from it and into the side of the surrounding alcove – the mask looked, horribly enough, as if it had grown *into* their faces, absorbing and reconfiguring living tissue. Some of the masks gave off a sickly yellow glow, echoed by the restraining devices and the complex biomedical support machinery surrounding the bodies.

The Doctor reeled at the scale of what he was seeing. It cut against everything he had ever believed possible, that a single Time Lord should have had so many incarnations. Everything that he had ever believed right.

'And the others?'

'I would have thought it obvious. These are incarnations that have yet to happen… from my present perspective. Or potential incarnations that may never happen at all.'

'This is an abomination.'

'The existence of so many facets of me, or the fact that all of them are here, gathered into this one place?'

'Both.'

The Master scuffed a sleeve across the glassy frontage of one of the cabinets, swiping away a broad band of dust. 'Take a look at this one. Quite the dapper young fellow, wouldn't you agree?'

It was no version of the Master that the Doctor recognised. A young man in a business suit, beardless, with a mop of boyish hair. His face, what the Doctor could see of it, seemed friendly and plausible. The face of a politician, the kind of man people would find it easy to trust. 'He could almost be you,' the Master commented.

'Low, even by your standards.'

The Master moved along a few spaces. Here was a version of himself reduced to a shrivelled corpse, a skeleton swaddled in a papery film of ash-grey flesh and dressed in a black suit with elaborate white sleeves and collar. The life-support mask, if that was what it was, gave off no illumination.

'Many of them, like this one, have perished,' the Master said, sweeping a hand around the chamber. 'The mechanism clearly failed. Careless of whoever brought me here, wouldn't you say?'

'Or merciful.'

The Doctor rubbed the dust from the next cabinet. This was a female version of the Master: still alive, if this ghastly state counted as life. Like the corpse, she also wore a frilled black outfit. Her hair was black, veined in white, combed back from her forehead. Unlike the Doctor's present companion, her face was beardless. The mask hid most of it. But he recognised something in her cheekbones and brow, a family likeness that was clearly intentional. Time Lords generally had their incarnations thrust upon them without the luxury of choice. But the Master had selected all his faces, and each bore the imprint of his mind.

'Your sonic screwdriver.' The Master had extended his hand, palm upraised, like a surgeon waiting to be handed a scalpel.

'What?'

'I have need of it for a moment. I wish to trace the neural connections between these life-support units.'

The Doctor hesitated. 'Look, I'm not sure…'

'My dear fellow, if we are to make any progress, we must trust each other.'

'I trust you about as far as…' But the Doctor knew that the Master had a point, as unpalatable as he found it. 'Here,' he said, slipping out the sonic screwdriver and thumping it onto the Master's palm with bad grace. 'And I'd like it back in one piece, if that isn't too much trouble.'

The Master made a few deft adjustments to the sonic screwdriver's settings and pointed it at the nearest cabinet. The screwdriver emitted a whining hum. The Master jiggled it and the pitch of the hum varied. 'Picking up an active neural connection,' he said. 'The cabinets aren't just linked; there is still mental activity flowing between them.'

'All of them?'

'The ones that are still alive, at any rate. They're coupled together, forming a single vast intellect.'

'One of you's bad enough,' the Doctor said.

'And in this instance, given that I did not submit to this condition voluntarily, I am inclined to agree with you.' The Master continued sweeping the screwdriver, the pitch rising and falling as he traced the neural connections. Without warning, something appeared in the air above them, billowing as if caught on a breeze. It was a long chain of mathematical symbols. Slowly the chain faded, and a second took its place. Then a third appeared at the same time as the second, and the chains seemed to dance around each other. Now more symbols appeared, strings of them spiralling and inter-penetrating faster than the eye could track, like the banners and scarves of a dancer.

'The pure mathematics of advanced time engineering,' the Doctor said, unable to hide the awe he felt. There was a searing beauty to this mathematics. It was the clockwork of the universe laid bare, in all its glittering, meshing harmony.

'I agree,' the Master said. 'The screwdriver must have triggered this holographic realisation. I believe it represents a distillation of the current mental state of the linked minds. They are thinking about the manipulation of time, and very little else.'

'Or being made to think.'

'Quite. A totality of minds, each of which was *already* superlatively attuned to the task of solving the thorniest time equations... There is almost nothing that the totality could not accomplish!'

'But to what purpose now? This ship feels deserted.'

The Master was continuing his sweep of the chamber. 'This really is fascinating, Doctor. All the cabinets are cross-linked to one degree or another but there are certain nodes which have stronger and more numerous connections than the others – almost as if these represent more dominant incarnations, versions of me which are assigned more authority and influence in the network.'

The Doctor, despite himself, could not help but be swept along by the sheer thrill of scientific enquiry. 'A scale-free network with a small number of hubs. Compared to a network in which the nodes have equal value, it's a vastly more efficient way of processing information.'

'With the sole disadvantage that the network is reliant on those few hubs,' the Master said. He swivelled on his heels, raising and lowering the screwdriver. 'Ah, now *this* is remarkable. Even the nodes are cross-linked at different potentialities! One node in particular is stronger than all the others...'

'The *Master* Master?'

'A little less of your paltry attempts at wit, Doctor, while I concentrate.'

'I'd get a move on, if I were you.'

Irritated, the Master lowered the screwdriver. 'Why, exactly?'

'Because something's coming towards us.' The Doctor pointed to the entrance on the opposite side of the chamber. What had been a dark maw was now beginning to lighten, as if some illuminated thing were approaching them. The approaching glow was red, and as it neared the Doctor made out many complex whisking shadows, in addition to the glow.

'A moment,' the Master said distractedly. The screwdriver's hum rose decisively. The Master strode forward, then pointed high up at the rows of alcoves. 'There, Doctor. That one. Of all the nodes, that is the most powerfully connected. That incarnation above all others...' But the Master faltered, as his sharp eyes picked out the still-living form. 'No. It's not possible.'

'I really think we ought to be giving some consideration to leaving,' the Doctor said.

'Wait. Don't you see?'

'I see it all right, old chap. It's you.'

The Master lowered the screwdriver until it hung limply at his side. 'My present incarnation – the body I am in now. Up there. How can this be?'

'My guess,' the Doctor said, 'is that the Sild have messed things up so thoroughly that all classes of time paradox are now allowed. Even a type three Blinovitch crossover.' Gently, feeling something not entirely distanced from compassion, he took the screwdriver out of the Master's hand and made a few quick adjustments to its settings. Then he nodded at the approaching light. 'We really must be on our way.'

The Doctor slipped the screwdriver back into his pocket.

The Master was at last able to tear himself away from the spectacle of himself, masked and still animate, high above them. 'For once, Doctor, we find ourselves as of one mind.'

'Let's not make a habit of it,' the Doctor said.

That was when the red metal spider burst into the chamber.

It was a vile thought to entertain, but McCrimmon kept coming back to the same thing: thank God that Lovelace was dead. Not because she hated him that much, even after what he had done to her – it was more a case of pitying men like that, bullies who got their kicks from asserting their authority over others – but because only Lovelace had known the combination for the door. The aliens, the crab things, whatever these monsters were, they obviously didn't know the code. They had no choice but to go through the combinations one by one, methodical as clockwork. If Lovelace had still been on the rig, then there might have been a way for them to torture it out of him, or use him as one of these puppets, the way they were using dear Tom Irwin, her closest friend on Mike Oscar Six. But she hated Irwin now, or at least the mindless thing Irwin had been turned into. A machine for opening doors.

Tap, tap, tap, tap, glance. Tap, tap, tap, tap, glance. How far had they come? She had been so shocked that she hadn't looked at her watch until long after the tapping began, but it had already been more than an hour since she had checked the time. Enough to work through hundreds of combinations, perhaps more than a thousand. What if, by some horrible twist, Lovelace had chosen the year of his birth – or the date of the Battle of Hastings?

Stuck behind the door, there was nothing McCrimmon could do. She had gone from desperately wanting to break down that door, to hoping it stayed shut as long as possible. There was nowhere else for her to go, no windows or ducts to escape through into the rest of the rig. Callow and Lovelace had been much too thorough for that.

So what did the crabs want? As much as it suited her ego to believe otherwise, she had a feeling she wasn't the immediate objective. She was just something that was going to get in their way temporarily, before being brushed aside or made into one of those puppets. The aliens were fairly obviously trying to reach the MERMAN equipment. It meant something to them. They either wanted to smash it or secure it, one of the two.

What had Irwin told her, before the crabs took him over? She thought back to the words he'd scrawled, done in his handwriting, rather than the robot-like script he had used last time. Something about Lovelace planning to destroy the equipment, but chickening out. And now Irwin reckoned they had to do it instead.

But the MERMAN gear was behind another security door, just as inaccessible to McCrimmon as McCrimmon was to the monsters.

Suddenly a possibility presented itself. Not much of one, it was true. But if the aliens were prepared to go through the combinations on their lock, she could do the same thing with the door to the MERMAN gear. She wouldn't be as quick as Irwin, or as methodical – she was bound to skip a few numbers – and Irwin already had a massive head start. But it was still a numbers game, wasn't it? Luck *could* still be on her side.

She left the door, ran back to the sealed entrance to the equipment room. Punched zero, zero, zero, zero into the pad. The lock flashed red, gave an alarm buzz which was all but inaudible over the still-sounding emergency alarms.

No, that was stupid. Assume – assume – that Irwin had started with four zeroes as well. If they were chasing the same combination, then it was pointless trying to catch up. She might as well start with four nines and count down.

What if Irwin had started at the top as well? What if the combinations were not the same? What was the optimum search strategy?

To hell with it.

She entered four nines. Then nine, nine, nine eight. Then nine, nine, nine, seven. She wasn't as fast as Irwin, her hands were shaking and sweaty, and she kept fumbling the digits.

But she was doing something now, not just waiting for the inevitable.

Big Cal would have approved.

CHAPTER TWENTY-FOUR

It was a robot, a thing as a big as a house. It had a spherical body, a smaller spherical head equipped with talons, pincers and probes, and attached to the body a multitude of powerful hinged and piston-driven legs, each of which ended in a barbed point sharp enough (the Doctor felt sure) to pierce a man right through. The spider's two multifaceted eyes were blazing red carnelians, the source of the glow and the shadows he had already seen.

The spider, having eased its bulk into the chamber, paused to study the two newcomers. The Doctor had seen nothing like it. Still he sensed a curious mechanical belligerence, a kind of dim-witted malevolence rather than outright calculating evil. Some of his best friends had been robots. But it was equally the case that among robots he had also made some splendid enemies.

The Doctor, always willing to give someone or something the benefit of the doubt, took a few cautious steps in the direction of the spider.

'I say!' he bellowed. 'Would you mind answering a few simple questions? We find ourselves at a bit of a loss as to where and when we are. Are you the custodian of this ship?' The Doctor, cautiously encouraged, took another step. 'It's just that...'

227

The spider sprang forward, leaping into the air and coming down with an audible clang a few tens of feet from the Doctor. He stumbled back, only just keeping his footing. The spider made a low, purposeful humming.

'I only asked!'

'Doubtless a very simple machine,' the Master said. 'Well, Doctor, how would you rate your chances of making it back to the TARDIS?'

The Doctor stared up at the spider's blazing red eyes. 'Rather less than excellent.'

'I concur. The sonic screwdriver again, if you would be so kind.'

The Doctor had trusted the Master once; it was not so very hard to do so again.

'What do you have in mind?'

'This.' The Master, having adjusted the screwdriver to his own satisfaction, levelled it at the spider and emitted an energy pulse. The spider's eyes dimmed and the robot sank down, its body lowering to the ground as if its legs could no longer support it. 'I recommend haste,' the Master said. 'I have merely incapacitated it.'

'Getting soft in your old age?'

'Believe me, Doctor, if your sonic screwdriver had the power to kill it, I would have taken that option. Here.'

The Master had thrown the Doctor his sonic screwdriver. The Doctor caught it deftly, and slipped it back into his pocket.

They ran out of the chamber, back along the connecting throat, past the great window with its periodic view of the passing planet, back up the rubble heap. The TARDIS was still where they had left it, yellow windows aglow.

'It's coming!' The Doctor shouted, aware that the spider had picked itself up and was gaining ground on them.

The Master, who had a head start on the Doctor, was the first at the TARDIS. He was looking over the Doctor's shoulder. The Doctor did not dare risk looking back, but even as he neared the TARDIS he heard the sound of rubble moving around behind him, and the rising hum that told him the robot spider was now very near.

'Quickly!' The Master hissed.

The Doctor thought, for a moment, of throwing the Master the keys to the TARDIS. It cut against every instinct he knew. But at least one of them would survive, and if it took the Master to undo the work of the Sild, then that was a vastly better outcome than both of them dying here.

But sense or caution prevailed. The Doctor reached the TARDIS, opened the door, and the two of them fell inside. The Doctor slammed the door and dashed to the console. He started throwing switches, looking anxiously at the central column. It rose and fell, but stiffly. The Doctor tugged some levers and adjusted some knobs. On the external viewer, the spider's red eyes glared like binary suns. It was circling the TARDIS.

'What are you waiting for?' the Master said. 'Commence dematerialisation!'

'The TARDIS suffered a power drain during our emergence – it was too violent. The accumulators are taking their time coming back to strength.'

'And you only thought to mention this to me now?'

'I assumed we'd take a little longer to look around.' The Doctor moved to another segment of the console and made some further adjustments. 'There's nothing to worry about. We're quite safe in here, and the TARDIS will be back to operational power in a very short while.'

The TARDIS lurched. They felt the shove even inside the control room, despite its artificial gravity. The view through the monitor tilted abruptly.

'It has us!' The Master called. 'The machine's picked us up!'

'The TARDIS is still quite safe.' The Doctor coughed. 'Whether we are is another question.'

'If your inertial compensators were working properly, we

wouldn't be thrown around like this!'

'It's on my list of things to fix,' the Doctor said.

The view, red-lit by the glow from the spider's eyes, showed that they were being carried down the rubble pile.

'Do something! For all we know this thing wants to throw us into an annihilation furnace.' The Master moved to the console and tried to shove the Doctor away from the controls.

'It's no use. We can't dematerialise. The TARDIS has just enough power to maintain dimensional coherence and generate a protective field.'

The Master was undeterred. 'If we re-route power from the dimension stabiliser… there should be enough inertial lag to give us the time we need.'

'You can't do that in a Type Forty, not unless you fancy living in a space the size of a shoebox.'

'If we had taken *my* TARDIS…' The Master left the statement unfinished.

'We'd almost certainly still be in a mess of some kind,' the Doctor said.

At length even the Master came to accept that there was nothing to be done except wait for the power to be restored. The spider had tucked the TARDIS under its belly, clutching it as if it was a tasty morsel to be taken back home and consumed at leisure. The spider scuttled through the dark warrens of the ship, as if on some urgent errand.

Eventually it came to a spherical room not much larger than the spider itself. It squeezed itself inside, and a heavy doorway irised shut, sealing off the entrance. The Doctor and the Master exchanged apprehensive glances. Perhaps this was where the spider planned to eat the TARDIS.

But after a few moments the door irised open again. They had come along a corridor, but now the view was of unremitting blackness. 'Vacuum,' the Doctor said, directing the Master's attention to the environmental controls. 'The air's been sucked away.'

'This must be some huge airlock,' the Master said.

The airlock was obviously like an eyeball in a socket. They had come in along the 'optic nerve', and now the eyeball had swivelled around so that the entrance door – the eye's retinal patch – was facing the other direction, into open space.

The spider scuttled outside, and with a propulsive twitch of its legs, flung itself away from the ship.

The Master and the Doctor stared at the view screen, watching as the hull receded and more and more of the enormous craft came into view. It was vast and scarred and impossibly ancient, a humpback whale of a spaceship, miles wide and tens of miles long. Lit only by the red light of a dying sun, just the outline and highlights of the ship were visible; the rest was as black as the space beyond it. There were no lights, no illuminated windows, no obvious evidence that the ship was anything but a derelict.

'I know it now,' the Master said, quietly.

'The *Consolidator*,' the Doctor confirmed. 'We should both have guessed a lot sooner than we did. But what is it doing here? It was destroyed! We both saw it destroyed!'

'It would seem we were mistaken.'

The spider was accelerating, by some unknown means, towards the planet that the dark ship orbited. For the first time, as their point of view changed, the Doctor made out the bloated dim sphere which was the star around which this world and ship orbited. It was a red giant, a star nearing the end of its Main Sequence lifetime. Once, not so many millions of years ago, it would have been bright and compact, undergoing steady fusion. But as the star gradually exhausted its supply of hydrogen, so its envelope swelled to hundreds of times its former radius.

In his travels the Doctor had witnessed the deaths of many worlds. He had even seen the Earth itself incinerated, as the enlarging Sun spread its envelope nearly all the way to the orbit of Mars. Time Lords, more than anyone else, understood the awesome fragility of worlds. They grasped the moth-like impermanence of stars. All was flux, all was change, all was death and renewal. Nothing endured, except nothing itself.

The Doctor imagined this world in better times, before sickness swelled its star. It was still possible to tell where there had been oceans and continents. Their outlines were still there, as if pressed into clay. Mountain ranges, mid-ocean ridges, chains of islands and deep benthic gorges. He had seen enough worlds to imagine seas and forests and a mantle of luscious white clouds, pressed beneath the merest kiss of indigo atmosphere. There was a time when he would have wept to see a world reduced to this. But there had been too many, and even a Time Lord's tears were exhaustible.

The spider took them down. They swept low over the world, untroubled by atmosphere. The surface rocketed by at orbital speed, the spider plunging through the notches in mountain ridges, along canyons so deep and wide you could have bowled a moon down them, across ocean beds and continental plains strewn with odd jagged formations. It took the Doctor a few moments to realise that these were the remains of cities, melted into blobby chrome slag by waves of stellar heat. Their architecture, in so far as it could be inferred from these molten ruins, was of towering, tapering palaces supported above the ground on mighty straddling legs. But it had clearly been aeons since these cities had known life and commerce.

'If I am not mistaken,' the Master said, 'we now have sufficient power to attempt dematerialisation. I wonder why you hesitate, Doctor?'

The Doctor allowed himself a smile. 'I'm surprised you have to ask.'

The Master nodded. 'We're being taken somewhere, do not seem to be in immediate peril, and one cannot help but be curious as to the destination.'

'There's also the matter of *why*.'

'I won't deny that that is also of interest. But let me be plain about one thing. My sole thought is for my own self-preservation. While that modest little objective happens to align with your own trifling concerns, we shall have no cause for disharmony. But should I find myself obstructed, do not imagine that I will let you stand in my way.'

'And they say gratitude is a dying art.'

'Ought I to be grateful, Doctor? It's true that you rescued me from Durlston A. But let's not pretend that you were in any way motivated by concern for my welfare.' The Master pointed to the view screen. 'Well, we seem to arriving somewhere, if I'm not mistaken.'

It was a city, perhaps the largest that they had yet seen. It rose in tiers, each smaller than the one below and supported on legs, a sagging chrome wedding cake, rising from a craquelured plain of radiation-blasted ochre, taller than any surviving mountain on this corpse of a world. Tall enough, indeed, that the city's topmost levels might once have pushed beyond the atmosphere, into lofty near-vacuum. Yet in all essential respects the city seemed as dead and decayed as any they had observed. The Master scrutinised displays, shaking his head at the antiquated and unreliable sensors. 'There is a trickle of energy coming from somewhere near the middle levels, but so little that it barely registers. Perhaps enough to sustain a few simple machines, but no more than that.'

'Someone sent this spider,' the Doctor said.

'But that spider may have been in that ship for a very long while.'

They descended. The spider took them down between four of the highest spires, descending through a thickening confusion of buttresses and bridges, until at last no part of the world beyond the city was visible. And still they descended, and descended, until eventually the spider entered another eye-like airlock, perhaps close to the energy source that the Master had detected. The airlock swivelled, and its door opened to admit a gush of stale cold air.

The spider, still clutching its payload, scuttled out of the airlock. And with an unceremonious jolt, the TARDIS was set down like a chess piece.

'Wherever we are,' the Doctor said, 'we would appear to have arrived.'

'Your talent for the pointlessly tautological statement remains unsurpassed,' the Master said, bending to consult instruments. 'It's a vault, as large as any of the chambers on the ship. Energy sources nearby. Atmosphere breathable, if a little on the cold side. Gravity close to terrestrial normal. Radiation and pathogen levels tolerable.'

'What about the spider?'

'It's just stopped. I think it was programmed to bring us here, and then await further orders.' The Master extended an inviting hand to the door. 'It would be rude not to see who had summoned us. Shall we investigate?'

'After you, dear fellow.'

'No, I insist. After you.'

'And leave you alone in here, even for a second? Not much chance of that.'

The Master chuckled and flung open the TARDIS door. 'Universes will evaporate, before you and I change our ways.'

The Doctor felt the gasp of cold, even in the control room. He locked the TARDIS controls, reassured himself that the sonic screwdriver was still snug in his pocket, and followed the Master.

They were in an arched space of supreme gloominess. The spider, as the Master had intimated, was looming over the TARDIS but now otherwise inert. Dim red light filtered through tall stained-glass windows, soaring up into the vaulted obscurity of a distant ceiling. The Doctor, in his travels, had acquired a keen sense of antiquity – an almost subliminal impression of time hanging heavy, of ages and aeons having passed. He had felt it on the ship, but he felt it even more acutely now, perhaps more powerfully than at almost any time in his life. Vast unremembered eternities had passed in this place.

There had been a visitor before them, the Doctor observed.

A space-suited body lay slumped on the ground at the foot of a flight of broad stone stairs. The stairs led up to a kind of throne.

It was complex. The throne was situated in the space formed between three fluted gold columns, which rose up to form a kind of plinth or cradle, upon which, tilted at an angle, rested what was unmistakeably a small saucer-shaped spacecraft. The Doctor had seen nothing exactly like it, but its basic design was typical enough of a small scout vehicle. The saucer's middle was domed, bulging above and below the midline. There were portholes in the dome, and space inside for anything between one and a dozen occupants, depending on how cramped the conditions they were prepared to tolerate.

The saucer was obviously incredibly old, covered in gold and jewelled ornamentation that appeared to have been worked into place after the saucer had been fixed above the three columns. This ornamentation obscured much of the original hull. It seemed to be made of bare metal, but here and there the Doctor detected the orange or red chips of what must have been the original paint scheme. That the saucer had some connection with the occupant of the throne was beyond doubt.

But of that occupant, much less was clear.

The throne was a heavy gold chair, surrounded not only by the bases of the three columns but also what the Doctor immediately recognised as rudimentary time-management technology.

'Stasis generators,' the Master confirmed, stooping down to examine the space-suited figure. 'Time dams, of a particularly crude and inefficient variety.'

The stasis-generators formed a bubble of retarded time – slowed down, but not stopped – just large enough to encompass the throne and its occupant. The Doctor made out the trembling blurred edge where the boundary of the retarded time commenced. The metal outside the bubble, even the gold, was duller than that within.

The throne's occupant was a humanoid woman of tremendous age. The Doctor wondered if he had ever seen so visibly ancient a specimen. She was clearly near the end of a very long life, at least by normal human standards. Everything about her was pale or translucent, like a picture that had been exposed to too much light. She wore a high-collared gown of white, grey and silver brocade. Her hair, held back by a delicate silver crown, was so white and fine that it more resembled a spray of fibre-optic threads erupting from her scalp. Her skin was colourless, like very old bones or driftwood. One hand, gloved, clutched the end of the chair's armrest. The other, ungloved, maintained an equally firm grip on the end of a plain golden rod, fixed to the chair's side like a walking stick.

'How long do you think she's been here?' the Doctor asked.

The Master's black-gloved hand pushed right through the helmet of the fallen figure. It crumbled into grey dust, as if it had never been made of anything more substantial than compacted ash. 'More than a little while, if this fellow's any indication. I wonder if he came for an audience with the queen, or to rob her tomb?'

The spacesuit's bulbous, top-heavy proportions spoke of alien anatomy. The Doctor caught a glimpse of a fish-like skull with saucer-sized eye sockets, before that too crumbled away.

'Ring any bells?'

'No...' the Master said, on a troubled note. But then something caught his eye. He reached for something clutched in the alien's glove. Strangely, the glove was still intact. There was a bubble of dust around it, which popped into nothingness as the Master broke the integrity of some field-generated membrane.

He levered apart the fingers and prised loose a sleek object of black and chrome.

'What is it?'

'A weapon, generating a self-preservation aura.' The Master inspected the pistol-like device, touched a stud in its side and aimed it nonchalantly at the Doctor, tucking his finger into the trigger guard.

'What are you doing?'

'My dear fellow, I thought it was self-explanatory. Aiming a neutron blaster at you.'

Eight thousand, eight hundred and fifty-one. Red light, alarm. Eight thousand, eight hundred and fifty. Red light, alarm. Eight thousand, eight hundred and forty-eight... no nine, she'd skipped one. Go back, do it again. Damn, but her fingers were useless! There was almost no illumination now, which made things even harder. The main power supply had cut out, the rig switching to back-up generators and batteries. The emergency lights were not much use.

McCrimmon had worked steadily for the first thousand combinations, ninety minutes by her watch, but she had stopped before proceeding with the numbers below nine thousand, unable to resist returning to the outer door. There had been no noise, at least none that she stood a chance of hearing over the multiple alarms, and she had allowed herself to hope that the others had abandoned their efforts to get through the door. But this was not the case. They were still at it, Irwin tapping in the combinations with a tirelessness that she could not hope to emulate. She hardly dared wonder where he had got to now. Up into the three, four thousands? Any minute, any second, he might hit the right sequence. And all she had done was waste precious time of her own.

From somewhere else in the fabric of Mike Oscar Six there came a muted metallic crash, and then another. The floor under her feet tremored, and then seemed to give, gaining a slight but ominous tilt that had not been there before. In the absence of windows, it was hard to be certain. But it seemed likely that something catastrophic was in the process of happening to the rig.

Her rig.

Jo tucked the MERMAN dossier under her seat. She had read it front to back, back to front, three times, but now her eyes were having trouble focusing on the text – and not just the blurred parts that referred to... *him*, the man whose name she was now in the habit of forgetting more than she liked. The helicopters were encountering increasingly rough weather, bucking and pitching in a most unsettling manner. It was one thing to hit choppy skies over land, where you always had the option of finding somewhere to touch down. But under them now was just swirling, turbulent sea, grey as slate, slimed with huge rafts of mucus-like foam.

The omens were not auspicious. They had already passed one oil platform that was on fire, its entire upper structure wreathed in flames, and another that was simply *gone*, with just three concrete leg stumps jutting from the water as evidence that it had ever existed. They had passed an oil tanker, snapped in two like a big bar of chocolate, the edges of the bite unnervingly clean and circular, down to polished metal, and as they overflew the wounded ship they had watched both parts gradually pitch end-up and lower into the water. They had seen, halfway to the horizon, a hemisphere of water disappear, scooped out of existence – and then watched as the sea reclaimed itself, walls of water closing in like a puckering mouth. They had watched columns of water rain out of the heavens. They had seen whirlpools of air open in clear sky, sucking atmosphere to who knew where.

Clearly the Sild offensive was taking more than one form, with time ruptures snatching entire structures and vessels out of existence, while the Sild who managed to come through with the ruptures were attempting the takeover of any kind of human installation, seaborne or dry land. Contact had now been lost with almost all North Sea maritime traffic and production platforms, including Mike Oscar Six. Isolated incidents were coming in from further afield. Trouble in the Irish Sea, the English Channel, the Bay of Biscay. The Sild had concentrated their initial efforts in the vicinity of the United Kingdom because that was where the Master was being held. But no part of the planet would eventually be spared.

There was still no absolute confirmation that the Doctor had survived the attack on Durlston Heath. Equally, the TARDIS had not been seen in the wreckage. Soon, according to the Brigadier, it would be possible to send men into the area, wearing radiological protective gear. The Sild had abandoned their interest in the power station, appearing more intent on gathering hosts for a push toward larger population centres. UNIT forces were trying to move civilians out of the path of the Sild advance, clearing whole villages, but it was bound to be a losing battle.

Jo had to believe that the Doctor was *somewhere*, doing something that might make a difference. Equally, she had to believe that there was something to be gained in this risky expedition out to the now silent rig. Eddie McCrimmon might have cried wolf once, but she had asked for help a second time, speaking to Jo personally. Jo felt a personal connection with the woman now, an obligation to answer her call. Whatever had happened to her, Jo would not be able to live with her conscience if they did not make an effort to investigate.

Why did she feel this way, she wondered? Was she that good a person, or did spending time with the Doctor make her want to be better than she was? Was that, ultimately, the Doctor's greatest achievement – not the deeds he himself did, but the deeds he inspired in others? The Doctor was one man, but he had touched countless lives.

Jo was ruminating on this when a time rupture opened right next to them, a hole in the sky that sucked in and then swallowed one of the three helicopters. She watched it tumble into a dark throat that had no business being in the air, rotors slowing and crumpling, air and life gasping from the cabin.

Then it was gone.

She looked at Yates, reading the shock in his eyes. But there was nothing to discuss. They had to keep going now.

CHAPTER TWENTY-FIVE

The Doctor shook his head pityingly. 'You don't even know if it works.'

'If it's still capable of generating an aura,' the Master said, admiring the gleaming shaft of his neutron blaster, 'I'd wager this weapon still has some potency.'

'Very good. And are you willing to wager you can get that thing to work before I trigger the device around your neck?'

'Ah, that.' The Master chuckled. 'A ruse, I confess. To inspire your confidence, your willingness to let me accompany you. I'm afraid I disarmed the triggering mechanism before I ever set foot in your TARDIS. Your control over me has been illusory.'

'You're bluffing.'

'In which case I invite you to test that presumption. Meanwhile, be so good as to throw down the TARDIS key and kick it to me.'

'Kill me and take it yourself.'

'No, Doctor. If I killed you, I would miss the satisfaction of abandoning you here, without a time machine, beyond any hope of salvation.' The Master waggled the blaster. 'The key.'

'Not on your nellie.'

'Very well, Doctor: you leave me with no choice. With regret...' The Master aimed the blaster squarely at the

241

Doctor's abdomen, and squeezed the trigger.

The Doctor should not have been surprised; he had been on the end of the Master's homicidal ruthlessness on many occasions. That was what made the Master's charm all the more twisted: that it could so easily transform itself into vicious single-mindedness. A dagger in the back, strangulation, the discharge from a neutron blaster... it mattered little, how the end would eventually come. There would always be that implacably composed face, dispensing murder as effortlessly as it dispensed the most vacuous of pleasantries.

But the Master yelped. The blaster had failed to discharge, and had instead self-destructed in a flash of pink that left the Master clutching one hand in the other, staggering back, pain and fury and indignation in his eyes. He stumbled and fell.

The Doctor too had fallen back. He had not been clutching a weapon, but in the same instant that the blaster disintegrated, a similar pink energy burst had impacted him hard in the chest. The Doctor landed on his back, his hands out of his pockets.

'At least,' he said, coughing, 'we know where we stand now.'

Dusting himself off, the Master rose unsteadily to his feet. 'A malfunction, for which you should count yourself very fortunate.'

'I'm not sure it *was* a malfunction, actually.'

The Master followed the Doctor's gaze. The suited alien was fading away. Even the bits of it that had shattered under the Master's examination were disappearing.

'What is this?'

The Doctor rubbed his chin, sitting upright. The pink energy burst had knocked the air out of him just as thoroughly as if he'd been whacked in the solar plexus.

'What is this?'

'Some kind of test, by the looks of things. Which we've either passed with flying colours, or flunked rather badly.'

The Doctor and the Master had both moved to the foot of

the steps. A pattern of lights had begun to race up and down the three columns around the throne. The stasis machines began to emit a rising drone.

The Doctor and the Master climbed the stairs side by side. It was obvious that this woman had directed the spider to bring them here, and very likely that she had been responsible for the illusion that had tricked the Master.

'A face you know?' he whispered.

'No,' the Doctor said, and in the instant it was as true a thing as he had ever uttered. But a moment later, the tiniest of doubts struck him. He was sure he had never met this woman in her present condition. But Time Lords were very good with faces, and at stripping away the effects of time. It was an occupational hazard to bump into the same individuals at different points in their lives, often only hours or days apart from the time traveller's perspective.

Had he once known this person, when they were much younger?

The rising drone reached a plateau, then quietened. The blur around the time bubble was now absent. The pocket of retarded time had been accelerated into the normal flow.

The woman moved her head. Her eyes, closed until now, opened wearily. She looked down at the two visitors, and her voice boomed and echoed from all corners of the vaulted chamber.

'I was beginning to think you'd never come.'

'Was there some point to that infantile trickery?' the Master said.

'To establish your intentions, violent or otherwise. Consider them established.' The woman paused. 'And for an infantile trick, it seemed more than convincing to you. Be warned that any further violent acts will be punished by your immediate destruction. I may not have much energy left, but I have enough for *that*. I know who you are – both of you.'

'I'm afraid you have us at a bit of a disadvantage,' the Doctor said.

The Master snarled: 'Identify this world. What is its name and location? Confirm the identity of the spacecraft orbiting it. What is *your* name, and how did you come here?'

By way of reply, the woman said: 'Did you explore the ship, before my robot found you?'

'We had a pleasant enough stroll,' the Doctor said.

'And did you find your way to the place where the copies of *him* are kept?' Her gaze, unmistakeably, was upon the Master.

'Incarnations,' he corrected. 'Not copies.'

'It is of no consequence. What matters is that you arrived too late, after the work was done.'

'Too late for whose work?' the Doctor asked.

'Who else, but the Sild?'

The Doctor shot a look at the Master. Much was confusing, but at least the woman had mentioned something that made a kind of sense. The strange thing, until now, had been the utter absence of the Sild at this end of time.

'Where are the Sild?' the Doctor asked.

'They achieved their goal. They gained access to a piece of technology aboard the ship. A forbidden machine, a device for opening ruptures in time, bridging the past and the present... their control over it was imperfect, to begin with.'

The Master could not hide his smirk.

'What did they do?' the Doctor asked.

'The Sild detected the Master's signal. At first they had no idea of its origin, but the psychokinetic imprint encoded into the signal enabled them to identify the sender. The records aboard the *Consolidator* told them who he was – who he had been, who he would be – a Time Lord with an unparalleled command of temporal engineering. They also discovered that he had played a part in their imprisonment – in the construction of the *Consolidator* itself. For the Sild the discovery of the psychokinetic signal could not have been more fortuitous. It gave them the means to reach back into history – to isolate and extract multiple facets of the Master, and to harness those facets to make their control over time even more powerful. And at the same time, to inflict eternal torment upon their Time Lord enemy!'

The Doctor glanced at the Master. 'Not looking so cocky now, are you?'

'The Sild harvested him,' the woman went on. 'Unstitched him from history, made him their prisoner, locked his minds together into a single Assemblage, a living computer linked directly to the time apparatus! His will was as nothing against their methods of neural control and coercion. The Sild have always been masters of pain and terror!'

'And with this... Assemblage?' the Doctor asked.

'His mind gave them absolute control of the apparatus. The work of unstitching him from history was but the prelude, barely tapping the potential of the equipment. With his mind solving the ever-shifting time equations... compensating for micro-changes in temporal flux, the ebb and flow of chrono-synclastic feedback patterns... the Sild were able to open vast portals into the past. Pathways and corridors into history, sufficient to bleed dry an entire world! They sucked the life from my world – drained Praxilion's oceans and skies. Then they left, escaping into time through those same ruptures.'

'To forge a new Sild dominion,' the Master said. 'Rewriting galactic history!'

'How long ago was it when they finished?' the Doctor asked, certain this was the first time he had heard of a world named Praxilion. 'By how many centuries did we overshoot?'

The woman pushed her head back into the padded embrace of her throne. She emitted a retching cough of dry laughter. Whatever he had said plainly amused her. 'Centuries, Doctor? Think again. You are *ten million years* too late.'

The Doctor scratched at his hair. 'Well, the thing is, you see...'

'If he had allowed me to navigate from the outset,' the Master cut in, 'that error would have been much reduced.'

The Doctor opted to ignore this criticism. 'You said that the robot was yours, and you've obviously been expecting us. Were you alive when the Sild did... whatever they did?'

'In the technical sense of the word, yes. But even then, I was confined to this stasis throne. I felt older than time – and yet from my present perspective, in those days I was almost youthful.' The woman closed her eyes again, and for a few seconds it seemed as if she had fallen asleep. 'I had another name once, but it is lost to time. To the people I governed – I will not say "ruled" – I was Her Imperial Majesty Uxury Scuita. They knew me better as the Red Queen. That is the only name that matters now. When I am gone, no one will remain to remember it.'

'And these people...' the Master said. 'Were they also citizens of this world?'

'Praxilion was theirs; they had evolved here. But it is not *my* world. I came to them in their hour of need. Twelve million years ago.' With evident effort, she craned back in her seat to take in something of the saucer, suspended far above the throne. 'My ship. I was its only pilot. My craft was... damaged, I suppose. Impaired, I made a crash-landing on this world. I remember little of that. But they found me, pulled me out of the craft. When they saw what I was, they made me their queen.'

'Just like that?' the Doctor asked. 'You drop out of the sky, and they popped a crown on you?'

'There was more to it than that.'

'Twelve million years,' the Master said, 'still places us many billions of years beyond the EMTT.'

'Quite correct,' the Red Queen said. 'This world, its creatures, its very ecosystem, all came into being long after what you think of as galactic history. Praxilion was not even a glint in creation's eye when Gallifrey knew its last hour.'

'But the ship?' the Doctor asked.

'Its name is the *Consolidator*, as you doubtless know.'

The Master had stopped clutching his hand – clearly the

hurt had been superficial. 'Are you certain of the identity of the ship?'

'There is no doubt.'

The Master eyed the Doctor. For the moment the two of them were exactly as equals.

'It can't be the same craft,' the Doctor said. 'Not unless a very important piece of Gallifreyan history is a complete lie.'

'I fear that may well be the case,' the Master said.

The Doctor was doing his best to keep all this organised in his head, but it was becoming an effort. 'So when you arrived, your Majesty – long before the ship – you must have seemed like something from the pages of myth.'

'To the citizens of this world, I was no less than a god.'

'And the citizens of this world?' The Master asked. 'Where are they, exactly?'

'All gone. Extinct or annihilated. After the Sild onslaught, only a few lonely pockets remained – isolated groups of survivors, struggling to survive in a world stripped to the bone. The rest had died in their billions, under the vengeance and cruelty of the Sild.'

'And you?' the Doctor asked.

'When all else was gone, they managed to keep me alive. This... stasis apparatus... was almost the last functioning machine on Praxilion. And for millions of years I have been here, as the support systems fail and I approach my last conscious thought, waiting for you.'

'To toy with us?' the Master asked.

'No,' the Red Queen said. 'To send you back. Not to that remote time from which you have travelled, but a mere ten million years, into the earliest days of the Sild onslaught. I have a temporal coordinate lock, maintained by a bound-tachyon pair. You will neither overshoot, nor undershoot.'

'And when we get there?' the Doctor enquired.

'You will give the Sild what they wish.' Her gaze fell on the Master. 'Him. The last piece of their puzzle.'

'No,' the Master said. 'This *will* not be.'

247

The Doctor raised a hand. 'We came here to find out what the Sild wanted, and then to stop them... not to surrender him to them!'

'My argument is not with you, or even the Master. His crimes merit punishment, but that is not my concern. My duty is to appease the Sild. If they have the last component of the Assemblage, they may spare Praxilion. The desolation they wrought on this world and its people may be undone. There can be no other way.'

'I assure you,' the Doctor said, 'that in my experience there are almost invariably about nine other ways. And it's useless to bargain with the Sild!'

The queen moved her ancient limbs. The Doctor could almost feel the creaking of sinews, like an old tree bending in the wind. The queen worked a ring from one of the fingers of her ungloved hand, then tossed it to the ground. It came to rest at the base of the stairs: a gold hoop with a glittering red gem, twinkling with an inner spark.

'One half of the tachyon pair. Cross-link it to your time machine, and it will carry you back to the other half. Travel back in time.'

'I have no intention of submitting to your will,' the Master said. 'I do not *obey*. I *am* obeyed!'

The queen pointed a now ringless finger at the Master. She mouthed an incantation. The Master groaned and dropped to his knees, clutching his head.

'You are damaged,' the queen said. 'That neural pulse was at the lowest setting... it should barely have troubled you.' A trace of contrition crossed her face. 'I did not mean to cause him pain... merely to assert my authority, and warn him that the next pulse would be worse.'

'The Sild touched him,' the Doctor said softly. 'Just before we left Earth. Evidently the contact did more damage than he's letting on. He must be using phenomenal powers of self-control, blocking the pain and re-routing thought processes around compromised brain areas.'

'A Time Lord's mental resilience is legendary. But even you have your limits.'

The Master forced himself to stand, although the evidence of the queen's neural attack remained in the tense muscles of his face. 'I am… weakened. But far from incapacitated.'

'But even the strongest mind will eventually wither, after it has known Sild contact. Or do you deny this?'

'She's right,' the Doctor said. 'I thought you'd got off lightly, but I should have known better. There's no good way to have a Sild shoving its feelers into your brain!'

'Thank you, Doctor, for your tender sympathies.'

'There's medical equipment on the TARDIS. If you will allow me to carry out a full examination…'

'Your medicine is useless in the face of Sild contact,' the queen said. 'But on Praxilion we lived under their oppression for half a million years! Once in a while, with the aid of an alien machine, we were able to spare those who had known the touch.'

'And do you have this treatment now?' the Doctor asked, guessing what the answer was likely to be.

'No. The machine was lost, even before the end. But at the time of my earlier self, the one who holds the other tachyon pair… she will have the means. Ask her to show you the Infinite Cocoon.'

'You cannot have such a thing,' the Master said.

'He's right,' the Doctor said. 'Only a handful of those abominations were ever made!'

'Nonetheless, my people found an Infinite Cocoon inside the ship. It had been put there, along with much else that ought to have been destroyed.'

The Master regarded the Doctor. 'With the correct programming, it might be able to heal me.'

The Doctor nodded – he could see the possibilities, even as it appalled him to think of what else the Infinite Cocoon could do. 'But only if the queen lets us use it,' he said.

'That is a chance you must take,' the Red Queen answered.

'I can guarantee that *without* her assistance, the Master will surely die.'

The Doctor nodded slowly. He had come to the same grim conclusion. From the moment the TARDIS was sucked into the future, they had always been meant to confront the Sild. This audience with the Red Queen, at the dismal end of her reign, was merely a postponement of that confrontation.

He stooped down and picked up the tachyon ring. He thought of its counterpart, ten million years in the past. In a sense, they were the same object, existing co-temporaneously. In the absence of the Time Lord reference signal, a bound-tachyon pair offered the surest aid to long-range chronic navigation.

'Thank you for waiting,' the Doctor said, pocketing the ring.

'I have a question for the Master, before you depart – and then one for you, Doctor.'

The Master stood with his hands clasped behind him. 'I am waiting.'

'The ship is abandoned. It served its purpose to the Sild, as have you. Now all it does is orbit Praxilion, a monument to a crime greater even than the entire sum your misdeeds.'

'Continue,' the Master said.

'My robot… the one that brought you here. Long ago it was able to implant a destructive device at the heart of the ship.'

'A bomb?' the Doctor asked.

'The Axumillary Orb. A weapon so potent it was among those made safe and locked away in the *Consolidator* itself. But we found it and made it very *unsafe*.'

The Doctor and the Master exchanged glances. Both knew of the Axumillary Orb, and its fabled destructive potential. The energy to turn a world into a cloud of gravel, in a device small enough to slip into a pocket.

'You have the means to trigger it?' the Doctor asked.

'In an instant, I can end ten million years of torment.'

250

'And me,' the Master said.

The Red Queen nodded at this blunt assessment. 'You are already on the point of not existing, Master. The destruction of the ship would change very little. But it would be a final kindness.'

The Doctor said: 'This can only be your decision, not mine.'

'Of course,' the Master said.

'Do you want a moment alone with the queen?'

'If you'd be so... kind.'

'I'll start hooking up the tachyon pair,' the Doctor said decisively, glad that it gave him an excuse to depart. 'It'll take a few minutes.'

'I have one question for you, before you leave. I cannot speak for the Master. But there is a chance you will return to your own time – or whatever remains of it, after the Sild have rewritten history. Back to the EMTT, the Epoch of Mass Time Travel.'

The Doctor glanced at the Master. He hardly dared speculate about their mutual fates. 'It's a bad habit, but I always try to look on the bright side.'

'It seems so long ago now, the EMTT. But it must have been something to behold. All those worlds, all those civilisations. All the wonder and terror of life and possibility, more than any living thing could ever begin to tire of. It must have been glorious.'

'It was,' the Doctor said. 'It was and is and always will be.'

CHAPTER TWENTY-SIX

At last the two remaining helicopters of the UNIT expedition came within visual range of Mike Oscar Six. They had survived the rest of the crossing, despite another time rupture opening up very close to Jo's helicopter. For a moment, they had been pulled toward that sucking absence. But the rupture had snapped shut and the pilots had been able to wrestle their craft back under control.

There was good news and bad news, Jo reflected.

The good news was that there was still a rig. It hadn't been sheared off at the legs like some of the platforms they had passed, and it wasn't totally ablaze, like a torch held up from the waves. The bad news – actually, the *very* bad news – was that the rig was indeed on fire in places, and there was ample evidence of structural damage to the main block, with parts of it sagging away from the whole, and what appeared to be a pronounced and worrying lean to the entire rig, as if the seabed itself had ceased to offer any kind of firm foundation.

But still. There was a rig. And just as crucially, the helipad looked more or less intact. The UNIT forces would have abseiled onto the platform if they hadn't been able to land, but this made life easier.

'Still no contact,' Yates said. 'And no welcoming party, either.'

'Perhaps we'll have the run of the place,' Benton said optimistically.

Jo pointed down at a red craft bobbing in the water. It was a saucer-shaped lifeboat, completely enclosed, the kind that could be dropped from the rig in emergency conditions.

'Somebody made it out. Should we see if we can help?'

'They'll have to take their chances for now,' Yates said. 'If they've survived, they should be safe in that thing for a while. It'll have an emergency beacon, so we can leave the rescue team to pick them up later. I'm afraid our priority now is to disable the MERMAN equipment.'

While the helicopters completed a circle of the burning rig, Yates called back to base and updated the Brigadier on events, including the loss of the third helicopter. He listened carefully, then signed off. 'The Brig says McCrimmon's mainland office had a wireless transmission just before they went off the air – they had an idea Edwina McCrimmon was being held in the secure zone reserved for the equipment. That's obviously the first place we'll look. The Brig's also had our people talk to Callow.'

Jo remembered the name from the briefing notes. 'One of the men working for the project?'

'Callow weaselled his way back to Whitehall, but he's in a spot of bother now.'

'Aren't we all!'

'I mean, Callow's going to be in hot water even if the rest of us get out of this mess. Turns out him and Lovelace have been up to some very naughty business indeed, breaking ministerial rules left, right and centre to get their test up and running – blackmail, theft of government materials, the lot. Callow's career's all but over. But he's given us the likely code for the MERMAN secure zone. Even if Lovelace locked the doors, we should be able to get through.'

'Provided Lovelace didn't change them,' Jo said.

'Well, that's what plastic explosives are for,' Yates said. 'And we'll use them if we have to.'

Rotors almost meshing, the two helicopters settled in towards the helipad.

The Master was alone. He had ventured outside, onto a small balcony projecting from the side of the queen's tower. Miles above the ground, the balcony lacked walls or railings. The air that he breathed was trapped by a field which extended only as far as it needed to: he could push his hand through the field's gentle resistance and feel the hard vacuum beyond, clawing at the fabric of his glove.

It was late in what passed for the afternoon. The dying red sun hung low behind the Master, pushing the buildings' shadows out to an impossibly sharp, airless horizon. Here and there, tilted at odd angles, were the technological ruins of earlier ages. It was hard to tell what had once been rockets, what had once been cities. Time and physics had turned them into abstract sculptures.

Above the horizon, the sky was a magnificent black, its absolute absence of light marred only by a dismal clutch of weary stars. The Master imagined worlds around those stars, just as barren and exhausted as Praxilion. There had never been a time when the universe had not felt entropy's hand, reminding it that all processes, all histories, all hopes and dreams, must eventually come to an end. For billions of years, though, life managed to delude itself that it had some gambit or strategy capable of outwitting entropy. It was a fallacy, as this cheerless spectacle confirmed. Late in the afternoon of both this world and time itself, entropy's touch had become an iron death grip. The universe was a clock winding down to its last exhausted tick.

The Master chuckled. It was a thought to stir the soul.

But now he made out the swift rise of another star. It was so dim as to be almost invisible, but the Master had been expecting it and he had known where to look.

This was the *Consolidator*, and if the name of the ship was correct, it carried the most infamous cargo in all of history.

Early in their existence, the Time Lords had taken a momentous decision. From across the galaxy, from across many eras, drawing on their combined wisdom and influence, they had gathered much that was evil or dangerous or destabilising. Not just weapons or technologies, but – where such collection was feasible – even entire species.

By their nature, the Time Lords were not about to be seen to be engaging in open warfare or xenocide. They were cleverer than that. They sought, instead, those hostile alien cultures that had already been locked away or entombed. Rather than leave these aggressive species lying around the galaxy, at risk of being rediscovered, they were brought into the limitless holds of the *Consolidator*. There, kept frozen or in stasis, they would wait out the centuries like a kind of toxic waste. The ship was built to stop its cargo from escaping, and armoured against intruders. Self-repairing, autonomous, it was designed to last indefinitely.

But that wasn't enough.

The Time Lords squabbled. Some thought that the *Consolidator* should be destroyed, now that it contained all the galaxy's old evils: smashed into a star, perhaps, just to be sure. Others argued that many of the dark technologies and sciences contained in the ship might turn out to have as yet unforeseen benevolent applications. It was even suggested that some of the hostile species might be subject to rehabilitation, perhaps to the point where they could be allowed to re-join civil galactic society.

Argument raged for centuries. No agreement could be found. In the end, a tawdry compromise was settled on.

If the Time Lords of the present could not decide what to do with the ship, the problem would be handed down to their distant descendants. A time rift would be opened, large enough to swallow the *Consolidator*. When it emerged, the Time Lords would have had long enough to ponder their ultimate decision – and in the meanwhile, traversing the time rift, the *Consolidator* would pose no risk to galactic stability.

But there was a problem. Even Gallifreyan science was not up to generating a rift of the required dimensions.

When orthodox approaches had failed, when the finest senior minds had admitted defeat, two young candidate Time Lords, promising graduates, were assigned the task of finding a mathematical solution to the problem. Both struggled with the arcane demands of the exercise. One of them was an undisciplined but brilliantly intuitive thinker. The other was a meticulous logician, able to view the thorniest problem in startlingly transparent terms.

The Doctor and the Master were friends and rivals. Both had their doubts about the wisdom of the *Consolidator* scheme, but they had been given a chance to prove their worth and so they put aside their private concerns. But the work proved almost beyond them. Opening a rift was hard enough, but maintaining it, achieving stability and a fixed temporal lock at either end, seemed to demand a completely new approach to the mechanics of time travel.

When at last it seemed that they had explored every possibility, to no avail, the Doctor confided in the Master that he was not necessarily sorry. Perhaps it was best to fail, rather than succeed and be complicit in the cowardly decision to foist the problem of the *Consolidator* on their descendants.

But the Master had a wild idea. For once, he was the intuitionist, not the Doctor. Gripped with the thrill of the hunt, the driven young man soon closed in on a possible solution. The collapse of the right kind of supermassive star could in turn create a black hole with a rare balance of charge, angular momentum and Hawking temperature... enough to cleft open time.

The Doctor checked the Master's work. It was watertight.

The Doctor begged the Master to abandon his work, to put aside thoughts of personal glory.

'Easy for you to say, when you are not the one who saw the solution,' the Master said.

'I will always know it was you. And you will always have

that satisfaction. You don't have to prove your genius to the world. It's enough that I've seen it.'

'For you, perhaps.' He did not call him Doctor then, just as the Doctor did not call him the Master. They had other names: strange and lovely as poems. 'For me, that would never be enough.'

'I beg of you.'

'I owe this to Gallifrey. I cannot *un-imagine* what has already come into being. I have seen time from a new perspective. It is both vastly simpler, and yet vastly more complex, than our foolish peers have ever dreamed.' The Master had paused, gripped by a sudden charitableness. 'I offer you this. Put your name to the work, and we will share it. I could not have found my way to this solution were it not for the blind alleys and dead ends you have already blundered down.'

'That's very magnanimous of you,' the Doctor said. 'But no. I don't want any part of this. And if you've a shred of decency left in you, you shouldn't either.'

'There's your answer, then. I am clearly beyond salvation.'

So the Master had taken his work to the High Council. There it had been subjected to thorough scrutiny – dismissed at first, then taken gradually more seriously as, one by one, he was able to answer his critics, to defend his most outrageous deductive leaps. Valiantly sure of himself, the Master remained steadfast in the face of the sternest cross-examination. In time, as he had always known it would be, the validity of his theory was accepted.

The Master, on the back of this work, could not help but be awarded the highest academic merit in his chosen discipline. And the Doctor, who had not won the academy's favour, was seen as something of a disappointment.

To the Master, that was as nothing. But it went some way to explaining the Doctor's lifelong sense of intellectual inadequacy, as measured against his old school friend.

As for the *Consolidator*, a star had eventually been found which was near to critical core collapse. On the moment of its implosion, the ship was sent hurtling toward the newly forming event horizon, exactly in accordance with the Master's scheme.

That was when everything went wrong.

The star's supernova collapse had not been perfectly balanced, and that in turn had led to an asymmetry in the formation of the event horizon... enough to spoil the perfection of the original calculations. Instead of falling into the time rift, the *Consolidator* had come in at an angle... and been destroyed in a mass-energy conflagration sufficient to rip every atom in the ship to its constituent particles.

It was a catastrophe, but it was also something infinitely worse than that. It was an embarrassment. The Time Lords had worked hard to maintain a façade of infallibility. There was only one possible resolution to the *Consolidator* fiasco. The whole sorry business had to be hushed up. Quietly, the entire existence of the *Consolidator* was pushed first into obscurity and then secrecy. No mention was to be made of it, ever again. There would be no punishment of those involved, because punishment would require the tacit acknowledgement that it had happened in the first place. Hands were washed, consciences salved. Everyone went free.

And time did that thing it was good at doing, which was to pass. The Master and the Doctor, in their different ways, broke free of Gallifrey. And no one, not even those involved in the *Consolidator* affair, dared to think that the ship might have survived.

How had it happened, the Master wondered now? Could the mass-energy conflagration have been misinterpreted? Had his calculations, far from being in error, been *more correct* than anyone had ever imagined? Had the *Consolidator* skipped not merely centuries, not merely thousands or tens of thousands of years, but millions of years?

Had it fallen through time while solar systems came and went, only to pop back into normal space on some unaccountably remote day, so far into the future that the

EMTT was a golden glow at the beginning of creation?

So, on the evidence of his eyes, it would appear.

It was almost a crime to destroy such a thing! It was, he knew, not too late to rescind the instruction. If he were to return inside, and make his case to the Red Queen, she would cancel the destruct order. This testament to his intellect would remain.

It was not like the Master to have doubts. But here they were. Second thoughts. Grave misgivings. These were novel feelings for him. He had been inside his own head long enough to think he had the measure of it. This was like finding a secret doorway, an aperture into some unknown part of himself.

The Master was psychic. All Time Lords had that talent, nurtured across patient generations of genetic intervention. It was a question of neural congruence, sympathetic resonance. Science, not magic: albeit science of a difficult, slippery kind. Some felt it more than others. Generally, the mental bond was strongest between Time Lords and their own kind. The literature on psychic communication between Time Lords and their *own* incarnations was, to say the least, sparse. Generally incarnations were prevented from meeting, but that was not to say that it had never happened. In times of crisis, in moments of great cosmic emergency, those appalling hypocrites on Gallifrey had been known to bend the odd rule or two.

The Master, speaking for himself, had never knowingly felt the psychic influence of his own counterparts.

Until this moment.

He had seen the versions of himself on the *Consolidator*, and known that many of them were dead. But that still left hundreds who were maintained in some quasi-life, with just enough mental activity to grasp that they were still alive, still captive, utterly without hope. They had been like that for ten million years.

He felt them. Their presence manifested as a kind of tight

headache, above and beyond what the Sild contact already made him feel. The headache was like a weathervane. Its axis was tilting, keeping track of the rising star.

And suddenly the star was a supernova. The Master swept up his hand to shield his eyes from the intense sphere of expanding light. For a moment there was a white beyond white, as if the white he had always known was merely an imposter, a tawdry approximation of the real thing. And then the sphere was fading at its margins, dulling to purple.

The psychic severance was sudden and shocking. It felt as if the weathervane in his skull had been jerked, set spinning. The pain, like the colour white, had become a thing beyond itself. The Master realised that he had in fact never really known pain, only pain's shadow.

Until this moment.

The Master fell to the ground, screaming, clutching his head. Above him, the sphere faded into the sky's perfect limitless black.

Praxilion was once more without a moon.

The Doctor knelt down to examine the unconscious form. The Master had collapsed to the floor of the balcony, his arm dangling limply over the side. The arm glittered with frost, commencing in a sharp line just beyond the Master's elbow. It was a most beguiling effect, as if the arm had been dipped in sugar.

The Master's eyes were closed, his face calm. He looked gentle, in a state of serene repose. The Doctor pondered all the evils this man had perpetrated, down through the long centuries of his existence, the crimes and the cruelties. It was impossible to square that knowledge with the helpless sleeping form before him. It would only have taken a shove to send him over the edge. With no air to slow him, the Master's body would be travelling at a fearsome speed when it hit the Praxilion surface. But there was no need to kill him that way. Left out here, with his arm exposed to vacuum, he would not have lasted long.

It would be a lie to say that the Doctor did not give some thought to leaving him. Not that the Red Queen would have allowed him to do that, of course. She wanted the Master to travel back with the Doctor, and the Doctor had no reason to doubt her powers of coercion. And he, too, wanted to undo the harm that the Sild had already wrought on time. If the Master was the key to that, so be it.

But deep down, even without those factors, the Doctor could not have left him there. They were both of Gallifrey. Wayward sons, it was true. But even a rogue Time Lord deserved better than death at the cold end of time.

The Doctor took the Master by the armpits and heaved him out of harm's way.

CHAPTER TWENTY-SEVEN

She would not have heard it if the main alarm had still been sounding, but at some point that electrical system had stopped working. Now there was only the muted crash and rumble of the dying rig, her own breathing, her own frantic tapping of the keypad, the wasp-like buzz from the door each time she hit the wrong combination. The door needed electrical power to work, but evidently Callow and Lovelace had made sure it was not dependent on the main supply. The same was presumably true of the door Irwin and the others were trying to get through.

So she heard the sound when it came. It was a distinct mechanical clunk, as of a gate latch being thrown. And she knew in that moment that she had failed in this last and bravest test of her life. Seven thousand eight hundred and thirty-three... more than two thousand combinations, and she still hadn't found the right one.

Not that it would have made much difference to her chances, but it had been worth a try. She might at least have been able to put an axe to the MERMAN equipment, and thereby put it beyond the reach of the monsters... whatever they wanted with it. They would surely have killed or converted her anyway, but there would have been a slim measure of satisfaction in spoiling their plans. Really, you had to take what you could get.

'Eddie!'

The voice had come from down the corridor but it did not belong to Tom Irwin, or indeed to any of her people. That was easily established. The voice was a woman's. McCrimmon was still the only female employee on Mike Oscar Six.

He heart raced. 'Who is it?'

'UNIT! It's me, Jo Grant!'

And suddenly they were coming down the corridor, torches bright, heavy in their boots, wearing military gear, with helmets and body armour and dangerous-looking guns.

'How did you...? What...?' She had far too many questions. 'You came!'

'Are you all right?' asked Jo Grant.

McCrimmon nodded, stunned and overwhelmed. 'More or less. But what about Tom and the others?'

'Tom?' asked Mike Yates.

'They were trying to get through the door, to get to me and the equipment. They didn't know the combination, but they were working through the numbers. They'd been taken over by... things.'

'Sild,' Jo Grant said, pushing back her fringe. 'That's what they're called. Mike's men hit them with stun grenades – the Sild came off their hosts and scuttled away.'

'We managed to shoot a few of them,' said Yates. 'The rest have probably made it to open water by now. They know the rig hasn't got long. We need to get you to the helipad, before this whole place falls apart under us.'

'OK,' McCrimmon said, holding her hand up against the dazzle of the torches they were still waggling about. 'So these things were using my men as hosts, is that it? But you've stunned the men now? Does that mean...'

'I'm really sorry,' Jo Grant said. 'But those men are all dead. When the Sild touched them, it was all over. There's nothing that anyone could do for them. You're really lucky to still be alive.'

'But we have to move fast,' said Yates. 'We need to disable the MERMAN equipment. Is it somewhere down here?' His men were already shrugging off heavy backpacks, tearing them open to spill out cables and electrical equipment.

McCrimmon was swinging between shock and elation. It was wonderful to have been rescued, but terrible to know that her friends and colleagues were gone for ever.

'What the hell is going on?'

'An alien invasion,' Yates said. 'Creatures coming through time, from somewhere else in the galaxy, to take over our planet. They've been homing in on the MERMAN signals – it's where this trouble all started. If we block the signal, we might slow or stop the invasion. Maybe.'

'Alien invaders? Are you serious?'

'Do we look like we're making it up?' asked Yates. 'We've lost a helicopter full of men on our way here, Miss McCrimmon.'

'It's not our first time,' Jo Grant said. 'Or second. But alien invaders are never the same twice. We've never dealt with the Sild before and we're a bit in the dark about the best way to fight them. Cutting off the signal is our best guess right now.'

'You don't sound confident.'

'We're not,' Jo Grant said. 'But this is about all we can do at our end.'

'Who's taking care of the other end?'

'The Doctor,' Jo said, with a strained smile. 'We hope.'

The Doctor had produced an old wickerwork garden chair and set the Master down in it, arms draped either side, exactly as if he had fallen into a lazy snooze on a warm summer's afternoon.

'Where are we?' the Master asked, sounding like a man roused from aeons of sleep.

'On our way to an earlier meeting with the Red Queen.' The Doctor stepped away from the TARDIS console, satisfied for the moment that all was in hand. 'How do you feel? You were unconscious when I found you. Your arm was exposed to vacuum, but beyond some mild frostbite I don't think there's any lasting damage.'

'I feel… different. Strangely different.' The Master opened his eyes fully, and raised himself from his slump into a proper sitting position. 'Doctor, something quite odd has happened to me.'

'You must have felt some kind of psychic severance when the *Consolidator* exploded, losing contact with all those counterparts of yourself.'

'I did.' The Master rubbed at the back of his head. 'I still feel the Sild's presence, Doctor. That hasn't gone away. But something *else* has.'

The Doctor also sensed a change in his adversary, but for now it was hard to say exactly where it lay. It was like the subtle change of light on a landscape, as clouds first occluded then revealed the sun.

'You've had a nasty shock.'

'It's more than that, Doctor. I feel quite profoundly altered.' The Master seemed, for a moment, utterly lost for words. 'Doctor, I hardly know how to begin expressing this. But for the first time in my life, I feel free of myself.'

'I'm not sure I follow.'

'I have never pretended to be anything other than what I am, Doctor. An agent of chaos, disorder, corruption. I have embraced these things just as vigorously as you have embraced life and possibility. But only now do I realise that my state of being did not come from within me. It was imposed from without.'

The Doctor looked at him guardedly, well accustomed to the Master's mind games. 'You'll need to be a bit clearer.'

'I need hardly ask if you are familiar with emergent systems, Doctor. Consider a flock of birds, thousands of them, swooping and moving as one mass. Almost as if they were a single living thing, rather than a mass of individuals. And indeed, in the flock, they *become* one entity, an emergent system, a gestalt organism whose rules cannot be inferred from the behaviour of any one element.'

'I see. And...'

'I have *been* that flock, Doctor. That gestalt. What I am, what I have done, cannot be ascribed to any single incarnation of me. It is an emergent effect, a property borne of the combined sum of all my identities, across all the time streams. Each and every one of me has felt that influence, the dark psychic pressure to conform to the gestalt. And in turn, by obeying that group will, we have done truly wicked things – deeds which only serve to reinforce the gestalt!'

'Well, that's awfully nice for you, but...'

'Don't you see, Doctor? I was present at the collective death of my remaining selves! In that moment I felt the worst pain I have known. But that severance was also a liberation! I am free of the gestalt! Whatever the Master was, it is not me!'

'And you expect me to believe that, do you?'

'Doctor, you of all people have always been ready to see the best in people, even in their darkest hours. I am asking you now to see the best in me. I have changed. I am truly not the man I was. And I weep for the things I have done.'

'Mm. Crocodile tears, I think the phrase is.'

The Master, still enfeebled, tried and failed to rise from the chair. 'Doctor, now of all times, you must believe me. This changes everything!'

'I'm not sure it does.'

'You cannot risk my return into time, at least not in the Red Queen's era. My other selves still exist around Praxilion – stronger, too, since there are more of them than at the end of time!'

'If you're free of their influence now, you'll be free of them when we arrive.'

'I fear not, Doctor. I am free now because of the shock of the psychic severance. The Vortex gives me some isolation, some psychic buffering. But when we emerge, who is to say what will happen? The effect of my collective selves, gathered in one point in space and time... I doubt very much that I will be able to resist them.'

'So what's your proposal? We spend the rest of eternity shuttling up and down the Vortex, like some demented elevator?'

'No, Doctor – while that fate might guard me against my other selves, it would be a cruel imposition on you.' Reaching out to brace himself against the Doctor, the Master finally succeeded in rising from the chair. 'But my selves are gathered around Praxilion, long after the EMTT. If we travel deeper into time... perhaps even before the EMTT itself... it could be sufficient!'

'You were never immune to their influence before.'

'No, but that was before I'd been vouchsafed a glimpse of what else could be!' The Master's voice was rising, but not in his usual hectoring, authoritative way. He was pleading with the Doctor. 'I beg of you. I believe I am strong enough to resist myself, provided we do not emerge in the Red Queen's time. Now I know what I could be... what I could have been... I can see a better path.'

'And what would that better path be? Galactic domination?'

The Master shook his head, smiling sadly. 'I can hardly blame you for mocking, Doctor. But I am quite sincere. I realise the monster I have become, and I wish to begin making some small amends. I could be like you: a force for good.' Slowly the Master returned to the seat – standing had worn him out. 'No; I couldn't begin to be like you. But I could be something better than I was. Wouldn't that be enough?'

Now it was the Doctor's turn to shake his head. 'I'm sorry. I'd like to believe you. But no one changes that easily.'

'But no one experiences what just happened to me!' Then an idea seemed to seize the Master. 'A psychic bridge, Doctor: between the two of us. If you could see into my mind, understand my good intentions...'

'And open my own mind up to Sild contamination?'

'Believe me!'

The console chimed. The Doctor returned to it and made a few trifling adjustments to the controls. 'We're approaching the other half of the bound-tachyon pair. We'll be there in a few seconds.'

'Please do not materialise. You will destroy me.'

'And how many times have you tried to do just that to me? Now I need to concentrate, if you don't mind. This is a very tricky manoeuvre.'

'As one Time Lord to another. We were friends once. Let me live. Don't make me become that *thing* again.'

'You've never changed,' the Doctor said, only half listening. He needed to judge the moment exactly… 'You've always been the Master. You will always *be* the Master.'

The Master fell to the Doctor's feet, clutching his trouser legs. 'I beg of you. Put aside all I have done to you…'

But the central column of the console had ceased its rise and fall. The Doctor stepped away from the pathetic, kneeling figure. The Master was sobbing.

'It was a nice try,' the Doctor said, not without a certain fondness. 'But really, after all we've been through, did you honestly expect me to fall for it?'

The console indications showed that they had arrived back on Praxilion, ten million years before they had roused the Red Queen from her stasis. They were in a building, almost certainly the same one they had already visited, except this was much earlier in its life. Air and gravity readings were almost identical to those encountered previously, although background radiation – while remaining within tolerable limits – was considerably enhanced.

The Doctor detached the queen's ring from its harness on the console, slipped it into his pocket, and opened the door. 'Look,' he said to the still-kneeling, still-sobbing form, 'you can cut out the amateur dramatics now.'

The Master did seem to gain some measure of composure. He ceased his sobbing, took a deep breath, and forced himself to stand. His eyes were red with tears.

'You're right, Doctor,' he said, with an air of absolute resignation. 'What's done is done. I can already feel them, you know. From the moment we re-entered normal time. Their influence is as strong as I feared.'

The Doctor stepped out of the TARDIS. He took in his surroundings. They were in the same vaulted space as before, except this time it was somehow grander, the decoration more ornate and ostentatious. At the limit of his hearing, he picked up the throb and hum of machines. He had not checked the energy readings, but it was clear that there was vastly more power here than in the future.

The TARDIS had come to rest – materialised – on a heavy golden plinth, equipped with three swooping arms that rose up around it, clenching it like a three-fingered claw.

The Master stepped out beside him. He took a deep breath, closed his eyes, and tipped back his head.

'I was not wrong,' he said, in little more than a whisper. 'The gestalt is reasserting its hold on me. A moment ago it revolted me to think what I was about to become again. Now it revolts me that I ever begged for your mercy!'

And with a strength that the Doctor had not seen in him since he found him slumped on the balcony, the Master laughed.

'Do you understand what I am saying, Doctor? I am becoming myself again! That thing that pleaded with you was but an aberration!' The Master smiled triumphantly. 'That pitiful, mewling part of me is dead! Let the Master be reborn!'

The Doctor wondered if the Master was simply up to more trickery and gamesmanship. But some vile intuition told him otherwise. The Master was being sincere now, as he had been sincere in the TARDIS. And that could only mean that the Doctor had committed perhaps the gravest error of judgement in all his years.

The Master's words tolled in his head like a cracked bell. *You of all people have always been ready to see the best in people,*

even in their darkest hours
     And that was true, most of the time.
     'I'm terribly sorry,' the Doctor said, quietly.

Chapter Twenty-Eight

The rig lurched again. From somewhere above came a sustained roar, signalling the collapse of some major structure.

'Pilots are getting itchy feet!' Benton said, coming back down the corridor after communicating by wireless with the helicopter crews still waiting on the helipad. 'They reckon we've only got a few minutes before it's too dangerous to stay put. Might have to take off sooner, if the angle on the pad worsens.'

'Tell them we're nearly done,' Yates said, keeping up an impressive façade of military calm as his men came back from placing the demolition charges in the MERMAN chamber.

'Can't you just... pull the plug out or something?' Jo asked, with what she assumed would be regarded as touching naivety. 'Won't that make it stop working?'

'We didn't build this equipment,' Yates said, 'and we don't know how much we can trust what Callow told his interrogators about the design. For all we know the thing can keep transmitting its signal even without an external power source.'

'It's not going to last long once the rig collapses, all the same,' Jo said.

'Maybe not, but we don't want the ruddy crabs getting their claws on it. This is the only way to be sure.'

Jo had been into the chamber, but only for a few seconds. Callow's combination had worked on the inner door as well, the one that Edwina McCrimmon had been trying to get through, and it had turned out that she had been very close to hitting the right set of digits – four 7s. The equipment had not been very impressive to look at, considering all the trouble it had brought: several upright silver cylinders, the size of beer barrels, connected to numerous grey-cased electronic boxes and spooling tape reels, the whole lot still whirring and clicking. There were cables and cooling pipes and computer terminals.

Jo thought of *him* being in here, the one whose name was now all but lost to her, helping the government men but at the same time helping himself, tweaking their equipment to serve his own ends. How simple it must have been, to take these boxes and cylinders and cables and make them do his bidding. The Doctor was good at that sort of thing, it was true – improvising, make-do-and-mend. It was the only way he stayed sane, on this primitive backwater of a planet. But *him*… the other one… he was in a different league. He could make *anything* into *anything*, given time. What fools his captors had been, to imagine they had any kind of hold over him.

But not so different to UNIT and the Brigadier, really, thinking they had a hold on the Doctor.

'Ready to go, sir!'

Yates's men had spooled out two lines of fuse, all the way back along the corridor to the first door, and they had connected these dual fuse lines into a box about the size of a biscuit tin. This was a radio detonator, Jo was given to understand. Yates had a similar-sized box in his hands, a corresponding transmitter unit would be used to detonate the charges when they had returned to the helipad. Given the structural damage already sustained by the rig, it was much too hazardous to blow the charges until they were outside and ready to leave.

'Arm,' Yates said.

One of the men flicked a sturdy switch on the lid of the receiver box. An amber light came on.

'Armed.'

Yates flicked one of two switches on his own box. A similar light came on. The two boxes were now linked by radio, ready for the transmission of the final triggering command.

So they pulled out, doing their best to respect the bodies of the dead men on the other side of the door, but knowing there was nothing they could do for them now. Jo watched Eddie McCrimmon with guarded admiration, knowing what she had been through these last few hours. She had not only confronted her own imminent death, but lost good friends and come to a sobering understanding that Earth was not exactly alone. And still she was functioning, keeping it together.

'That'll do it?' McCrimmon asked. 'Those little charges you placed?'

'They'll bring the roof down,' Yates said. 'Literally, if this place is as rickety as it feels.'

'The time ruptures have undermined the rig,' Jo said. 'It's happening everywhere, not just here.'

'We'd better get a crack on,' Benton said, as if any of them needed that spelling out.

They passed more bodies on the way to the top of the rig. The route they had come in by was blocked by fire, so they had to take a lengthy diversion through a different part of the rig, trusting to Eddie McCrimmon's flawless local knowledge. Through a canteen, through a common room, down a corridor lined with recently abandoned bedrooms. All the while Yates was cradling his transmitter box, watching the indicator light on its top. 'Bother,' he said, as the amber light flickered and returned. 'Signal's weak!'

'Had trouble reaching the helicopters, sir,' Benton said. 'Must be all the metal in this place. It's not like a normal building.'

By the time they reached daylight, the amber light had

gone out completely. Yates swore at it, turning the box this way and that to see if he could get a signal.

The rig jolted again. Jo watched in appalled wonder as one of the tower cranes buckled and fell into the seething grey seas below. 'How long?' she asked Eddie McCrimmon.

'Dunno. Feels as if one of the legs is crumbling away under us by the minute.'

Yates nodded grimly. 'Back aboard the helicopters, everyone. Including you, Jo – and Miss McCrimmon!'

'I'm not setting foot off this rig until I know the rest of you are safe,' Eddie said. 'Sorry, but I'm still the boss of this thing and you are still my guests.'

'At least get on the helipad,' Yates said. 'The rest of you, move it! Benton – you're staying with me.'

Benton responded to this with cheerful equanimity. 'What's the plan, sir?'

'The plan is that some poor mug's got to go back inside. We'll just have to trigger it and hope for the best.'

'I stopped hoping for the best around breakfast time, sir. It's been downhill ever since.'

Half the squad was now back aboard one of the helicopters. Jo watched as it lifted off from the perilously tilting helipad. Part of her desperately wanted to get aboard the other machine, but she kept thinking of what the Doctor would do.

'I'd better come with you,' Eddie said.

'No chance,' Yates said. 'Get aboard that helicopter, Miss McCrimmon.'

'Is this a civilian facility, Captain?'

The question seemed to puzzle Yates. 'Last time I checked.'

'Then I'll do as I jolly well please, thank you. Or do you really think you know your way around the rig well enough? There are new fires breaking out all the while – thing's going to be the Towering ruddy Inferno before you can blink.'

'I won't allow a civilian...'

'Then we'll all go, shall we? Take a picnic? Look, the time

276

we've been standing around arguing, I could have been halfway to the secure area – and stopped for a pee on the way. That gadget of yours doesn't look very complicated.'

'She's right,' Jo said. 'It makes sense.'

'Thank you, Miss Grant,' Eddie McCrimmon said, with an edge of doubt in her voice.

'But I'll come with you. No ifs, no buts.'

'You're all barmpots, I swear. But if you insist… Captain, give me that transmitter.'

'No,' Yates said forcefully. 'We'll go. The three of us. Benton – get everyone else aboard the second helicopter, and pull clear of the helipad. Hover at a safe distance. You should see the blast when it happens. If there's no sign of us within five minutes of the explosion, start heading for the mainland. We're low on fuel as it is – last thing we want to do is ditch in this weather.'

Benton hesitated.

Yates yelled: 'That's an order, sergeant!'

The Master took the Doctor's hand in his, clutching his sleeve with the other. 'Sorry? My dear fellow, no apologies are called for! You have done *absolutely* the right and proper thing! You have given me back to myself! You have made me whole again! You have my undying gratitude!'

A phalanx of alien guards surrounded the plinth on which the TARDIS rested. These, the Doctor supposed, were the native citizens of Praxilion. He had seen nothing quite like them. They were furry creatures with multiple legs, like fat hairy caterpillars, except that each was longer than a man was tall. They were all bent into right angles, upright 'L's with their rear halves horizontal to the floor, each supported by six pairs of thick muscular legs, splayed out from the body rather than supporting it directly from underneath. The other half of each creature, bent perpendicular to the floor, came equipped with a head and just as many limbs, except that the upper three pairs were longer and more obviously dextrous, being tipped with mitten-like hands, each hand consisting of a flat leaf-shaped palm and an opposable 'thumb'. The creatures' heads were almost mammalian, with snouts, broad smiling mouths and darkly intelligent eyes. Their fur, from head to tail, was organised into red and white stripes, like toothpaste squeezed from a tube. They gave off a sweet, honey-like odour.

All were armed. Over their fur they wore belts and harnesses and elaborate cross-webbing. Each Praxilion carried in two of its hands a thing like a cattle prod, a golden staff tipped with a glass muzzle and connected to a cylindrical backpack by a flexible tube. These weapons, whatever their nature, were pointed at the Doctor and the Master.

'Step down from the platform,' buzzed a synthetic voice, emanating from the nearest Praxilion.

The Doctor and the Master did as they were instructed, both men instinctively raising their arms to show that they carried no weapons of their own.

'State your identities,' buzzed the voice again.

'I am the Doctor... this – as you undoubtedly know – is the Master. And if you don't mind, a little courtesy might not go amiss. We were sent here by your queen, so the least we deserve...'

This insolence earned the Doctor a crackle of purple energy from the nearest cattle prod. He staggered and was about to drop to the ground when the Master caught him.

'Do not hurt the Doctor! Not if you want my continued cooperation.'

'What are *you* to us?' buzzed the voice contemptuously.

'Your miserable planet's salvation. Why else would your queen have gone to the trouble of sending me back here?' The Master, satisfied that the Doctor had recovered from the energy burst, folded his arms haughtily. 'I presume we have arrived during the Sild onslaught? I presume also that the *Consolidator* is presently in orbit around Praxilion?'

Now there was a note of guarded respect in the alien's

voice. 'You know much of our world.'

'I also know how it ends. In abject desolation. In ten million years your kind will be extinct and all but forgotten.' The Praxilion raised its lance threateningly, but the Master countered by raising the black-gloved palm of his own hand. 'Trifle with me if you wish, but you will find it profoundly counterproductive.'

'Let them approach. If they have found their way to this time, it can only be because I sent them.'

It was a different voice this time. Amplified, but recognisably human in intonation. Indeed, they both recognised the speaker. The Doctor and the Master looked over the heads of the Praxilion phalanx to the throne of the Red Queen, her Imperial Majesty Uxury Scuita. She sat in the chair, between hefty banks of throbbing stasis equipment.

She was visibly younger, although only relatively speaking. This was still a tremendously old woman. The Doctor reminded himself that even now, it was two million years since the Red Queen's arrival on this world. She was already rationing the finite remaining seconds of her life.

'You sent us,' the Doctor said. He made to reach into his pocket, only halting when the phalanx jabbed their staffs threateningly. 'Steady on! I only want to show you the other half of the bound-tachyon pair.'

'Allow me to see it,' the Red Queen commanded.

Slowly, the Doctor withdrew the ring and rested it on his upturned palm. 'May I?' he asked, indicating the stone steps at the base of the throne.

'Approach.'

Leaving the Master standing at the foot of the steps with his arms still crossed, the Doctor ascended to the throne. 'We met you in the future,' he told her. 'You'd been waiting for us, just so you could direct us back to this moment if we overshot.'

The Red Queen nodded. She seemed less a prisoner of the throne than she had been in the future, her bearing more regal. She still had the glove on her right hand, the golden rod gripped in the left. But something was different about the rod, the Doctor noticed. It had gained a gold-encrusted sphere on its top, which now served as a handle.

'And how long did I have to wait? I assume the worst. A million years? Two?'

'Ten,' the Doctor said. 'You were near the end of your stasis capacity. If we'd have arrived even a little later, I doubt that you'd have been there to greet us.'

'And Praxilion? What of it? Had better days come? Tell me we overcame the Sild, reversed the harm they have done to our world. Tell me I did *not* let my people down.'

'You didn't let your people down. But I can't tell you things were much better.'

'You could have consoled me with a white lie, Doctor.'

The Doctor hesitated, trying to find some crumb of consolation in what he had to report. 'What the Master and I witnessed in the future is just one time stream. Our travelling back will almost certainly shift events onto a different one. That's what you hoped for, isn't it? To alter history from this point on?'

'We *had* a history, Doctor. A past and the hope of a future. The Sild destroyed all that. Now we'd like it back again.' The Red Queen outstretched her hand. 'May I see the ring? It's not that I doubt you.'

'Of course not.'

The Doctor passed the ring to the queen. She held it up to her eye, examining it carefully, its ruby light pulsating and wavering as if the fire in it had been quickened. 'Astonishing to think this thing was touched by myself, ten million years from now.' She looked at him marvellingly. 'You are a time traveller. You must be used to this sort of thing.'

'The day time travel stops astonishing you,' the Doctor said, 'is generally the day something ghastly goes wrong.'

The queen stretched out the ring finger of her ungloved hand. She was already wearing what appeared to be a duplicate of the ring containing the bound-tachyon pair. She slipped the new ring onto the same finger, and worked it up the length of the wrinkled, bony digit until it was in the contact with the first. She pressed them together, and the rings blurred and merged, the ruby glow intensifying and then settling down to its former brightness.

'I did not doubt your word, Doctor. But it is as well to be certain of these things.'

'I agree wholeheartedly.'

'And your associate – the Master? He presents himself willingly? I'm surprised not to see him in shackles.'

The Master, unbidden, ascended the steps to stand next to the Doctor. 'The Sild have made an enemy of me, your Majesty. But I confess there is another reason for my apparent submission.'

'Go on.'

'I have need of urgent medical intervention. I have been touched by the Sild.'

'Then you are fortunate to be alive.'

'The contact was brief, and I am a Time Lord. Nonetheless, my mental fortitude is not limitless.'

'You would seek my help.'

'I was told you had some experience in this matter.' The Master spoke carefully. 'Mention was made of an Infinite Cocoon.'

After a long interval the queen said: 'It is true. We have such a machine, although we scarcely understand all that it is capable of. Even so, in the most extreme cases, it has saved the lives of Praxilion citizens who were touched by the Sild. But all paid a price! Most we tried to save did not survive their time in the Infinite Cocoon. They came out changed. Sometimes horribly.'

'I am willing to take my chances.'

'And then what? If you survive the machine, you will accept to be handed over to the Sild?'

'I must confront them eventually, whatever happens.

Now is as good a time as ever.'

'Wait,' the Doctor said, raising his hand. 'I have done what was demanded of me, by bringing him back to this time. But I will not be party to an injustice! The Master has committed great crimes, it's true. But he should answer to the Time Lords, not the Sild!'

'I am afraid, Doctor,' the Master stated, 'it is rather late in the day for qualms.'

The Red Queen called to her aides. 'Prepare the Infinite Cocoon!'

Chapter Twenty-Nine

Jo, Yates and Eddie McCrimmon went back into the rig, fighting every rational human impulse to get as far away from it as possible. Yates kept trying the detonator, trying to get a signal through, but so far there was too much interference. Jo wondered how much time they had left. Mike Oscar Six was burning, at risk of explosion or runaway inferno at any moment; it was also undergoing a slow but steady structural failure, which might at any second result in it collapsing back into the sea. There was the very real possibility, too, that elements of the Sild were still present, lurking in shadows and corners. No sane person would rather have been down in these hot corridors than up in one of the UNIT helicopters, Jo thought.

'You seem to be taking this in your stride,' Eddie said to Jo, when they were passing through a recreation area, set with rows of orange seats before a blank white projection screen. 'Rigs disappearing into thin air, robot crabs taking over people... You're acting like it's all in a day's work.'

'That's not far off the truth,' Jo said.

'When you first came to see me, you had a feeling something more was going on.'

'Let's just say that this isn't the first time UNIT has dealt with some pretty strange stuff.'

'And this friend of yours – the Doctor? Where does he fit into things?'

'He doesn't, really. The Doctor's the ultimate square peg.'

'The third man – the one with Callow and Lovelace – he knew your friend, didn't he?'

'They go back a bit.'

'The third man said they were at school.'

'They were, I think. But when we say "school"... that's where it gets complicated.'

'Is the Doctor all right?'

'I don't know.' Jo had to swallow hard. 'He left us. Took off in the... that's what we're hoping, anyway. He might be trying to fix things at his end.'

'His end?'

'There's this thing he can do. It's a bit difficult to accept, unless you know him.'

'Thing?'

'He travels.'

'And have you ever... gone with him?'

'Once or twice.'

'When I was a little girl,' Eddie said after a long silence, 'I had these books. Ten of them. They were blank to start with. I filled them up with stories about this woman, this queen, who lived on another planet. I had a big biscuit tin of felt-tips, all the colours you could get. That was where I got the name of the queen from, from the words on the side of the tin: Luxury Shortbread Biscuit Assortment. Her Imperial Majesty Uxury Scuita! She was in charge of this kingdom, full of talking animals... I did all the stories, drew pictures and made up facts and stuff about the queen's world. How the money worked, how the magic operated, what kind of clothes the queen wore, the customs... I lived in that world, Jo. I was *on* another planet. But only in my head.'

'That's also a kind of travel.'

'It was, I suppose. Then one day – actually it was on my 12th birthday – my dad found the books and threw them in

284

the bin. I was doing badly at school and he thought they were a distraction, that I was spending too much time off in my imagination. When I should have been knuckling down.'

Yates, who had not spoken for some time, said: 'Looks like they were wrong to doubt you, Miss McCrimmon.'

'I never forgave my dad. I only saved one of the books, the one that was under my pillow. I hadn't filled more than half of it. But the others were gone for good. And now I can't even remember anything that was in them. Just childish nonsense, I suppose. What's it like, Jo? To travel? To really travel?'

'Fun,' Jo said. 'Most of the time.'

Eddie coughed something from her voice. 'How's that transmitter, Captain? The MERMAN gear is two floors right under us. If you can't get a signal here, we'll need to go through C section, which'll take us close to that fire we saw on the way up.'

'Signal's still flaky, but better than it was. If it doesn't work here we're stuffed anyway. Right below us, you say? I'm not sure I like the idea of blowing charges under my feet!'

'The floor should hold,' Eddie said. 'Provided it hasn't been compromised by fire or structural damage elsewhere.'

Jo couldn't help laughing. 'That's not much of a guarantee!'

'About as good as you're going to get. I wouldn't want to risk being much closer, Captain – we'll start narrowing down our options for escape, and that helicopter of yours isn't going to be able to hang around for ever.'

'I agree,' Yates said. He knelt, setting the transmitter box on the ground. 'Things might get a bit wobbly, so make sure you're ready.' He flipped back the safety cover on the detonating switch. 'Firing in three... two... one...'

He flicked the switch.

Jo held her breath, counted to three in her head. That was more than enough time.

'Nothing,' she said.

'Wait,' Yates said. 'I'll try again.'

But a second and a third attempt proved no more

successful than the first. 'Too much interference, assuming the receiver hasn't been tampered with. We'll need to get closer.'

'Mike, look out!'

Jo had seen it first: a door easing open in the wall along one side of the recreation room, a figure coming out of a small office or pantry beyond the door. It was a bearded man, an oil worker, wearing an orange one-piece boiler suit and a white safety helmet. Jo recognised the man: he had been the first person to speak to them when they first came to the rig.

'Tom?' Eddie said, questioningly. 'How are you... I thought you were dead!'

'He was!' Yates said, looking up from the transmitter. 'I stepped over his body!'

'But the Sild... you said they'd left them. Tom – are you all right?'

'He's not all right,' Jo said.

The man called Tom was pulling something out of the pocket of his boiler suit. Jo's world seemed to slow down. Even the UNIT soldiers had not seemed to give any thought to the possibility that the hosts on the platform might have weapons of their own. The Sild could only make use of what they found, and why would there be guns on an oil rig?

Tom pulled a heavy-looking thing from his pocket. He took it in both hands and aimed it at Mike Yates.

It looked awfully like a gun.

'Flare pistol!' Eddie McCrimmon said. 'Get down! He's going to shoot!'

Yates was fast, but not quite fast enough. Tom fired the flare pistol straight at him. The gun cracked, the flare rocketing into Yates, clipping him on the side of the head, sending him tumbling away from the transmitter. The flare continued, ricocheting off a wall, rocketing back. Yates's head hit the floor with a jolt. The flare whooshed.

Eddie McCrimmon snatched up Yates's automatic, gripped it double-handed, echoing Tom's stance, and fired one bullet after another into the huge man. At the fourth or fifth discharge, a silver thing detached itself from the back of his neck, fell to the ground and began to scuttle toward the open door. Eddie lowered the automatic and blasted it. The Sild twitched and was still.

Eddie went over to the shattered thing.

'There's something still alive in it,' she said. 'Squirming around in there.'

'That's the alien itself,' Jo said, kneeling down next to Mike Yates.

'It looks totally harmless. Like a little wee seahorse or something. Almost pretty.'

Eddie laid down the heel of her shoe and moved it back and forth, putting her weight into it. Jo heard a glassy crunch.

'I'm sorry about that man,' Jo said. 'I liked him, when we met. You mustn't blame him for what happened.'

'I don't,' Eddie said.

Jo returned her attention to Yates. 'Mike's hurt,' she said. 'The flare nearly hit him face-on. There's a bad cut on the side of his head. Mike, can you hear me?'

Yates had been knocked out for a few seconds. He was coming around now, but remained groggy.

'Jo,' he said.

'You've had a nasty knock, and you're losing blood. Hold on.' Jo dug into her pocket for her handkerchief and pressed it hard against the wound in the side of Yates's head. The gash was as long as her finger, and deep enough to be almost to the bone. It could have been much more serious, of course, but Yates was clearly in no condition to continue.

'Where are we?'

'In the platform. We were trying to let off the charges. Do you remember that much?'

Yates was having trouble opening his eyes. 'Where's Benton and the Brig?'

'Benton's on the helicopter, waiting for us, and the Brig is a few hundred miles away.'

'Your man's in a spot of bother,' Eddie said. 'Could be some internal bleeding there, apart from the visible wound. You'd better get him back to the top – he's a good couple of hours from the nearest hospital. Think you can manage him, Jo?'

'I don't know... between us, maybe.'

'You'll have to cope on your own. One of us still has to blow up those charges. I'm going into C section. If it doesn't work, I'll come straight back.'

'I don't know—' Jo started.

'No arguing – your top priority is to get the Captain off the rig.'

'How are you going to get off, if you get stuck down there?'

'There's a lifeboat left, and I can easily reach it from C section.'

'And release it?' Jo asked.

'Been over it about a thousand times. Wee bit of a bump when you hit the water, but it's a lot better than drowning. Once I'm down, I'll just sit tight until someone can come and rescue me.'

'Might be a little while, with everyone tied up.'

'It'll only be me, so there'll be no problem making the emergency rations and water last.'

'Tell me what to do, I'll do it,' Yates said groggily.

'Aye, and you've had all the training about how to launch a lifeboat, have you? No, didn't think so.'

'This is a military oper...' Yates began, then trailed off, like a drunk man who had lost the thread of his thought.

Eddie hefted the transmitter box, no more impressed than if it contained a new pair of shoes. 'Looks like a pretty simple piece of kit.'

'Here,' Jo said. 'Take my walkie-talkie. I've still got Mike's. It's set for the right channel.'

Eddie took the walkie-talkie – it was clear she knew her way around one from the nonchalant manner in which she slipped it into her coat pocket. 'You'd best be on your way. Watch your back on the way out.'

'And yours,' Jo said.

'You know,' Eddie said, 'the next time you hear me complaining about not wanting a boring desk job on the mainland, do tell me to shut up.'

They were airborne, travelling in a saucer-shaped golden flier. In outline and proportions it was similar to the queen's own spacecraft, almost as if copied from that machine, although several times larger. They had passed through the force-field bubble protecting the capital city and were now travelling unprotected, save for the defensive shield generated by the craft itself. A landscape streaked below – mostly parched, but with the occasional dwindling lake or sea as evidence of better times. Above, the sky was a deep blue, streaked with the white cottontails of high altitude clouds. There was atmosphere here now, instead of the vacuum of ten million years ahead.

'The *Consolidator* – is it up there now?' the Doctor asked.

'In orbit, as it has been for two million years,' the Red Queen said, her throne now inside the flier, guarded by a small detachment of Praxilions. 'Under Sild occupation, the fulcrum of their control of time. Our weapons are quite impotent against it.'

'Never mind your weapons,' the Master said. 'I'm surprised the Sild allow you to move around at all. Why aren't we being shot at?'

'We're of little concern to them,' the queen answered. 'Occasionally, just to remind us of their power, they will strike against us – that's why we have force fields. But mostly we pose no threat to their ambitions. They also need the material resources of our planet – its air and water – so they cannot use heavy weapons against us, for fear of incinerating the very things they crave. More than that, my people are useful to them. I'm sure you are both familiar with Sild invasive methods?'

DOCTOR WHO

'We've learned a thing or two,' the Doctor said. He was standing, surveying the view through the flier's wide sweep of a window, while the Master sat on one of the human-compatible seats that had evidently been provided for their benefit.

'If the Sild can,' the queen went on, 'they would rather control a population than destroy it. It gives them an army or labour force, or both, depending on their needs. Obviously, we have resisted. But periodically Sild forces manage to capture Praxilions, sometimes in great numbers. They become Sild hosts, helping to run their machines.'

'To what end?' the Master enquired.

'Before we get to that,' the Doctor interrupted, 'it might help if we knew a thing or two about how the Sild arrived around this planet in the first place. And while we're at it, I might ask the same thing of you, your Majesty.'

'What did my counterpart have to say?'

'Very little, I'm afraid. But then again it *had* been ten million years.'

'Do not expect me to much more forthcoming. I've already been here for two million years.'

'But not conscious for all that time,' the Master said.

'No – I would be mad if that were the case. But I have lived a long life, all the same. I came to this world… you saw my vehicle, I presume?'

'I'd like a closer look at it,' the Doctor said, something stirring at the back of his mind again. 'But it looked like a very small ship to me – a scout or shuttle, from a larger mother vessel.'

'Yes, that was my conclusion. And there are times when I swear I can almost remember a mother vessel. It was a huge craft, like a city – a ship with hundreds of people on it, all busy, all doing something important. *My* people, then. But something was wrong with the mother vessel – it was under attack. There was a monster… I managed to escape in the pod. That's what I called it, I think. After that, I can't be

290

certain. But somehow I ended up on Praxilion.'

'Before or after the coming of the Sild?'

'Long before, Master. There were no Sild then, and no *Consolidator* in orbit around Praxilion. There was just this world and its people. It was a beautiful planet, with great shimmering oceans, lush forests and lovely powder-blue skies. Its people lived simple lives, in peace and harmony with both themselves and their world.' As she uttered these words, the flier skimmed low over the ruins of a city, blasted into a series of cratered outlines, like a blueprint for itself.

The Master smiled. 'So where did it all go right?'

'When I arrived, they treated me as a god, even though I was very different to them. It took me a while to understand why. The Praxilion society was a very old one. It had been through a technological golden age, perhaps more than one, then collapsed back to peaceful agrarianism. But the people remembered. Their world was littered with ancient technologies they were now too fearful to use again. And in their oldest records they carried some dim recollection of the galaxy's history, right back to the EMTT. Their knowledge was muddled. But they remembered enough to understand that there had been a time when humanoids like me wielded immense political and economic power. Rightly or wrongly, they saw me as the key to returning Praxilion to its former magnificence.'

'I assume you refused?' the Doctor asked sharply.

'I wanted to help them.'

'You were meddling with fire!'

'You'll have to excuse my associate,' the Master said. 'He has this strange notion that it is perfectly acceptable for him to tamper in the affairs of other cultures, but utterly wrong for anyone else to do so. It's the worst kind of moral arrogance.'

'I don't need a lecture,' the Red Queen said. 'I know that I set these people on a path to catastrophe. But I *meant* well.' She turned away as one of her Praxilion aides scuttled alongside her throne to whisper something. 'You may find this interesting, gentlemen. The Sild have opened one of their atmospheric suction portals within the last few minutes. We're about to skirt its margins. I'll take us in as close as it's safe to go.'

The Master extended his hand. 'Doctor – might I beg your assistance?'

The Doctor helped the Master to rise. The two of them stood next to each other before the flier's window.

'There,' the queen said sharply. 'At eight o' clock. Do you see it?'

The Doctor squinted. There was something up there, a whorl-like tightening of the clouds, like the eye of a storm. It was all purple and white spirals, whipping around at astonishing speed. A whirlpool in the sky.

No, he corrected. Not a whirlpool. A *mouth*. A ghastly swallowing mouth, gorging itself on what remained of Praxilion's atmosphere.

CHAPTER THIRTY

Jo and Yates staggered out onto the open deck of Mike Oscar Six. Yates was only just capable of walking, and for much of the time had to rely on Jo for balance and direction. It did not help that the angle of the rig was tilting ever more steeply away from vertical, meaning that even Jo was finding it hard to maintain her orientation. With some regularity now, booms and crashes signalled the platform's on-going structural failure. Each lurch brought a moment of heart-stopping terror, as if it might be the last. Clearly there was not long to go.

The helipad was empty, but Jo had expected that. With all the smoke billowing up from the rig's sides, she couldn't see Benton's helicopter at all.

Resting at the base of the helipad, she used their walkie-talkie. 'Windmill 635, come in. We're in position.'

She had to strain to hear the answer. 'Benton here. We haven't seen the blast!'

'Eddie's still getting into place – she's got the transmitter.'

'What about the Captain?'

'Mike's hurt – we need to get him off the rig immediately.'

'Roger. We're descending. Keep your head down!'

To Jo's intense relief the helicopter nosed cautiously through the smoke, then started lowering back down to the pad. Though much of the rig's superstructure had collapsed, there were still many obstacles that the pilots had to avoid. Jo could only admire their skill and courage in returning under such conditions.

The helicopter touched its skids to the ground, but kept nearly full power on the rotors. Benton slid open the door, hopped out and helped get Yates aboard.

'What happened?'

'Flare pistol!' Jo said. 'Probably worse than it looks. But we couldn't get the charges to blow.'

'And Miss McCrimmon? Is she going to come back this way?'

'I hope so. Can we still hover for a bit?'

'Couple of minutes, and then you're pushing your luck.'

Jo and Benton squeezed back into the helicopter. They pulled off the pad, then slid sideways, through the curtain of smoke. It was only when she saw it from the outside that she appreciated what a perilous state the platform was now in. It was teetering like a bar-stool with unequal legs, threatening to topple into the sea at the slightest provocation. Flames were curtaining out of the superstructure at a dozen locations. Large parts of the rig were already burned out, reduced to edifices of black char. Jo thought of Eddie still somewhere inside all that, and wondered why she had ever allowed herself to be persuaded that splitting up was a sensible idea.

'Oh, Eddie – you didn't have to do this...'

Her walkie-talkie squawked. She lifted it to her ear. 'Jo?' came the voice.

Jo had to shout over the noise of the rotor. 'Are you all right?'

'Yes! I'm in C section – ready to detonate! Thought I should let you know. With all the crashing and banging going on in here, I'm not sure I'll ever be able to tell if the charges blow!'

'We're in the air,' Jo said. 'We should be able to see something.'

'Well, here goes.'

Jo waited a second. Nothing happened. She was starting to think that even this attempt had gone wrong, that perhaps the receiver and charges had failed, when a fireball blew out from the nearest side of the rig. The explosion was huge – much larger than she had been expecting. When the blast had cleared, she could see right through the walls, into a cross-section of floors and walls and rooms. New flames were already beginning to spread, anxious to consume.

'Eddie?'

'I'm here! That was a bang and a half! I felt the whole rig shudder!'

'It's probably not helped matters! You'd better get back up to the pad as quickly as you can. We're not far off!'

'Get yourselves clear, just in case the whole place blows up. I'm not going to risk going back through C, it's too dicey. I'm not far from the lifeboat station now. Can you see it?'

'Not yet,' Jo said.

'Fly around until you can. It'll be good to have visual confirmation that it's still there. You can't miss it, big red saucer-shaped thing.'

Jo gesticulated to Benton, who in turn relayed commands to the pilots. The helicopter circled slowly around the rig, until the next face of the platform came into view.

'Got it, Eddie. It's still there. Can you get to it easily?'

'Nearly there!'

Jo watched the lifeboat, hanging on the rig like the last red apple on a tree, willing it to drop.

'Remarkable,' the Master said. 'By my estimation, the width of that portal must be in the order of 500 metres!'

'At least,' the queen said. 'It's transient, of course – they only open for a few seconds or minutes at best. But the fact that they can do that at all…'

'It speaks of impressive temporal control,' the Master said.

'Even more so when you know how far back into the past that portal extends.'

'Billions of years,' the Doctor said. 'Back to a small blue planet I happen to know very well. The Sild are draining the air from Praxilion and feeding it back to Earth: thickening it up in readiness for their full-scale invasion through time!'

'Not just the air,' the queen said. 'Our oceans, too. For every suction portal they open in the sky, there's been another in our seas. You've seen what's left of them. Before very long, they'll have been drained away completely. Praxilion will be as dry and airless as an asteroid.'

'I'm afraid you're correct,' the Doctor said.

'The fault is mine. If I had not arrived on this world, the Praxilions would still be living in peace, with all they need.'

'You showed them how to use the old technologies?' the Master asked.

'Yes, although I barely understood them myself. But I gave the Praxilions the courage to try, to relearn the old secrets for themselves. That was really all they needed. Guidance. A shove in the right direction. Before very long they were on the way to a full-scale industrial revolution.'

The flier was accelerating away from the suction portal. As they watched, the swallowing mouth snapped abruptly shut. Where it had been, the sky was still wrinkled with knots of furious cloud, flickering with lightning discharges.

'They'll open another soon enough,' the queen said. 'And another. Their control has been improving all the while. But still they want to do more than this.'

'And the *Consolidator*,' the Master asked. 'It just… arrived?'

'Found its way to us. It was very old, as we later learned, and it had been wandering the galaxy for an unimaginable length of time, its creators dead, its ultimate purpose forgotten. I think it was lonely. Or possibly a little insane. Whatever the case, our industrial activity must have drawn the ship's attention. We altered the chemistry of our atmosphere, warmed our world – unmistakeable indicators of intelligent activity. The *Consolidator* sought out Praxilion and fell into orbit around our world.'

'With, one assumed, the Sild aboard,' the Doctor said.

'Yes, but we didn't know that at the time. In fact we didn't wake the Sild until centuries after our first exploration of the *Consolidator*. To begin with, we could only find our way into small areas of the ship. It was huge, like exploring a lost continent. But even in those first few years, what we found was enough to change Praxilion out of all recognition. New technologies, new materials… the life-extension equipment was one of our early finds. Fortunate for me, or I'd never have lived to see what came after – I was already old when the ship came.' The queen qualified herself. 'If you can call that *fortunate*…'

'Stasis alone cannot account for your age,' the Doctor said, thinking of the creature he had met at the end of time.

'No, it's true. There were also therapies – drugs, regimens, strange machines. They held death at bay, even reversed its progression, for a little while. But always *time* would find a way to win.'

'It has a habit of doing that,' the Doctor said. 'I suppose you never took a chance with the Infinite Cocoon?'

'I was never that courageous, Doctor. I have seen what it can do.'

'Tell us of the Sild,' the Master said, with a note of irritation. Perhaps he did not care to be reminded of the hazards that awaited him in the Infinite Cocoon.

'It was six thousand years before we found our way into that part of the *Consolidator*. Six thousand years! Of course I saw only a fraction of it. The Praxilions woke me only when they needed my counsel…' The Red Queen faltered in her account. 'But the error was mine. I should never have advised them as I did. I should have seen that it was a trap.'

'A trap?' the Master asked.

'We sent two explorers into that part of the *Consolidator*. Their names were Hox and Loi. They were very brave: both had accepted to be altered by the Infinite Cocoon, so that they might pass as humanoid. Many volunteers preceded them, but they were… less fortunate. They either died or had to be euthanised.'

'Why did you have to put them through that?'

'The *Consolidator* was built by humanoids, Doctor. There were parts of the ship where only a humanoid could safely pass. So the Praxilions had to become humanoid.'

'And you didn't think of volunteering yourself?' the Master asked.

'I was too frail. Believe me, I would have done anything to spare the world another of those screaming abominations created by the Infinite Cocoon.'

'And what became of Hox and Loi?' the Doctor enquired.

'They were not looking for the Sild. They didn't even know about the Sild. They were looking for the secret of time travel: the means to reconnect Praxilion with the glory of the past.'

'Various forms of time manipulation,' the Master mused, 'would certainly have been among the restricted secrets placed aboard the *Consolidator*.'

'Placed there for a good reason!' the Doctor said vehemently. 'Some of those time-travel techniques are extremely dangerous!'

'You were masters of time,' the Red Queen said. 'You had that capability. Why should we not have it as well?'

'A fair observation,' the Master said, with a supercilious smile.

'It scarcely matters now. Hox and Loi failed. They were tricked into releasing one of the Sild, in return for information about the time apparatus. Hox was taken over – became the first Sild host. Loi managed to survive long enough to get word to us. But by then it was too late. With Hox under their control, the Sild were able to release the rest of their kind. It was the beginning of the end. They were free, and they had ready access to all the deadly technologies aboard the *Consolidator*. Including rudimentary time travel.'

'Rudimentary enough to delve back into time and scoop

incarnations of the Master out of history,' the Doctor said. 'But that was only the beginning!'

'With the Assemblage, there was no limit to their power,' the Red Queen said. 'The Master's intellect gave them ultimate control of time!'

'I have always chosen my enemies well,' the Master said, as if this was something to be proud of.

'You made it easy for them. From your prison in the past, you injected a distress message into time. You imprinted your own psychokinetic signature on the transmission, like a fingerprint, so that your authenticity would not be in doubt. But you made a terrible mistake! When those signals interacted with other versions of you, the psychokinetic imprinting set up resonances – ripples on the psychic sea. Flares in the night! That was enough for the Sild to lock on to your counterparts – all your other incarnations, strewn through space and time. They could begin their harvest! They could begin unstitching you from history, as if you had never existed!'

'They failed to capture *me*.'

'They did, eventually,' the Doctor said. 'We saw your counterpart, aboard the derelict. The Sild triumphed!'

'They always triumph,' the Red Queen said. 'But at the present moment, here and now, they do not yet possess your current incarnation. And they need it, to make the Assemblage function at its maximum effectiveness!'

'They won't cut you a deal, you know,' the Doctor said. 'They'll take the Master and still turn Praxilion into an airless, waterless husk – only faster than before! That's how they operate!'

'When you only have one bargaining chip, you had better make the best of it,' said the Red Queen. 'The Master is the only thing I have that they want.' She paused. 'Once upon a time I used to think that running a planet would be easy. But it isn't, you know. Not at all. It's the hardest thing imaginable.'

*

Jo clenched her fist in delight as the lifeboat dropped from the side of the rig. Her emotions were so heightened that time seemed to slow, the lifeboat taking an agonisingly long time to fight its way down through the air, through the smoke and the flames licking from the platform's lowest levels, toward the surging grey waves below. Eddie was all right, though. That was all that mattered.

There was a crackle from the walkie-talkie, something garbled coming through.

'Eddie!' Jo said excitedly. 'We can see you – you made it!'

Her reply was crackly but audible. 'That was a bump and a half! They make us use these things in training, but I'd forgotten how far down it is!'

'Are you all right?'

'Aye, I think so. Boat's watertight, I've a few bruises but nothing that won't mend.'

'Pilot says we've got to leave!' Benton said. 'But there'll be search and rescue people out here as soon as possible.'

'Did you get that, Eddie? You shouldn't have to put up with it for long.'

'Don't worry about me. I'm clear of the rig now and I've got rations and water to last a good couple of days. Probably a nice drinks bar somewhere here if I look hard enough. If you *could* speed up things a bit, that would be great.'

'It's not going to take days,' Jo said.

'You think it made a difference, that big bang?' Eddie asked.

'We're just going to have to wait and see,' Jo said.

Benton grinned. 'You're starting to sound like the Doctor!'

'One of us— wait.' Jo was looking at the sea with ominous expectation. The lifeboat was bobbing up and down, being carried away from the platform by the swell. But something was opening up in the water next to it. A growing absence, walls of water being pushed apart by an invisible barrier, defining a hemispherical void in the sea itself.

'It's a rupture!' Benton shouted. 'The Sild are still coming through!'

'No,' Jo said, disbelieving. 'Not now. Not here! Eddie – can you hear me?

'What's the matter?'

'Can you… *steer* that lifeboat?'

'Oh, sure – I'll just open one of the windows and use this little plastic cup as an oar. No, it's a lifeboat. Um – is there a problem?'

'There's a time rupture right next to you.'

The void was growing, its circular edge expanding to meet the tiny red disk of the lifeboat.

'I can't see it. But there's a heck of a swell here, feels like I'm going over the top of a rollercoaster—'

'She's going in! Get us down!' Benton said. 'Maybe we can get the winch on—'

'It's too late,' Jo said. 'Eddie!'

And it was. The rupture appeared to have reached its maximum aperture, holding back a circular cliff of sea. Over the sharp lip of this aperture, the lifeboat toppled and fell. They watched it tumble. The rupture began to collapse. In an eye-blink, the lifeboat was simply gone. It had not vanished under the waters. It had ceased to be.

The walkie-talkie had gone dead. Jo squeezed the talk switch a couple of times. 'Eddie? Can you hear me? Eddie?'

But there was no answer.

CHAPTER THIRTY-ONE

'No greater evil has ever existed,' the Red Queen declared. 'But we have never had the courage to destroy it, as we should have done. Perhaps it would never have allowed us, even if we'd tried.'

'You could have locked it away,' the Doctor said. 'Buried it underground, or something.'

'No, it was always too useful for that. When it wasn't making monsters. We never had the strength of will to place it beyond all use.'

The Infinite Cocoon was smaller than the Doctor had been expecting. He had read of it before, seen reconstructions, life-sized holograms. But his memory had tricked him. The marbled grey machine was only just large enough to take a human form, lying down inside it. A large creature, such as an Ice Warrior or Judoon, would never have fitted within. So it was not Infinite at all, but in fact rather depressingly finite in its potential. Just another piece of over-inflated advertising, in other words. The universe was full of things like that.

The Master pecked at the control panel, jutting from one end of the machine. 'Simple enough, Doctor, I think you'll agree. I recognise most of these pictograms from our schooldays, and the meaning of the rest is easily inferred. Linear C, with some digression into the D and E variants.'

'We never understood more than a fraction of the controls,' the Red Queen said.

'Then it's no wonder you were in the habit of making monsters,' the Master said.

'Don't underestimate it,' the Doctor said warningly. 'The Praxilions weren't fools.'

'Fortunately, neither are we.' The Master was quickening the pace of his inputs. He had started with just his index fingers, hunting and pecking like a novice typist, but had now progressed to all five fingers of both hands. The keypad clattered. Patterns of illuminations surged and ebbed across the control matrix. The Infinite Cocoon hummed and gurgled in eager anticipation of its next guest.

'I hope you know what you're doing.'

'It's my brain, Doctor. I trust you'll accept that I am the one best placed to repair it?'

'He's already entered a far more complex stream of instructions than any of my technicians,' the Red Queen said.

'The damage done by the Sild is not trivial,' the Master said, pausing to look up from the panel.

'Can I help?' the Doctor asked.

'You will help by arranging my delivery to the Sild. When I emerge from the Cocoon, I expect to experience a degree of functional impairment.'

'Let's hope they don't mind damaged goods.'

'I assure you that the damage will be temporary, Doctor. Now if you would both allow me to complete my work?'

In fact it did not take the Master very long to complete the entry of his string of commands. He stepped back from the console, appraised it guardedly, then nodded. 'I am done. The Cocoon is prepared. There is no sense in delaying matters.'

'I wish there were another way,' the Doctor said.

'I will die unless I submit to the Cocoon.'

'Perhaps that would be better than becoming part of the Assemblage.'

'You might make that fatalistic choice, Doctor. Please leave me to make mine.'

'Of course.'

The lid of the Infinite Cocoon slid off to one side, until it was supported along one long edge. Yellow light spilled from the machine's interior. The Master braced two hands along the open side, ready to climb in. 'The process will begin automatically, once I am inside. There will be no need for outside intervention.'

'Nonetheless,' the Red Queen said, 'my technicians are standing by.'

'Tell them not to touch a thing.' The Master made to climb over the lip, but at the last moment his strength seemed to escape him. The Doctor moved to his side and gave support. 'Good luck,' he said.

'Sincerely meant, Doctor?'

'Of course.'

'Then I take it in the spirit with which it was intended.'

The Doctor helped the Master into the box. The Master settled himself inside it, arms crossed over his chest. The lid began to close on him.

The Doctor stepped back. He had glanced at the control matrix and recognised the form and meaning of many of the symbols. But the Master's knowledge of such matters was superlative. The Doctor knew that he would be powerless to offer much assistance if the process began to go wrong.

The lid shut tight. The machine increased its humming and gurgling. It rocked slightly.

'When my people submitted to the Cocoon,' the Red Queen said, 'we were always ready for the worst. We had a retinue of guards on hand ready to kill the thing inside.'

'Hopefully that won't be necessary. The Master isn't trying to turn himself into a completely different form, just repair damage done to his existing body. That should offer less scope for error.'

'You hope he comes through, don't you?'

'Why shouldn't I?'

'You and he are hardly allies. I've learned that much.'

'You need him alive at the end of this, to hand over to the Sild. Of course I don't want him to die.'

The machine continued its gurgling work. Patterns played across the input console. The Doctor could only assume that matters were proceeding according to the Master's intentions.

But what now remained of the Master, he wondered? The Cocoon might not be turning him into a completely different form, but to access the deep structures of his brain it must still be dissolving him down to a more basic level. The Doctor imagined a soup with the half-formed shape of a man floating in it, a kind of gooey homunculus. His greatest adversary, reduced to a kind of living stew. The Infinite Cocoon was formidable and ancient technology, but it was surely not invulnerable. If he sabotaged it now, or just entered a random string of commands, that might be the end of the Master.

Or the creation of something worse?

'It will be a little while, if I'm not mistaken,' the Red Queen said.

'Good. There's something I've been meaning to ask you, and now's as good a time as any.'

'Go ahead, Doctor.'

'Two things, actually. My taking the Master to the *Consolidator* is your last best hope for the survival of this planet, wouldn't you agree? If the Sild don't agree to spare the survivors, it will all have been for nothing.'

'Your point being?'

'Now may be your only chance to strike back at the Sild. They will be expecting me to arrive with the Master, so their defences will be lowered. I could also carry the Axumillary Orb.'

'How could you know of such a thing?'

'Because I saw it being used.'

'There is only one Axumillary Orb, Doctor, and I assure you it has never been used.'

306

'But it will be,' the Doctor said. 'In the future, you succeeded in smuggling it aboard the ship. You used it to destroy the *Consolidator*, along with the Master's final surviving incarnations. But this is an earlier timeframe. The Axumillary Orb still exists – it has yet to be taken aboard the ship, let alone detonated. I know. You're holding it in your ungloved hand. It's the sphere on the end of your sceptre. It wasn't there when I met your future self.'

'You are very perspicacious, Doctor.'

'I've been called worse. I take it I'm right, though?'

'Of course. Why pretend otherwise? And yes, I have often wished I could find a way to bring the reactivated device aboard the *Consolidator*. You say I succeed?'

'Yes, but by then it's too late to save Praxilion. But now it isn't!'

'I will consider it. Why did you wait until now, before discussing this matter?'

'Because I'd rather the Master didn't know I was prepared to blow him and me into the middle of next week.'

'You would be ready to make that sacrifice, Doctor?'

'If there was no other choice.'

The Red Queen nodded sagely. 'I have met many brave individuals in my time, and many that consider themselves brave, until the moment of testing. I believe I have learned enough to know the difference by now.'

'None of us really know, until the time comes.'

'But the time has come for you, over and over. I see it in your eyes.' The Red Queen clutched the Axumillary Orb and unscrewed if from the rod. 'If there is a way to trigger it remotely, I'm afraid my technicians haven't yet figured it out. I'm afraid it can only be detonated manually, by twisting the two parallel rings until they line up. You'd have a few seconds, no more, before the device activates.'

'It's a shame we don't know the remote trigger. I wish I'd asked yourself when I had the chance.'

'Too bad, Doctor. Catch!'

She tossed him the Axumillary Orb. The Doctor caught it deftly, hefted the dense metal sphere, then slipped it into his pocket. 'Thank you, your Majesty. I sincerely hope I don't have to put it to good use.'

'I'm sure you'll do your best. And the other thing?'

For a moment the Doctor's absentmindedness had the better of him. 'The other thing?'

'You said there were two things you wanted to ask, Doctor. The Master is still… preoccupied. Now's your chance.'

'Ah, yes. Well, it was about your ship, actually – the one you came in on. Would you mind awfully if I took a closer look at it?'

'There's nothing to be learned from it, I'm afraid. My technicians have searched every inch of the thing, from top to bottom. There's no visible means of propulsion, no obvious control or navigation systems. They must be incorporated into the basic form of the vehicle at an extremely high level of integration.'

'Or not there at all,' the Doctor said.

'Why do you say that?'

'Because I don't believe that saucer is a spacecraft at all, your Majesty. The reason you haven't found any control systems is that none are present.'

'Preposterous if you don't mind my saying so. How did I fly my ship to Praxilion?'

'You didn't. You simply tumbled through a rupture in time, out of control. Your ship was not a ship at all.'

'What was it then?'

'A simple escape pod, an airtight metal shell with just enough integrity to cope with passage through time.'

'And what brings you to this shattering conclusion?'

'Because I've seen your ship before, your Majesty. Or something very like it, on the side of an oil platform. It's a lifeboat, designed to be dropped into the sea. The saucer shape is simply the most efficient form for an airtight vessel, designed to weather the worst storms.'

'You are making very little sense, Doctor.'

'That's because you've forgotten who you are and where you came from. I don't blame you; it was a long time ago after all. But somehow you were caught up in the Sild time ruptures, sucked through eternity, across an immensity of space and time.'

'I arrived on this world long before we woke the Sild. How can I have *caused* my own arrival?'

'Very easily, I'm afraid – just as the Master and I overshot, you *under*shot.'

'This is absurd.'

'But true. You came from the twentieth century, your Majesty. You were caught up in the Sild time disturbances happening in the North Sea, and hurled into this future. How, I don't know – you probably didn't intend this to happen. But I do know that we've already met.'

'In my future. Yes, we know. It's how you knew about the Axumillary Orb.'

'Also in your past. Hold up your hand, your Majesty – the one you keep in the glove.'

'Why?'

'Because I want to see if I can spot the missing fingers.'

'How could you…'

'Your name, your *real* name, is Edwina McCrimmon. You lost two fingers in an industrial accident, proving your mettle in the oil industry.'

'How dare…'

'The name means something, doesn't it? You haven't heard it for millions of years. Who would know it, here on Praxilion? But it's your name. You know it. You *own* it.'

The Infinite Cocoon stopped gurgling. It was still now. The dance of lights on the control matrix had ceased. The lid began to slide off to one side, a bar of yellow light ramming up from the interior.

The Doctor dashed to the side and looked into the machine with supreme apprehension.

But it was as if nothing had happened. The Master was still there, lying on his back, arms folded across his chest. His clothes were as immaculate as when he had entered. His eyes were closed. He almost looked serene.

'Well?'

'He's breathing.' The Doctor leaned down, stationed an ear over the Master's chest and listened carefully. 'Two heartbeats. Regular pulses. He's alive. He's come through the Infinite Cocoon!'

Yet the Master was deeply unconscious. The Doctor extracted him from the Cocoon with great effort, two of the Praxilions assisting with the job. They placed the Master onto a kind of stretcher. Externally, he appeared intact. There was no guessing what had happened to his mind.

'Will you take him?' the Red Queen asked.

'That was the arrangement.'

'You'll consent to deliver your enemy to the Sild?'

'It's the worst thing I've ever had to do. But there is no alternative. We could run, now, but the Sild will always find him. Help me take him to the TARDIS.'

'And have you escape with him into time? I'm afraid not, Doctor. It's nothing personal, but for the sake of Praxilion, I simply cannot take that chance. You will ride my flier up to the *Consolidator*. It has the necessary range, and the Sild will not attack if they believe you have the Master.'

'It would be quicker and easier by TARDIS.'

'This is the way it happens, Doctor. Please do not argue unnecessarily.' She had made her mind up, clearly.

'The Sild may not be in a hurry to see me leave,' the Doctor said.

'Then I wish you the best of luck. I am sorry that circumstances have… reunited us in this fashion. You seem like a good man, but I also have my people to think about. They have suffered enough for my errors. I will not perpetuate their misery.'

The Praxilions helped the Doctor and the recumbent

310

Master to the flier. They would be travelling alone, with no other crew, but the flier would be on automatic pilot, its course locked against outside interference.

The Doctor kept an eye on the Master as the Praxilions readied the craft for flight. He remained comatose, breathing slowly but regularly. As vulnerable, in his way, as when he had been inside the Infinite Cocoon.

'If our positions were reversed,' the Doctor whispered, 'what would you do? Smother me? Something worse? Or accept that there's a part of me in you, a part of you in me?'

The craft had sealed itself for departure. The Doctor strode to the broad sweep of the forward window and watched the city fall away below. The saucer-shaped flier accelerated steadily and had soon slipped free of Praxilion's thinning atmosphere. The craft bucked and swayed as it made the transition to flight through vacuum, but artificial gravity allowed the Doctor to remain standing. He returned to the Master.

'Doctor…' his lips moved, shaping the word at the limit of audibility. The Master's eyes were still closed.

The Doctor leaned closer. 'How do you feel?'

'Very tired.'

'You came through the Infinite Cocoon. If you remember me, I think that is a good sign.'

'I am free of it. Whatever it was.'

'The Sild.' For now, the Doctor thought. The Master would have died without the Cocoon's intervention. But this was only the most temporary of respites. He added: 'Do you remember where we're going?'

'I remember that there is something that must be done.' There was a long interval before the Master spoke again. 'Forgive me, Doctor. I make a poor conversationalist.'

'Rest. There's nothing more you need to do now.'

The Doctor returned to the window. There, coming up fast, was the vast dark bulk of the *Consolidator*, backlit by the purple and red glory of some squid-like stellar nebula.

CHAPTER THIRTY-TWO

When the helicopters landed in Aberdeen, nearly exhausted of fuel, Jo was still numb from what had happened at the rig. Everything they had done – had it been for nothing? And Eddie McCrimmon's bravery – had all that been futile? It was so unfair. How could the universe be this callous, this unfeeling?

And the Doctor – still no word on him. So they had both failed. Blowing up the MERMAN equipment had not had any effect, and whatever had happened to the Doctor and him, the other one, good or bad, it had also had no influence on the Sild's ambitions. Failure on two fronts. Failure and futility and death. And this was just the start of it – the beginning of the beginning of the end. That was what the Doctor had promised. Sild takeover was inevitable, once they gained a claw-hold. And this was starting to look very much like a claw-hold, wasn't it?

A military ambulance was waiting to collect the injured Yates. He had been in and out of consciousness all the way back, disorientated and rambling about his situation. Jo was almost on the point of envying him. Perhaps the greatest kindness of all would be to die, now, in a state of blissful confusion.

But Jo and Benton were ushered into a white wooden

313

cabin near the landing area, and in the cabin was a telephone, and on the other end of the telephone was Brigadier Alistair Lethbridge-Stewart, and something in the Brig's voice had the effect of snapping Jo out of her funk almost from the first word.

'Miss Grant. So glad you've made it back to dry land. I am very sorry to hear about Miss McCrimmon – she did a very courageous thing, and she has our utmost gratitude.'

The Brig had obviously been briefed on events at Mike Oscar Six. 'I'm sorry, too,' Jo said. 'But it counted for nothing, did it. The time ruptures kept on happening. That's why she fell into one.'

'That was unfortunate. But I am pleased to say that Miss McCrimmon's actions may have had some consequence. We have been tracking the frequency of time ruptures, Miss Grant. They are still continuing, but the interval between them is increasing and the scale of the ruptures appears to be diminishing. There is no doubt in my mind that the destruction of the MERMAN equipment has had a very detrimental effect on Sild operations. They obviously needed that signal to fine-tune their temporal incursions, like a homing beacon. We've denied them that, and now their attacks are becoming scattershot.' The Brigadier coughed. 'Of course the war isn't won yet – not by a long margin. Sild parties are still advancing inland, and more of them are coming ashore by the hour. But if we are beginning to stem their arrival through time, we may yet have a chance.'

'But the Doctor…'

'Still no word, Miss Grant. Rest assured that you'll be the first to be informed if there are developments.'

It was hard to shake the sense that he was returning to the *Consolidator*. They had been aboard it, witnessed its destruction, and yet all that lay in the future.

The flier jolted. Some violent force had seized it. The Doctor guessed that it had been intercepted by the approach and docking systems of the *Consolidator* itself: tractor fields powerful enough to crush an unwanted visitor like an ant under a heel. He glanced at the Master but the man was deeply unconscious again.

A mouth opened in the forward hull of the ship, gaping wide like a whale's jaw. Inside was a ruddy red docking bay. The flier slid into that mouth as if riding rails. The Doctor very much doubted that he could have done anything to resist the tractor fields, even if he had had control of the flier's motive systems. The *Consolidator* was much too powerful for that. They were being reeled in like an insect on a chameleon's sticky tongue.

Ribbed red walls slid by on either side. The mouth began to close. The Doctor felt a few more surges and bucks and then the flier came to rest with a definite bump. They were in a large interior space, similar perhaps to one of the chambers the Master and he had already explored in the future.

The Doctor returned to his passenger. The jolt of landing had stirred the Master.

'I think we've arrived,' the Doctor said gently. 'Here. Let me help you to your feet.'

The Master was groggy, weak, but just about able to support himself with the Doctor's assistance. Together they hobbled toward the flier's door. They had not reached it when it began to open on its own, even though the Doctor had yet to verify that there was breathable air outside. He felt a pop of equalising pressure, but the differential could not have been great.

They hobbled down the short disembarkation ramp.

'It was good of you to bring me here,' the Master said, wheezing between words. 'You should leave now, while you're able.' He coughed. 'Frankly, I fear for your welfare.'

'And dump you here like a parcel? Sorry, but that's not really my style.'

'I will grant you this. You have always had an idiotic attachment to style.'

'Why, thank you.'

The two men made their way out from under the overhang of the flier. The red-lit chamber soared far above them. The atmosphere was forbidding.

'No welcome party,' said the Doctor.

'I believe you may have spoken too soon.' The Master jabbed his chin into the gloom. 'Here they come. Whatever *they* may be.'

It was an amorphous, shuffling thing – not one type of creature, but dozens of different ones, all under Sild control. This made perfect sense, in hindsight. Aboard the *Consolidator*, held in stasis for eternity, were countless examples of alien intelligences deemed too malevolent or aggressive to remain at large. The welcoming party was made up of individuals from a couple of dozen of these hostile species, no two of them even remotely alike. There was a towering, grey-furred, hunchbacked thing with two red eyes set somewhere in the middle of its sternum; there was a thing like a brain moving around on three prehensile spinal cords; there was a thing like a cactus; there was an alien that seemed to be made entirely of water, a single wobbling blob of it, contained by some impossible, directed surface tension, with coloured organs floating around inside. There were half a dozen species that the Doctor thought he recognised. A Quagulan, in its glittering, knife-edged armour. A Social Craint, half organism, half unicycle. A multi-legged sting-tailed Mepuloid, fixing him with a cluster of eyestalks.

All that they had in common was the fact that each was controlled by an ambulator, and that each ambulator contained a tiny Sild pilot.

'Friendly-looking bunch,' the Doctor whispered to the Master. 'All they need are some burning torches, and we'd really feel at home.'

'The Master will step forward!' commanded a shrill electronic voice.

'What do you want with him?' demanded the Doctor.

'What do you hope to achieve?'

'Completion! Fulfilment of the Assemblage!' It was impossible to know which of the creatures was addressing him. 'This is the final element. It will bring about our total mastery of time!'

'To what end? So you can leave Praxilion a shrivelled husk, and turn Earth into a drowned world? It won't get you anywhere, you know! The civilised species of the galaxy united against you once; they'll do so again.'

'Enough,' the Master said wearily. 'I thank you for your efforts, Doctor, but I fear they are wasted.' He released himself from the Doctor's support and stepped unsteadily toward the waiting party. 'I am ready. I am yours. Do with me as you would.' He raised his arms in surrender.

'I'm sorry,' the Doctor called after him. 'I'll do what I can, I promise.'

'The fault is mine,' the Master said, turning back to look at him. 'If I had not shone so brightly, I would not have come to their attention.'

And then he winked.

The Doctor knew instantly that something was not as it seemed; that the Master had gained, or believed himself to have gained, the upper hand. How could this be?

'Wait!' the Doctor shouted, addressing now the Sild rather than their prisoner. 'He's cleverer than you! Whatever hold you think you have over him, it's not strong enough!'

But the Sild had no interest in the Doctor's words. They knew only that the final piece of the Assemblage was now in their possession.

'You may leave,' the voice informed the Doctor. 'Or stay. The choice is yours. You are of no consequence to us.'

The Doctor glanced back at the waiting flier. It would return on automatic pilot to Praxilion, and once there the Red Queen would have no reason to deny him the TARDIS.

But he could not leave.

'If you don't mind,' he said, 'I'll hang around.'

'Concern for your friend?'

'Actually,' the Doctor said, 'it's you I'd be more worried about.'

They promenaded the vast and gloomy bowels of the ship, until at last they arrived at a place the Doctor recognised. It was the hemispherical chamber where they had seen the Master's other incarnations, rows and rows of them, stacked all the way to the dizzying zenith. All the iterations of the Master, all faces and forms, unstitched from time.

It was different now, as of course it had to be. There were very few unoccupied positions, and all the incarnations appeared to be alive, if this dismal condition could be dignified by such a term. Once more, the Doctor marvelled at the variety of guises his adversary had worn, from the faces and bodies of children to the greyest of wraiths. Men, women, humanoids and aliens – all human and non-human life was here. The Master had been all of these things. Would be, the Doctor corrected himself, needing a constant reminder that many of these incarnations were in fact from the Master's future, or rather the future that now only existed as a shadow of itself.

One position, in the lowest ring, was conspicuously vacant. This was where they were taking their prisoner. The Master, for his part, offered no visible resistance. He was still putting on an act, stumbling and wheezing, giving an impression of only feeble awareness of his predicament. But that wink had given the Doctor the lie. The Master, he was certain, was in total command of his faculties. He had been so from the moment the Infinite Cocoon released him.

What had happened in there? What had the Master *done*?

His Sild captors brought him to the empty position. There was a man-shaped aperture, around which was arranged the life-support and neural interface systems, the mechanisms which would keep him alive and connected into the Assemblage. The Master slotted into the gap like a precisely made puzzle piece. 'Please,' he wailed, with suitable histrionics. 'Spare me this! I beg you!'

'He's pulling your leg, you know,' the Doctor said, arms folded.

The Sild-controlled aliens fixed the breathing mask over the Master's face. There was just time for the eyes to swivel onto the Doctor, a definite mischief in them.

A curving glass door hinged into place.

'Initiate neural connection! Bring the final unit into the Assemblage!'

From around the snug-fitting aperture, various silvery lines snaked out and began to probe the Master's form. He wriggled slightly, but gave no indication of great discomfort. Not even when the lines pushed through the skin of his skull, and wormed visibly under the skin.

'Contact established! Beginning integration!'

All around the chamber, the other versions of the Master were responding to the introduction of the new element. They twitched and squirmed. Their eyes blinked or slid under tight eyelids.

'The Assemblage recognises the final element! The symmetry is complete!'

Patterns of light now danced across the chamber, following geometric pathways from one element to the another. At first the Doctor could follow the dance, but it soon became too rapid and complicated for study. It was like a speeded-up film of traffic moving through a city's grid, accelerating into a blur of frenzied motion. These were the neural impulses flowing between different elements of the Assemblage. Any one version of the Master was potent enough, but linked together the effect was equivalent to a massively parallel supercomputer, executing many instruction steps simultaneously. This was what the Sild had wanted; this was what they had got.

So far.

'The Assemblage is stable! Mental power is now exceeding all previous limits! Initiate time rupture!'

The Doctor remembered the window in the adjoining chamber, where they had first glimpsed the ruined husk of Praxilion. He ran to it, the Sild oblivious to his movements, and again found the tall curving pane. He did not have long to wait before the world swung into view, descending from top to bottom.

Praxilion had changed since that last view from orbit, but he had seen the world as it now was from the flier. He recognised the shrivelled remnants of oceans, not yet totally sucked dry. The atmosphere was an indigo soap bubble. But still, an atmosphere and seas. Where there was life, there was yet hope.

'Time rupture commencing! Magnitude and stability of rupture already exceeding all prior efforts!'

The Doctor noticed now that a glowing control panel had appeared on the pane, annotated in Gallifreyan. It had not been there in the future, but by then many of the *Consolidator*'s less essential systems must have broken down. He waited until the planet had come into view again, then tapped a series of commands onto the glass. The planet froze, then swelled. The Doctor zoomed in closer, directing his attention on one of the larger remaining oceans. There, in the middle of it, was an appalling thing to behold. The waters were spiralling around the open mouth of a time rupture many tens of kilometres across, creating a terrifying, island-sized whirlpool. Then, not too far to the north, another rupture opened and held. The Doctor touched the controls again. The view jerked west. Here was another rupture, opening into the atmosphere – an air-swallowing void so enormous that it was visible from space, like the giant storm on Jupiter.

The Doctor reeled at the destruction he was witnessing. Had he misjudged things? Was the Master not, in fact, putting on any sort of act? Had the Sild got exactly what they had always sought: absolute control of time, achieved by harnessing the Master's unsurpassed command of temporal physics?

So it seemed. At this rate, Praxilion would be a dry and airless husk in mere weeks – if not sooner. The Master was only just getting into his stride, after all.

The Doctor had seen enough. He dashed back into the main chamber. 'Stop this! You're butchering a world! Nothing can justify this crime!'

'Why do you protest now?' the electronic voice asked. 'You must always have known this would be the outcome!'

'You gave us no choice! At least spare the Praxilions. You've ruined their world. Let the survivors live in peace.'

'Increase the time ruptures. We have what we need now. The Praxilions have no further strategic value. Their continued existence is an unnecessary detail.'

'No!' the Doctor shouted. 'That was never the arrangement! You told the Queen you'd spare her people, in return for the Master!'

'A necessary lie.'

The Doctor sprinted to the compartment where the final incarnation had only recently been installed, slipping easily between the Sild-controlled aliens. He dug his fingers into the seam where the glass cover had closed over the Master, trying to lever it open.

'Cease.'

'No! I should never have let this happen!'

The Doctor redoubled his efforts. With a crack, the glass cover sprung open. The Master, masked, seemed unaware of the intrusion. The Doctor tried to rip the neural connections free, but as soon as he had wrenched one of the silver lines from the Master's flesh, another slithered in and replaced it. It was hopeless.

The Sild had him. It was the Quagulan and the water-creature, the latter flowing itself over him, exerting a soft but irresistible pressure. They tugged the Doctor away from the Master. With a free hand he tried to rip loose the Quagulan's ambulator, but it was too firmly attached. His fingers closed around the cylinder containing the Sild pilot, but before he could do any harm the water-creature had smothered him, so that he was literally inside it, goggling at its floating, disconnected organs, like multicoloured goldfish in a plastic bag, the ambulator also floating inside. And then he was on his back, struggling for breath, before the water-creature flowed off him.

'He is too unpredictable. He must die, or he must become Sild!'

The fight had knocked the wind out of him. He tried to get to his feet, but his muscles had turned to jelly. The walking brain toppled slowly over, its spine-like legs tangled and limp. The brain's ambulator had detached itself, abandoning its host organism. Now it was scuttling over the hard metal floor, heading straight for him.

The Doctor had no strength. Everything seemed to close down as the Sild neared. He was looking down a swirling, rushing tunnel – his own imminent annihilation. The Master had barely been able to endure the briefest of contacts with the Sild. The Doctor, much less mentally resilient, had no hope whatsoever.

The ambulator vanished. It did not simply cease to exist on its own. So, too, had the circle of flooring immediately beneath it. And in the instant of its disappearance, there had been a cold cosmic chill. A time rupture, no larger than a beach ball, had swallowed the ambulator.

The Doctor found some strength. He struggled to his feet. The Sild seemed confused, as well they might.

From the Master, muffled by his breather mask, came the unmistakeable sound of laughter.

'Send another unit!'

Now it was the turn of the Social Craint to lose its controlling organism. The silver crab scuttled off the top-heavy creature, balanced on its strange cartilaginous unicycle. The Social Craint fell over. The crab whisked toward the Doctor.

It too vanished. The rupture had been bigger this time.

The laughter was spreading now. It had started with one

facet, the version of the Master who had travelled with the Doctor from Earth, but others were joining in. Ones and twos, quietly at first, but echoing from one side of the chamber to the other. It was like a conversation, conducted in a particular sort of manic chuckling laughter.

The Doctor said: 'Of course! I should have known – it's the Master, don't you see? He's achieved independent control! He can make the time ruptures happen whether you want him to or not!'

'This is not possible! The Assemblage is our instrument! We are its master!'

'I've a feeling the tables have just been turned.' The Doctor was bent over, like a runner with a stitch. 'But don't say I didn't warn you.'

The Master's laughter was becoming contagious.

Men, women, children, aliens... they were joining in. The laughter amplified itself. It built and swelled in definite waves. It rose and fell. It was a cackle, then a shriek, then a dark burbling undercurrent. It was a thing with a mind of its own. The Doctor swivelled around, his eyes darting from one incarnation to the next. Though they were masked, their faces moved with laughter.

Convulsions of laughter. An audience of Masters, in hysterics.

CHAPTER THIRTY-THREE

'There is a fault with the Assemblage! Contain and rectify the fault!'

'Rather too late for that,' the Doctor said, a dim sort of understanding coming upon him. 'He's fooled you. Fooled me, come to think of it.'

'This is not possible!'

'He's found a way to turn the Assemblage against you!'

'This cannot be! The Assemblage is our own invention!'

'Then you shouldn't have left it lying around once you were finished with it!' The Doctor could only see one way that the Master could possibly have triumphed. When they had overshot, visiting the future version of this ship, the Master had had time to study the architecture and logic of the Assemblage, tracing its connections with the Doctor's own sonic screwdriver.

It had seemed like innocent curiosity at the time. But nothing was ever innocent where the Master was concerned. He had used that information to shape his own mind in the Infinite Cocoon – not merely healing himself, but making himself into a kind of mental weapon. When the Sild probes sank into his mind, they had provided the means for the Master to begin his takeover.

Not for the first time, the Doctor was forced to admire the

extreme resourcefulness of his old adversary.

'You have betrayed us!' the Sild voice declared, trying to make itself heard over the laughter. 'We trusted you to bring the Master to us! You will be punished!'

'You've tried that!'

'Destroy him!'

The Quagulan raised an armoured arm. The armour adjusted itself in a complex manner, allowing a gleaming little weapon to pop out of the Quagulan's sleeve. The weapon swivelled on a little turret, and its barrel clicked open.

'Now steady on!' the Doctor said.

The Quagulan weapon fired, or began to fire – it would never be clear which. Either way, the Quagulan would not be shooting at anything else again. Its entire arm had vanished, along with a sizable chunk of its upper torso. The edges, where the body part had been scooped away, formed a perfect glistening concavity. The Quagulan dropped to the ground. The Doctor felt the faintest ghost of an energy pulse waft over him, no worse in its way than a pleasant summer breeze.

Now it was the turn of the water-creature. It began to wobble its way toward the Doctor, shimmering and rippling like a single bloated raindrop – it moved itself like a man in a potato sack, forming two stubby foot-like appendages – before some sudden and violent force ripped it into a thousand wet pieces. The bits of the water-creature rained down around them. Its internal organs, separated from their support medium, twitched and spasmed in a most unpleasant fashion.

The Doctor had both hands raised. 'Enough!'

The laughter ebbed away, until there was a kind of watchful silence. The Sild did not know what to do next. Nor, for that matter, did the Doctor.

Suddenly there was movement, one of the glass covers being pushed aside. The Master, the familiar incarnation who had travelled with the Doctor, stepped out of his Master-shaped alcove, peeling away the breather mask and allowing the neural probes to slither from his flesh. He stopped, adjusted his sleeves and gloves, and took a moment to groom his hair, for all the world as if he had just stepped out of a changing room.

'Destroy him!' the Sild called. 'He is the weapon! He is the one that has damaged the Assemblage!'

But the Master raised a gloved hand, quite calmly. 'I strongly suggest that you do nothing of the sort. I may no longer be physically bound to the Assemblage, but my control over it remains absolute. I can and will exercise my time control to eliminate you all. In fact I have every intention of doing so.'

'Destroy him now!'

The Master turned to face the remaining party of Sild-controlled aliens. He pointed his hand at them, palm raised, fingers spread, and made two of the aliens disappear.

'You doubt my sincerity?' he asked.

'I think they're getting the message,' the Doctor said. 'And I suppose I should offer my congratulations. You've done what you always do – turned the tables.'

'Indeed, Doctor. But the Sild have only themselves to blame.' Casually, he made another two aliens disappear. The Doctor wondered to what far corner of space and time they had been consigned, whether it was the airless cold of interstellar space or the blazing dense core of a star. He doubted very much that the Master had spared his victims. He had standards to live up to.

But there were more Sild than the relative handful controlling these alien hosts. They must have been on their way for some while, drawn by the time ruptures, sweeping through the great corridors and halls of the *Consolidator* like a silver tide, until at last they began to approach the Assemblage. The Doctor heard them before he saw them: it was a low metallic rumbling, the sound of a million whisking metal legs. When the front of the stampede reached the chamber's low-ceiling entrance, it paused. The Doctor and the Master had by then both turned to greet the oncoming army.

It was a shifting, teetering wall of silver, easily as high as a man. Crab upon crab, thousands of them just in the very front of the advancing mass. Beyond, there must have been millions. They were locked together into a single organisational unit, bound by legs and tentacles, and packed so tightly that there was very little space between their bodies. The Doctor made out countless glass cylinders on the backs of the crabs, and within those cylinders countless squirming thumb-sized Sild, no two distinguishable. He understood then what he had always known, but until that moment not properly appreciated: the Sild had no conception of the individual. That was how they had conquered worlds and empires. They were the ultimate cannon fodder. And yet they came in such overwhelming numbers that they could absorb the most appalling losses. They had no fear, no remorse, no sense of loss at their fallen comrades. That was why they always won; why they would always win in the future.

'Very good,' the Master said. 'You've spared me the trouble of demanding your presence.' And he extended his hand and punched a hemispherical hole in the wall, vanishing perhaps a hundred Sild in one instant. But the hole quickly healed itself, as the Sild readjusted themselves to once again form a seamless surface.

The Master chuckled and did it again, twice this time. The Sild reorganised.

'Stop!' the Doctor said. 'You're killing them for the sake of killing!'

'Would you rather I destroyed all of them in an instant, Doctor? It is fully within my capabilities.'

'I'd rather you didn't kill them at all. There has to be a better way!'

'Not with the Sild. I would have thought that was obvious by now.'

Without warning, the entire chamber shook as if struck by a titanic hammer. The floor shuddered beneath the Doctor's feet. He had to paddle his arms to regain his balance. Then the hammer blow came again.

'What are you doing?' he asked the Master.

'Nothing. I believe the Sild are using the *Consolidator*'s defences against the surface of Praxilion.'

The Doctor would have rushed to the window again, but the wall of Sild blocked his way. But he could imagine the spectacle well enough. Weapons of awesome destructive potential, raining energy down on the scattered remnants of that once great civilisation.

'Stop!' the Doctor shouted, hoping that he was addressing the Sild. 'The Praxilions have done you no harm! They delivered the Master! You have no reason to punish them further!'

'We have every reason!' came back the reply. 'They delivered a trick!'

'That was the Master's own doing – even I didn't know what he was planning!'

'Ignorance is no excuse. The bombardments will continue!'

The chamber shook again.

The Doctor reached into his pocket and found the object waiting there. He produced it slowly, allowing all a good chance to see it. Then he tossed the golden sphere from his palm once, as one might a cricket ball, before catching it deftly. 'This ends now! No more deaths! No more punishment! There's been enough!'

The Master, his arm still outstretched, eyed the fist-sized sphere. His eyes met the Doctor's questioningly.

The Doctor nodded. 'The Red Queen's sceptre. The Axumillary Orb.'

'The most concentrated explosive device in history,' the Master said. 'How strange, to see it now! The paradoxes of time travel never cease to fascinate.'

'It's the same device that the Red Queen used,' the Doctor

confirmed. 'But earlier in its existence. The Red Queen hadn't yet learned how to operate it by remote control. But she showed me how to trigger it manually.' The Doctor rolled the sphere in his fingers.

The Master's smile was tight.

'Would you?'

'If it meant an end to this butchery.'

'It would mean an end to you. To both of us. To all of me.'

'I'm afraid that strikes me as a small price to pay.' The Doctor paused. 'But this is an instrument of last resort. The Sild will cease their attacks against Praxilion. You will cease your attacks against the Sild.'

The Master tilted his chin. 'Sympathy for them, Doctor? After all they've done?'

'There's no crime in the universe large enough to justify genocide.'

'Tell that to the Time Lords, who made this ship.'

'We made a terrible mistake. I'm not about to make a second.' The chamber clanged again. The Doctor shouted: 'The attacks will cease! You will obey me!'

The Master nodded appreciatively. 'I couldn't have put it better myself.'

The Doctor shuddered. He had held this much power only once or twice in his career. It was not a feeling he much cared for.

'And you will stop attacking the Sild.'

'Very well.' Slowly, the Master lowered his outspread hand, tightening it to a fist as he did so. 'I believe the point has been made. So what do we have now, Doctor? Stalemate?'

'I prefer ceasefire.'

A section of the wall of Sild vanished, leaving a scooped-out hollow. Another followed, to the right. A moment later there was a third, to the left. The remaining Sild tumbled and scrambled to fill the voids. There seemed no end to them.

'You contemptible...' the Doctor began.

The Master's eyes were wide. His arms were at his side. 'I

did not do that!' Then he looked around, up and up, taking in the Assemblage, all the masked faces. 'I did not do it,' he repeated, with an urgency the Doctor found hard to dismiss. 'They did.'

'They are you.'

'My control over them is… not absolute.' There was fear in his eyes now. 'They seem unwilling to accept your terms, Doctor. They seem not to believe that you would really destroy us all.'

'Then you'd better convince them!'

'I have seen the Axumillary Orb in action – they have not!'

More Sild vanished. In retaliation, the Sild reinitiated their planetary bombardment. The chamber resonated, as if it had been hammer-struck. The Doctor nearly went stumbling. He flailed for balance, but by some great good fortune managed not to lose his grip on the sphere.

The Master spread his arms, a theatrical impresario greeting his audience. 'Listen to me! The Doctor is sincere! He will bring destruction down upon us all!'

More Sild vanished – along with a sizable chunk of the chamber's own floor. This was met by another assault against Praxilion.

'They're not listening,' the Doctor said.

'They will.' The Master now outstretched his hand and directed it at one of the elements in the Assemblage – one of the versions of himself. He set his jaw, his face tensing with effort, his eyes narrowed to concentrated slits. A circle of distortion began to form around the incarnation that the Master had selected – it was the beardless young man in a suit that the Doctor remembered from their first visit to this chamber. The circle wobbled, as if its integrity were being resisted. The Master grimaced. The circle stabilised, gained definition, and with a pop the space inside it – including the alcove, and the young man in a suit – ceased to exist.

'No!' the Doctor said, horrified at what he'd just witnessed. 'You can't wage war on yourself!'

'If it is a matter of self-preservation...' the Master said, straining with the effort, 'then I am more than willing.' He pivoted on his heels, his outstretched arm rising and falling as he sought another victim. This time it was a child, no more than a boy. The Master scrunched up his face again. He grunted with the exertion. The circle – the surface defining the time rupture's volume – began to form.

But the Master went flying, knocked back by an invisible force. 'They resist!' he said, struggling back to his feet. 'But I am stronger! Are they so foolish to think their combined will is superior to mine?'

'You can't hope to win!' the Doctor said. 'They're you!'

'And my mind has been reshaped to exploit the Assemblage,' the Master said, pausing to wipe spittle from his chin. 'I will triumph!' He raised his hand again, but this time the Doctor could not help but notice a tremor in the outstretched limb, a quivering in the fingertips. The Master shut his eyes and tried to project another time rupture. But a similar rupture was starting to form around the Master himself. The Assemblage was trying to spit him out of this timeframe.

'They're fighting back!' the Doctor shouted.

'Let them! I am stronger!'

Even the Doctor was beginning to feel the desperate crackle of psychokinetic energies, as the Master warred with the ranked counterparts of himself. Both time ruptures had collapsed before they had a chance to stabilise, but now others were opening and collapsing all around. There were dozens – some as large as beach balls, some as small as soap bubbles. They quivered and popped too rapidly for the Doctor to track. It was almost pretty. It was also war, as both sides grappled with the ancient time machinery and tried to gain a decisive advantage.

Civil war amongst the incarnations of the Master? The Doctor realised that the universe still had some surprises up its sleeve. Not that he had ever come close to doubting that.

Cautiously, he slipped the golden sphere back into his pocket. He had a feeling it had outlasted its usefulness, at least for the moment.

'I should have known it,' he said. 'I can barely get on with myself, and I'm not half as vain and arrogant as you.'

The Master went sprawling again. It was a wonder he had managed to avoid being ejected into time. But there was something new in his expression now. He looked around the chamber anxiously, sweeping his gaze along the rows and ranks of himself. Time ruptures were opening and closing at random, biting spherical chunks out of the Assemblage. Spheres and partial spheres were appearing in the floor, in the wall of the Sild, in the very fabric of the *Consolidator*. The Doctor danced to one side as a void opened under his feet.

'Runaway instability!' the Master declared. 'The time equipment is going into overload!'

'Can you stop it?'

'No! It's beyond my control now – beyond all control!'

The Doctor watched, numbed, as the Master's incarnations vanished in ones and twos, scooped out of existence.

'Where are they going?'

'Anywhere, anywhen – back where they originally came from! I'm being scattered back into time!'

The pace of the time ruptures was growing furious now. Even the Sild could barely maintain their wall. They too were being snatched out of existence, hurled into the vastness of eternity.

'The ship won't last much longer,' the Doctor said.

The Master's chest heaved up and down with the effort of breathing. 'I concur. From this point on, the runaway instability will only escalate. We may have only minutes...'

The Doctor dug his hand into his pocket. 'You've seen the Axumillary Orb! Don't think I won't use it!' He began to walk toward the Sild. 'You're going to give us passage. Both of us. That's all we want.'

'They won't listen to you.'

'They will. The Sild wanted to escape into time. That's what they're getting! Not as an all-conquering military force, focused on one objective – but hurled at random into all time and space! They'll all be scattered and divided, militarily useless! But that's better than annihilation!'

'I hope they see it that way.'

The Doctor advanced on the wall of silver crabs. It began to part, cleaving wide to allow the two Time Lords to walk down it, the Doctor first, his hand still in his pocket, the Master close behind, the silver sea closing on them the moment they had passed. Time ruptures continued – even deep within the mass of Sild. Parts of the ship were disappearing at an alarming rate. Before very long, its basic integrity would be weakened.

'We had best make haste,' the Doctor said.

'After you,' the Master said.

CHAPTER THIRTY-FOUR

By the time they reached the flier it was clear that the *Consolidator* did not have long to live. Awful groans sounded throughout its fabric, as if a living thing were suffering the torments of the damned. Blasts of wind now howled down corridors where the air had been crypt-still for a thousand centuries. Artificial gravity surged and faded, making the ship feel like a roller-coaster ride. The hull was holed. The vessel was surrendering to the void, even as the time ruptures consumed it from within.

But the flier was mercifully intact. The Doctor and the Master raced up the connecting ramp, having long since seen the last of the Sild. Working together, they operated the alien controls as if born to them. The autopilot systems began to lift the flier and spin it around for departure. They had no need to wait for the great door to open, for the time ruptures were serving the same purpose. The fabric of the *Consolidator* was winking out of existence even as they watched. The flier's navigational computer selected one of these holes and shot them through it.

'One question,' the Master said, bracing himself against a console, when they had regained something like level flight. 'How confident were you that the Sild – not to mention my counterparts – would fall for your bluff?'

'My bluff?' the Doctor asked, surprised.

'The Axumillary Orb. A weapon of unspeakable destructive potency, Doctor. If the Sild had bothered to learn the slightest thing about you, they would have known of your spineless inability to deliver on a threat.'

'I just saved your life. Lives. Don't I deserve a little gratitude?'

'You deserve nothing, Doctor, save my undying contempt.'

'Coming from you, that's not far off a compliment.' But the Doctor's levity was short lived. 'There she goes,' he said, nodding to the rear window.

The *Consolidator* was breaking up, becoming a disconnected cloud of pieces, drifting slowly apart in a pale nimbus of escaping atmosphere.

'We should consider ourselves fortunate,' the Master said. 'Very few individuals have ever seen the same ship destroyed *twice*. Your precious Blinovitch would be spinning in his grave, if he were anything but a myth.'

'Time is resilient,' the Doctor said. 'It can stand the odd paradox or two.'

The flier pitched, nosing down toward Praxilion. The Doctor had been doing his best not to dwell on what the Sild had done to that already ruined world, but the evidence was now hard to ignore. New craters, still livid from the heat of their creation, pocked the surface. Mountains of shattered crust had been lofted into orbit, blanketing the world from pole to pole. The Red Queen could not possibly have survived the bombardment, could she?

But the flier was heading home regardless.

'What of us now, Doctor?' the Master asked, as the flier approached the smoking stump that had been the palace. 'It would seem we find ourselves at something of a crossroads.'

'Will you consent to return to the twentieth century?'

'Back to a miserable prison cell, with only a colour television for company? Why yes, Doctor: what a splendid suggestion.'

'Then you're going to be stranded here on a dying world, at the end of time, with no possible hope of escape. That television set's looking better and better, isn't it?'

'There are ways and means.'

'You mean, stealing my TARDIS?'

The Master looked affronted. 'My dear fellow, the thought had not even begun to cross my mind.'

'Good, because it won't do you an ounce of good trying. And remember, I've still got this.' The Doctor pulled the Axumillary Orb from his pocket.

'It's good that we understand each other,' the Master said. 'No room for doubt.'

'None at all.'

The flier nosed its way between the still-smoking spires of the palace. The Doctor felt a deep apprehension as they came in for landing. The palace was a wreck, blasted and gutted. The TARDIS might have survived – even that was not guaranteed – but he had grave fears for the Red Queen.

'She's endured so much,' he said. 'Millions of years. All that accumulated wisdom. It can't end like this.'

'Everything ends,' the Master said. 'That's the beauty of it.'

They landed, settling in through a faint but still active pressure containment field. The flier touched down on rubble, the remains of part of the palace which had collapsed in on itself.

The Doctor and the Master stepped out into clouds of dust, both men shielding their mouths.

'I fear the worst,' the Master said.

'That she might have survived?'

'No, Doctor. That she might have died.' Then the Master halted, and pointed to three small forms waiting in the dust-haze. 'Praxilions! Some of them are still alive!'

The Doctor and the Master stepped over obstacles, batting dust from their faces. 'Your queen!' the Doctor called. 'Is she…?'

'Come quickly,' said one of the Praxilions. 'There isn't much time.'

'She's still alive?'

'On the edge of death. But the machine... you have used it once, and proven your control of it. Could you use it again?'

'The Infinite Cocoon?' the Doctor asked.

'It is her only chance.'

They brought the Doctor and the Master to the machine. Praxilions waited next to it, with the queen's exhausted and injured form cradled between them. Both men regarded the alien machine with foreboding. There could be no mastery of this technology, only a temporary truce with it.

'Well?' the Master asked. 'Is it damaged?'

The Doctor used his sleeve to wipe a layer of whitish dust from the lid. 'It should still function – it's very sturdy technology. But I don't suppose I have to tell any of you that there's a terrible risk in using it.'

'Do what you must,' said the Praxilion. 'Without it, she has nothing left to lose.'

The Doctor stationed himself at the control panel. He touched buttons. Yellow light fanned in a widening arc as the lid slid to one side. 'Place her inside,' he told the aliens. 'Carefully!'

'It's hopeless,' the Master said, his arms crossed. 'The woman is beyond salvation.'

'Her neural patterns should still be recoverable,' the Doctor said. 'Maybe not the most recent additions, but the deep structures... her oldest memories. It has to be worth a try!'

'To what end?' the Master asked sceptically. 'So she can govern a ruined world?'

The Praxilions had lowered the Red Queen into the machine. The Doctor tapped controls, desperately trying to recover his rusty knowledge of this ancient alien symbolic language, its subtleties and pitfalls. He was sure that the

Cocoon had the capability to bring Edwina McCrimmon back to life. Equally sure that the slightest error could prove catastrophic. Nor was there much time to ponder the exercise. The palace was shaking on its foundations. It would not be long now.

'There. I've done what I can. It's up to the machine now.' The Doctor glared at the Master. 'No help from you!'

'The difference between you and me, Doctor, is that I understand when something is futile.'

The lid began to close. The machine commenced its humming and gurgling. Patterns of illumination began to chase themselves around the control matrix, gaining in speed and complexity.

'It's starting,' the Doctor said. 'Support medium flooding in… metabolic breakdown beginning.' He tapped a set of commands. 'You've been through this. What was it like?'

'A cleansing. But I recovered.'

'More's the pity.'

'We are what we are, Doctor. If I did not exist, the universe would soon fill the void left by my absence. You could almost say that the universe *requires* us. We are order and disorder. We balance each other very effectively.'

'Yes. Well I'd almost started to get used to the idea of the universe without you. I'm not sure I like this new turn of events.'

'My coming back, you mean? The reversal of time-fade? Now that my selves have been threaded back into time – some of them, at least? But take heart, Doctor: they could be anywhere. Some of me probably didn't survive the transition through time. Who knows where we came out?'

'They turned against you, at the end. Is it all going to be forgiven now?'

'You mean, can I expect to be at war with my other selves, for the rest of time?' The Master seemed to consider the possibility for the first time. 'I relish the prospect. I have always been the strongest of them. You saw it yourself. The

339

Sild needed me more than they needed any other of my incarnations.'

'Only you could feel contempt for yourself!'

'With justification. I am still here. They were scattered at the mercy of the time ruptures.'

'Something's wrong,' the Doctor said suddenly. 'Metabolic breakdown's proceeding too far. It should have started reversing by now, reassembling her.' Anxiously he tapped controls. 'No… it's not meant to do that.' He looked up. 'Morphological coherence fading. I'm losing her.'

'I always said it was futile.'

'Don't just stand there!' The Doctor continued to do his best, but the pattern of lights was dancing beyond his control. The Infinite Cocoon's humming and gurgling had ratcheted to a new level, like a cement mixer about to shake itself to pieces. 'If you've a shred of decency anywhere left in you, you must assist!'

'She's too far gone.'

'I don't believe you. When you programmed the Cocoon to work on your own mind, it was like child's play. You understand these symbols, these controls, far better than I ever did. Now put that genius to good use!'

The Master closed his eyes, sighed. 'I still maintain that there is nothing we can do for her. But if you will insist on my demonstrating that futility…' He opened his eyes, walking to the Doctor's side. 'For the sake of argument, I shall assign basic regenerative parameters to your side of the control matrix.' He executed a quick, fluent sequence of commands. 'I shall take care of the higher functions. You need only follow my lead, and attempt not to make too much of a hash of things.' The Master made a show of cracking his gloved knuckles. 'Are we ready?'

'Get on with it!'

The Master's hands became a blur of motion. 'Re-imprinting morphic boundaries. Locking anatomical control parameters. Why did you not do this before?'

'Because… never mind.' It was all the Doctor could do now to match the Master's work.

'Chemical gradients normalising. Flow rates asymptotic. You're drifting: stay with me, Doctor.'

'I'm doing my best.'

'Yes, and therein lies the tragedy.' The Master's fingers were an arpeggiating blur, like a concert pianist navigating the most technically difficult of passages. 'Neural forms re-branching. Track those growth vectors, Doctor! Track and anticipate – work *with* the Cocoon, not against it. Yes, good. Good! You're learning!'

'She's coming back.'

'I hardly dare believe it.' But it was true. The pattern of lights on the control matrix was slowing, the Cocoon easing its humming and gurgling. 'Indications show normal human physiology, all biological functions restored and stable.'

'We did it,' the Doctor said.

It fell to the Master to sound a cautionary note. 'Let us not get ahead of ourselves – we have no idea what her mental state has become. The Cocoon may have wiped her clean, left her with a complete absence of memory and personality.'

The machine had stopped. The lid began to slide open. The Doctor and the Master left their positions and moved to the side opposite the opening lid. Both of them seemed to hesitate before looking inside.

'She's alive,' the Doctor said, observing the slow rise and fall of her chest.

'Not just alive, Doctor!' The Master shook his head in obvious amazement. 'She is physiologically much younger than when she went in! How remarkable!'

'Almost as if she's been regenerated,' the Doctor said.

'The power of this device… complete control over the biology of living forms… in the wrong hands, it could do terrible things!'

'Don't start getting ideas, old chap. Here. Help me get her out.'

The two men leaned in and extracted Edwina McCrimmon from the Infinite Cocoon. The machine had digested, and then reconstituted, exactly the clothes she had been wearing when lowered into the interior. But they no longer fitted her very well. Her figure was fuller, that of a healthy middle aged woman rather than an incredibly old and frail woman. The Doctor's hand brushed through her hair – no longer entirely white, but a coppery red, shot through with fine threads of grey. The broad freckled face was that of the woman he had met on Mike Oscar Six.

'Bring her throne!' the Master ordered the waiting Praxilions.

They lowered her into the chair. She was coming round, mumbling incoherently as she surfaced from the profound unconsciousness of the Cocoon. The Doctor produced his sonic screwdriver and swept it back and forth before McCrimmon's closed eyes. 'Normal optic nerve function,' he told the Master. 'Everything seems ship-shape. She's just a bit groggy.' The Doctor pocketed the sonic screwdriver and clicked his fingers loudly. 'Edwina! It's me, the Doctor! Can you hear me? Try and open your eyes!'

'Where am I?'

'On Praxilion,' the Master said. 'Do you remember Praxilion?'

'Of course I…' Her eyes were open now. She looked first to the Doctor, then to the Master, then down at her hands, one of them still gloved, but the other unblemished by time. 'The Sild… What happened to me?'

'You've been through the Infinite Cocoon,' the Doctor said. 'It read your genetic structure, restored you to an earlier state of youthfulness. You should also have access to memories that have been locked away for many years.'

'The Sild are gone,' the Master said. 'From here and from Earth. Blasted back into time. You need not fear them now.'

'What about my people?'

'I'm afraid Praxilion is no longer inhabitable,' the Doctor

answered. 'The palace itself won't last much longer. But we have the TARDIS! The survivors are moving aboard, and I can take them somewhere safer. You'll come with us.'

'I remember something,' McCrimmon said, with an awed fascination entering her voice. 'It's always been there, in my head! But it's been so long. How could I have forgotten?'

'What?' the Master asked.

'Scotland. I remember Scotland.'

'We'll take you home,' the Doctor said. 'You should never have left. But now you have a life to start living again.'

'And my people... the Praxilions?'

The Doctor smiled gently. 'You've given them enough guidance. I think it's about time they started governing themselves, wouldn't you say?'

The palace shook again. There were only a handful of Praxilions left inside it now.

'We have to go!' the Doctor declared. 'Edwina – can you walk, if the Master and I help you? It's not very far.'

'I'll do my best.'

The two men took her under each arm and assisted her as she hobbled toward the TARDIS. It was not that she was injured, the Doctor knew, just that she would take a little while to get used to this sprightly new version of herself again. He knew that feeling well enough.

But when they were nearly at the TARDIS there came a savage jolt as some part of the palace's fabric finally gave way, collapsing beneath them, and the floor tilted so sharply that all three of them lost their footing, and then had to scramble for purchase as what had been a level floor became a slowly steepening ramp. The collapse was continuing – the very fabric of the palace finally giving way. The Doctor eyed the TARDIS – it looked fit to topple at any moment.

'Come on! We only have a few seconds!'

But when he had hit the ground the bump had sent something tumbling from his pocket. The Doctor watched it roll away, gathering speed down the steepening incline. It was the Axumillary Orb.

The Master looked at it. He could not tear his eyes from the object, even as it rolled further and further beyond his reach. One of the most devastating destructive devices in the history of invention? A bomb powerful enough to shatter a world, and yet which could be stuffed into a pocket? How could the Master fail to be entranced?

'Wait!' he called, beginning to scuttle back down the slope, even as the Orb rolled off the ledge, falling out of sight. 'I must have it!'

'Leave it!' the Doctor shouted. 'You don't have time!'

The Master, for an instant, seemed to grasp the sense in the Doctor's words. He began to creep back up the slope, crouching to keep his centre of gravity low. The palace's collapse was continuing – cracks and fissures beginning to spread through the floor as the structural stresses took their toll.

'You are right, Doctor… for once.'

'Good!' the Doctor called, his hand on the TARDIS at last, the door still open to admit the last of the Praxilions. 'I'd like that in writing, if at all possible!' He urged Edwina McCrimmon aside, trusting she could take care of herself these last few footsteps.

'Good grief,' he heard her call, as she slipped through. 'It's bigger on the…'

But the Master had stopped again. There was no guessing how far the Axumillary Orb had fallen, when it rolled over the edge. Yet the possibility existed that it might still be in reach, and the Master could not resist that temptation. The slope was steep, getting steeper, but still traversable.

The Master began to creep down the slope.

'I must have it, Doctor. I must and will. Surely you understand?'

'You're a fool! We have to leave now!'

The Master scuttled further down the slope, almost sliding on his back as the angle steepened. 'This is a power too great to be left lying around, Doctor! Someone must possess it! It may as well be me!'

'Leave it! I give you my word that I'll drop you off in time, somewhere other than Earth!'

'You'd do that for me, Doctor? How very touching.'

But behind the Master, between him and the TARDIS, a crack spread with sudden speed. It deepened and widened. The TARDIS pitched, as the entire structure shifted by degrees. There were only seconds left now: to delay dematerialisation any longer was the height of recklessness.

The Master had reached the end of the ledge. He knelt down, stretching his arms down into the void. The Master grunted with the exertion. The ground tilted, and he had to scramble not to slide over the edge.

Then suddenly he jerked back, holding up the little sphere. 'I have it! I have the Axumillary Orb!'

The TARDIS leaned again. Outside of its own internal gravity field, the Doctor could only just hold on. In moments it would topple into the abyss.

'I'm sorry,' the Doctor called. 'I can't wait any longer.'

The Master had reached the widening crack. It was still possible to crawl across it, for the moment. 'No, Doctor! Wait for me!'

'I'm sorry.'

The Doctor made to close the door. The Master was halfway across the crack, legs spread like a rooftop thief striding between two buildings. Seeing what was about to transpire, realising that he could not possibly make it back to the TARDIS now, the Master froze. 'No. You can't do this. You can't leave me here.' But they both knew there was nothing the Doctor could do.

'You brought this on yourself,' the Doctor said. 'Like you always do.'

He slipped through the door, fell into the TARDIS interior. There was no sense that they were on a slope now: McCrimmon and the Praxilions stood at right angles to the floor, as if all was normal. His hearts racing, the Doctor rushed to the central console. He closed the door. He initiated dematerialisation.

Before he changed his mind.

CHAPTER THIRTY-FIVE

There were two points of immediate business to be attended to, before the Doctor could consider his work done. Both depended, to an improbable degree, on the reliable functioning of the TARDIS. Not only was it required to get him home, across a greater span of time than he had ever crossed, but it needed to hit two accurate targets. This was, in all frankness, asking rather a lot of the old girl. But she had, it had to be said, seldom let him down when he most needed her.

The first stop required little or no spatial travel, since it was the planet Praxilion, ten million years and a bit of loose change into the past. On the way, the Doctor explained to his passengers what he had in mind. There were, of course, many more Praxilions travelling as refugees in the TARDIS than could easily be accommodated in the control room. The TARDIS could swallow multitudes. But those present would pass the word on to others, and so on.

'We'll arrive a century or so before the time when the Red Queen first landed on your planet – back before you'd even begun to have the first stirrings of your industrial revolution,' the Doctor said.

'What will we tell the Red Queen, when she arrives?' asked one of the natives.

'In all likelihood, she never *will* arrive. Time is unknotting itself – or making itself into a slightly different knot.'

'Our industrial activity brought the *Consolidator*,' said another. 'If we don't have an industrial revolution, all will be well. We will live in peace and harmony with nature.'

The Doctor scratched at the back of his head. 'Yes. Well you see it doesn't have to be all or nothing. You can still have your industrial revolution: scientific and technological progress has its up sides as well. Unless you were happy with a very short lifespan, no sophisticated medicine, and no way at all with dealing with natural disasters? No, I didn't think so. But just take it a bit more slowly this time. You only have one planet; you don't want to burn it up twice.'

'And the *Consolidator*?' the Praxilion persisted. 'Will it still come?'

'Hard to tell, old chap. There's a good chance it will still pop back into the galaxy, since its origin isn't causally bound to the fate of the Sild. Er, yes.' The Doctor was looking at a sea of blank faces. 'What I mean is, everything that went wrong with the *Consolidator* will probably still go wrong, second time round. But it only homed in on Praxilion because of your runaway industrial activity! If you keep that in check, you shouldn't attract it. And even if you did…you'd still know better than to go poking around inside it, wouldn't you?'

'If we remember,' a third said.

'You will,' McCrimmon said. 'I have no doubt about that. You never really needed me – you just thought you did. But all I did was make things worse for you.'

'Your intentions were good,' the Doctor said.

'Does that excuse me?'

'Not really. But it's about the best most of us can hope for.'

Before long the console signalled their imminent arrival. The Doctor whispered an incantation. Let it be Praxilion, not some airless asteroid or sweltering hot swamp world. He studied the external indicators, none of them giving immediate cause for alarm. It was almost too good. With a degree of apprehension he risked the viewer. He panned the camera around. Blue skies, green grasslands falling away in gentle terraces.

'Praxilion!' he announced. 'All change!'

When the door was opened a lovely fragrance filled the control room. It was early evening, judging by the angle of Praxilion's sun. The air was cool but not cold. The clouds were flecked with glorious accents of rose and cream.

It was the end of a perfect summer's day.

'It's an old sun,' the Doctor said. 'But it still has millions of years of life in it.'

McCrimmon stood by him as the Praxilions filed out. An astonishing number of them had survived the end of the world. Out there somewhere, in hamlets and villages, their pre-industrial ancestors were going to have to adapt to some strange new arrivals, with a funny way of talking and heads full of odd ideas.

'I almost want to go with them,' McCrimmon said. 'It's such a beautiful place. I'd forgotten quite how lovely it was.'

'All planets have their moment,' the Doctor said. 'Their finest day. This might be Praxilion's.'

'I can't stay, can I? No, of course not. There's another world for me. And it's not like I don't want to go back.'

Outside, the Praxilions were assembling on the gentle green slope. Comical red and white caterpillars, bent into 'L' shapes. Some of them were already collecting flowers. They had never seen flowers before. Far in the distance, a coil of smoke rose up from a little thatched cottage.

'They'll be fine,' the Doctor said. 'But if you'd like a little time with them… I do need to recalibrate the TARDIS, before we set off again. We've a much greater crossing ahead of us.'

It was a lie, albeit a white one. He had no need to calibrate. But it was good to allow her time with her people. He watched from within the TARDIS, as she went out onto the cooling hillside. A breeze was picking up, flicking her hair across her face. She went from Praxilion to Praxilion, bending down to speak to them. There was laughter and tears. She had come to have affection for these gentle, brave creatures, and they in turn had come to have affection for this ungainly humanoid.

But all things had to come to an end eventually. That was time's hardest lesson. One that not even Time Lords ever fully accepted.

The Doctor watched as they said goodbye to one another. Farewell to the Red Queen.

And then it was time to be on their way again, back into history.

'Will I remember all of it?' she asked, when the TARDIS was under way, and she had had time to herself, time perhaps to come to some accommodation with what the future now held. 'Praxilion, travelling in time, all that madness?'

'Some of it. Maybe not all. It's probably too much for one head, anyway. Deep down you'll always have the knowledge, the wisdom, that you acquired during the millions of years you lived on Praxilion. But you may not know where that wisdom comes from. It'll just be there, when you need it.'

'I'll miss them.'

'They'll miss you.'

'There's a wee problem. It's going to look a bit odd when I pop back again.'

'You must have been lost at sea,' the Doctor said. 'That's the only explanation. And it very likely happened at the height of the Sild crisis. All we have to do is bring you back a bit after that, and no one will be any the wiser. Say, a day or two. I've already got the coordinates locked in. I'll drop you at a convenient stretch of deserted coastline, let you find your way inland. Provided you look sufficiently tired and bedraggled, there's no reason for them not to accept your story.'

'In these clothes?'

'Have a rummage in the TARDIS wardrobe. I'm sure you'll turn up something suitable.'

'That's not the main problem, though. This is.'

McCrimmon took off her glove, held up her hand for the Doctor's benefit.

Four fingers and a thumb. All present and correct.

'Ah.'

'The Infinite Cocoon didn't just make me younger. It *fixed* me. Put right that old injury.' She waggled her new digits. 'How the heck am I ever going to explain this?'

'I suppose I should apologise. But the Master and I had slightly more on our minds than making sure you ended up with the right number of fingers. You could always keep wearing the glove, you know. People will just assume you've become self-conscious about the missing fingers. It won't ever cross anyone's mind that the fingers have come back!'

'A glove, Doctor? On just the one hand?'

'Who knows?' he said. 'Perhaps you'll start a fashion.'

A weary Lethbridge-Stewart was making his way down the grey corridors of UNIT headquarters, much on his mind – it was going to take months to clear up this latest mess – when something caught his eye, fluttering in the breeze from a draughty window. It was one of the posters they had been putting up, when the crisis had been building. To the Brigadier's knowledge all the others had been removed, but this one had obviously escaped attention.

The Brigadier paused and read the heavy text, scanning down the authoritative words until he reached the last two lines.

TOGETHER WE CAN RESIST THIS INFLUENCE!
REMEMBER THE MASTER!

Remember the Master, indeed. It was strange now to think that they had ever needed to be encouraged into that act of recollection. The hard part, indeed, was going to be remembering a time when it been hard to hold on to the Master as a concept. That whole episode would come to seem surreal and faintly dreamlike. But there was no doubt at all that it had happened. The Master had begun to slip from their minds, like water running out of a sieve. To begin with, it had been possible to resist the forgetting – the posters were part of that, and the armbands, and the simple strategies like wearing one's wristwatch the wrong way around. But none of that had really made a jot of difference in the long run. The Brigadier remembered how terribly, terribly hard it had become near the end, when the Sild were breaking into Durlston Heath. Just trying to hold the idea of the Master in his head for the duration of a sentence had required phenomenal mental fortitude. Ultimately, it was not a battle any of them could win. Even the ink on the posters had begun to fade and smudge at an accelerated rate. In a week or two all they would have been was blocky smears of unreadable grey, like some dreadful piece of modern art.

But the process had begun to undo itself. The posters had begun to un-fade, un-blur. The Master had begun to pop into the Brigadier's head, unbidden. He began to have less and less difficulty reconstructing the sequence of recent events. The Master had been in prison, now the Master was somewhere else. But at least it was clear that there *was* a Master and that the chap was a thoroughgoing nuisance.

Whatever injury had been done to time, it was evidently in the process of healing itself again. All was well with the world, in other words. Until, with grim inevitability, the next crisis popped up. How would they cope, the Brigadier wondered? There had been a time before the Doctor, it was true. But it was impossible to imagine how they could manage without him now. The Doctor could also be a thoroughgoing nuisance, but at least he was *their* nuisance.

Was it time to face the inevitable: that the Doctor was gone for good? Lost in time, his fate unknown – assuming he had not died that day at Durlston Heath. But no, something had happened, somewhere in time and space – or else why would the memory of the Master be coming back so strongly? If that was not the Doctor's doing, then…

The Brigadier ripped the poster from the wall. He

scrunched it up into a tight little ball, mashing the Master's leering face. On the way to his office he passed a red wastepaper bin.

Good bloody riddance.

But as the paper hit the bin, something gave the Brigadier pause. It was a distant sound, but clearly coming from within UNIT headquarters. A familiar rushing, wheezing noise, as of some clapped-out machine about to give up the ghost.

It sounded very much as if it was coming from the laboratory.

The Brigadier did not hasten there, but instead continued his way to his office, where he settled himself behind his desk and picked up one of his several telephones. He asked the operator to put him through to the army medical centre, where he knew Mike Yates was recovering from his injuries on the platform.

'Lethbridge-Stewart here, Miss Grant – I thought I'd find you at the hospital. No, no, I... Yes, I appreciate it's late. Indeed. But I think you may want to come here with all haste. Yes, I can send a car. Good news, Miss Grant? Yes, I rather fear that may be the case.'

The Brigadier placed the telephone back down on the handset and allowed himself the briefest of smiles. In a little while his world was going to get awfully complicated and irritating again, as it was inclined to do.

But he would not have had it any other way.

EPILOGUE

The Doctor brought Bessie to a halt next to one of the white generator lorries owned by the many television companies covering the McCrimmon press conference. The lorries were all modern and large, some of them functioning as miniature studios and broadcast suites. Some of them even had satellite dishes on their tops, aimed at the drizzling grey sky. Although the exact nature of Edwina McCrimmon's statement was still a matter of speculation, word had already got around that it was going to be something big, implying a major shake-up of both the company and its objectives. Stocks were jittery, not just in London but all around the world. The other players in the petrochemical industry looked on warily. Sudden press conferences made everyone nervous. It wasn't the way things used to be done. Say what you would about Big Cal, and he'd made his share of enemies over the years, but he'd never have kept everyone in the dark like this. There'd have been a quiet whispered word in the smoking room, fair warning. A good man, Big Cal. Not like that upstart daughter of his and her new ideas.

Jo and the Doctor fought their way through the thicket of press and oil people crowding the McCrimmon Industries lobby. It was like a cold Scottish sauna, with all the drizzle that people had brought in on their anoraks and umbrellas turning to steam. It was standing room only in the main conference room, and the frustration of those who couldn't get in was palpable. Jo felt a little guilty, using her UNIT accreditation to barge her way through the hordes. But then there were very few doors that a UNIT pass wouldn't open.

McCrimmon was already part way through her speech when the Doctor and Jo shuffled into the back of the room, Jo having to tiptoe to see over the shoulders of a pair of burly oilmen stationed in front of her. McCrimmon was standing up on a platform, with a lectern in front of her – it had the McCrimmon 'M' fixed to the front on a piece of card. She wore a colour-coordinated blouse and skirt. Her gently accented voice was being picked up by a microphone and amplified through the speakers at the back of the room.

'… simply not sustainable in the long term,' she was saying. 'We can pretend otherwise, but the problem won't go away just because we bury our heads in the sand like ostriches.' Behind her, projected down from the ceiling, was a photograph of a cluster of oil platforms at twilight, almost pretty with their yellow lights and orange flames, against a cloud-streaked pink sky. 'We are sucking a resource out of the Earth that exists in a finite, non-renewable quantity – it cannot go on for ever. But even if it could, we would still need to change our game. Our dependence on fossil fuels cannot continue indefinitely. We are polluting our planet, warming our atmosphere, and worst of all we are doing so with dreadful inefficiency!'

The image behind her changed. Now it was a shot of some gridlocked American multi-lane superhighway, with cars nose to tail all the way to the horizon, under an orange-brown sky of pure smog. 'We at McCrimmon Industries understand that things can't change overnight. It will take many decades to move from *this* to something more elegant and less polluting. Electricity, perhaps, or hydrogen power. But make no mistake. History will force this change on us whether we like it or not – at least if we want to retain something resembling a global technological civilisation. But why wait until things are desperate? Why not begin to adapt and anticipate now, while there is still time? We have lost many of our platforms, suffered great damage to others. We have no choice but to rebuild – but why not seize the chance to do things differently, for once? Those of us at the forefront of the petrochemical industry have the influence to begin making these changes now. What we lack is courage and imagination. The problem is that we see ourselves in the oil industry. Really, though, we're in the energy business. Oil has served us very well, but it's no way to carry things forward. I happen to be very proud of the company my father built up, but I don't want to see that company become obsolete by the turn of the century. No, I want us to become stronger, more competitive – more agile. And fully able to face the challenges ahead of us, however difficult they may be.'

'She's in for a rough ride,' Jo whispered.

'No rougher than the one she's already been on,' the Doctor said. 'She'll cope, I'm sure.'

The picture behind McCrimmon had changed again. Now it was that famous photograph taken by the Apollo astronauts, of the Earth, rising above the Moon.

'Lately,' McCrimmon said, 'I've had a chance to put things into perspective. I think it fair to say that it's given me a fresh slant on things. I've had… I won't call it a vision, because you'll all start thinking I'm mad. But a very forceful realisation of what could happen to this planet, this Earth of ours, if we keep going down the wrong road. I've seen a world drained of its resources, literally sucked dry. A dry and barren rock, all but lifeless. But it doesn't have to be that way. We can make the right choices, starting here and now. We can choose our own future.' McCrimmon paused, and lowered her hand to the top of the lectern. 'McCrimmon Industries is committing itself to change, to bringing about a better world. But we can't face up to the future while we're burdened with the past. I am proud of my name, proud of who I am

357

– proud of the man who built this firm up from nothing. But McCrimmon Industries is a name for the twentieth century. We need to start looking further ahead than that.'

The 'M' dropped away from the front of the lectern. Behind it, hidden until now, was a second card on which an entirely new corporate logo had been printed.

It was an arc of grey cratered landscape, and above that the rising Earth. But the blue and green globe was also the sun. It threw off yellow rays. Beneath the arc, in pale red letters, was a single word:

Praxilion

'This is the new name for what we are, what we do,' McCrimmon said. 'Praxilion is much more than just an oil company. In fact, I confidently predict that our oil activities will take up a smaller and smaller slice of our business. Energy is what we're about, ladies and gentlemen. Finding new ways to generate, store and utilise energy – ways that will help our planet, not harm it. It's not going to be easy, I know. Aye, as matter of fact it's going to be awfully difficult! But what are the alternatives?'

She thanked her audience, and reminded them that brochures were available, and that she'd be ready to take questions from the audience. There was a smattering of lukewarm applause, mixed in with some discontented muttering from certain quarters.

'Praxilion,' Jo heard someone say. 'What an absolute load of cobblers!'

'Well, that went down about as well as I expected,' the Doctor said when they were out in the lobby again, jostling cameras and big, fuzzy microphones.

'They didn't like it much, did they?'

'No, Jo, they didn't. Not at all. But I doubt very much that Edwina McCrimmon anticipated anything else. She's well aware that people take a long time to come round to genuinely new ideas.'

'Do you think they will, in the end?'

The Doctor smiled. 'For the sake of your planet, I sincerely hope so.'

'All that time she spent in the future… does she remember any of it?' Jo was flicking through one of the Praxilion brochures. It was all very glossy and vague, like a political manifesto.

'If she remembered all of it, it would drive her quite insane. But she remembers enough, I think. She had the strangest dream, Jo – a dream that seemed to last a thousand lifetimes. She was the queen of a dying civilisation. She saw all the mistakes a world can make, through ignorance and greed. Now she has the chance to make sure we do a little better.'

'I feel sorry for the Praxilions.'

'Remember, Jo, they haven't evolved yet. History is fluid. A tiny input here, a tiny change there, can make a vast difference to the outcome further down the line. The Time Lords were supposed to stop that sort of chaotic disruption from growing too large, but Praxilion lies far beyond their reach. The Sild's own actions may have introduced a perturbation sufficiently large to change Praxilion's destiny.'

'So they might avoid all that the second time round?'

'More or less.'

Jo closed the brochure and left it on a table for someone else to pick up. She couldn't tell if the Doctor was just saying all this to cheer her up. It was hard to know sometimes. Being a Time Lord meant seeing the best and worst of what creation offered. Light and darkness, evil and benevolence, existence and annihilation. All were unified in the Time Lord's unwavering gaze. She wondered how it was possible not to grow a little hardened and detached at the prospect of something as thoroughly inconsequential as a single human life. If a Time Lord could feel indifferent to fate of an entire civilisation, then what did a person mean to them?

'Any thoughts, miss, on what you just heard?'

It was a bearded BBC reporter, shoving a woolly

microphone under Jo's chin.

'Good luck to her, I say.'

'Some of our listeners will naturally assume that you're just saying that because you're a woman.'

'No,' Jo corrected patiently. 'I'm just saying that because I'm a not a complete—'

The Doctor had taken the opportunity to snatch the microphone away from his colleague. 'I trust your listeners will be intelligent enough to make up their own minds. The fact of the matter is that I've just heard more sense coming out of Edwina McCrimmon than from almost any personal acquaintance of mine since Leonardo da Vinci.'

'Leonardo da Vinci.' The reporter winked at his sound man – they had a right one here, obviously. 'Met him, did you, sir?'

'Met him?' The Doctor feigned grave personal offence. 'I was his personal instructor in the arts of draughtsmanship, fencing...'

Jo tucked an arm around the Doctor's sleeve. 'C'mon. We're leaving. Before you get yourself locked away.'

'Doctor! Jo!'

It was Eddie McCrimmon, barging her way through a thicket of microphones to reach the two of them.

'We thought you'd be a bit busy after all that!' Jo said.

'I will be – Q and A session in ten minutes – but I wanted to speak to you before you left. Thanks for everything, both of you.'

'You're the one who should be thanked,' the Doctor said.

'The hard work's still ahead. But look, something amazing happened. Jo: do you remember those books I told you about, when we were on the platform?'

'The ones your dad threw in the bin?'

'He called me yesterday. He knew about the press conference going ahead, so I thought he was going to give me a hard time about steering the firm in a different direction, letting down his legacy, all that sort of nonsense.'

'And?' the Doctor asked.

'There was none of that. It's like he's finally decided to let go. That whole business with Callow and Lovelace... I think that was the last straw for Big Cal. He's withdrawing from direct control of the company's affairs, letting me run the whole operation... it's as if he's seen the light, after all these years.'

'Better late than never,' the Doctor said.

'But that's not all. He could barely contain himself. Said Morag had found something, when she was tidying his office – a little plastic bag with nine books in it, tucked away at the back of a desk.'

'Your books?' Jo asked.

'I haven't seen them yet. Dad and I are meeting up tomorrow. He'll give them to me then. But he says they're mine. He says it's my writing in them, my drawings... but that's not possible, is it? Those books went in the bin when I was 12. I know! As soon as I found out what he'd done I went tearing down the road, trying to catch up with the bin men. But it was too late – they'd gone in the back of the lorry, with that big crushing thing! There's no way these books have just turned up now, all these years later. How is that possible?'

'How indeed?' the Doctor asked.

'But if Big Cal says they've turned up...' Jo said.

'I'll find out tomorrow, I suppose. And if he's right...'

'You could start to forgive him,' the Doctor said gently.

'I could try. It's been hard, you know, what he did. But I suppose he only wanted to do the best for me.'

'Forgiveness is good,' the Doctor told her. 'It's the grease that makes the universe turn.'

Outside it was still drizzling. They picked their way through boggy grass, over a snake's nest of thick black electrical cables laid out between the TV lorries and their generators. The satellite dishes hummed. The news of McCrimmon's bombshell press conference would already be winging its way around the world by now.

'So that's that then,' Jo said. 'All's well. The world is on a better course.'

'For now.'

But it had not been the Doctor speaking. It was the Master, blocking their path between two of the slab-sided white BBC outdoor broadcast lorries. His black suit was immaculate. His beard and hair were neatly groomed.

'Well, well,' the Doctor said, not without a certain fondness. 'So you made it back after all.'

The Master was tightening his gloves. 'Never underestimate me.'

'I wouldn't dream of it. I gather you found a TARDIS?'

'Eventually. As a matter of fact I found one abandoned, at the end of time. A Type Forty, a little worn around the edges, but only one previous owner. Oddly enough, the chameleon circuit was damaged. I repaired it easily enough.'

The Doctor nodded. He wondered if the Master was telling the truth. As usual, it was impossible to tell. 'Well it's very good of you to drop back in on us. I presume you've come to strangle the new world order at birth?'

'I have more pressing concerns than the future of this miserable little planet. I merely stopped by to bid farewell, at least for the time being.'

'Were you at the press conference?' Jo asked.

'Listening in.' The Master patted the side of one of the white lorries. 'McCrimmon will undoubtedly fail, but I cannot help but admire her boldness.'

'You can take some credit,' the Doctor said. 'If you hadn't intervened, the Infinite Cocoon would have killed her. Or something worse.'

For a second, no more than that, the Master seemed bashful. 'It was a mere trifle.'

'But still you helped. You gave her back her mind and body. You had nothing to gain from it. Why did you do it?'

'Why did I commit an altruistic act, you mean?' The

Master, momentarily, appeared at least as befuddled as the Doctor. 'Because it cost me nothing. Because what use is a lifetime of villainy, without the counterpoint of at least one good deed?'

'So you did this one decent thing,' Jo said, 'to make the rest of your crimes stand out even more?'

'Crudely put, Miss Grant, but in essence correct.'

'I don't believe you,' she said forcefully. 'I think you did it because… you're still capable of goodness. You're not totally lost. There's still that glimmer of humanity in you.'

'On the contrary, Miss Grant, it was as calculated an act as anything in my career. And with that behind me I may now rededicate myself to the perfection of chaos.' The Master opened the door into the side of one of the outside broadcast vehicles. 'I'll be leaving now. I have an appointment in London, at the Ministry of Defence… a score to settle.' He prepared to step up into the lorry, one booted foot already off the ground. 'Doctor: I believe I owe you a debt of gratitude.'

'For not listening to you, when we were in the Vortex and you warned me you'd turn back into a monster?'

'That,' the Master said. 'But also the other thing. You could have destroyed me. You chose not to.'

'You needn't thank me.'

'Then I won't.' The Master was about to slip into the vehicle and close the door behind him. But on the threshold he hesitated. 'I will say this. That time we spent together, exploring the *Consolidator*, the ruins of Praxilion… I cannot say that it was entirely unenjoyable. Almost like…'

'Old times?' the Doctor finished for him.

'We were quite good, weren't we?' And the Master chuckled. 'Well, goodbye, Doctor. Goodbye, Miss Grant. Doubtless we will meet again.'

There was a click, and then another click, and then a volley of clicks. They were the clicks of automatic weapons being readied for use. Slowly, with no great consternation, the Master looked up onto the roof of the adjoining broadcast vehicle. Two UNIT soldiers were kneeling up there, guns aimed squarely at the Master. They were not the only ones. UNIT personnel were closing in from all sides, on the roofs of the lorries and creeping along the narrow spaces between them.

Jo heard the bass thump of a heavy military helicopter.

The Master eyed the door, as if weighing his chances of making it into his TARDIS before the soldiers had a chance to open fire. For a moment, he seemed on the verge of giving it a go. Then he shook his head, smiling through his beard.

'I should have known, Doctor.'

'Known what?'

'That you'd betray me. Some radio signal, I presume, to alert UNIT to my presence? Or must I apportion the blame upon the shoulders of the charming Miss Grant?'

'Neither of us,' the Doctor said. 'I'm sorry, old chap, but we didn't have the foggiest idea. I suppose they must been tailing Jo and me, on the off-chance you wouldn't be able to resist showing up.'

The Master nodded, seeming to accept this version of events. 'Next time, Doctor, I will not make the mistake of renewing our acquaintance. And there will be a next time.'

The UNIT soldiers soon had the Master handcuffed, gagged and blindfolded – they were taking no chances, Jo saw. She watched as they marched him away, feeling an odd sadness.

'You know what this means, don't you?' she asked, as they made their way back to Bessie.

The Doctor looked at her but said nothing.

'He got his wish. He sent a message into the future, and he ended up escaping. I know he's just been recaptured, but for all we know he's had centuries of freedom since you last saw him.'

'He paid a stiff price.' The Doctor invited Jo to step onto Bessie. 'Millions of years of torment at the hands of the Sild, and then a glimpse in the Vortex of what he could have been, without the influence of his other selves... I wouldn't wish that on my worst enemy. Even him.'

'You think any of that left its mark? He still seemed like the Master to me.'

'Time will tell, Jo. It usually does.' The Doctor turned Bessie's ignition. After a few false starts she clattered into reassuring life. 'Now about that hydrogen conversion I've been meaning to do...'

Jo laughed. 'Are you talking to me or the car?'

'Well, both of course,' the Doctor said. 'Anything else would be the height of rudeness.'

He put Bessie in gear, and they began to make their way out of the mass of parked lorries, out towards the road that would eventually take them home.

It was a marvellous feeling.

ACKNOWLEDGEMENTS

Writing this book would have been a thrill under any almost circumstances, but it has been a particular delight to work with Justin Richards, as knowledgeable and sympathetic an editor as one could wish for, as well as a limitless mine of *Who*-related lore. Thanks, Justin! It has also been a tremendous pleasure to work with commissioning editor Albert DePetrillo, who very generously provided exactly the visual inspiration I needed at exactly the right time. Thanks, Albert! Finally, I am indebted to my long-standing agent, Robert Kirby, for helping set up the book deal in the first place. The news, arriving on a sunny morning in Florida a day before I got to see a space shuttle launch, could not have been more welcome. More than anything, though, I would like to express my gratitude to all who were involved in *Doctor Who* during the Pertwee years and beyond. You brought a tiny flickering rectangle of black and white terror into my world, and I will be forever grateful.

Alastair Reynolds, behind the settee, March 2013